PRAISE FOR UNDER THE LESSER MOON

"Lush emotions, vivid characters, and a world rich with history—I didn't want this journey to end."

— ESSA HANSEN, AUTHOR OF *NOPHEK GLOSS*

"Stunning. The world building is some of the best I've ever read, and the main character, Akrist, has left me with a permanent ache in my heart. Set in a brutal, often merciless world, the story kept me breathlessly turning pages to the very end. Clear your calendar, because you won't be able to put this one down."

— JULIE ESHBAUGH, AUTHOR OF *IVORY AND BONE* AND ITS SEQUEL, *OBSIDIAN AND STARS*

"A compelling story like none other, told in an incredibly crafted world. I can't wait for Book Two!"

— DAN VADEBONCOEUR, CO-HOST OF THE MEDIA NERDS PODCAST

To: Steena thanks for
the support!

Feed Your Imagination!

SHELLY
CAMPBELL

UNDER THE
LESSER MOON

THE MARKED SON
BOOK ONE

🌸 MYTHOS & INK

Cover design by James T. Egan of Bookfly Design.

ISBN 978-1-989423-18-9 (softcover), 978-1-989423-19-6 (ebook)

Library and Archives Canada Cataloguing in Publication

Title: Under the lesser moon / Shelly Campbell.
Names: Campbell, Shelly, author.
Description: Series statement: The marked son ; book 1
Identifiers: Canadiana (print) 20200297430 | Canadiana (ebook) 20200297449 | ISBN 9781989423189
(softcover) | ISBN 9781989423196 (ebook)
Classification: LCC PS8605.A5487 U54 2020 | DDC C813/.6—dc23

Published by Mythos & Ink
Winnipeg, Manitoba, Canada
www.mythosink.com

To Colin, Liam and Finn. Life with you boys is the greatest adventure. Thank you for that, and bless you for tolerating me when I'm lost in imaginary adventures in my head.

PART ONE
"DAESON"

CHAPTER ONE

Shortly after my birth, a flash flood plucked my three-year-old sister, Tasie, from a riverbank and swallowed her whole. One muddy gulp and Tasie was gone. Aella, my mother, never forgave me for that. In her mind, *I* killed my sister. Forget the icy water, crushing logs, and unforgiving slabs of submerged stone. I—Aella's firstborn son—did it.

My mother and father still fought about it six years later. Tonight, as always, I heard them through the walls of my tiny, solitary hut.

"It's *my* fault," Aella wailed.

"Nonsense," my father's deep voice rumbled. "How many times do I have to say it, Aella? Nasheira's will. A goddess wants a soul to come back home, she takes it. That's it."

"No," Aella barked. "No, *I* let her touch my stomach to feel the baby kick. She was so excited at the idea of a sister, Hasev. I didn't know! I *should* have known. It *felt* like another girl," she sobbed. "How could I let her touch it? A *daeson!*"

My mother spat the last word like the bitter curse it was. The title *daeson* literally meant *damned son* in the old tongue.

Daeson Akrist. That was me. Cursed enough to kill my

older sister from within the womb. And my mother was not the only one in camp who believed that.

I scrunched my eyes shut and pressed my blanket against my ears. *Six years old and you still cling to your blanket like a baby.* Squashing the thought, I breathed in the comforting smell of familiar fabric. Aella's sharp words muffled to dull taps, like a woodpecker chipping away at Hasev's dry assurances. Nothing my father said could appease her. She didn't stop until he stormed out of their hut. That's how all their arguments ended. I hummed a gathering song to myself and filled my skull with the grating squeak of my molars grinding together until there wasn't room for the memory of my parents' stony voices. Then I fell asleep and dreamed about the wurm. It was always the same dream.

Above my hut's door flap hangs the familiar symbol, a ghastly, twisted root that looks like a wurm—the icon that marks my dwelling as a daeson's. The moment I take my gaze off it, it wriggles and plops to the floor. As it writhes toward me, it swells to the size of a real wurm, waxy white, thicker than a man, and nearly twice as long. Moonlight quivers off its dry, maggot-like body. Dirt chuffs as it moves. Then the smell hits. Guides, what an appalling smell, like rancid fat and damp mould.

I can't move as it inches toward me. Bile rises in my throat and breath tangles between my ribs while I wait for the creature to feel its way to my bedroll.

Wurms have no eyes. There's something horrifying about that blindness and those feelers wriggling out of its head like thousands of beckoning fingers.

Knowing that you have not yet been discovered, knowing you will be.

Behind the twitching feelers, a cruel mouth quivers, jawless and malformed, a black funnel filled with circles of triangular teeth, and a milky, paralyzing poison.

The wurm bumps the edge of my mat, sampling, exploring. A single, swaying feeler brushes across my stomach. Its spineless body jerks. Eager feelers flock onto me, poking, peeling back my shirt, and stretching my skin. I scream when the first row of teeth snag across my belly. I always scream.

🕊

I BOLTED UPRIGHT, panting and swallowing dizziness. Over the pounding at my temples, I heard feet trudging from the family hut toward my small shelter.

Hasev. I buried my nose in the hem of my scalloped blanket. You must have screamed aloud. Stupid. Now he's going to make you recite the whole creation story. Again. Hasev used to share the same story every night I couldn't sleep. He'd told it so many times, I'd memorized which words made his voice drop and which ones made his eyebrows rise. I had to, because Hasev didn't tell the story anymore. He made me recite it instead, like a punishment.

A wedge of blinding lamplight squeezed past my door flap, followed by a broad, bearded face. "Well, boy?" Hasev huffed, squatting so he didn't smack his head on the curved ceiling.

I squinted, dipped my chin to my chest, and mumbled, "Nasheira had two sons."

"Can't hear you."

I wiped my damp cheeks with quivering hands and focused on the moss wick of Hasev's stone lamp. My voice steadied. "She created them herself, the first out of soil and the second out of sky. She named them Pau and Yurrii." I paused and wrinkled my nose. "Why did she name them after the moons?"

Hasev sighed. "You know the story, boy. She named the moons after the sons, not the other way around."

"Oh." I puffed out my cheeks. I liked making the story last longer. Hasev always left when it finished, and I didn't want to be alone out here, not after the dream. "Pau of Earth hated Yurrii of Sky, who floated amongst the stars, while Pau curled like a slug in the dirt.

"Nasheira told him that, although his little brother had the company of const—" I wriggled under the weighty word. "Constell..."

"Constellations," Hasev prompted with a small smile.

"Stars is easier to say."

"Fine then. Say stars."

"Although his brother had the company of stars, Pau could breathe life into soil. But Pau was jealous. He shook his earth and spat poison about him so no life could grow. Yurrii shined the light of his sun down, cooled Pau with his rain, and shaded him with his clouds, but Pau hated him and still would not let life grow." I licked my lips before continuing.

"So, Yurrii took pity upon his elder brother. He told him that if he would allow life to grow, if he created a human whose feet walked on soil and fingers touched the sky, Yurrii would travel through the fingers to the feet and take Pau's place in the ground. Then Pau could travel through the feet to the fingers and have Yurrii's sky." I scratched my eyebrow and cocked my head toward the ceiling. "I wish I could switch places like that."

Something in Hasev's small, warm eyes turned cold. It made the smile on his face look like it was trying too hard. "Me too, but we're not gods, are we?"

I didn't care that his smile had looked sour: it still counted as a smile. Leaning forward, I nodded seriously. "Pau agreed. He grew a human woman on his soil, but when Yurrii came through her fingers into the ground, Pau killed him. Then he pushed his brother's body out of the ground into a great rock that became the moon. Now Pau owned both the sky and the earth, and Yurrii was entombed. What does entombed mean?"

"I told you last time."

"But how can you get buried in a rock? It's a rock. It's too hard."

"Not for Pau." Hasev motioned impatiently for me to continue.

I bit at a hangnail. I didn't like the end of the story. "Nasheira saw what Pau had done, and she took him and trapped him in a moon beside Yurrii, and said, 'My first son, you shall never again grow the seed of life on this barren rock.'

"Then she took a pebble from Yurrii's moon and a pebble from Pau's. She planted the stones in the human woman's womb, and the woman birthed. Out of Yurrii's stone grew a golden angel of the skies, a dragon to guide and protect in Yurrii's memory.

"And out of Pau's stone grew a monster, a wurm larger than a human that burrowed into the ground. It would forever remind people of Pau's evil. Pau was the first daeson."

I swallowed and glanced at the top of my doorway. The pale chunk of gnarled root reminded me of what I was, what the eldest son of every family was.

Hasev cleared his throat and shifted his weight. Between us, his lamp guttered and threw flitting shadows at the walls.

"I'm not like Pau," I whispered.

Hasev exhaled through his teeth. "I know, boy."

"I didn't kill anyone. I didn't do anything." Hot tears streamed from my swollen eyes.

"I know, Akrist."

"Then why does Aella hate me?" My voice cracked.

"She doesn't. Your mother doesn't hate you."

I studied my father's feet. He always held them so still when he lied.

AFTER HASEV LEFT, I sang to myself in the dark. My wobbling voice wove through the starting lines of a lullaby, one that Aella often sang to my little brothers, before I pursed my lips and fell silent.

Lullabies only work if someone else sings them to you, stupid.

Creeping off my bedroll, I peered through the crack above my door flap to the slim wedge of night sky beyond. Pau and Yurrii hung half-faced against a black canvas. Closing one eye, I blotted Pau out of my view and inhaled as I squinted at his smaller brother.

Mothers used Pau and his wurms as a threat to unruly children. "Do as you're told, or Pau's wurms will eat you! Go to sleep or Pau will trap you in his moon!" They'd grin as they said it and their children would giggle.

I didn't think it was funny. I'd never seen a wurm in real life, just the one in my dream, but our hunters often found knots of them tunnelling amongst our trap lines. They culled every wurm they found without mercy. Left uncontrolled, the hideous creatures would strip every animal from our traps and starve us. We knew whenever the hunters killed one because they returned to camp still reeking of the foul creature's blood.

I inhaled deeply. The night outside only smelled like dew, chasing the stench of wurm from my memory. Pushing the flap aside, I crouched at the entry to my hut. The camp's domed huts huddled together like turtles in the moonlight. At the centre, protected like a soft-bellied beast, lay the Speaker's hulking home with the other huts surrounding it. I didn't reside in my family's house. No daeson did. Close contact with unholy eldest sons caused illness, miscarriages in women, and sterility in men.

Drowned sisters, too. Don't forget drowned sisters.

My runt of a hut crouched at the outskirts of camp, on the north side where Pau reared his pale head to follow Yurrii through the sky. My family's hut hunched ten paces south of mine. I studied it with bleary eyes, hitching my blanket around my shoulders and padding towards it. Its roof sloped like a tortoise shell and the weave of the grass panels beneath were tighter and tidier than my hut's. Hasev had helped me build mine, but he couldn't weave like Aella could.

As I crept by the wall, I cringed at the memory of Aella arguing with Hasev, but the hut sat silent as I passed. Other sounds twisted in the breeze as I went—a cough, a stream of urine hitting the ground, a footstep—but nobody saw me as I snaked my way through the sleeping camp.

I heard the vaiyas before I saw them. Scratching noises, choppy words, and the occasional cluck of displeasure. A moment later, all nine of them came into view, clumped comfortably together in the dust. Their rounded backs and slender arched necks glowed in the soft starlight. A few dainty heads turned at my approach. One of the figures staggered to its feet with a drawn-out groan and spoke something I couldn't understand.

Vaiyas were our pack birds—large, long-necked creatures with scales instead of feathers and a knack for imitating human speech. A soft huff reached my ears as the silver-backed vaiya tipped its beak and identified my smell. The spiked crest on his head drooped, and the animal whistled and picked his way through his lazing flock to reach me. It was Vax, the patriarch.

No one else held much of a place in their hearts for our vaiya flock. Since they were an unpopular chore, naturally their care shifted to the daeson of camp, and right now, I was the only one.

I'd named all nine of the camp's vaiyas. Five females: Vina, Veset, Voru, Vala, and Vir. And four males: little Vable, Vust, Voti and, the largest, Vax. He was my favourite, and he stood before me now, complaining of an itch.

"Where?" I whispered, the tightness between my shoulders easing as I inhaled Vax's sweet, musty scent.

He blinked, his eyes dark and long-lashed. "Itchy?" he rasped in a shrill voice.

"*Where*, Vax?"

Clicking his huge hooked beak, he swung his head down to his right ankle, gnawing at it. Then he bobbed up and extended his two-toed foot.

Avoiding the long spur higher up his leg, I bent over to fold up a few scales, exposing two bury bugs. Picking them off, I crushed them under my boot. By the time I'd finished a cursory search for more, my stomach had unclenched from my nightmare. The flock's soft whistles surrounded me. I dropped Vax's foot and patted him solidly on the flank. I had to stand on the tips of my toes to reach that high. The vaiya's head hovered at twice my height.

Squinting up at him, I admired his sleek form in the moonlight, the curve of his neck, the lazy flick of his serpent tail and the scale-studded round of his chest with no upper limbs. Vax was a handsome bird and smart for a vaiya, too. He'd learned a healthy vocabulary of spoken words and asked for water and food by name. I watched as he flared the spiked crest on the top of his head and ducked toward me, eyes flashing beneath reptilian ridges.

"Overcooked," he lamented with a sigh.

I slapped both hands over my mouth to suppress a giggle at the word the vaiya must have picked up earlier.

Buoyed by my response, Vax repeated the word robustly, and the rest of the flock echoed it.

"Shhh! No!" I chided.

The vaiyas flinched and then hushed, trailing apologetic whimpers of "No."

They'd wake everyone if they wound themselves up. "Quiet," I whispered.

Vax nibbled at my fingers.

"Let's go to sleep." I led Vax around two bedded females—Vina and Vir—to sit in the middle of the group. The big vaiya nested behind me, snapping at the other crowding birds as I leaned against his haunch.

"No!" they hissed. I heard one animal try "overcooked" one last time before the flock settled. I breathed in the dusty, sweet smell of them, and burrowed into Vax's warmth at my back.

As I pulled my blanket up to my chin, I recalled Aella's harsh whispers. She never spoke of my brothers with such venom in her voice.

Would she hate me so much if Tasie were still here? If I hadn't come right before her daughter drowned? My eyes blurred and Vir leaned closer to me. Despite Vax's clucking warnings, she picked at my wet cheeks with a gentle beak.

"Water," she crooned.

Eventually, I drifted to sleep with the vaiyas soft murmurs humming in my ears. "No... sharpened... inside... fire... overcooked..."

CHAPTER TWO

I was eleven when the other dreams started, the ones that came true. The first one started the same as my wurm dream. In the dream, I was paralyzed by fear, but instead of that wretched smell under my door flap, I found a dragon scale.

Ridged and marbled with golden tones, it lay in the middle of my floor as if someone had set it there. Something about it made my stomach recoil and my breath sour in my throat. I couldn't sort out why. It was just a dragon scale. Why would the sight of it raise such foreboding in me?

I found the real dragon scale the next day, wedged amongst a patch of kiro grass. We valued kiro for its sweet scent, using it for bedding and incense. Alone on the hillside, cutting and bundling swathes of the fragrant stuff, I paused when a patch of sunlight winked at me from deep within the turf. Tilting my head, I squinted at the flat disc of gold about the size of my palm, ridged and flecked with rich brown. My chest tingled.

I swallowed, clenched my fists, and pinned them to my sides. *Don't touch it.*

Hasev had drilled it into me enough times. "Scales belong to Na-Jhalar. You ever find one, don't touch it. Come and get me."

I couldn't understand why scales were so special if dragons just shed them like peeled-off toenails, and I said so.

"Have you ever seen a dragon?" Hasev had asked.

"No."

"When I was your age, I'd already seen more than I could count with both hands. My father told me that, in his youth, the sky was sometimes so full of them it looked more gold than blue. Camps had more Speakers than they ever needed, and dragons guided them away from storms and toward the finest hunting grounds." He sighed. "But Guides are rare now, and so are their scales."

It's my fault. I swallowed guilt. *Like everything else is.* My father wouldn't come out and say it, but the creation story spelled it out well enough. Dragons were good. Wurms were evil, and the two didn't mix. As a descendent of Pau, a brother of wurms, I hadn't seen a dragon because my birth had driven them all away. *And you killed your sister just like Pau killed Yurrii. Dragons must be able to smell evil on you.*

Hasev carried on. "Scales are rare gifts from the Guides to the Speakers, amulets that provide protection and inspire wisdom." Then he mumbled sourly, "Nasheira knows the man needs it..."

I don't think he'd meant for me to hear that last part. The elders whispered that Na-Jhalar's older sister was more suited to lead, but Nasheira chose as she wished, and she'd chosen Na-Jhalar, not Arsu.

I frowned at the scale nested in the grass. Vibrant gold with delicate veins of turquoise, it was stunning compared to the vaiyas' grey scales. I was overcome with the urge to touch it.

If I told Hasev about the scale, Na-Jhalar would add it to the stack on his necklace and never consider it again.

How will he even know you touched it? It's as close to a Guide as you're ever going to get. Perhaps Nasheira sent you a dream so you could find it first.

My tongue pressed through the gap of my missing front tooth. A swell of heat bloomed in my stomach as I bent and picked up the scale. It was lighter than I thought it would be.

Sunshine blazed through its filmy width, and its surface glowed amber. I'd never seen a dragon, but I imagined I was one now, soaring effortlessly on gusting winds, crying in triumph at those pathetic, earth-bound beings below. Closing my eyes, I tipped backwards. Air punched past my lips as my backside hit the ground. I relished the breeze against my face, held the scale over my heart, and flew far away from the camp.

I didn't remember falling asleep. A gasp woke me with a start.

Someone's shadow blocked the sun. Raven hair whipped past her proud jaw and curled around her neck. Aella.

You're not supposed to be anywhere near her.

But she towered over me with raw eyes and thin lips. I'd never seen my mother's pretty face so disfigured, so furious, so *close.*

Look away.

Swallowing, I sat up and gaped around me. The sun was low on the horizon, and behind my mother stood *all* the camp's gatherers and half the vaiyas. They had returned from foraging in the south.

I gulped and a shiver shot through me.

"You are to remain a respectful distance from your mother," Hasev had ordered. It was my duty as an eldest son to prevent situations like this.

Why was she standing so close? My mouth trembled. To speak, even to look directly at her, was blasphemy.

Why doesn't she step back? They could just skirt around—

The sensation of an object pinching my palms snagged my breath in my throat as I remembered what I held.

Oh, no. Oh, no. Sweet Nasheira! Aella was staring at the dragon scale.

They *all* were.

She stood like a wooden carving with flint for eyes.

A moan crawled up my throat as I glanced at the lovely scale sandwiched between my dirty hands. I couldn't drop it, couldn't think. Hot tears scrambled down my face and, for a single moment, I met Aella's gaze.

She has brown eyes. I'd never been close enough to see their colour.

My mother reacted as if I'd burned her. Her whole body twitched. Jerking forward, she tore the scale out of my hands. The gatherers behind her yelped and the vaiyas pranced and hissed, but I didn't make a noise as the scale sliced through the meat of my fingers. For a long second, Aella's eyes bulged at the hot blood smearing the sacred gift.

Past the rushing in my ears, I heard the gatherers mumble prayers; saw them press the index and middle finger of their right hands to their foreheads. It was a holy gesture, symbolizing the placement of responsibility for the death of Nasheira's second son on the head of the daeson.

Fat drops of blood patted onto my lap from the cut on my fingers, but I barely felt the pain. I wanted to apologize, to say something, but a boulder had settled between my ribs.

Aella wailed. The jagged noise tore through the still air and several vaiyas rolled their eyes and cried a frantic echo.

Hands shaking, Aella bent and wiped the scale on the front of her dress. Where my blood had smeared the gold, a marbled pink stain remained.

She spun and sprinted down the hillside. The other gatherers snatched up their children, praying loudly as they scuttled into the valley with the vaiyas bouncing behind them.

Your dirty blood is smeared all over a Speaker's gift. My stomach lurched. *They'll brand you for this.*

❧

I WAS TOO terrified to return to camp on my own. Aella had to send Hasev to fetch me. He grabbed my shirt sleeve and dragged me toward camp with pursed lips and red cheeks. Before we reached the bordering huts, he pinned me with his dark, ever-changing eyes, and I shrunk under the intensity of this glare.

"Na-Jhalar likes to hurt people," he whispered under his breath. "Don't let him see you cry, understand?"

I avoided those eyes and focused instead on the modest scar on my father's chest, tracing its elegant edges. It was a rite of passage, the mark every adult inflicted upon themselves to honour Nasheira. Daeson didn't get one. I'd asked.

"Do you understand?" he repeated, turning to grip my shoulders so tight I suspected he'd leave bruises.

I froze under his sudden touch. I didn't understand, but I wiped my nose and nodded. *I'm in trouble.* I knew that much.

Our camp had been without a Speaker for a very long time before Na-Jhalar, so I guess we were lucky to have him. Hasev said generosity from the dragons happened less and less. They didn't pick Speakers for every camp anymore, and they didn't guide us away from storms like in the elders' stories.

And now I'd defiled one of their scales.

Hasev let go of me, and my mind locked onto the image of Na-Jhalar's twisted face, eyes protruding beneath a single wiry eyebrow that spanned his entire forehead. The way spit sprayed like rain from his sausage lips whenever he shouted —which was all the time.

"Will I be shunned?" I gulped, trotting to keep up with Hasev as he pulled me. Our Speaker had branded a man once, a stranger who'd wandered into camp, eyes bulging and hands full of dragon eggshells. *No one* touched dragon eggs, not even the Speakers. Our elders screamed when they saw those crushed shells in the babbling man's hands. I still remembered the awful smell as Na-Jhalar pressed that glowing ember into the poor man's cheek, that clinging stench of burnt hide. If you bore the S-shape scar on your face, the whole world left you alone. Camps abandoned you, and no one would speak or trade with you ever again. It was a death mark.

"Guides, no," Hasev replied, but he didn't tell me what *was* about to happen. A sawing sound clawed up my throat as we closed on the main hearth and Na-Jhalar's hut.

"Remember what I said," Hasev hissed.

Don't cry.

He shoved me to my knees at the main hearth and when Na-Jhalar turned, he already held the dragon scale stained pink by my own blood.

"Defiler!" he bellowed, raining spit in his anger. He dwarfed me. He outsized everyone else in camp. Only a Speaker could afford to eat enough food to maintain such a figure. The rest of us shared his spoils. His impressive girth was a sign of his status as surely as the dragon scale necklace was. "This wurm's descendent has defiled a holy dragon scale!" he announced over my head.

"Shall we brand it?" Arsu smirked behind her brother and my blood turned to ice.

Oh Nasheira! Tears burned my eyes. I gaped back at my father.

"Holy Speaker," Hasev cleared his throat, "Forgive me, but isn't branding reserved for high sins?"

Murder and desecrating a dragon's nest. Those were the only high sins I knew of. Mother of Yurrii, was touching a dragon scale among them? Aella had touched it. So had Na-Jhalar. Blood roared in my ears as Na-Jhalar sniffed and nodded.

"Yes, high sins," he said.

Stop crying. He'll see it. Distract yourself. Pinning my gaze to Na-Jhalar's scar, I lost myself in its odd details—a puckering, roped river map utterly unlike any other adult's mark. Scar tissue rolled over his chest in elegant parallel patterns, like a current slipping around half-submerged stones.

I glanced to where Arsu stood behind her brother. The slashing scars ribboning her exposed belly looked like childish imitations of Na-Jhalar's mark.

People chose different methods to mark their passage to adulthood. Some cut themselves. Others, like my father, preferred branding. Influenced by how their parents had crafted their marks, some scrubbed ashes or injected dyes into the raw wound to stand out; young men and women were drawn to the virility of an artful scar, after all.

But no scar bested the one that inspired them all, the Speaker's mark. Speakers didn't scar themselves. Nasheira herself chose Jhalar when he was a twelve-year-old boy. The Speaker often had Arsu retell the story around the main hearth at night, because his sister had witnessed the whole thing. One of Nasheira's dragons gave Jhalar his mark, and he'd been *Na*-Jhalar ever since. That short title tacked to the beginning of his name meant he could do whatever he wanted, including publicly humiliating an eleven-year-old daeson.

While people spoke Na-Jhalar's name in reverence, they said *daeson* with a sneer, like the word burned bitter on their tongues. I was a wurm to them, the furthest thing in the world from a Goddess-chosen Speaker.

How I wished to be further from our Speaker now, as he seemed to reach some sort of internal decision and lunged toward me, meaty fist raised. When the first blow struck the side of my head, I didn't cry out.

I didn't scream when his next punch raised a swelling squeal in my ears and made my nose bleed. I didn't fall over, either. When blood dribbled over my lip and down my chin, I found my father's face in the crowd, and he nodded.

I cringed when Na-Jhalar knocked me onto my back and leaned over me wafting sour breath. My vision blurred as I stared carefully past Na-Jhalar's shoulder while he panted like a winded ox. He didn't need horns. My eyes stung with unshed tears. *Idiot. Hasev said not to cry.* My breath hitched. I feared what might slip out of my mouth if he hit me again.

Swallowing the building ache in my throat, I tried to blink away my tears, but they slipped down my cheeks. And that's when I spotted the dragon. Far up in the sky, over the Speaker's left shoulder, a burst of gold against pale blue. I watched her wheel silently, translucent wings shivering as they hooked the heavens and spun upward. Her hide rippled like sunlight on water. *A dragon. An actual Guide from Nasheira.* And I was the only one who saw her.

A slow ache gathered between my ribs, the same earnest tension that built when I held my breath for too long, but this tightness didn't unspool when I exhaled. It grew until Na-Jhalar booted me in the ribs, curling me up like a poked caterpillar. By the time I could inhale, the dragon was gone, the Speaker no longer stood over me, and the crowd had parted. My two younger brothers, Jin and Dero, squatted in the dust at my mother's feet.

Both boys gawked at me, fascinated, wrapped like vines around her ankles. Aella watched as if she'd witnessed nothing more than Na-Jhalar stomping a rat. Then she stepped out of my brothers' grasp, steered them away, and left me lying in the dirt.

I'M WATCHING *our camp from the south slope, where I found the dragon scale. Petrified, swallowing against a swelling, prickly feeling in my stomach, I spot something across the valley, emerging from the woods. Something enormous.*

I can't make it out yet, but its passing uproots trees as if they're blades of grass. No one else in camp has noticed it. Immersed in their daily routine, they don't know what's coming.

I do.

I try to yell but no sound comes out. Dream air is like sap, and the noise sticks in my throat. Trees at the edge of the valley teeter wildly. Swarms of birds scatter. Jaundiced segments of white peek between trunks. Quivering, stocky feelers curl around branches.

The wurm's girth alone stretches wider than the entire circumference of our camp.

People see it now. It breaks, like a pulpy avalanche, through the north side and winds toward the river, oblivious to what lies in its expansive path. My hut folds like a crushed bug beneath it. People run, open-mouthed, screaming soundlessly.

Gevi, Arsu's mate, pumps his arms as he sprints toward his hut where I know their baby is napping, but he's not fast enough. The wurm ploughs over the hut while Gevi falls back in horror.

Saliva floods my mouth, and I gag, crashing to my knees.

Gevi crumples like someone's just snapped the line holding him up and he lies there, waiting, until the maggoty wave of flesh swallows him as well.

"No!" I shriek, but the vision swallows the sound. Tears stream down my face as I scramble to run down the slope, to stab at that repulsive, sightless face, anything to stop it. But I hold no weapon,

and my legs won't move. Beneath my feet the ground shudders under the weight of the wurm as it passes. The world shakes.

✣

STINGING pain blossomed across my cheek, and I came to the sluggish realization that someone was hitting me. All around me swam noise, thick and overwhelming. I couldn't grasp it. Babies crying. People shouting. The shrill calls of vaiyas. And someone's screaming drilling into my ears.

The ground is shaking. It's not just the dream, the whole world is rocking.

I had crawled back to my hut and fallen asleep after Na-Jhalar's beating. My father's face loomed in the chaotic darkness, fear in his eyes.

As Hasev raised his hand, I understood that he had been slapping me. *It's me.* I was the one screaming, so loudly that I couldn't hear what Hasev bellowed as my hut shuddered and the earth growled and rocks squealed around us.

I struggled out of my father's grip. Some small part of my mind balked, appalled by my actions, but the tremendous drive to run drowned everything else out.

"Daeson!" Hasev managed to grab me as I lunged for the hut's opening, and I gagged and shrivelled under his touch. "It's just an earthshake. Calm down!" My foot struck out as though I had no control over it, meeting his knee with a crack. He fell over, surprised, and the next thing I knew, I was outside and running, only vaguely aware of the vaiyas' shadows sprinting beside me in the moonlight as the world shuddered and yawed to the right. I scrambled to stay on my feet.

My flight was arrested by the river bordering our camp. I lost my footing, sank ankle-deep into the sandy bank, and skidded to my hands and knees. Pain radiated from my temples—echoes of Na-Jhalar's beating—all the way down to my sliced fingers. Gulping air, heart rattling at my ribs, I knelt with visions of that hideous, enormous wurm congealing like glue in my brain.

In the dim moonlight, the river sloshed, milled, and settled. Tremors beneath my knees thrummed and then finally subsided, but my neck still prickled with anxiety. I looked up.

Across the river stood a boy with red hair and a twisted root tied around his neck. There were others standing behind him, men and women. A trio of unfamiliar vaiyas screamed over their shoulders and my flock answered with challenges of their own, but their cries faded in my ears. My focus pinned to the necklace with the root because I knew what it meant. It was as if I had known he would be here. As if I had known I would find something at this river that would completely change the course of my life.

A daeson. It's another daeson.

CHAPTER THREE

It seemed fitting that the new tribe arrived on the heels of an earthshake, since their daeson shook everything I knew from its foundations. After I spotted him at the river, our camp moved quickly to separate our vaiyas—Vax would spar with any males and steal females if he won. Once both flocks were shackled and hooded, Na-Jhalar met with the visitors at our main hearth to negotiate their shelter.

Since they weren't dressed in the bright garb of Aeni—nomadic tribesfolk who blew like seeds between settlements—they were probably a group like us, perhaps refugees looking for a night of haven. Just as Nasheira's Guides were meant to shelter us from our harsh world, camps were expected, as a courtesy, to offer any travellers—except those who were branded—one night's worth of food and shelter.

Once, I complained about it to Hasev, as he'd always told me that food and shelter came at a cost, and if I didn't work for mine I wouldn't have them. "Why do travellers get one night free of food and rest, then?"

He snorted. "It isn't free. It's a fair exchange because

anyone who travels faster than the camps shares information about herd movements and trade routes."

More than one night shelter, however, required a more valuable trade, and if a group wished to join our camp permanently, Na-Jhalar weighed their supplies, skills, and herd animals against any disadvantages of taking them in. If this group wished to join ours, a daeson in their midst would be a significant mark against them. Lucky for them, this group also brought with them three breeding-age female vaiyas, an impressive stock of medicinal herbs, four hunters, three children, and two gatherers. One of the women was young, and Na-Jhalar's eyes lit up with desire when he saw her. When the daeson's group asked to join our camp for the week, I wasn't surprised that he said yes immediately and asked the girl to be his chani.

A chani was a Speaker's mate, set apart because, if she said yes, she was not allowed to mate with anyone else. A Speaker could have as many chani as they liked, male or female. To be asked was a great honour. Chani's immediate families received luxurious gifts and were held in high esteem. It was said that in times past, Speakers had provided for entire camps of chani and their families. Our camp was a small one. Na-Jhalar had only two chani. This new girl would make three.

The red-headed daeson appeared at my hut that evening. He stood at the entry for a ridiculously long time, staring at the symbol above the threshold.

I sat on my bedroll, too uncomfortable to invite him in, but also curious. I let him stand there, shifting his feet, while I examined the scrapes on his knees and bruises on his face.

One of his green eyes was blackened and swollen to a crescent slit and the other squinted back at me, hard and appraising, before we both looked away.

"I'm supposed to sleep here," he said. Then, apparently

deciding he didn't need an invitation, he entered the hut and stood above me. I suddenly wished I was standing too.

"You're a daeson?" I asked.

He sneered. "Obviously." He dropped his bedroll as far away from mine as possible, which wasn't very far.

"Are you the only daeson in your group?" I asked, and he ignored me, looking over the paltry contents of my home. He picked up the wooden bowl Hasev hadn't retrieved yet and turned it over.

"You're the only one I've ever met," I added. Hasev always dodged the question when I asked why there weren't more in our camp.

Silence.

"What's your name?" I asked.

The seconds drew out. I stared at his hair. The colour of ula leaves in the fall, redder than a sunset, it poked out of his head like it was trying to escape, but couldn't decide which direction to go. I'd never seen hair like it. Just as I decided he wasn't going to answer, he said, "Tanar." Then he grinned, an ugly smirk that pinched his freckled face.

"In Aeni, it means *trouble*," he added. Laying down on his mat, he turned his back to me. "You mind putting out that lamp?" I obeyed without thinking, and then I sat there in the dark while Tanar's breath became deep and even. A thousand questions burned on my tongue and I didn't have enough bile to ask any of them.

A baby cried from the opposite direction of camp, across the river. Tanar stirred once at the sound and then lay still.

As I lay awake wondering at Tanar's bruises and whether his name would prove prescient, I heard Aella and Hasev arguing again. Their voices grew so loud that Tanar woke with a snort.

"You encourage it, Hasev!" My mother's voice stung, venomous. "You treat it like your own son!"

"Aella, the boy screamed. I thought he'd been hurt." Hasev snapped.

"By what? That little shiver in the night? It always screams. Screaming brings your attention, and that's what it wants." Her voice broke. "It's as if you enjoy caring for it."

"*By the Guides*, would you rather I let the boy wake the whole camp? Should I let him starve? Would you have murder on our heads?"

"It's eleven years old! It can fend for itself!" She shouted now. The startled mew of my youngest brother, Dero, punctuated her words. "You treat it like a son, Hasev! You talk to it and teach it like a *son*! It is *daeson*!"

In the dark, I could see that Tanar's eyes were open. He was looking at me, and even though I knew it was far too dark for him to see it, the burning in my cheeks appalled me.

"It is *my* duty!" Hasev bellowed.

Aella's words changed from fire to ice. "Do you forget *my* duty, Hasev?" For a long moment, I heard nothing at all except Tanar fidgeting with his blanket and the blood pounding between my ears.

"Aella." My father's voice was soft, compassionate.

"Do you think you make it easier for me?" My mother sobbed now. Enough pain radiated from her words that my throat closed.

What duty is she talking about?

"Aella. I didn't think. Please..."

"It's daeson," she returned, through choking sobs. "It's *daeson*. Please, Hasev, treat it as such."

I clasped my hands over my ears and squeezed my eyes shut, wondering if all that had happened since I picked up the dragon scale—the earthshake, the dream, the stranger in my hut—was a result of my disobedience. *Why did I pick up the dragon scale? Why didn't I just leave it?*

TANAR'S TRIBE requested to join ours. They didn't have a healer of their own and one of their babies was sick, the one I'd heard crying from across the river. Our healer, Fraesh, had kept the baby's family away from the rest of camp until he could be sure the illness wasn't something catching. Once he assured Na-Jhalar it was safe, the Speaker accepted Tanar's tribe into ours at evening prayers.

Two weeks passed, and I learned just how much trouble Tanar was. While I tried to be as invisible as possible, Tanar made his intentions obvious, and they didn't include pleasing anyone. He fascinated me.

I'd spent my entire life moving, working, and hiding, driven by the urge to please the people around me. My inconspicuousness was perhaps the only thing that *did* please them.

When I caught Tanar dulling the edge of a blade he was meant to be sharpening, he looked up with that grin that didn't meet his eyes and said, "Since I can't do anything right, I'll do everything wrong!"

The boy was a mirror image of Pau himself, disobeying rules and making mischief. Everything about him seemed a blatant act of defiance. He wore black eyes like badges, and it didn't take long for him to draw the loathing of Na-Jhalar like a raw hide absorbs water.

Tanar took immense pleasure in maddening our Speaker. He taught the vaiyas unspeakable vulgarities, all of them referencing the leader of our camp.

It took me two frantic days to break the flock's new, offensive habit. I didn't doubt I would have been flailed for their misconduct, except for the fact that Tanar also taught the birds to announce his name at the end of their proclamations. He took several cruel beatings in his first weeks with us, and required considerable care afterwards. Although he preferred to sleep outside when the weather allowed it (I preferred it too), he spent more than one night in my cramped hut too weak and bloody to crawl elsewhere.

The wurm dream haunted me several nights a week, the cold vision creeping under my door flap and pinning me under its horrible weight.

✣

SOMEONE ROUSED me from restless sleep, and I screamed, swatting the hand away. I sat up, panting.

Muted light filtered through the space under my door, but not enough to identify the shadow swaying before me.

"Who's there?" I coughed, pulling my clammy blanket up to my chin. The unsteady form crumpled over and curled into a ball, sniffling once. Squinting, I glimpsed dishevelled red hair.

"Tanar?" I leaned forward, my head still swimming with sleep.

Nothing but an inhuman gurgling came from the pile on my floor. My stomach clenched as I remembered the wurm dream. Stumbling to my hands and knees, I crawled past the prostrate form and pulled back the door flap to let in the moonlight. Soft silver beams fell upon Tanar, revealing glistening ribbons of blood running from his nostrils to his chin. For some reason, I was instantly angry at him. I gagged down the urge to shove him back out my door.

"What did you do?" I shouted.

Tanar gurgled.

Letting go of the curtain, I stumbled over his feet, cursing as I felt my way back to my bedroll. I grabbed some rags and hurried outside toward the river.

The water looked dark and bottomless, like a door to the

middle of the earth. Shivering, I dunked the rags under and wrung them out. From my hut, Tanar groaned loudly enough for half the camp to hear.

Tanar blinked rapidly as I re-entered and pinned the door flap open. He still lay on his back with a stupid, half grin pasted across his lips even now. I wanted to drop all of the soggy rags onto his face. Instead, I dabbed at the drying streaks on his chin.

"Guides, why do you do it?"

He didn't answer.

"He'll kill you one of these times, and even Nasheira won't fault him for it!"

He sneered.

I pulled the rag away and leaned back.

"He can't hurt me," Tanar said. His teeth flashed, and he tossed his shoulders and squealed in a high, giddy voice, "No one can hurt me!"

"Be quiet!" I hissed.

He fell silent, still grinning as I mopped at his face hard enough to make him flinch. I wanted to scrub the smile right off his lips. It was making me shiver, like it always did.

"Why can't you just act like a normal daeson?" I mumbled.

"Normal." Tanar snorted, and I jumped as fresh blood sprayed out of his nose. "Normal like you?" His face bunched into an ugly scowl. "Pretending that everything is fine? Ignoring what's going to happen in the end? You're the one who's not normal."

Oily smoke from the lamp swirled around us. My throat ached as I swallowed against the cold churning in my stomach.

He analyzed my face and his grin faltered. "Your dutiful father didn't have the stones to tell you, did he?"

Staring at him, I felt a terrible, prickling sense of doom squeezing me.

"Do they brand us?" I asked.

He shook his head.

"What then?" I snapped.

Tanar's head rolled back, like I wasn't worth his attention.

Heat clotted in my stomach. I gripped his shoulder and shook him. "Tell me what they do, Tanar!" He lurched up, shoulders hunched, back rigid, and I recoiled at the instant anger pinching his face.

"They sacrifice us."

"What?"

"They bind us and cut us when Pau swallows Yurrii." He giggled.

"You're not making sense."

"They cut us. They. Cut. Us!" he screeched.

"Stop it!" I shouted and shoved him back down. He wouldn't stop laughing, but he didn't rise again.

"Do you remember the creation story?" Tanar asked with morbid calmness now. "Remember Pau's punishment?"

I was silent. I couldn't make myself leave. I had to know.

"Nasheira takes Pau's seed," he urged hoarsely. "His mother takes his seed."

"I don't understand." I swallowed. It was a lie. I didn't want to understand.

Tanar clutched my arm. "She takes away the gift of life. She makes him barren." He slumped back onto the mat.

"You're lying," I said. "They're not allowed to kill us."

He shrugged. "They don't kill us. Technically. They cut us and leave us bleeding. But we're as good as dead."

"Who told you this?" I didn't know why I asked. I didn't want an answer. I wanted Tanar gone.

His eyes unfocused and his lips trembled before he answered. "My mother used to come stand outside of my hut every morning to tell me."

I could only stare.

"And your pretty little mother will cut you."

"Stop it!" I shouted.

Tanar giggled deliriously now. He made a slicing motion across his crotch with one hand.

"Get out!" I hauled him toward the door. I wanted to hit him. It took everything I had not to. "Get out. Get out!" I shrieked.

He did. And I was alone, sitting in the dirt in the middle of my hut. I held my head in my hands like it would break apart if I let go. I couldn't breathe.

"No," I said aloud. "No, no, no." Not true. Tanar lied. Even as I clamped my hands over my ears, words of the creation story came to me.

"My first son, you shall never again grow the seed of life."

How could I have been so stupid? There were no other daeson in our camp, and Hasev would never tell me why. They weren't banished. They were butchered.

"It's not true," I sobbed rocking back and forth. "Not true."

Familiar numbness gripped me, like falling through ice and slipping into the authority of dark waters. It pulled my panic from me in cold waves of shock. I stumbled out my door, past the twisted wurm above my head and past Tanar.

I don't recall whether I found Vax, or he found me. I just remember flopping at his feet, the strength of his elegant neck curling around me, and his hot breath against my cold, slack face.

"Safe," the vaiya crooned, as I curled against his solid warmth, but I knew with wretched certainty that I'd never be safe again.

CHAPTER FOUR

"Tanar is sick." My voice sounded grainy and foreign. I felt numb and far away from the cold hut where Hasev squatted across from me. I'd called him here before dawn, after Tanar had crawled away to Nasheira knows where, but long before the hunters left for the day. "Does he have to stay here?"

My father scratched at his beard and shrugged. He wouldn't meet my gaze. He'd been coming to see me less and less since the new daeson had arrived. I wondered if he was afraid Tanar would tell me the truth.

"Is that what this is about?" he huffed. "You call me out here before dawn to whine about sharing your hut?"

"I don't want to catch it. I think it's what the baby across the river had." This wasn't really what I wanted to talk about. I didn't care about the sickness or Tanar.

Hasev let out a short burst of nervous laughter, one that shook his frame like the trees in the earthshake. Wiping the sweat from his brow with the back of his arm, he blurted, "What would you have me do, daeson, eh?" When he spread his arms, they nearly brushed both walls. He actually waited to see if I'd answer, but when I didn't, he scrutinized me, leaning forward and lowering his voice as if he were sharing a secret. "Akrist."

I flinched at the unexpected use of my name. For a second, I couldn't help it; I felt like I was just a normal boy. Then it was gone.

"You are old enough to sort out small problems like this for yourself. The boy can sleep outside for all I care, or you can. It's warm. He can build his own hut soon."

My stomach collapsed, sucked at my ribs and pulled at my throat. Aella was wrong. Hasev didn't care about me. I couldn't keep the words burning my throat buried any longer.

"What happens to us?" I spat.

"What?" Hasev's eyebrows drew together.

"What happens?" I enunciated each word with careful measure. "What happens to the daeson?" I raised my gaze even though tears pricked my eyes. I stared at my father and willed him to answer me, to tell me that it was all a mistake. I'd never stood up to him like this.

Hasev pressed his lips together and stared back, his face folding into misery. "We're not talking about this."

Yes we are. "You say I'm old enough to sort out my own problems. Don't treat me like a child then. Tell me what happens."

Silence yawned between us. Hasev curled into it and clamped his fists.

"Tell me, please."

Silence.

"Do our mothers cut us and leave us to die?" My voice wobbled, and I jammed my fingernails into the soft flesh of my palms to steady myself. *Say it isn't true, Hasev. Please, just say it.* But Hasev's eyes hardened and he looked right through me.

"Say it isn't true," I choked.

Tears filled his eyes and the sight of them undid me. I sagged, mouth opening and closing like a beached fish, thoughts sloshing through my head like scalding water.

"The creation story," I whispered, cold shock slipping through my veins. "You made me tell it over and over again."

Hasev's shoulders dropped and his smallness left room for rage to thicken the air between us. "What was it to you, some sort of riddle?" I rasped. "Was I supposed to figure *this* out from repeating it?"

He said nothing, looking so defeated that I almost pitied him. But instead, I continued yelling. "You are a coward! You made me dance around the truth! You pretended to care!" Heat filled my chest, burning up any air that I had left. Nausea followed like thick smoke.

Hasev shifted. "Let me—"

"Get out," I barked, clutching my stomach.

"I never—"

"GET OUT!" I screeched. It was the second time in as many hours that I'd chased someone from my hut with those words.

I DIDN'T LEAVE my hut that day or night. I clapped my hands over my ears and covered my head with my blanket to block out the outside world. Even Vax chirping and clicking his beak forlornly outside my door couldn't rouse me. By the time I did emerge, my head felt stuffed full of cobwebs and I was shocked to see a small hut had been erected just north of mine. I recognized Tanar's wurm necklace hanging above its entry. He must have built it yesterday. Dawn hadn't kissed the horizon yet, but lamplight seeped beneath the crack in

Tanar's door flap, so I cleared my dry throat and asked to come in.

And what I found in the red-headed daeson's new hut sent a fresh plume of shame hissing through me.

A baby. *It must be another daeson from their camp, because no mother would allow her child this close to a son of Pau otherwise.*

"Pin the door shut behind you." The red-headed boy curled on his side in the dirt, his back toward me while the baby lay gurgling on Tanar's bedroll. An ugly X-shaped scar marred the child's wrinkled forehead.

"Why is he marked like that?" I asked, aghast.

Blood still caked Tanar's hair. He smelled like he hadn't washed, and the sickly whistle of his breathing made me edgy. I opened my mouth to repeat my question and Tanar rolled toward me.

I clamped my mouth shut. His wounds oozed, purple and green, possibly infected, and his nose was bent so badly that I didn't think he'd ever breathe normally again.

"He's a twin." Tanar replied. "Did you see the other baby with its mother? They're brothers. Identical. This one was born first but his parents hate the second-born boy almost as much as him. They think he's tainted from sharing the womb."

Just like touching my mother's stomach tainted Tasie.

Tanar shrugged. "But there's only one true daeson in the pair. His parents can only sacrifice one, and they couldn't risk mixing up the two of them."

"Guides," I hissed. *A baby. They did this to a baby. They'll have no problem at all cutting you.*

"Aye, Guides." Tanar grinned.

"Why is he here?"

"He's feeling better now. Your healer said he didn't have to stay across the river anymore. And his father was barely feeding him over there anyways. I take care of him so he doesn't starve. I call him Xen." The baby reached for Tanar, so he extended his hand and let those chubby fingers grip his as if it were the most natural thing in the world. I had never seen him look so at peace.

The baby from across this river. A daeson all this time, and I didn't know it.

Except for the whistle of his breathing, the red-headed boy sat silently regarding the daeson infant. I realized he was waiting for me, for the questions he knew were coming.

I swallowed and braced myself. "Do they cut everything?"

"Some mothers do."

I looked up and, although Tanar's eyes had nearly swollen shut, he studied me coolly. I found no anger in the green.

Mother of Yurrii, why can't there be anger? Something normal, something expected? Tanar, I was learning, never did what was expected.

"They're only supposed to cut off your stones, but sometimes they cut everything off. You'll never last the two days if that happens." Tanar shrugged and smiled sadly. "I heard a few mothers get so upset they can't do it, and another has to cut their daeson for them. It's the worst shame a woman can have, to fail Nasheira like that. Most make the cut themselves, no matter how upset they are. Some do a good job. Others…" His lips twitched. "Others make mistakes." Tanar looked down and frowned. "It's not murder if it's an accident." His voice soured with sarcasm. "It's Nasheira's will then."

My skin crawled as I asked, "When?"

"When Pau swallows Yurrii." Before I could question him, he added, "I don't know what it means. I just know we won't make it to manhood."

A boy was considered a man only after his twelfth year. He was allowed to scar his chest after that.

Tanar reached into his pocket, peeled a long strip of dried

meat from a meager bundle and offered it to the baby. When the child squealed and released Tanar's finger to latch onto the jerky, the red-headed boy smiled, a genuine smile, the first I'd ever seen from him.

"Who told you all this?" I whispered finally. My voice sounded brittle.

"A daeson," Tanar replied. "One who lived through the sacrifice."

"How old was he?" I asked.

Tanar shrugged. "Twenty years maybe."

"From your camp? They took him back after the sacrifice?" I couldn't hide the pathetic hope in those questions.

"Guides, no." Tanar shook his head. "The camp always journeys after a sacrifice. Even if a daeson lives through the cutting, he is Nasheira's for two days. He's tied so he can't escape and find his camp, and it's forbidden for a camp to take him, or any other daeson, back before the two days. Afterwards, the aeni found him and took him in."

Aeni were the fastest of travellers, they lived out of tents and the packs on their backs, gathering and hunting as they went. And they were forever sweeping into camps, depleting stocks, drawing impressionable youth into their colourful, carefree midst, and flitting off with new followers. It made sense that they'd pick up straggling daeson too. They were keen traders who'd know the value of a life saved. Aeni didn't do anything for free. A life saved was a life owed. How would a daeson with nothing possibly repay such a debt?

"The daeson smiled as he told me, laughed at the look on my face. I told him he was a liar. I was only six and even though my mother had told me every day, I still didn't believe she'd cut me. He showed me how they'd cut him, and I ran to my father, clutching at him, begging him to tell me it wasn't true."

I did the same. I'm eleven and I still ran to Hasev like a toddler wanting reassurance.

Tanar grinned that awful grin. "He slapped me, looked at me like I was a wurm, and told me it was true."

"What did you do?" I whispered. *What should I do?*

"I ran away and nearly starved to death before I crawled back again. I've stayed since then, until our Speaker died and our camp split and we found you." The smile slid from his face coldly.

"You want to die?" I winced as I said it.

Tanar shrugged, tugging the blanket down as Xen yanked it over his own face. "I want to be a sliver under their skin."

I stared at my feet in the dust. A long, lifeless silence swallowed us. The numbness grasping me now was a blessed release.

"What if we leave?"

Tanar shook his head. "Won't work. We'll starve. I steal enough to feed Xen and me day-to-day, but I can't stockpile anything," he sighed. "My father searches my hut too often."

"Mine doesn't," I croaked and Tanar fixed me with a strange, hungry gaze before breaking into a genuine smile, one that lit up his face.

CHAPTER FIVE

I returned to my hut before the rest of the camp woke and lay with the weight of my fate paralyzing me. It was an odd, indignant feeling, listening while daily life churned around me as it always had, oblivious to my world turned on its head.

South of my hut, Aella cooed as she gathered my sleepy brothers onto vaiyas, strapped on her carry baskets, and followed the gatherers walking up the south side of the valley. In mornings past, I'd sometimes followed and foraged too. As long as I stayed respectfully distant from the others, no one told me where to go or what to do.

Other mornings, I had stayed with the elders. They huddled around fires as I mended, scraped, or sliced food for drying. No one thanked me for my contributions or chided me if I shirked because no one spoke to me. My camp considered everything I gathered, mended, gutted, or skinned to be tainted and only safe for adults to use. Children were too vulnerable to risk exposure to anything gathered by my cursed hand. Hasev had always told me I had to earn my shelter and everybody was needed for a camp to prosper. But, I realized now, that's all I was to them. A *body.* A tool for picking and carrying, not even as valuable as a vaiya.

Your work won't be trivial now. You have to gather and hide enough food for you, Tanar, and the baby to escape. We hadn't been taught to hunt and my head hurt thinking about how much the three of us would need to stockpile to survive the winter alone. *How in Nasheira's name are you going to find enough food?*

Tanar had warmed considerably, and though I barely knew him, I craved the closeness of a friend. I wanted to prove to him that I could do this, and I needed to keep my mind off the fact that my own family intended to mutilate me.

And then it clicked. An idea. I knew where to start, but I'd have to wait until the hunters left.

Sitting up, I listened as hunters gulped down the last drops of hot tea from clay mugs and stood tolerantly while their elders crammed leaf packets of leftovers into every fold of their clothing. Cradling familiar weapons, the hunters marched past my hut to the north with our three quietest vaiyas in tow. *Only the Speaker and the elders are left now.*

Some mornings, the Speaker commandeered Vax to carry him up the valley to follow the gatherers. Other days, he chewed gifen leaves until his eyes blurred. Today, I had to know for certain if he was staying in camp or going because I needed Vax for what I was about to attempt.

I trotted toward the centre of camp in time to see Na-Jhalar duck back into his hut with his favourite chani, the new girl—Tanar said her name was Delani. I winced at the thought of her under him. Three times in the past two weeks, I'd seen the slight girl leaving the Speaker's hut with her sleeve pulled over her wrist, dabbing her bleeding nose.

Na-Jhalar likes to hit.

Chani had the choice to accept or reject a Speaker's proposal. But I suddenly wondered if Na-Jhalar would have been so agreeable to Tanar's camp joining ours if she had said no.

With the Speaker in camp for the day, nobody would miss Vax. The big vaiya was too unruly for the gatherers, and too loud for the hunters. I could steal away and be back before anyone noticed Vax was missing.

I whistled for him, a low warble of a common day bird, and the big vaiya rounded a hut behind me with a squawk that made me start.

"Bird brain," I chided with a grin as he nudged his head into my chest. "Were you following me?"

"Hide and seek!" he crowed.

"Shhh." I patted down his crest and untied his shackles. "Not now. I have a job for you. Want cobnuts?"

"Cobnuts. Yes!" Vax tossed his head and shifted on his two-toed feet, kicking up dust.

"Come on then." The patriarch trailed me back to my hut where I retrieved my carry bag and climbing rope. At my hand signal, he crouched, curled his neck behind me and tucked his head under my shoulders to boost me onto his back. I gripped his neck rope. Before I'd finished swinging my leg over his back, we were off.

With the lightest touch of my legs, I steered Vax through the advancing trees on the northern face. The wind howled past my ears and I couldn't contain a grin of exhilaration.

I had a plan now, and riding tall on the silver back of a powerful vaiya, I was beginning to think maybe I could do it. *We could escape. This could work.* I pressed Vax northward and he trilled and lengthened his stride until my hair blew wildly in the wind and my eyes watered.

Gatherers weren't allowed here. The northern hunting territory was riddled with pit traps and snares that could cause deadly accidents to those unfamiliar with their location.

Weeks ago, the hunters had found a grove of cobnuts at the end of the eastern trapline. They'd brought home basketfuls of the nuts, but cobnut trees grew tall, and I wagered that the hunters hadn't stripped the grove as efficiently as the gatherers would have. As long as I stayed off the trap lines and away from the hunters, I could make a healthy start to our cache, unwitnessed.

The grove was easy to find. The east trap line followed the river. Hasev had warned me of its proximity because the vaiyas had a favourite beach near it, and I visited it with them often. At the end of the trapline, where the river curved east, a clump of gnarled, multi-stemmed trees displayed their pale yellow leaves like a banner. As I'd suspected, a heavy harvest still clung to the topmost branches, out of reach of even the tallest vaiya.

"Cobnuts!" Vax demanded, stretching his neck and clicking his beak in frustration.

"Patience." I unfurled my climbing rope. The trees were easily fifteen hands high, but too spindly to climb. "Stand still, Vax. Don't move or I'll fall."

"Still." He bobbed his head.

I planted my feet on the small of my vaiya's back and stood with my arms wide.

"Cobnuts now." He whistled.

Gathering the rope in one hand, I tossed one end overhead, aiming to loop it over the closest branch.

"Missed," Vax lamented.

"Critic," I murmured and tried again, this time snagging the branch enough to bend it toward us.

Vax shifted.

"Hey!" I shouted, clinging to the rope. "Stay still." He settled obediently.

We gathered enough cobnuts to appease Vax and fill half my carry bag. I stashed the bag under a pile of rocks near the river within walking distance of camp. If any of the elders spotted me arriving with gathered goods, Hasev would be sure to ask me to produce them later.

Shouts greeted me as Vax and I entered the camp, and I realized something was terribly wrong. Our Speaker rounded the closest hut like a charging bull.

"Daeson!" he barked. Delani and the elders fanned out behind him. "Did you take my bird?" He clutched Vax's neck rope even as the vaiya shied away.

I pressed two fingers to my forehead, crumpled to the ground and nodded.

Na-Jhalar's foot slammed into my side, and all the air left my lungs.

"No!" Vax hissed.

"Shut up!" Na-Jhalar held fast to the neck strap.

The big vaiya's crest flared and he dropped into a defensive stance. He was picking up the Speaker's emotion, amplifying it. All vaiyas did it. If I didn't diffuse this soon, Vax could get agitated enough to strike.

It's okay, Vax. I wanted to say, but I couldn't inhale. When I could, I blurted, "I'm sorry. He just wanted a run. I thought you weren't using him. I'm sorry."

Na-Jhalar kicked me a third time, but it was half-hearted. "You will be," he muttered. Pulling Vax into crouching position, he hoisted himself onto the vaiya's back. I had a horrible feeling in the pit of my stomach.

Vax lurched to a stand, wide-eyed and trembling.

"With undisciplined animals," The Speaker announced, "If one method doesn't reach them, you find another that does." He turned to Delani. "There's always a method that reaches them, isn't that right?"

She nodded, pale-faced.

"Go get me a rock from the hearth."

Delani nodded again and trotted away.

Oh Guides. I'd seen him break a man's fingers like this once. For brushing up against one of his chani. I clutched my hands to my chest. "Please." the word slipped past my lips, high-pitched and desperate.

Vax stamped his foot. Dust billowed around us while elders coughed and looked at their feet.

"Please don't." I whimpered again as Delani trotted back toward us lugging a boulder half the size of her head.

"No hurt!" Vax barked and moved to block me.

The Speaker jerked at the vaiya's harness and steered him away. "Hand it over." He leaned down and Delani passed the rock up to him.

I cringed, bracing myself for the pain that would follow.

Na-Jhalar hoisted the rock above his head and smashed it into the side of Vax's face. It hit with a wet crack. The vaiya squealed, staggered and pitched sideways, toppling the Speaker.

"Vax!" I screeched.

Several people screamed with me as Na-Jhalar rolled to his feet with the rock still in his fist and brought it down on Vax's head again.

"Speaker, stop!" Someone staggered forward and snatched his wrist.

I scrambled toward Vax on my belly.

Blood dribbled onto the dust in front of me, alarmingly red.

Vax's legs kicked. I couldn't reach him without getting gored by his spurs.

"It's useless, just like this daeson is." Na-Jhalar sneered and hefted the rock again.

"It's the patriarch! Please, Speaker," the elder who held him rasped while my vaiya's sides heaved.

He's breathing. I sobbed loudly. *Please Nasheira. He can't die.*

"It's no good for hunting or gathering. It's only good as an example." The Speaker sniffed.

An awful keening sound pressed out of my vaiya.

"If you kill it, the whole flock will scatter. There isn't a male bird old enough to take over. We'll lose them all. The whole flock. Please, Na-Jhalar. Put the rock down!" I recognized the elder now—Iva, our storyteller. Her position was nearly as important as the Speaker's.

He might listen to her.

Na-Jhalar stared at Iva. His face twisted and hung there. Then he blinked, refocused on me, and grinned at the tears rolling down my face. He let the rock roll out of his hand. It hit the ground beside me with a thud.

I flinched as he leaned close enough for me to smell rotting teeth and gifen on his breath. "If I catch you stealing from me again—dragon scale or vaiya or a bloody blade of kiro grass—I'll make you sorry you ever lived. Understand?"

I nodded and sobbed, unable to pull my gaze away from my writhing vaiya.

The Speaker seemed to delight in my tears. He straightened and walked back toward the centre of camp with his crowd following behind him.

"Vax," I croaked, scrambling around his flailing legs. My breath cut off as his face came into view. "Oh, no, Vax," I blurted. "Oh, Nasheira, no!"

Thick blood oozed from the right side of his face. The ridge above his bony brow pressed into his skull like a crushed egg, and his eye was a jellied mess.

"Ouch," he whimpered, and I folded as nausea overpowered me.

Mother of Yurrii, it's my fault. Na-Jhalar maimed him to hurt me.

"I'm sorry, Vax," I choked. "I'm so sorry."

Blood spattered my thigh as the vaiya lifted his head and nuzzled my outstretched hand. I leaned my head against the good side of Vax's face as wretched sobs tore at my chest. Stroking his crest, I babbled, "It's going to be okay, Vax. I'm sorry. It's going to be okay." The lie stung my mouth.

CHAPTER SIX

The night after Na-Jhalar tried to kill Vax, the moons tracked through the sky. Pau followed behind the lesser moon, bloated and full, overpowering his little brother's pale light with sallow yellow tones.

My people believed that Nasheira's sons were most powerful at their fullest, and since Pau was bigger, his malevolence peaked on nights like this. We held a ceremony to balance it, an arrangement of long-winded patterned prayers, and a double mark on Na-Jhalar's wooden slab calendar. The ceremony was sealed with the drinking of a special tea, steeped with the leaves of a rare plant whose foliage resembled dragon scales. Drinking Guide's leaf tea was supposed to counteract Pau's evil with the blessings of Yurrii.

I'd always hated the tea's bitter taste. The whole idea that drinking the disgusting brew would somehow thwart misfortune seemed ridiculous. But tonight, under the moons, I sat with Vax's head in my lap, holding a poultice over the swelling, ugly wound, and I guzzled Guide's leaf tea until my stomach ached. I prayed. Sweet Nasheira, how I prayed.

Iva had been right about Vax's importance. While the big vaiya wasn't suited for hunting or gathering, he was indispensable to the flock. Without him, our socially dependent group of vaiyas would disintegrate. We had no male old enough to take Vax's place so the females would seek out wild flocks with a big male to take them in. That's why Tanar's tribe had been so desperate to join ours. It wasn't just our healer that attracted them. It was Vax. They'd have eventually lost their vaiya hens without a male to hold them.

A week after the full moon ceremony, the elders convened and Na-Jhalar announced that we'd be following the gazelle herds south.

Vax's wounds were still pus-filled and red. He picked at his bandages every time I changed them. Guides, I'd never felt so helpless. *He's not fit to travel, and if he dies during a journey, your camp will be stranded, and it will be your fault.*

My only relief came from an unexpected source. Tanar had opened up completely, and we had started planning our escape. He helped me with Vax and added his daily stolen rations to our cache. We'd buried our cobnuts and some dried meat under my sleeping mat, but we hadn't had time to stash more. Vax and Xen took most of our time. As our camp packed around us, we hastily sewed false bottoms into our carry bags and divided our paltry stash between us. We'd need to steal more if we were going to survive, but I couldn't get Na-Jhalar's warning out of my head. *If I catch you stealing from me again, I'll make you sorry you ever lived.*

WE BURIED OUR PIT TRAPS, dug up Na-Jhalar's precious patch of gifen plants, and journeyed south. Our camp followed the river through the valley and into a broad forest of pechi trees. When we reached a waterfall, the forest parted like a sliced loaf, with trees hanging horizontally into the abyss. We couldn't scale the cliff to follow the river, so Na-Jhalar chose to steer us west. We filled our water bags and obeyed. Two days later, as we followed the ridge ever further from the river, we spied a golden Guide, silent and circling high in the heavens above our caravan—confirmation that our Speaker had made the right choice.

We had a festival that night.

"This is our chance," I murmured to Tanar as Na-Jhalar announced it. "They'll lay out more food than anyone can eat tonight, and Hasev always forgets to feed me when there's a festival. It's the only time he chews gifen. Everyone will be distracted."

We decided I would steal the food and Tanar would act as lookout. Sweet Nasheira, I'd rather do anything else, but this wasn't a chance I'd get again. Festivals were rare. We needed food to escape, and Tanar's red hair, bruised face, and ugly sneer drew too much attention. It had to be me.

That night, we watched as people set out platters of roasted tubers and nutty bread on bright blankets south of a temporary hearth.

The children had raided two bird nests this afternoon, and now the eggs sat freshly boiled, like speckled pearls on a bed of greens. Blood sausages and rounds of soft vaiya cheese all awaited the stomach of the Speaker and his chani. Pots of scalding tea and little clay bowls of gifen leaves lined the centre of the spread.

Elders helped women and children unpack their elegant beaded tunics. The beads were made of painted wood or tiny rounds of bone. The children's were relatively simple, but the women stitched their tunics in complicated, enchanting patterns with so much beadwork they clattered when they moved. When the women lifted their arms in dance, the splayed fabric of their wide, swirling sleeves would look like the wings of a dragon, glinting in the firelight.

Everyone will be watching them. They won't see you.

The men wandered bare-chested, wearing only soft breechcloths, belts, and leggings like mine. Their faces blazed with glowing white paint, and feathered armbands wrapped their upper arms. Most carried hollow, decorated rhythm sticks, and some still smeared finishing touches of speckled red paint to the scars on their wide chests.

"Come on." I beckoned to Tanar.

We herded the excited vaiyas away from the bright, flapping dancers who made my birds stamp their feet and squawk loudly. If I didn't settle them somewhere quiet, I risked a beating, and the thought of Na-Jhalar standing over me again tightened my chest so hard I could barely breathe.

"You all right?" Tanar glanced sideways at me. "It's not too late to switch. I can steal."

"I'm fine," I lied.

We sat with the flock for a while. I hummed tunelessly under my breath in an effort to calm Vax enough to change his bandage. A horrible heat rose in my cheeks and my vision blurred every time I peeled back the padding over his crushed eye socket. *My fault.*

"Stay up." He nudged his head against my chest defiantly as I secured a fresh bandage, and I obligingly stroked his crest.

"No, Vax," I spoke firmly.

"Itchy?" he persisted.

"You are not. Where, Vax?" I sighed. "Where are you itchy?" When he didn't answer, I made him promise to stay and protect the flock.

He settled with an exaggerated huff, and Tanar and I returned to the main hearth. Elba, a young woman, saw us and clutched her arms, frowning pointedly at the ground between us. People held varying opinions on what close contact with a daeson was. Elba preferred half a camp away, it seemed.

"If I see anyone looking your way, I'll make some noise." Tanar grinned.

The dancers stood in twos and threes, shifting their costumes and hushing their children. They waited, their gaze on the tree line crowning the northern ridge, where Yurrii had already risen, and Pau's light shone like lace through inky, fanned branches. A rehearsed silence fell over the crowd when the second moon crested the tree line, and I knew, even before I looked, that Na-Jhalar had emerged.

I skirted the dancers, edging toward the blanket full of food and craning my neck to see the Speaker. I glimpsed the single blushing dragon scale against its golden backdrop. My throat closed, and heat rushed to my head. *Easy. You can do this.* I stroked my hand where four bulging scars traced a red path through the creases of my fingers. The necklace shifted, and the pink sliver slipped from my view. I eased into position behind the tent closest to the food.

Apart from his holy neckwear, Na-Jhalar stood completely naked. Tradition dictated that, on such sacred occasions as this, the proper formal wear for a Speaker was nothing at all. After all, what human-made adornment could improve that which Nasheira had hand-picked? Standing beside his quietly radiant girls in their simple white tunics, Na-Jhalar barely looked human at all.

The Speaker cleared his throat and raised his arms. The skin beneath dangled as he recited the day of the year and plunged into the opening words of a prayer. The circle around the main hearth answered in practised monotone.

I knew the prayer well and mouthed the words through gritted teeth until it wove to a finish as the Speaker lowered his arms.

Delani presented him his meal, and he plopped down, penis flopping against his thigh. The chani sat at his feet, offering him morsels of food, half of which fell out of his mouth as he chewed, rolled down his belly, and lodged between his legs never to see the light of day again. The food he wasted could have fed me for a week.

The dancers stood in their opening stance, circling the fire. The women moved first. Silent, floating, the beads on their costumes shivering like dew, and their faces glowing in the firelight. My mother stood above the crowd. She'd braided her hair in a twisting knot at the base of her neck that made her look girlish, yet she moved like an untamed thing, with the unrehearsed grace of a creature in its element.

I shuddered. She didn't *look* like a murderer.

The other women churned about her like water, fabric frothing and slapping at bare thighs. The slow crescendo of rhythm sticks beat in time with the dancer's footsteps. As the hollow sound grew, the women transformed. Their steps were weighted and inhuman. Heat flashed in their eyes, wild and piercing. In a flash, the armoured tunics unfurled, and a million shining points rippled against the glow of the fire. Sweat gleamed like tiny scales on their temples. They were dragons just like the one we'd seen today. Spinning and wheeling effortlessly through swaths of smoke.

Pay attention. It's almost time. My mouth dried out, my attention divided between the dancers and the elders closest to the food.

Rhythm sticks cracked like thunder, drumming through my chest. I held my breath and watched the white faces of the men bobbing like tiny moons cresting a smoky storm. They jumped in time with the women now, leaping so high, they could have reached up and plucked Yurrii right out of his stony grave.

And then the singing started. The elders, children, and the dancers began to harmonize. It was a wordless, powerful melody, rising like an unsettled wind, tugging at the dancers, thrusting them into ever faster spins and leaps, rising in breathtaking intensity.

Go now. I held my breath, lunged around the hut and skidded to a stop at the edge of the blanket. My hands shook as I shovelled handful after handful of blood sausages into the front of my shirt. There was a roaring in my ears, louder than the song. Feet stomped and beads flashed. Noise swamped my mind. My legs froze beneath me. I saw Tanar's bright hair and wide eyes between the jostling limbs of the dancers.

Move, he mouthed and pointed.

One of the children spun toward me, heedless of my presence as they giggled and broke the dance formation.

Tanar whistled loudly and the child turned and balked at the sight of a daeson. Several other dancers turned to Tanar and glared, herding the child away from him. Daeson were forbidden from touching or even drawing near to other children. The close call shook everyone who saw it, distracting them from me.

I stumbled backward, clutching the greasy sausages against me, and turning my back on them all. It took everything I had not to run back to my tent. Every agonizing second, I expected someone to shout and point. Yet as I ducked into my tent, there were no shouts. I fell to my hands and knees gulping for air and pressing my forehead to the ground.

Outside, the dance ended and folded into silence as my heart sang in my head. Na-Jhalar recited a listless blessing as I dumped the sausages onto my bedroll and hastily unpicked the stitches on the false bottom of my carry sack. By the time the happy clatter of dishes settled outside, I'd tucked them all in. Blood sausages could keep for a whole season. We were well on our way to caching enough to escape.

I jumped as my tent flap opened, ready to bolt past whoever had come to capture me.

"It's just me." Tanar grinned. "You did it."

A nervous laugh barked out of me. "We did it." I hid my carry sack in case Hasev came to feed me later, but he never came.

You don't need him anymore. I mused, chewing on a chunk of rich blood sausage. *You can take care of yourself.*

CHAPTER SEVEN

Days after the festival, we found the desert. We skirted east along its sandy edge, trying to link back to the river we'd parted from at the ridge, but we couldn't find it, and vicious windstorms pressed us southward, surrounding us with dunes.

Our water supply dwindled. We switched to travelling at night and the flock lost rations first. Vaiyas could survive without drinking for weeks, but not without suffering. They stopped begging for water after three nights. Then they stopped speaking. I considered stealing water for them, but Na-Jhalar posted Darvie and Iva as guards, two of the camp's most vigilant hunters.

The sand dunes gave way to pale, weathered rock formations. Some were small enough to skirt, others impassable. Many hills, with their smooth, worn surfaces, presented a deceivingly easy climb but were dangerous to navigate, riddled with hidden cracks.

We shifted the vaiyas' diminutive water bags so that they could carry a few of the spent adults and children, and we trod carefully onward.

One morning, a few hours before sunrise, as I trudged behind the strung-out caravan with the vaiya flock, a cry peeled across the rocks. As I turned toward it, I heard an awful, gurgling yell followed by the shocking thud of a large body collapsing. The vaiya flock burst into startled alarm, their crests raised. Another sharp cry howled through me.

Vir had miss-stepped, perhaps due to the poor lighting. Most likely though, dehydration and exhaustion caused the vaiya to slip into the narrow crevasse that broke her leg.

She'd pitched forward, partially throwing her passengers before skidding further down the hill. What I saw next pounded the breath out of me.

Gevi's legs were pinned underneath a thrashing, screeching Vir. He lay on his stomach, and I knew by the way he arched his back that his baby was at his chest. He was trying to save his child from being crushed, his face drawn in agony just as I'd seen it in the wurm vision.

My downed vaiya screamed and whipped her tail as I crawled closer.

Then Gevi saw me.

Automatically, I averted my eyes, some small, unconscious part of me squirming. When I glanced up, his gaze met mine, wide and white. Blood streamed from his nose. One hand reached toward me, pleadingly.

Gevi did not see a daeson. As Vir screeched again, he mouthed the words, "My baby!"

My gaze flew to the caravan far ahead. Bodies jostled back toward Vir's agonized calls. *Almost at the top of the next ridge! They're too far.*

Swallowing, I mustered every soothing thought I could, and hoped it was enough to settle Vir, as I scrambled into striking range. Fighting against all I'd ever been taught, I grabbed for Gevi's outstretched arm.

He twisted out of my reach.

"My baby!" he gasped again, desperately, and I nodded, ducking and pressing close enough to feel his ragged breathing and his hair across my cheek. Reaching under him, I pulled the small, unmoving bundle to my chest. I dared not look down, but instead shifted the baby to one arm and pulled at Gevi with the other. I couldn't move him.

"Vir," I wailed. "Vir! Up!" I wanted to put the baby down so I could use my arms, but the flock had packed too tightly around us now.

"Vir! Up!" I pleaded, tears springing to my eyes.

The baby isn't moving, isn't crying.

"Please, Vir!" But the animal was beyond hearing. This time, when she rolled her eyes and thrashed, her tail snapped back and caught my shoulder, tearing my shirt and leaving a bloodied welt. I sank back to my knees, heaving on Gevi's arm as hard as I could, openly sobbing because it wasn't working.

Strong arms crowded around me, pushing against Vir's writhing body, clasping onto Gevi. Hands swept me aside as others took over, straining, sweating, and grunting clipped assurances to the trapped man.

Vir panicked. Her head crashed into the ground. Froth sprayed from her beak. Dumbfounded, I watched as the vaiya's tail struck Iva like a serpent.

"Calm her!" she bellowed. At the same instant, someone snatched Gevi's baby from my arms.

For the first time, my focus turned to my fallen vaiya, and my heart dropped.

Vir looked like a crushed bird, her right leg folded under her at an impossible angle. Amidst the blood, something sharp protruded, like the end of a spear. When the patchy moonlight caught it, I realized it was a bone, glowing ghostly and pale. I groaned and crawled to the vaiya's flailing head, tears running down my face.

"Shhh. Vir. Pretty bird," I crooned, "Shhh, I'm here. I'm right here."

Her gaze rolled toward me. The defeat in its dark depths broke me.

Vir wanted to get up. She *knew* that Gevi was under her.

"Oh, Vir," I blubbered, and flung my arms around her soft neck despite her violent struggling. "It's all right. It's all right. It's over, pretty bird," I sobbed. "You don't have to get up, Vir."

She relaxed, and I buried my wet face in her neck, terrified that death had already pulled her away.

"Stay with me," I whimpered. "You're going to be all right." The last words sat like stones in my belly because they were a lie.

I didn't remember when the others pulled Gevi free, didn't recall them ferrying her down the hill to Fraesh, the healer. I didn't remember everyone leaving. For a long time, I sat with Vir's head in my lap.

A hand on my shoulder made me wince. It brushed across the welt from Vir's whipping tail. When I turned, Hasev's face loomed over me.

"It's my fault," I choked.

Hasev looked at Vir. "It's suffering," he said.

At the edge of my sight, the tip of Hasev's spear dipped toward the dust. "I know," I sobbed.

Vir's big head lolled in my lap. She panted, eyes half-closed. *She's leaving me.*

Vax hovered over Hasev's shoulder. I shook my head, sniffling. "He won't let you kill her."

Hasev glanced behind him, made a sound in his throat, and nodded. A long silence swam between us. My shoulders hunched, and a horrible, aching sob rose in my chest.

"They're going to eat her," I whispered, blinking at the tears spattering Vir's smooth beak.

Hasev's sigh sounded like the wind through an old, creaking tree. He squatted and ran his big, strong hand over Vir's neck. Still looking at the vaiya, he murmured, "I would be honoured to know my death would save so many, wouldn't you, daeson?"

I curled away from him, head sinking to my chest. "Is that what you think sacrificing me will do?" I said the words quietly, but I knew he heard by the way his shoulders tensed.

"You wouldn't leave this vaiya for the wurms, would you?" he admonished, ignoring my question.

I shook my head.

"There's no other way. It's Nasheira's will."

I nodded. My chest was breaking, like the wurm vision was clawing out of me, hollowing me out.

Vir died that afternoon. I could give her no more comfort than my small presence and a tiny scrap of shade from the midday sun. She just stopped, like Nasheira had snuffed out a flame.

The entire vaiya flock started keening, a low, hollow mourning cry. And that's how I knew she was really gone. Vaiyas could sense when a spirit left a body, and they'd wail whenever they felt it happened. They did it for humans and for animals we speared while hunting, and they did it for Vir too.

When we gathered for evening prayers, Na-Jhalar raised his hand toward me and beckoned. "Bring the daeson here."

As I shuffled toward the Speaker, I had no doubt that I was about to be punished. I had touched a child.

⌒

TANAR DABBED at my split lip in his tent. There was no water to share and Xen was alternately grabbing for Tanar and wailing forlornly. The red-headed boy spoke between the cries.

"I was coming down the hill to help, but the others got there first."

I nodded slowly, ears ringing and face numb.

"The baby's mother pulled her from your arms. She went straight to your Speaker afterwards."

Arsu. Gevi's mate. I save her baby and she has me beaten.

"Who is she to shout orders at your Speaker?" Tanar asked.

"His sister," I slurred. "Arsu is Na-Jhalar's older sister. My father says she wishes she was chosen Speaker instead."

Tanar nodded, patting Xen's stomach as the infant howled again. In the pause following, the red-headed boy pinned me with a hard gaze I couldn't avoid. "Watch that one. She's hungry for your blood."

COLD WATER DRIPS *on my cheeks. I wake among the vaiyas with the sharp tang of rain filling my nostrils. The flock chirps and whistles. They push to their feet and crow as sheets of rain ripple through the desert, soaking us.*

I laugh, tipping my head back, and sticking out my tongue as the sky rumbles around us.

Then, I realize that the rumble isn't thunder. Something else scythes through the sky. My eyes catch the silhouette of membranous wings. Gold flashes.

A Dragon! She glides low over our caravan and rain pours from her wings, drenching us in waves. Everyone is praying, laughing and spreading out water bags while the Guide makes pass after pass, shaking sheets of water from her wings as she goes.

There are no clouds in the sky. The rain is coming from her.

IT WAS an awful thing to wake from a dream full of rain when your mouth tasted like dust. Tears pricked my eyes when I realized my reality was trudging through another night in the desert with Vir dead and nothing to drink, but the next day, something incredible happened.

I woke with the noise of vaiyas filling my ears and realized that the flock was calling a greeting. Vax stood. His neck craned at an awkward angle as he crowed to the sky above. The vaiya's crest had raised, but he was excited, not agitated.

I rolled to follow Vax's gaze skyward and heard it.

It shuddered through my chest like swelling thunder, a raw, powerful sound that instantly made me feel small. The hair at the back of my neck prickled, and I scrambled to my knees.

I know that sound.

I knew it in my bones and every fibre of my body. I knew it in the farthest shadowed corner of my mind. We all did. A dragon. A Guide.

Mother of Yurrii, my dream!

Some small part of me must have thought I knew what to expect, but as my eyes focused on the span of pale yellow gliding above, breath evaporated in my throat.

She was so close, maybe three times the height of a pechi tree. And she was incredible.

A low whistle of resistance sang over her wingtips as she turned her head and dipped a wing to bank left. The sun burned an opening in the milling clouds, and shadows rolled across the dragon's back, revealing the sculptured curve of a shoulder blade. Lean lengths of muscle and tendon tapered to a thin, delicate elbow.

As she banked further, the entire structure of her wing stretched into view. A sickle-shaped claw curved forward as she wheeled across the sun, her shadow slicing the ground. Every branching vein and puckered scar silhouetted like golden lace woven into the luminescent sails of her wings.

My heart thudded in my throat as the Guide manoeuvred back toward us, exposing her pale underside. She kept her forearms tucked against her chest and her legs pressed against a solid tail studded with three barbs.

She was close enough that I could see the stunning green of her eyes, deeply set beneath the ridge of her brow. As she stretched her neck, her mouth peeled open in a yawn of lethal teeth.

The sound of her call tore through me. The vaiyas crowed in excitement, but I barely heard them as the Guide wheeled above.

She's looking at me. A hungry pull balled in my chest, and I realized I held my breath. *She's looking right at me, calling to me.*

The emerald gaze fixed on me as she glided closer.

The weight in my chest tugged. I forced myself to breathe, to swallow, but it didn't seem to help. The pull between my ribs snapped tighter. Flames of panic licked my mind. That emerald eye regarded me, unblinking.

Don't be stupid. She's not here for a daeson.

The noise of the vaiyas crashed around me, unbearably sharp. I wanted to yell at the flock to stop, but I fell back into the sand, breaking eye contact with the dragon. Around me, the flock's trumpeting grew louder, warning of an intruder. The Guide blasted back a frustrated bellow.

She turned and flew toward the northern horizon. She didn't look back. Each solid cut of her wings pressed distance between us, and in less than a minute, she was no more than a smear of gold against the clouds.

I stared after her until my eyes burned. My lungs hurt.

Sagging, I rubbed my chest, ears ringing and breath bleeding past my parched lips.

The flock milled around me, anxiously barking. I recognized Vax beside me, but it was a while before I could gather my feet to stand with the vaiya's support. I leaned into him, despite his piercing bawls, and followed his glare. In front of me, the whole caravan was looking to the south, away from the dragon.

Scaling down the coarse rock slopes to the south with easy, practised strides, came a long line of colourful forms, leading half a dozen vaiyas with full water bags.

Aeni. Water. Oh Thank Nasheira. They have water.

CHAPTER EIGHT

Tanar joined me to restrain Vax.

"I've never seen a dragon that close," he whispered, fumbling with the shackles. "Have you?"

I shook my head, hands trembling as I pulled the hood over Vax's good eye and secured it under his beak.

"Mine!" one of our vaiyas hissed, crowding the flock, but only one ani approached. Aeni didn't trust their names to anyone but their closest kin. To us, they were all called ani.

"Nasheira's peace with you." The ani bobbed his head and wiped his nose, taking in our paltry supplies.

"May her Guides mark your skies." Na-Jhalar spoke the traditional response and puffed out his chest to display his dragon-scale necklace.

The ani brightened at the words. "Seems we did have one mark the skies just now, eh? What luck!" He gestured to the north where the dragon had flown. "We were following her and we found you. What are your needs then, Speaker?" The question wasn't one of compassion. Aeni didn't offer a night's food and shelter as courtesy like camps did. They traded. The question was the start of a bargain.

"Give us three of your water bags and lead us to the source," Na-Jhalar demanded.

The ani whistled through his teeth. "Those are big needs. We'd lose all the distance we gained this morning taking you back there. I could supply you with a map instead." Aeni were expert mapmakers. They travelled at a breakneck pace compared to camps and charted waterways and herd migrations as they went.

"Not good enough." Na-Jhalar crossed his arms over his barrel chest. "Give me your water and one of your people to guide us to the source." It was a badly veiled insult, insinuating that the ani might supply a false or inaccurate map.

The man bristled. "What do you offer in return?" he asked sharply.

"Two vaiya hens of breeding age."

My breath caught in my throat. *Please no. Say no.* I couldn't stand to lose another vaiya so soon after Vir.

"That would get you the water and a map, to be sure." The ani scrutinized our skinny flock. "But I'll need more than that for a guide, and our time." His eyes locked onto Na-Jhalar's necklace.

"Three dragon scales would suffice."

Our Speaker's face screwed up as he clutched his necklace. "They are sacred."

The ani shrugged. "Seems you've plenty to spare. You are free to reject my terms and we'll move on."

At Na-Jhalar's silent scowl, the ani started to move away.

"Wait," Na-Jhalar snarled, licking his dry lips. "We agree to your terms."

I could have kissed Hasev when he recommended two of the unnamed birds that had come with Tanar's group. The ani transferred their water bags, took their two new vaiyas and pushed one of their own men forward.

"Our servant, Latik, will stay to guide you to the water."

Tanar elbowed me. "They gave his name. He's not an ani. You know what that means?"

"Daeson?" I whispered, and Na-Jhalar echoed my question with obvious distaste twisting his face.

The ani shrugged again. "He's paid his debt. Do you want to see proof?"

Latik started undoing his breech cloth.

"No." Na-Jhalar snorted and waved him off.

I gaped at the silent man as he re-tightened his belt around the fat that settled around his girth. *A grown daeson. One who's survived the cutting.*

"What's to stop him from leaving the aeni?" Tanar asked. "Why do they trust him to come back when he's done guiding us?"

I shrugged. "I'll bet they treat him more like a human than any camp ever did."

As soon as the trade was settled, the aeni left with our two vaiyas in tow.

Tanar and I kept Vax hooded so the patriarch wouldn't chase down the vaiyas we'd traded.

Latik started walking north. He didn't beckon, or speak, he just started walking.

Our camp mobilized hastily and followed. As soon we felt it was safe to do so, Tanar and I whisked off Vax's hood, unshackled him, and left him with the flock so we could trot toward Latik before anyone could stop us.

His long-legged strides made him difficult to keep pace with. Before either of us could speak, he announced. "I can't help you, so don't ask." His voice was startlingly high and childlike.

"What makes you think we need help?" Tanar snapped.

Latik pointed a long finger towards our necklaces. "You're marked for sacrifice, and you think that since I survived, I can save you. Every daeson in every camp asks."

"Well, if being saved means following the aeni like a tethered vaiya, we're fine, thanks," Tanar's said.

"If you try to follow me after, I'll bring you back to your camp, and they'll reward me for it. I'm not showing you my scar. I'm not telling you my story, and I'm not saving you." Latik's words sounded tired, as if he'd recited them thousands of times before. He quickened his stride to break from us.

"We don't need your help." I trotted to keep up. "We want to trade."

That slowed him down. A sharp laugh burst out of him. "A trade? What in Nasheira's name would two daeson have to offer?"

"Depends on what you can give us." Tanar answered.

He chuckled. "I told you, I can't help—"

"We don't need you to help us escape." I interrupted. "We just need to know how much time we have. Tell us when it happens, the sacrifice."

Latik's shoulders twitched.

"What does it mean when Pau swallows Yurrii?" I pushed. "When does it happen?"

The older daeson shifted his carry bag on his shoulder and sniffed. "What will you give me in exchange for this information?"

"Five blood sausages." Tanar blurted and my eyes goggled. That was nearly a week's worth of our stash, and I'd risked my hide stealing those sausages.

"Ten." Latik countered.

"Eight," I snapped, determined to grasp some authority.

"Done. Bring them to me, and I'll give you your answer."

It was nearly an hour before we had the opportunity to stealthily retrieve the sausages from the bottom of my carry bag. By the time Tanar and I threaded back to the front of the caravan where Latik led, the sun was high in the sky, and I was dizzy and parched, despite my careful sips of water.

"Every twelve years, Pau swallows Yurrii. The greater moon covers the lesser one. That's when the sacrifice happens. Next fall, little less than a year from now." Latik's hard stare softened. "Nasheira help you both when it does."

He didn't speak to us again after that. I let the older daeson's strides carry him further and further from us until I was surrounded by the familiar smell of my own vaiyas. I couldn't decide which was worse, being blind to my fate, or knowing the exact date of its arrival.

Latik took half a day to lead our camp to the water source. Once there, he pointed to a valley to the North West and said to Na-Jhalar, "The desert ends just past those hills." Then he turned and started walking back south. He didn't even look at Tanar and me as he passed.

We made our plan to escape camp in spring because neither of us thought we could survive the coming winter in the wastelands with a baby. It gave us plenty of time to prepare.

But I wasn't prepared for the betrayal that was to come.

CHAPTER NINE

L ife inexorably returned to normal. I'd thought it would kill me, waiting until spring within a camp that meant to sacrifice me, but the truth was, regular life felt like a balm now that I wasn't pretending at it, now that I had a firm, achievable plan. I didn't tell Tanar, but I enjoyed it, this bland camp life that I'd never have again. I savoured each moment in hopes that I could remember a taste of it once it was gone.

The thought of the three of us fending for ourselves alone in the wastelands still quickened my breath and sent ice down my spine, but sometimes survival didn't mean obsessing about the larger plan. Often it meant tackling the next small task, and the next one, and the next, until they all added up to something bigger.

Tanar and I only stole what our camp wouldn't miss. We did our best not to draw attention to ourselves—notably harder for the red-headed boy than it was for me. Our cache grew sizable and we buried it deeper under my hut. We spent the rest of our time with Xen and the vaiyas.

As winter progressed, the gatherers' only bounty was dry wood. Hunting brought sparse returns, but occasionally, the hunters returned to camp with crows of triumph and Vust, Voti, and Veset pranced into camp slung with sleek carcasses from the trap lines.

Na-Jhalar would emerge from his hut to inspect the day's hunt with a pasty, drawn face. His duties included choosing a carcass for each chani's family. The heart of the largest animal was always reserved for the Speaker himself, but after that, his chani picked their choice cut or favourite organ from the chosen carcass, and the camp shared the rest.

Along with Delani from Tanar's group, Baline and Celi were Na-Jhalar's other two chani; they were tall sisters, with milky skin and hair the colour of mid-day sun. Their parents were Fraesh, the healer, and Iva, the storyteller.

It was a rare honour for a family to produce two chani, and Fraesh was a proud father. He accepted the chani's gifts from each hunt like a king and stubbornly argued whenever the Speaker reopened the tender issue that *one* family should only be allotted *one* gift.

"Then you will give me back one of my girls!" Fraesh always answered, his quiet chuckle at odds with the hard look in his eyes.

On warmer nights, everyone drifted to the main hearth in groups with hides to scrape or harek plates to carve. Na-Jhalar led us in prayer to the Guides, the sound of his voice echoing over a trapped audience. We recited the day of the year, and our Speaker added a mark to his slab of wood pocked with even rows of slashes. Then, Iva regaled us with cautionary tales and songs about our ancestors. We enjoyed listening to the keeper of our history far more than Na-Jhalar's nasal prayers. Afterwards, we offered scented smoke of mint and kiro grass, and little gifts of carved dragons with stone eyes.

On colder nights, evening prayers were as shallow as the ticks Na-Jhalar made on his calendar. We echoed our responses wreathed in the fog of our own breaths with fat snowflakes swarming around us. Iva kept her history lessons short and afterwards, everyone stamped their feet, wrapped their blankets tighter, and returned to their snow-blanketed huts.

This was the simple life that I'd miss when it was gone. Evening prayers around a hearth fire with dozens of people bunched around it. Iva's clear singing voice. The triumphant crows of the hunters returning to camp. Hasev's laugh, and Aella's voice when she sang to my brothers. And my vaiyas. Sweet Nasheira, I would miss them most of all.

IN LATE WINTER, Voru birthed three good-sized chicks—two males and a female. I named them Vell, Vyto, and Vuna. Hasev and Jin, who was training to replace me as vaiya keeper, had been there to see the births, watching quietly and ignoring my presence.

New life bloomed beyond my flock as well. Elba swelled so heavy with child that it looked like the poor girl might burst. Despite her constantly flushed cheeks, the woman looked radiant with the spirit of Nasheira. She and her mate, Darvie, couldn't wait to meet their first child, hoping that it was a girl.

When it happened, I was with the vaiyas. Two sickle moons hung above the frozen lake and the icy night air carried the racket of camp up the hill to where the flock had settled. As the vaiyas idly flicked their tails, I watched Darvie and his other mate, Mira, hover over Elba outside their hut. She wasn't swatting them away like she normally did when they fussed over her. I couldn't see their facial expressions, but as the trio walked, it was easy to read the pain in Elba's posture. The baby was coming.

They walked like that, in slow, quiet circles, at the grassy edge of camp, only stopping when Elba bent over, clutching her belly. Darvie would lean in, whisper in her ear, or Mira would stroke her back until Elba finally straightened, swallowed, and nodded.

Their quiet intimacy broke when Elba cried out during the ever-closer contractions. My four vaiya hens stood and crooned, silver backs flashing in the cool moonlight. I grinned as Vax and the other males eyed them warily. The females of a flock had a tendency to sing during a birth. It was a low warbling sound that thrummed through my chest.

Fraesh marched toward the couple, shooing Darvie off with flapping arms and steering Elba and Mira toward their hut.

Darvie paced outside. He clutched a birth blanket so dainty and lovely that I couldn't imagine his large hands making it. I clutched my own blanket closer. It was the only gift I'd ever received from Hasev, from anyone.

The labour went on for hours before a wet, primal howl cut through the night.

The vaiyas hushed.

"Let me see her," Elba exclaimed. When no one answered, she repeated, "I want to see her. Let me hold my baby." Her tired laugh echoed in the silence.

Fat flakes of snow wafted to the ground.

Darvie started toward the hut, but halted as Fraesh and Mira emerged, eyes red-rimmed and mouths tight.

Elba screamed inside the tent. "Let me see my baby! Bring her to me!"

Fraesh flipped back the door flap, balancing a wet, red infant in his arm.

"Is it...?" Darvie choked, even as he stepped back from the healer and pressed two fingers to his forehead.

Fraesh shifted the ruddy, splay-limbed baby into both

arms and handed the child to Darvie. The young father held his first son, his daeson, as if Fraesh had plopped a pile of shit on the pretty birth blanket. The healer mumbled something else, at which Darvie nodded dumbly, refusing to look down.

Fraesh patted him on the shoulder and turned back toward the hut.

I barely heard the screams of Elba and the agitated vaiyas around me. I watched the baby and Darvie, the way he held the infant at arm's length as those tiny arms flailed, searching for security.

My stomach folded into a tight, cold ball.

I will never in my life forget what happened next.

Darvie lowered his eyes to look at the baby he awkwardly held. The newborn cried.

And Darvie dropped him.

Like the daeson was a bag of maggots.

I screamed.

The baby's cry cut off mid-squeal as he struck the ground with an awful, flat thud. The small body flopped face down. Darvie wailed and jerked away as if he expected the sprawled bundle to attack.

Sharp silence, then a horrible, high-pitched scream from the baby, shrill and sustained.

Elba stopped shouting.

Fraesh turned back to Darvie, mouth hanging open as he spotted the source of the thump he'd heard.

The baby's jagged, shredded cry whipped the flock into an uproar. Vaiyas foamed around me like water. I fought to see past them.

Darvie and Fraesh stood rigid, staring at the howling infant sprawled between their feet.

The healer moved first. He ducked and grabbed the baby, brushing snow from the screaming child's cheeks with big, shaking hands. He swaddled the baby as if the birthing blanket was the only thing holding the daeson's tiny body together.

Darvie sobbed, shoulders jerking, one hand over his eyes. He breathed in strangled gulps.

The healer didn't speak until the baby was in his arms, and the man in front of him fell into a painful, hollow silence. "He is your duty. Your daeson."

"Mira's already had a daeson. She wears the mark on her arm. I don't want it," Darvie croaked.

It. I winced.

"Mira's firstborn doesn't cancel out Elba's." Fraesh blinked at the baby. "It's the woman's burden to bear a daeson, and the man's to raise one."

Inside the tent, Iva's voice rose firm, but oddly soothing, like she was telling one of her stories. "Elba, you are so lucky. Listen to me. I know. It's best to get this over with now. There are only seven months until the sacrifice. Before you know it, you'll have another beautiful little one on the way."

Sacrifice. The word struck me like a stone. *Oh Guides, we need to get out of here. Spring can't come soon enough.*

AFTER THE INITIAL SHOCK, Darvie named his daeson Enso and dutifully, if somewhat numbly, accepted his responsibility for keeping the child alive. Darvie was young, but not stupid. He knew that if he neglected Enso entirely, his camp would retaliate by cutting his food shares and forbidding him from ever serving on the elder's council. Elba and Mira would likely leave him if he dishonoured himself like that, never mind the consequences of angering his goddess by spurning what was meant to be her sacrifice. Darvie kept his honour, and the satisfaction of his goddess, safely intact, and my people were glad of it.

Whenever I saw Enso, I remembered Tanar offering his finger to Xen in his hut. It had seemed so strange that first time I saw it, almost foreign to see two daeson sharing such normal, human contact. I wondered vaguely how many other daeson babies ever had their little hands held before it was too late, before touching became unnatural and invasive. Before they grew into their curse.

I knew why Tanar needed Xen to be a secret, why he only brought the infant to his hut when no one was watching him. If Na-Jhalar ever dug out the fact that Tanar cared about something, if anyone suspected that the red-headed boy held a shred of compassion in him, they could hurt him with it.

Just like the Speaker had wounded me by striking Vax.

I wasn't as good as Tanar at keeping secrets. If I'd been smart like him, no one would have known about my attachment to my vaiyas. The guilty consideration washed through me that, if Darvie abandoned Enso, and I was left to care for the baby, it would plant one more weakness in me.

One more way our escape could fail.

"We have to go soon," I whispered to Tanar one night, and he nodded in agreement. "Next week on the night of the new moons. We'll go then, when it's darkest."

The following days passed by too slowly and too quickly. I was constantly looking over my shoulder, waiting for our plan to be discovered.

But no one was the wiser until the day before the new moons, with less than six months until the moons eclipsed, when I returned from gathering with soft leaves of junab tucked under my shirt. I ducked into my hut to add the pungent medicinal plant to our stores, and I froze.

My bedroll was flipped back and crumpled. An empty

crater yawned where my storage sack had been. My cache was gone.

Oh Guides, we've been caught! The thought strangled me. I dropped the junab and sprinted to Tanar's hut, but his bedroll was gone. The hut was empty.

"No," I gulped, head spinning. Stumbling back to my hut, I stared at the hole I'd worked an entire winter to fill. I flipped my bedroll over the crater and sagged over it, breathing in shallow gulps, my vision swimming.

It took hours to realize that nobody was coming for me because nobody had discovered our cache. Tanar had taken it. He had taken the cache and Xen, and he had left me. I expected rage to swallow me as I stood there in my gutted hut, gulping like a fish out of water. I waited for a red-hot wave of choking emotion, but there was only emptiness and a faint buzzing in my ears.

I'm dead.

CHAPTER TEN

The weeks after Tanar abandoned me are hazy. As soon as our camp discovered it had lost two of its precious offerings to Nasheira, Na-Jhalar took measures to ensure they didn't lose the daeson who remained. He ordered me confined to my hut, and hunters took turns posted at the entry day and night. They burned my boots in the hearth fire so that even if I somehow managed to slip past my sentries, I'd shred my feet if I ran.

Arsu volunteered for the majority of guard duty. I had no idea why, but the woman seemed to take pleasure pinning me with her cold gaze while I lay, still gripped by shock, in my prison hut.

I was allowed out for one hour per day to groom and tend the vaiyas. It was the only way Vax could be appeased. On the days my guards didn't let me out, the big vaiya howled and paced outside my hut.

I barely heard him.

My mind wrapped itself in knots like a tangled fishing line.

How had I not seen Tanar's betrayal coming? I couldn't

unhook the memories of camaraderie and Xen's grin when he learned my name. They kept snagging in my mind and tearing at every soft spot inside of me.

Tanar had used me.

You don't have to worry, I wanted to tell my sentries. *Even another daeson thinks I'm useless. There's nowhere to run.*

Hasev never visited. I could only assume he didn't want to face me.

Spring rains hung over our valley for weeks at a time. My hut leaked and I couldn't find a dry spot for my bedroll. I got sick. It started with a bone deep itching, a tortuous, irrepressible prickling that made me scratch at my arms and legs until my skin bled. The sores came next, a smattering of ugly ulcers across my back and chest, and then the illness quickly progressed to frothy coughing. My chest felt like it was filling with sap, and I couldn't lay down, so I dozed propped against my rolled bed mat. It wasn't just me, I soon realized. Within a week of the onset of my illness, many of our camp were infected. I could hear them all coughing at night.

One morning I awoke to the vaiya flock keening just as they had when Vir died.

Their mourning cry. Someone's died.

"Who was it?" I asked Darvie later as he stood at my entry. He was safe to speak to. Arsu kicked me every time I made a sound, but Darvie would sometimes answer when I spoke. Having his own daeson seemed to have softened him.

"Chan." He answered. One of the elders.

"The sickness?"

He nodded. "A third of the camp has it."

The next day, during a rare sunny break in the weather, Fraesh came into my hut. He squatted and reached toward me, and I cringed. Nobody ever touched me unless it was to strike. He looked into my eyes and asked me to stick out my tongue, then directed Darvie to let me sit outside. "It will burn out any yellow staining the spirit."

Darvie nodded and Fraesh left. I dozed outside all day with Vax. I couldn't do much more than sit, but I'd forgotten how good the sun felt, how that soft radiance melted right into my bones.

The next day Fraesh came again. "You've been itchy?" he pointed at the fresh-peeled scabs on my arms.

I shuddered and coughed. "I feel like I could scratch right down to my bones and it wouldn't be enough."

"Here," he tossed a small pot toward me. "It's junab. It should help numb the feeling a bit, but use it sparingly."

I nodded quickly, wanting him to leave so I could slather the stuff on in private.

"And the cough?"

"Worse at night."

"Take a big breath for me."

I inhaled, wheezed and broke off into a fit of wet coughing.

"I'll bring you some mint tea tomorrow. Keep outside as much as you can." And before I could thank him, the healer turned and left.

That night, as I sat against my bedroll, reeking of junab, it sounded like the whole camp was coughing. Ugly, barking noises ricocheted between the huts until sunrise, when the vaiyas called their mourning cry again.

I woke to the bustle of the camp packing up and getting ready to move.

I limped on tender bare feet as the storyteller steered me toward my vaiya flock.

"What happened?" I whispered.

Fraesh scrubbed at his face before answering. "The sickness killed Delani."

So. Na-Jhalar's favourite chani was dead. I tried to bring up remorse for the woman, but there were no feelings left in me.

"Half the camp is sick. Including Iva." His voice broke as he spoke his mate's name.

"I'm sorry." I said automatically, and Fraesh stared at me for several long seconds before clearing his throat.

"You have no boots. Ride on your big vaiya and control the flock. I'll be watching you and if you make any move to run, I won't hesitate. Understand?"

We cremated our dead and fled our camp, leaving our huts and any belongings we could spare as offerings to Nasheira burning in our wake.

I slowly recovered, and so did everyone else who was ill, but we all would bear puckering, pink scars and nagging coughs for the rest of our lives as reminders of the terrible illness.

Even once we'd settled into a new camp, and my guards had built me a caged hut, Fraesh still came to check on me. Iva took extra sentry shifts too, like Arsu did, and when I asked her why she wasn't spending more time hunting, her preferred activity, she shrugged. "I'm needed here," she said, and the concern in her eyes made sense when Fraesh admitted something to Darvie about Na-Jhalar on his next visit.

"The gifen has pulled him under," Fraesh murmured, but I had sharp ears. "He isn't taking Delani's death well. Baline and Celi do their best to take care of him, but I need to be close by to help."

I wasn't sure if Iva stayed close to make sure Na-Jhalar was safe, or if it was her daughters she was more worried about. With Delani dead, Fraesh and Iva's daughters were the only chani Na-Jhalar had left. I couldn't understand why anyone would willingly endure the man's company if they didn't have to and I said as much to Fraesh. "Why do they stay with him?" I asked. "They could step down at evening prayers any time they wanted. They just announce it, right?"

Fraesh sobered and scratched his chin slowly, keeping his back to me. "They could," he sighed. "But they won't. He's the Speaker. Who knows what he'd do to them if they stepped down."

There was frustration in his eyes, and I realized that Fraesh had shared a deep fear with me. I wasn't the only one who hated our Speaker. "My girls are your cousins," he said. "Did you know that?"

"What?" I gaped through the stout wooden bars across my entry.

"Hasev never told you?" The healer frowned as he turned to me. "Iva is his sister."

Hasev never told me a lot of things.

SPRING PASSED and gave way to a humid summer. Even with Fraesh and Iva's occasional company, my days confined inside were agonizing. I'd been imprisoned for almost three months and I itched to do something, anything, to get out of my own head. I begged for longer breaks with the vaiyas. I sometimes spoke to Arsu when she guarded me, even though I knew she'd come into my hut and strike me for doing so. It felt good to feel something other than the thoughts in my head, and the suffocating, ever-present weight of what was coming for me in three more months. I could see it now, through the wooden bars of my hut entry, the space between the moons was shrinking. It was a frighteningly obvious reminder of my fate. And the urge to run from it suffocated me on a daily basis.

One afternoon, Darvie let me have an extra hour with the vaiyas. His daeson started crying in the hut beside mine, and as soon as he ducked through the doorway to tend to the baby, I vaulted onto Vax's back, jammed my bare heels into his sides, and clung on as the big vaiya bolted.

"Run?" he crowed, peering back at me with one eye.

"Yes, run," I urged.

I didn't stop when I heard yelling behind us. I curled over Vax as he sprinted northward until the first spear whistled past my cheek and thudded into the ground ahead of us. My vaiya shied and another projectile sang as it shot past us.

"Stop," I gasped. "Vax. Stop!" I hauled back on the neck strap and held out my hands when my vaiya obediently skidded to a halt. "Don't kill him, please!" I yelled. *Mother of Yurrii, what did you expect would happen, you idiot?*

The hunters surrounded me and herded me back to camp, leaving my punishment to the Speaker. However, that night at evening prayers, Na-Jhalar was too wasted on gifen to deliver a prayer or a beating. Iva spoke the appropriate words and marked the calendar, and Arsu beat me instead. She had me lay on my belly so I couldn't see what she was doing. I'd been stripped of everything but my breechcloth, and I'd seen the sapling she was holding, so I expected a whipping. Instead, Arsu struck the soles of my feet, over and over again until the sapling was red with my blood.

My sentries had to drag me back to my hut.

"What were you thinking?" Fraesh asked me that night, standing outside my hut with a pot of junab in his hand.

I looked up at the tone of his question. It wasn't harsh or accusatory. Fraesh looked genuinely curious.

"I wasn't," I croaked. "How can I think at all, trapped in here all these months with nothing rolling around in my brain except for how I'll die soon?" My feet throbbed so hard that tears stung my eyes.

Fraesh pursed his lips and passed me the salve.

CHAPTER 10 | 87

"Thank you." I said. I'd never thanked him for everything he'd done when I was ill.

"Get some sleep," he huffed.

I DON'T KNOW how many times I suffered through the wurm dream before it struck on a night when Iva was guarding me.

"Hey," she called as I sat up gulping for air and shivering.

"Don't," I begged. "Shhh. It'll hear you."

"It's a nightmare. You're awake now."

I opened my eyes to see Iva gripping the bars and behind her, I saw nothing but the soft glow of a hearth fire. *No wurm.*

Hugging my chest, I turned away from the storyteller and whimpered as the after-effects of the dream pooled with the throbbing pain firing through my feet.

"Do you know how to play tavi?" she asked.

Tavi was a popular game with the hunters. I'd seen them pass the time engrossed in tavi matches while they guarded hanging carcasses from wurms on night shifts, but I'd never played it. I shook my head.

"Come here. I'll show you."

Wincing, I grabbed my blanket and crawled on my hands and knees toward the wooden bars the wurm had annihilated in my dream. Every movement jarred my bandaged feet.

Iva fished in her pockets and pulled out four rounds of polished bone. "These are the tavi pieces. You take two. One of each." She passed them through the bars. A dragon was carved into one and a wurm in the other.

"Now you need something to wager. We can use anything." The storyteller got to her feet, and sifted through the dirt around the hearth fire until she'd collected a handful of stones. She passed half to me. "Pile your stones together, and hide one tavi piece in each hand."

I closed my fists over both pieces.

"What was your dream about?" Iva asked, using one finger to push her stones into a neat row.

"A wurm," I swallowed and held out my fists.

"You must have it often. Darvie says you scream most nights."

My cheeks reddened, and when Iva moved her hand toward one of mine, I snatched it away. "It's the same dream each time." I said. Something about Iva's sharp brown eyes, and the fact that she was Fraesh's mate, made me trust her.

"This one." She pointed. "The dragon piece is in this hand."

I let the piece roll in my open palm.

"Ha! See. I won." Iva smiled.

I handed over one of my stones.

She held out her fists.

I pointed at her right hand, and she shook her head and revealed the wurm piece. "You have to learn your opponent's tells. Darvie's eyes dart toward the hand that holds his dragon piece, but you have to take a long time to choose before he'll do it. Pay up your stone."

I slid one of the rocks through the bars.

"You always have the same dream, every night?"

I held out my fists and shrugged. "I've had others, but this one the most." I paused, uncertain how much I should give away. Then I realized it didn't matter. "Sometimes my dreams come true."

Iva's finger hovered over my right fist. She pointed to my left fist and I grinned, shook my head and took one of her stones. "If a dream comes true, it's a vision."

I snorted. "Only Speakers have visions."

"Oh, I suppose you've confirmed that in your eleven years of infinite wisdom."

My cheeks reddened at her playful tone. I picked Iva's dragon piece, and she pushed another stone to my side with an exaggerated sigh.

She cocked her head at me with eyebrows raised until I cracked and told her everything. A warm wind ruffled my hair as I told her about the dragon scale dream, and the one where Gevi and his baby were crushed, and how I'd seen the Guide in the desert before she came.

She asked the occasional question, but when I was done, we played in silence for a long time. First my wager pile dwindled, and then Iva's. When she was down to her final stone, I pressed past the tightness in my throat and said, "Thank you for this." She smiled with her eyes, pointed at my fist, chose the wurm piece, and pushed her final stone over to me. "What did you dream about tonight?"

"It's nothing." I looked down at the stone to avoid Iva's eyes. It had felt good to talk to someone about the other dreams and not have them rebuff me as a fool, but my wurm dream, I had no wish to repeat it. It echoed enough on its own as it was.

"Your tell is that you tuck your hair behind your ear when you're uncomfortable. Just like you did now." Iva paused, inhaling. "If you are having visions, they could be important, Akrist. You could save someone, like you saved Gevi."

I flinched at the sound of my name. "I'm the only person who dies in this dream, and we already know that's going to happen soon." I held out the tavi pieces.

"Keep them."

"One more round then?" I offered.

"You already have all my stones." She held out her rough palms. "I don't have anything else to wager."

"Your wager can be an answer. If I win, I'll ask you a question and you have to answer it."

She laughed. "Deal. But if I win, you answer *my* question."

"Fair enough."

She deliberated for several seconds before pointing at my right fist. I opened my hand to display the wurm and she heaved an exaggerated sigh.

"What is your question?"

I licked my lips. "Did you ever have a daeson?"

The laughter drained from her face.

For a moment, I thought she wasn't going to say anything, or that she'd lie, but she rolled up her shirt sleeve and exposed the inside of her wrist instead, pointing to a bright blue circular mark surrounding a raised bump of skin.

"Do you know what this is?"

I shook my head.

"The raised bit is a pebble under my skin. That's meant to represent Pau and the blue is the sky around it. This is a rare ink. Only healers know the recipe for it, and only mothers who have survived the death of their daeson are allowed to wear it." She sighed and let her sleeve slide back down her arm. "Yes," she whispered. "We did have a daeson, after Baline and before Celi."

I didn't have to guess what happened to him.

Iva stood and turned her back to me, and we didn't speak for the rest of her shift.

After that night, Iva, and sometimes Fraesh, would bring something to occupy me. They would play tavi with me, or bring a garment with a seam to mend, a basket that needed patching, or a hide to scrape. We never spoke about it, but I knew what they were doing. Distracting me. Letting me keep some scrap of my sanity while I sat in my prison. I wasn't sure whether to thank them for it, or curse them for giving me a glimpse of what having parents who cared felt like. That is how we passed from summer into early fall.

Now, when I tended the vaiyas, my camp's people, who had easily overlooked me before, stared. Still, unshakable glares, like the eyes of a concentrating and capable predator locked onto its prey. Even when I kept my head down, I felt that cold, communal gaze crawling up my neck like a spider. My community anticipated my sacrifice, salivated over the very idea of it. I felt like a trapped animal or worse still, like something was trapped in my chest, rattling around my ribcage, trying to burst out.

Hasev told me once that the hunters came across two types of animals on the trap lines. Many would fight for their lives right down to the last second, chewing their limbs off to slip a snare. And there were those that, when you came upon them, lay there exhausted, petrified, and resigned.

In the late autumn weeks leading up to my sacrifice, I was the second type.

CHAPTER ELEVEN

The sky was achingly clear on the evening of the sacrifice, as if the clouds had scattered to roost beyond the horizon, unwilling to witness the coming brutality. Outwardly, I sat perfectly still, leaning against Vax and watching my camp solemnly don their holy costumes—beaded white shifts, painted chests, and feathered armbands.

Truthfully, I'd never been more terrified in my life, not during the wurm vision, not when Tanar told me what our fate was, not even when he left.

I leaned on Vax because I couldn't stand, because somehow there wasn't enough air outside tonight. My heart thrashed in my chest, churning up dizzy, shuddering waves. If I moved, surely I'd break into a million pieces.

The other vaiyas careened in frantic chaos, maddened by the waves of raw fear radiating from me. They packed around me like fish in a net, howling and hissing, snapping at the air. Moonlight glared coldly off the edges of their crests and the length of their spurs. It made them look like black-eyed demons with hungry jaws and writhing white tails.

Jin had long ago fled back to camp. Arsu, my guard, stood

as close as she could get to the edge of the flock, swearing and jabbing her spear to keep the vaiyas in check.

The whole flock reeled beyond any control but mine, and I couldn't even stand of my own volition. Vax and I were fixed figures in the eye of that silver storm. The big vaiya knew that if he moved from his faithful post, I'd tumble backwards into the trampling squall, so he stood rigidly. His tail flicked near my face. Against my back, the pounding thud of his brave heart and the barking of his calls shuddered through me. I had no doubt that Vax, or any of the other vaiyas, would kill anyone whose intent was to hurt me tonight.

Between the restless silver bodies, I saw my mother. She looked more broken than I.

Aella slumped in Hasev's arms. He held her head pressed against his shoulder with one hand tenderly stroking her raven hair as if she were a small child.

Odd to think of my mother, who stood even taller than Hasev, as small.

Usually, Aella handled herself with such adept grace that she wasn't noticed for her height. Tonight she seemed stretched and thin, almost translucent, and she stood so still in Hasev's embrace.

I wondered if she cried, if her heart beat at her throat and cut off her air. I wondered if she felt trapped. Which one of us would fall apart first when the time came?

Your pretty little mother will cut you. Tanar's words sang in my ears. I choked on hot tears.

Oh, Nasheira! What am I supposed to do? How could I live for two days tied down and bleeding beside Darvie and Elba's tiny baby? How could they do it to an infant? Blinking, I strained to suck in air that felt like syrup. The screams of the vaiyas were ear-splitting.

Hasev kissed Aella on the forehead before facing the

howling flock. The ceremonial white paint on his face masked his expression, but I saw a subtle pause and a tired slump in his broad shoulders before he walked toward me. My father didn't want to come see me. I was his duty. Those small, hesitating gestures never let me forget that, never allowed me to imagine I was his son. He nodded to Arsu, relieving her.

This is it. Oh, Nasheira, it's happening!

My knees buckled. I slid down Vax's side, slamming to my hands and knees in a plume of dust with the communal screams of the vaiyas closing over me like cold, black water. *No, I want my father.* If that small voice hadn't twanged through my mind just then, I think I would have fainted and been hauled away like waste. I didn't want that.

I wanted to talk to Hasev one last time before it was over. It was the last strand of comfort I could cling to. *Oh, Nasheira, if only I could breathe!* My heart cracked, and I wasn't sure if I actually spoke the words, or if my thoughts stemmed the chaos of my vaiya flock.

"Stop. Vax, tell them to stop it. Let Hasev come."

When the birds had subsided into sharp, scared silence, my father, the giant, stepped forward. His shoulders were bravely squared and his steps certain. He looked almost menacing, with feather armbands prickling like spikes around his upper arms and his scar painted blazing red. I'd often admired that scar, the suitably simple, yet artful pattern of it. If I wasn't a daeson, I'd have wanted a scar like my father's. Solid. Strong.

Only Hasev's eyes betrayed him tonight. They shone with tears, spilling out pain. Watery tracks carved through the white paint on his cheeks.

A deep, fresh fear tore through me and despite my best efforts, the vaiyas caught the emotion and started howling again.

"Stop it," I sobbed. *This is so wrong.* "Stop it!" I screamed again, and this time the flock obeyed.

Hasev crouched next to me. At the edge of my vision, he pulled his hand down his face before focusing his injured eyes at some point over my shoulder, just below whimpering Vax's belly. For a long time, the big vaiya's sympathetic cries and my panicked wheezing grated through the air.

I wanted to say something, *anything,* but I choked on my words and couldn't even look up at my father.

"Akrist." Hasev finally spoke, and his deep voice broke when he said it.

I wailed at the sound of my name.

"Akrist." He spoke again, gently, and this time I met his stare despite the tears streaming down both of our faces.

"You were a good boy..." Hasev faltered, his throat working, and tried again. "I want you to know that you were always a good boy."

Something in me shattered. Miserable sobs pressed out of me, and I couldn't say any of the things I'd wanted to tell my father. I couldn't breathe, and I could not stop the pathetic sounds tearing out of me.

Then my father's hand rested on my shoulder, and for the first time in my life, it felt *good.* The sensation was the most natural thing in the world, a father comforting his son. I had *never* had that.

I didn't want it to end. But it did. When sobs finished wracking through me, I sat up, stiff and stripped raw, like driftwood.

"Do not hate your mother," Hasev said.

I shook my head and swallowed.

"Akrist..." Hasev opened his big hands imploringly. They trembled. Tears dripped on them like rain. His next words sounded very hollow and yet they were brimming, swollen with hurt. "I am so sorry. We have to go now."

I just kept nodding stupidly and biting my lip against the pathetic sounds trying to crawl out of my throat.

"Jin will stay with the flock," my father said, thumbing over his shoulder, and I nodded.

"I'll go get him," he mumbled. I nodded again. I hadn't stopped nodding. My head bobbed up and down like a float in water as Hasev waded through the flock away from me.

He's leaving so that I can say goodbye to my vaiyas.

To Vax.

Mother of Yurrii, this is happening too fast.

I sagged forward. How could I say goodbye to Vax? I couldn't. Blessed Nasheira, I couldn't say it. *He won't understand.* I drank in the bright intelligence behind his dark eye, the dip in his skull and the pale scar where Na-Jhalar had wounded him. *He's been my real family. His trust never faltered, and he never left my side.* He'd try to follow us, and he wouldn't let them hurt me. The big vaiya would face all the spears in my camp before he'd let that happen. He'd done it without hesitation when I asked him to run this summer.

They'll kill him. Oh Nasheira, they'll do it.

I can't.

I can't.

Choking on my thoughts, I curled into a ball on the ground as if I could physically shield my explosive emotions from the flock, from the big vaiya whose single, warm eye focused on me even now. I was sliding into horrible, fragmented chaos, skidding down a sheer, shale cliff. I wished it were over. I wished I would hit the bottom and break into insanity. Anything was better than hanging on the edge like this.

"It's all right, pretty bird." Vax's coarse voice spoke close to my face. I hadn't heard him move, but now his big head hung inches from mine, his sweet breath warm against my cheek.

"It's all right," he repeated.

"Oh, Vax," I gulped, flung my arms around his strong neck, and pressed my face against warm hide. I couldn't look him in the eye. He'd see my fear. *Sweet Nasheira, if I say good-bye, he'll know what's happening.*

"I know," Vax said.

Snapping straight to stare at the vaiya, I stuttered. "W-what? What did you say?"

"I know. It's all right," Vax repeated, unruffled.

My gaze slid warily to the rest of the vaiyas who, until moments ago, had been hysterical and barely contained. A sudden calm settled on the flock. The change in them was surreal. I didn't understand it. Somehow this new composure terrified me more than the previous insanity.

"Vax..." I started hesitantly, and the vaiya nudged my chest consolingly.

"Call her," he said reverently, and the rest of the flock whistled in encouragement.

I wanted to ask Vax what he meant, wanted to know what had happened to my birds to make them quiet so suddenly, but Hasev approached.

"Call who?" I whispered to Vax, but the big vaiya didn't answer.

Jin hovered at the far edge of the flock.

"We have to go," Hasev repeated, and I nodded again on cue, like we were puppets doomed to repeat the same scene over and over. *If you look at Vax one more time, you'll break. Just move your feet. One in front of the other,* but I couldn't.

My father coughed and carefully held out a blanket, *my blanket*, the one he'd made when I was born. He also held a pale, gnarled root on a leather thong. My gaze darted from that to my father's painted face.

He cleared his throat again and peeled his gaze away from

me. Humiliation bruised his voice when he spoke. "You have to take your clothes off."

"Oh," I stammered, and nodded as I took the blanket and necklace. Hasev turned his back.

I undressed with awkward, stiff movements. Fall night air raked over my bare skin as I pulled the wurm necklace over my head. It felt like a collar. Draping the blanket around my shoulders, I folded my clothes into a neat pile on the ground, knowing that I would never wear them again.

Darkness closed in around me, cold, familiar waters coming to bear me. Woodenly, I walked into the camp where my death waited. My limbs swung heavy, like I really was wading through ice water.

Sweet Nasheira, let me drown in this fear before the cutting starts, let me die before then.

A horrible, binding pressure pulled at my chest with every breath. I feared I would collapse before I ever reached the northern edge where everyone waited in their festival clothes. But I walked on.

Aella stood like a delicate ice statue, ready to topple. Elba was with her. The harsh moonlight clung to them, hollowing out their faces, and showing their bones beneath their glittering garb.

Darvie held his shivering, wailing baby.

Na-Jhalar stood unclothed except for his holy necklace.

Mother of Yurrii, that we should share so much in common with our Speaker right now except trinkets.

If I wore the scales of the Guides around my neck, and Na-Jhalar had my dirty root tied to his, would Nasheira mistake us? Could a goddess not see through such primitive signs? Was I to die simply because there was a twisted piece of root bound at my throat?

Na-Jhalar recited the first words of our bloody ceremony.

My head rolled to see Yurrii and Pau hanging heavily above us.

They were touching. The black shadow of Pau already consumed the edge of Yurrii. Something recoiled in my stomach, and yet I couldn't stop watching. As the Speaker continued his address, Pau slid, almost undetectable to the eye, chewing into the side of his younger brother.

Swallowing him.

I willed it to stop. I stared as I had when I'd been little, cramming every ounce of my strength into forcing Pau's retreat, stopping the murder, turning time back.

Time did seem to slow a little. Voices grew garbled and drawn out. Every motion thickened. Each heartbeat pounded with the authority of a final strike. I passed through eternity as the Speaker recited verse after verse of memorized monotony, and the moons hung like watchful eyes over us all.

Eventually, time tripped, caught, and raced onward.

We began to move.

The pain in my chest and the roar of my heart drowned out the words that ended our leader's speech and started our journey north. The Speaker led, and only the fathers and mothers of the daeson followed him

Darvie went first, then Elba. She seemed torn between maintaining a distance from Enso, who was nestled in her mate's arms, and keeping well ahead of me. Hasev and my mother walked behind me, but I couldn't even hear their light footsteps.

The pull in my chest grew as we neared the northern border of camp. I stumbled, groaning as I tried to suck in air that wouldn't come. *Don't disgrace Hasev. Be a good boy.* But my head reeled messily now and any control I had over my body peeled away in layers.

How far north did we have to go? We were still within

sight of camp, but nearing the tree line now. It looked black, jagged and foreboding. The same black swallowed the edges of my vision. *Sweet Nasheira, what's happening to the air? Why can't I breathe?*

I stumbled, tried to focus on Elba's tunic, but she seemed to be tilting.

I winced as I heard Aella's voice, fuzzy and muted in my ears.

"What's wrong with it?" she asked Hasev.

Hot, white spots ignited like sparks across my vision. The wurm pendant pulled like a boulder around my neck. It choked me. I couldn't breathe. Dropping the blanket, I clawed at my throat.

Oh, Nasheira, what's happening to me? Am I dying? Is this how it feels, like a great hand crushing me?

My knees gave out. Slower still, the earth swung up to meet me. Ages passed as my jaw struck cold earth and my teeth cut into my tongue. Blood bubbled out of my mouth with all the speed of trickling sap, and yet another eternity meandered by before Hasev clutched my shoulder and rolled me over.

Blood, hot and bitter, slid down my throat. I made an awful gurgling sound as my hands clasped my chest. I couldn't cough, couldn't move. My father's solid silhouette faded.

Soon all I could see was the blazing white distortion of the brother moons mashing into each other in the inky sky above. Pau had consumed half of Yurrii now. Shadows crawled across craters like dark, pooling poison.

Then I saw something else.

Sliding across the macabre backdrop of the moons came the clawed point of a tapered wing. It blocked the brothers Pau and Yurrii for only a moment, but I caught every translucent, veined detail as it passed.

A Guide. Something in me clicked and connected with consciousness. My eyes widened. I sucked in a tremulous breath and coughed. I tried to tell Hasev, but couldn't speak.

Call her, Vax had said. I squirmed.

My father stood still, the hunter in him sensing something and searching for a source.

The leaden pressure in my chest felt like it was about to snap through my spine and sink ever-faster to the centre of the earth, dragging my broken body with it.

A realization struck me. *She's doing it to me, the dragon.*

Call her.

My mind spun back to the desert, when a golden Guide had dipped low over us; I'd dreamed of her beforehand, and I'd felt this pulling at my chest. It brought me to my knees then, too. I thought the dragon was calling me. She'd looked right at me. Had she been trying to ensnare me then? For what?

Please, I tested mentally, *come save me. Sweet Nasheira, you're crushing me to death!*

The pressure in my chest relaxed. A shuddering, grateful moan rushed past my lips as the darkness at the edges of my vision receded completely.

The morbid procession stood frozen and silent around me. Their heads cocked to the side like they were straining to hear what made their instincts hum with recognition.

Still, I couldn't move. Although I could breathe, it took all the strength I had to make my lungs expand.

I'm here. I squeezed my eyes closed. *Can you hear me? Please... you're hurting me.*

This time the weight lifted enough that the pain at my chest seeped away completely. While I could swallow against the sharp taste in my mouth, I couldn't lift a hand to wipe the blood that dribbled down my chin.

I can't move! Fresh panic boiled through me. *Please, they're going to kill me. What do you want?*

The reply blasting through the valley was the most beautiful and terrifying sound I'd ever heard. Every head in the procession swung up and to the southeast, where the trumpet of Nasheira's golden Guide had sounded. I heard the tiny sounds of the vaiya flock back in camp crooning their reverent greeting.

Then the golden angel arced into my view, pale, glowing, and sinuous in the moonlight.

My breath caught. Everybody's did. We were captured by the subtle, natural adjustments her wings made, reaching out and easily examining the current that bore them. We were so caught up in her detail that we didn't notice how fast the dragon approached until she hung right on top of us, back-winging, churning clouds of roiling dust, and whipping our hair back from our faces.

She was our entire sky, cutting a golden swathe through splintering moonbeams.

Everyone around me scrambled back and dropped to the ground, fingers pressed to their foreheads.

I lay alone with the dragon I'd called.

I wanted to scream and laugh and cry. I wanted to stand before her and to run as far and as fast as my legs would take me. I had never felt so utterly tiny and exposed in my life, lying naked in the dirt, pinned under the gaze of a golden Guide. I saw every detail of the dragon as she stretched her limbs to land.

Moonlight shone through the rippling membrane of her wings, highlighting puckered scars and needling through tiny holes. She touched down, and the ground at my bare back shivered from the substantial weight. Patches of scales were missing from her raptor feet. When she dipped her dainty head to regard me with one huge, emerald eye, shadowed spaces pocked her jaw where teeth were missing.

She was the most perfect creature I had ever seen in my life.

I was scared to death of her.

I couldn't move, could barely blink as the Guide slipped toward me. Even on the ground, she moved with fast and flexible grace. I forgot how to breathe as she delicately set the splayed claws of one forearm over my lower half and mantled her wings possessively over me. I'd seen hawks do the same thing, before they ate mice.

She's going to rip me in half.

This towering creature held enough power within one claw to reduce me to a bloodied mess with a single flick. I winced as the idle twitch of one thick and wickedly pointed talon prodded my left thigh.

Please, I whispered in my mind, *please don't kill me.*

My eyes slammed shut as that giant head swivelled and dropped downward. Resigned, I waited for the puncture of pointed ivory teeth through my soft bones, but nothing came except a burst of hot, humid air blanketing sweetly around me. It reminded me of the vaiyas. I kept my eyes closed, listening to the deep, hollow draw of the dragon breathing as moist blasts of air fluttered my eyelashes and raised goosebumps on my skin.

When I blinked and focused, a slotted nostril and the tips of two cone-shaped teeth hovered just above my face. As her jaws dropped open, a meaty, slightly sour smell greeted me and I saw right down the dragon's dark throat.

Guides, she could fit five of me in her mouth without swallowing.

There was a snorting huff, as if the Guide was insulted by my thought, and before I could think another, that ridged tongue slid out from between its ramparts and scraped across my chest. The touch of it was surprisingly and instantly agonizing. Tiny barbs bit into my skin and tore it away. I screamed, broken from my trance. She was *skinning* me. I squirmed like an earthworm on a hook as her tongue scoured my chest and impatient talons jammed into my thigh.

Oh, Nasheira, it hurts! Nothing had ever hurt this much. The Guide drew her tongue up my left shoulder, tearing at the skin even as I sobbed for her to stop. The world started spinning.

Then there was nothing. The pressure released from my chest like a taut rope snapping. I gasped as blood rushed to my prickling legs. Feebly, I tried to cross my arms over my burning chest and smeared something slimy and warm.

There was blood on the ground. I saw it as I pulled my legs up protectively and rolled to my side, blinking at a world that was shifting to black. The last thing stamped in my vision was the hideous sphere of Pau totally eclipsing Yurrii. The last sound I heard before sliding into unconsciousness was the beating of gossamer, golden wings.

Just like that, Nasheira had chosen me, had marked me in front of my entire camp.

Daeson Akrist was a Speaker.

PART TWO
"MARKED"

CHAPTER TWELVE

I awoke with the image of golden wings firmly in my mind and a wordless cry on my lips.

Sky scrolled by above. A shifting sense of motion disoriented me. Blinking at my surroundings, I realized I was in a travois towed by a vaiya. Strung out behind us, vaiyas loaded with supplies ambled in a serpentine line, chirping and whistling as they picked their way down the grassy slope. Scuffing feet and low, casual voices drifted from ahead. As I tried to sit up, a tightness pulled at my chest followed by hot pain.

I hissed, pressing my hands against my chest. It was bandaged. A crusted brown stain marred the fabric. An itchy trickle of something—sweat? blood?—ran down my ribs, and a long, low whimper escaped me before I realized the travois had stopped. A shadow fell over me.

I cringed.

"Akrist."

Fraesh's voice.

The healer slowly opened the bandage. "It's healing, but you need to stay still."

"Where is he?" I asked.

This is wrong. It was dark when the dragon came. Where had the daylight come from?

"Where's who, Akrist?"

"Enso," I blurted. "What happened to him?" An awful vision of the baby crying scuttled through my brain.

Fraesh stiffened like something had stung him. "The baby's gone, Akrist. He was sacrificed."

I tried to exhale, but couldn't. My throat closed completely and when I finally did manage a breath, it came out as a sob. Dizziness swamped me, and the world pooled into fuzzy oblivion before me. Frantic thoughts pressed past the heat, the fever, and the crying. *I lived and Enso died. I didn't even try to save him.*

"What does it mean?" I gingerly touched the swollen abrasion that skidded from my chest to my left shoulder. The strange infection, although ghastly, would pass quickly. Twisting, latticed lines of scar tissue drifted toward my shoulder, weaving in and out of smooth skin, like red serpents skimming through pale water.

Some tried to replicate the Guide's mark, cutting and burning themselves in an effort to wear that powerful scar by fraud, returning to their camps bleeding and screaming that they'd been chosen. But the way the infection branded the skin was beautifully singular. My mark was no fraud.

"It means we're not sacrificing you today." Hasev unrolled a strip of clean fabric. Fraesh and the rest of the elders' council had been called to another meeting in the Speaker's tent, so the healer had left my father to change my bandages. "Sit up."

I did as I was told, waiting for elaboration as he wound

the fresh bandage around my chest. Sitting up triggered the dizziness, like weakness had baked into my bones. The fever had broken. I felt its slow decline, like a curtain being pulled away. But my limbs still felt like lead, and I couldn't shake the smothering feeling that I stared out at the world through miles of sluggish, sleepy haze.

Familiar faces seemed skewed, slightly off. When Darvie or Fraesh spoke to me, they sounded like aeni actors in a play, pretending to be someone else, rigidly performing an unconvincing act of everyday life. Casual glances and common tasks seemed forced.

Hasev was a great, ungainly puppet, cocking his head to listen as Na-Jhalar's nasal, piercing voice cut like a spear through the tangle of words tumbling out of the Speaker's tent. Na-Jhalar had called his council, which included all of the elders, the storyteller, and the healer. While I couldn't hear their words, their subject was clear, even to me.

"He means to kill me, doesn't he?" I spoke carefully.

"Killing is not allowed."

But with the image of Darvie's screaming baby imprinted on my mind, I knew those words meant nothing.

"The Speaker must follow the word of Nasheira," Hasev added. "You're dragon-marked. Nasheira chose you for a reason. We just have to decipher what she means by it." He pointed at the Speaker's tent and I was suddenly aware of the heated voices coming from within.

I couldn't wait for the public proclamation to hear my fate. Later that night, while Hasev slept, I crept toward the Speaker's well-lit tent and eavesdropped on the heated, muffled voices within.

"He must be sacrificed!" Na-Jhalar demanded.

"Holy Speaker, we've gone over this." Iva said. "You do not wish to lose face just because of this boy, do you?"

"Of course not!" the Speaker spat.

"He's just a boy," the storyteller pressed softly.

"I know that!"

Iva spoke slowly. "No, *tell* your people he is *just* a boy."

Silence.

"Maybe Nasheira didn't mean to make him a Speaker. She already has you, Na-Jhalar," the storyteller explained. "Perhaps she just meant for him *not* to be a daeson. What if the mark was just to cancel his cursed birth? To redeem him? Tell your people he is neither Speaker nor daeson now. Just a boy. Nothing more or less. Nothing for them to worry over."

Just a boy. Sweet Nasheira, I'd waited my entire life to be just a boy.

A NORMAL BOY. I repeated that to myself as I removed the twisted root from the front of my tent, as I groomed vaiyas alongside Jin and gathered forage that wouldn't be marked and set aside as tainted.

The one wish I'd chased my entire life was nothing like I expected it would be.

I knew I couldn't simply cast off my old identity and fit into the camp like the missing shard of a broken pot. I'd always been the piece that didn't fit.

I had no idea how to gauge anyone I crossed. Before, as a daeson, I'd known my boundaries. My place in the world had been nothing if not clear. I was to stay distant from the children, and out of everyone else's way. But now it seemed Nasheira had turned my entire life into a tavi game. Forced to consider every person carefully, I had only subtle signs and instinct to guide me. I could not tell you how many times I made the wrong move.

I found by miscalculation that Elba now felt I should maintain twice the distance from her as I had previously, whereas her mate Mira conversed with me freely, often asking me to describe the Guide that marked me. My youngest brother, Dero, hated me, mostly because Jin often shrugged him off to shyly ask my advice on handling the vaiyas. Iva spoke with me constantly. Unabashed by the glares of many of her fellow council members, she enthusiastically questioned me about my vaiyas' reaction to the dragon, my visions, my choosing, and my scar.

Talking so much was exhausting. I wasn't used to lengthy conversation, and Sweet Nasheira, if idle chatter with Iva felt awkward, it was paralyzing for me to speak to anyone else. I choked mid-sentence, leaving my questioner staring while I gasped like a flopping fish on a sandy bank. Should someone lean too close, brush against my arm, or casually lay a hand on my shoulder, I flinched as if they'd burned me. Sometimes I felt like I was being suffocated by the people around me. They were all too close, too loud, and too clingy. To my shame, I often preferred the cold, hard-eyed, cursing faction of my camp to the friendly, personable ones who made the effort to comfort me.

Having grown up invisible, it was overwhelming to be thrown into such sudden focus.

I was embarrassed at not instantly becoming the person I'd always wanted to be and horrified by the habitual words and actions that automatically escaped me, revealing the daeson within.

During the early days of our journey after the sacrifice, while I searched the skies for the dragons that were supposed to come back, my father did his best to become my companion. For the first time in my life, Hasev did not want to spend time with me out of duty. He wanted to be my father. But I just couldn't let him.

Bitterness hardened my heart. Hasev hadn't visited me during my months of captivity, hadn't even taken a shift as my guard, and then he'd had the audacity to *cry* before he led me to sacrifice. I couldn't think of him as a father anymore, but I didn't have the strength to push him away.

I pasted on a brittle, tight smile as he stammered through sentences he would start with "daeson" before catching himself with a cough. How many times had I yearned to hear Hasev's steady, deep voice speaking my name as a boy? Now, it burned me.

Weeks after the moons eclipsed, Hasev quietly presented me with one of his spears.

"You're a man now. You should learn how to hunt, how to hold a weapon. I'll teach you when you're well enough."

My cheeks burned and I couldn't hold my words back. "You think you know my path so well? What if I've already chosen to be a gatherer?"

The spear sagged in Hasev's hands. "Oh." he said. "H-have you?"

Children chose their life paths soon after they scarred their chests. Hunter, gatherer, or—for a rare few who were taken as apprentices—healer or storyteller. My own father had no idea what direction my heart pulled me. He'd just assumed.

I let confusion and embarrassment fill his grey-blue eyes before putting him out of his misery. "I haven't chosen yet."

"Oh," he said again. "Well, take the spear. Either way, I'd like you to have it."

I didn't want to take it. Heat boiled up my throat, but I'd never been good at using words as weapons. I'd been invisible for too long.

So I took the spear. The balanced, elegant weight of it in my hands felt forbidden and beautiful at the same time, like the dragon scale I'd held years before. Part of me wanted to turn it in my hands and admire the way the sun warmed its angles, and part of me, the daeson part, wanted to drop it and run.

A year ago, I would have basked under the instruction of my father, would have given anything for him to teach me how he handled a weapon with such deft and familiar grace. I would have cherished every word. It was too late now.

Maybe that wound would have healed with time. Maybe I could have had a father again. But even if I had wanted him to, Hasev would not teach me to hunt when I got well. He'd never teach me to hunt.

My parents argued at night as I lay under a sky where Yurrii persistently followed Pau through a path of stars. The venom in their voices was unmistakable. Aella often hissed the word "Tasie." Speaking my sister's name usually silenced my father.

Hasev finally comprehended that his mate could never accept me as family. As far as Aella was concerned, I'd caused Tasie's drowning twelve years ago. I'd been born to die. She'd meant to cut me out of her life, literally. To avenge her drowned daughter. And it had not been allowed to happen. My father's choice was clear: it was me or Aella.

Hasev didn't tell me his decision, he just drifted away until there was a gap between us too big for either one of us to cross.

As Hasev withdrew, Iva and Fraesh swept in. I often wondered whether my father had asked his sister to watch me in his stead. I have no doubt I would have crumbled without their support.

I survived by losing myself in the busy and necessary tasks that came with setting up a camp. My new hut felt ridiculously large and out of place when I was done building it.

Although I was now allowed to reside in my family's hut, I was exceedingly uncomfortable with the very thought of it and unwilling to be the wedge that drove my parents even further apart. I built my new home on the opposite end of camp, not far from Fraesh and Iva's.

To my surprise, I missed the security of my family's hut nestled nearby. My first night alone, I felt deeply ashamed when I realized that I missed the bars of my old prison hut. *What is wrong with you? You are free now.* But, my cage had been secure from wurms.

There's too much room in this hut. A wurm could reach you before you ever woke. I shuddered.

I did not miss the symbolic root that previously marred my doorway. Iva taught me how to hone a flint until it was sharp enough to shave with, how to hunt: where to set a snare, how to track an animal, and techniques for aiming and throwing a spear. Fraesh brought me on gathering trips and taught me how to identify medicinal herbs. I chose my path. Iva grinned when I told her I was a hunter.

On cold mornings, when the hunters left camp, I joined them. I was touched and a little embarrassed when Fraesh stuffed leaf packets of food into my waistband and insisted on one more cup of tea before I left. I never thought I'd be beating a quick retreat from the clucking frenzy of morning gatherers with a spear—my father's spear—resting against my shoulder.

It brought a peace that I'd never known, hiking north-ward from the camp with strong, quiet hunters at my back, and Vust, Voti, and Veset as tactfully silent as I'd ever known them. I liked being a part of an essential and efficient group.

Winter arrived with no more dragons in the sky than there'd been before the eclipse. I passed into my twelfth year and began to wear my black hair braided away from my face in the style of the hunters. I didn't even flinch when, in a snow-blanketed gully, I made my first kill and the hunters clapped me on the back, whooping enthusiastically as if it was the first time they'd ever seen a gazelle dropped by a spear.

Hasev said nothing, but nodded proudly with a wide, wistful smile brightening his eyes. I forgave him a little then.

When we returned to camp, Iva winked as her daughter Celi chose the lungs of my animal, her mother's favourite, for her chani share. Na-Jhalar was too lost in a gifen trance to choose for his chani at all that day. It was often that way now. That evening, I flopped against the warmth of a dozing Vax while Jin pressed me for every detail of the hunt.

And that was how life continued for us, with slow, rolling normalcy. It was as normal as we could expect in our hard world, with our incompetent leader slipping ever further into the languid addiction of gifen.

With my mark no longer a threat to his leadership, the Speaker's sober moments dwindled. As our leader decayed into dependency, we flourished. Camps often looked to their storyteller for leadership when they didn't have a speaker. Often, a storyteller's knowledge of the past gave them a keen eye for navigating the future, and they already played a key part in evening prayers. So naturally our camp gravitated toward Iva. She led fairly, readily took advice from her elders, and our camp existed in happy, busy efficiency.

In late spring, Baline gave birth to a healthy, blessed boy, Galeed. He was saved from the cursed fate of daeson because of a grisly but valuable reminder Baline kept all these years.

A mummified stillborn baby. A boy.

Fraesh had been there that night, years earlier, when Baline's daeson was born dead. Since such occasions were usually painfully private affairs that could occur before a woman's pregnancy was prominently showing, a camp often demanded more proof of a daeson's existence and expiry than a blue circle tattoo from the healer. Presumably, Fraesh had preserved the stillborn baby so Galeed could live without the fate of the damned sons pinned to him.

Whether the mummified child was actually Baline's or not, I didn't know. It was not unheard of for a woman to discreetly purchase a dead baby from the aeni: they confidentially supplied such stock for the right trade. Similarly, it was not unknown for women to try to fake a daeson's tattoo themselves, or bribe a healer to mark them fraudulently to avoid having a daeson at all, even though they risked getting branded and banished by doing so. It was, however, much rarer to find a healer who'd face the wrath of Nasheira by denying her goddess's rightful offering.

I didn't think Fraesh would condone such deceit, nor the market of stillborn babies, but either seemed preferable to the ritual that was the culmination of a daeson's horrible life, the fate I'd somehow sidestepped while Enso had not. I thought often and bitterly of Darvie's son, an utterly useless sacrifice. It hadn't pleased Nasheira. She hadn't sent any more dragons to guide us. We were still alone. Our goddess didn't care about us.

CHAPTER THIRTEEN

Three years after my choosing, daeson Sivi was born into our camp by Arsu's womb. Her mate, Gevi, wouldn't pick up the boy. He fed him vaiya milk and changed him at arm's length, but never cradled or spoke to his first-born son. I had seen him bear crushing weight to save his daughter, but he couldn't be bothered to touch his son. Daeson Sivi's mewling cries echoed through camp day and night. By the third night, I couldn't stand it anymore.

Tanar had enough compassion to save Xen. He would have done something by now. You're fifteen years old. Act like it.

Swatting aside my blanket, I marched toward the diminutive new hut on the north side. Those shredding cries pierced my ears as I closed the distance, and I faltered when I saw lamplight under the door flap of the daeson's hut.

Clearing my throat, I waited for a pause between Sivi's howls. "Gevi?"

Feet scuffed and shadows shifted inside. "Who is it?"

This is stupid. The baby's not alone. Go back. But I couldn't. I hadn't saved Enso. I needed to make that right somehow and this felt like a start.

"I could t-take the boy for a while," I stammered. "If you want a break from the crying."

The door flap eased open and Gevi stood there swaying, mouth slack and eyes ringed by dark circles, like he'd forgotten what sleep was.

"If you want to go back to your daughter. I can take him for a bit."

Gevi didn't give any indication that he'd heard me, but he shuffled out of the hut and toward his family home without even taking the lamp.

I stiffened as I passed under the root symbol and ducked into the tiny hut. Daeson Sivi howled, red-faced and oblivious to my presence.

I reached out and covered his tiny clenched fist with my own hand, but it didn't feel natural like when Tanar did it with Xen.

"Hey. It's all right," I murmured, but the baby's cries drowned out my words.

Pick him up. Hold him. I knew that was what he needed, but I'd never held a newborn before. I hadn't even held Xen, just his hand. The rule to avoid other children had been beaten into me too firmly. Holding Sivi's fist right now, as he flailed, was making me nauseated and it didn't seem to be calming him down.

The door flap whipped open and Arsu squinted before recognizing me. "You," she hissed, stabbing a finger toward me.

I shrank at the venom in her voice, but couldn't retreat. The hut was too small. "H-he needs someone to hold him," I blurted.

"What did you say?" She enunciated each word slowly.

"I-I could hold him and give Gevi a break—"

The woman moved fast. She gripped my arm and tore me out of the hut so quickly I nearly tripped on her screaming daeson. Her fist cracked into my cheek and I toppled back into the dirt. White swarmed my vision, so I didn't see Arsu line up to kick me in the ribs. The blow pounded air out of me, and I lay there wriggling as she straddled me and bent to speak in my ear.

"You remember what happened to you last time you laid hands on my child, daeson?"

I coughed and curled away from her, but she grabbed me by the hair and shook me.

"Answer me."

I nodded, mouth opening and closing like a fish, unable to draw breath.

"Your feet must still bear the scars."

I flinched.

"That was nothing, you hear?" Arsu growled. "You ever come near my family again and I'll kill you. I'll stuff you into a hole so deep, no one will ever find out what happened to you. Do you understand, you miserable little wurm shit?"

I nodded. I kept nodding until Arsu turned and left. Daeson Sivi's cries drowned out my whimpering as I pressed my arm against my side, and limped back to my own hut. I couldn't breathe without pain firing through my ribs. Laying on my bedroll, gritting my teeth and swallowing tears, I closed my eyes as Sivi's wailing sawed through me in the dark. *Never again,* I vowed silently. *I'll stop it somehow. They won't sacrifice their daeson ever again. I'll steal them all away.*

Daeson Sivi died two days later.

Fraesh determined he was healthy in body and that Gevi wasn't responsible for his death. "Some go like that." His face pinched as he bound my broken ribs. "Well fed, but starving to be held. Can't be helped, boy."

Yes it can. Any one of you could help, but you don't. I wanted to tell him, but it hurt to talk.

When such bitter thoughts consumed me, I did my best to

bury them. I told myself that a normal person wouldn't harbour such vindictive emotion. Sometimes I could push it all down and forget I was ever anything but Akrist, a regular fifteen-year-old boy. I covered my Speaker's scar when people looked too long, and I almost never flinched when I was touched.

I acted my part until it convinced those close to me. I almost convinced myself.

THE MOONS REMAINED our macabre timekeepers. After daeson Sivi died, Pau and Yurrii separated so that we never saw the moons in the sky together. Mates who'd yet to birth their first sons abstained from sex, or drank special tinctures purchased from the aeni intended to prevent pregnancies—a dangerous gamble as Fraesh insisted that none of the drinks worked. But twelve years was a long cycle, no matter how determined mates were, and it was a long time to be childless. Early cycle daeson like me were rare, but not unheard of. We had daeson Sivi, but after he died, we had no more damned sons until the end of the moons cycle.

By the time I turned twenty-one, Pau began tracking Yurrii through the same night sky again, marking less than three years until the next eclipse. There tended to be a general surge in births around this time. Young women who had yet to bear their first son tended to share themselves more freely, for if they did birth a daeson, they were guaranteed to be rid of it within a few short years.

Groups who sought shelter within our camps often contained pregnant women and babes-in-arms now. We could tell which ones had daeson from a distance by the way the fathers held them. Arsu loudly pressed to turn such groups away after the traditional one night's courtesy, but

Iva considered each applicant fairly regardless of their damned sons, taking in capable hunters and gatherers for as long as they wished to stay.

By the time I turned twenty three, with less than a year until the next sacrifice, we'd gained four daeson; two red, wrinkled newborns, and two toddlers who were old enough to care for themselves, one dark-haired and thin, one fair and inexplicably round.

Somewhere along the way, I'd grown into a man I was ashamed of.

Every time I resolved to approach the daeson, my ribs hurt where Arsu had broken them and my breathing became heavier and faster until dizziness swamped me. My hands shook for hours afterwards, and I hated myself for it. *They repulse you now? Physically? These boys who you were once? You've sworn to save them. You have less than a year, and you can't even gather the strength to talk to them.*

I'd had nearly eleven years to prepare, yet here I was, running out of time, just as it had happened with Tanar. And what had I done with my time?

By my age, a normal man had long ago found a mate, perhaps a few. Most were well into starting families, with two or three children. I was over halfway through my journey to becoming an elder and had neither a mate nor children. Fraesh asked me gently if I knew my path concerning a potential mate, and I blushed and couldn't answer him. I wasn't attracted to men, not like my brother Jin was. Certainly, women were allured and intrigued when they learned of my Speaker's scar. The mark of Nasheira held a definite magnetism, and I'd been told before that mine was particularly attractive.

A lot of good it did me.

When new women in the camp investigated the story behind my scar, most withdrew, horrified. A few were curious enough to continue courting, some despite my history, and some because of it. But their efforts were always in vain.

The truth was I'd spent half a lifetime avoiding intimacy of any kind. In the company of women, other young men turned into endearing creatures with all the awkwardness of vaiya chicks.

I was not like that.

I was what the vaiya chick grew into if you kicked it every time it nuzzled your hand. For a daeson, being intimate wasn't just some broken rule, it was something beaten out of us. It felt instinctively wrong and unnatural.

That said, I was an otherwise healthy male of twenty-three years. Certainly, I was attracted to women and wanted to touch them. But when it came right down to the moment, a wave of nauseating guilt from my past always drowned out any natural longing in me.

Crippled by the company of women and daeson alike, I whittled my life down to its simplest form possible. Hunting, scouting with Vax, and avoiding almost everyone else.

That was my life. That was how I wasted eleven entire years, pretending to be normal, denying that I was a Speaker, and ignoring the daeson I'd once promised to save.

I may have continued my selfish existence forever if Nasheira—bless her—hadn't sent me another sign. This time she didn't send a Guide. She sent an angel.

Her name was Yara. And she saw right through me.

OUR GATHERERS POURED into camp on the first evening of winter, having collected two travellers along with their day's bounty. It had been a cold day full of frost and fat snowflakes. I crouched by my fire when I heard their rebel-liously warm voices carrying up the hillside.

The gatherers sang a bright, bouncing tune, something ridiculous about springtime and summer festivals.

I smiled as Vable trotted buoyantly into view with three bundled children wedged between the gathering sacks on his back. All of them, including the vaiya, were excitedly crowing something I could not hear as the children waved bunches of wild onions like flags. Shaking my head, I wondered how the gatherers kept such hearty cheer on a blustery day like this.

Then the main group crested the hill, and I heard the most incredible, contagious laugh. I lifted my head at the pleasant sound and saw her through the flames.

She was wreathed in a fog of her breath and a swirl of lazy snowflakes. Warm amber curls spilled around the edges of her fur-lined hood. Her cheeks glowed, and a smile still played at her lips and danced in her eyes as she sang. There was something regal about the way she held herself, yet entirely natural, like the proud curve of a vaiya's neck, or the perfect fold of a dragon's wing. It was instantly and abso-lutely fascinating.

With a casual shift of dark eyes, she saw me.

A warm wash of primal emotion overcame me. My breath caught, my heart stumbled, and I felt the gentle, tugging throb of a more basic male response. On its heels, expected and familiar, came the guilt, that horrible, humiliating sense of immorality, the sickening reminder that I was a bad person—no—that I wasn't a person at all.

Dropping my head, I blinked rapidly at the fire that suddenly felt too hot. I tried to push the fresh image of her out of my head because I didn't want it soiled by that ugly, plaguing guilt. Guides, I wished I'd brought something to occupy my hands.

I hated being reminded that I was a daeson. *Oh, Nasheira,* I hated the confusion that rolled around inside me now.

Can you not just act normal? Breathe!

Against my will, my gaze lifted away from the coals, but the radiant woman was no longer there. There was just a girl in her place, slouching to duck further into her hood. Her tan curls nearly hid her sombre face.

I asked after her the next day as casually as I knew how. Iva told me that the two women heard the gatherers yesterday and crashed through the woods to seek them out.

"Aeni?" I asked.

Iva shook her head. "Mother and daughter. Lost from their camp nearly a year. Journeyed with an aeni group though, until a month ago when a sickness struck so hard they fled in fear for their lives. Do you remember the one that came through camp when you were a boy?" Iva squinted at me.

"The one what?" I asked and she huffed.

"The sickness! Your head is in the clouds. She's got you, hasn't she?"

"Who's got me?"

"The girl, the plain one with the tan curls. Her name is Yara. Her mother is Enna." Iva glanced up from the spear shaft she was fire-hardening, sly eyes dancing. "That's what you came here to ask, isn't it?"

Yara. My heart skipped foolishly. I had a name. *Yara.*

I really meant to leave it at that, to pretend that I felt nothing but idle curiosity when Yara and I exchanged glances. I intended to avoid her as I did all other women, address her politely when forced to, and never again make eye contact.

But I couldn't erase that fleeting, celestial image. Her halo of snowflakes, her warm lips. I was torn between disgust at my attraction and longing to witness that marvellous vision again. Was that all it had been, a vision? A wishful exaggeration of character and features caused by a hurried glance?

Was it possible that I'd imagined that glowing, smiling face? I'd not seen it since. Certainly, I saw Yara. We were a small camp, and crossing paths was an eventual inevitability. But I'd not found that vivacious woman who met my glance over the fire. The Yara I'd seen since was a shuffling, silent ghost of a girl whose only outstanding trait was an uncanny ability to be invisible. She just disappeared in a crowd, like a sleek sparrow joining a flock mid-flight, capable of effortless adjustment to every turn and bank in the natural formation, until she was no longer an individual, but just a tiny part of a much larger thing.

I'd worked my entire life to go unnoticed like that, but I would never be the sparrow. No matter how I tried to hide them, my differences still marked me, especially when the choice gossip of my past made its rounds.

I could tell when Yara had heard my story. One morning when we passed, her gaze slid my way and settled on my chest, not my face, as if she could peer through my heavy overcoat to see the Guide's mark beneath.

I felt exposed. Clenching my teeth, I held my breath until she passed. *Sweet Nasheira, what has she been told? What does she think of me now that she knows what I was?* To most people, I became one of three things when they learned of my mark: a horrible misfit who should never have been allowed to live, a modest, mysterious Speaker in disguise, or an acceptable outlet for all of the dark and twisted fantasies they'd ever held about daeson.

And I don't want Yara to think any of those things.

Sighing, I considered talking to Jin. My brother and I had become closer than I'd ever hoped, but not familiar enough to discuss much more than hunting and vaiya maintenance. Besides, his mate, Aaron, threw cold glares my way when he knew Jin wasn't looking. I didn't want to cause tension between the two men by vying for Jin's ear over my trivial worries. Apprehensions about Yara would have to chew through my lonely mind unadvised.

Perhaps the only soul who sensed my private dilemma was Vax, and the old bird's only consolatory words were: "Pretty girl."

Two days passed before Yara sought me out. She approached me one afternoon while I checked Vax for bury bugs. My back was to the camp, so I didn't see her coming, but Vax whistled and nudged me playfully.

The big vaiya always whistled at girls he found pleasant. Tanar had taught him that.

"Shhh. Crazy bird," I scolded lightly, without turning.

The one-eyed vaiya warbled and nibbled at my hair before crowing, "Pretty girl!"

"Vax!" I snapped and stumbled as I turned. *Mother of Yurrii, you are an idiot!*

Yara was right in front of me. I stared at her feet as my face turned bright as a sunset.

"Did you teach him that?" she asked.

"No," I blurted and glared back at Vax, who frolicked merrily out of my reach. "I'm sorry, he just..." Swallowing, I ducked my head, defeated. "No."

Yara looked past me now. I could tell because she shifted her stance and stretched on her toes to see over my shoulder. Amazing what you could tell by staring at people's feet your entire life.

"What happened to him?"

"What?" I glanced up at Yara's frowning face only long enough to catch the direction of her gaze. "Oh, Vax? He lost his eye."

I realized I had only stated the obvious but couldn't say anything more. Invisible fingers tightened around my throat.

Yara waited for more detail as my thoughts raced.

Stop talking to her. Turn around, and she'll leave. She shouldn't be seen with you. Ignoring the thought, I opened my mouth to speak, but the guilt persisted.

Tell her you are a sick, perverted little wurm who's attracted to her, why don't you tell her that?

Swallowing, I tried again. "H-he was hit with a rock."

"Oh." She shifted nervously before straightening and walking toward Vax.

Horrified by the possibility of the big vaiya spooking, and well aware of his defensive nature, I scrambled after her, but Vax only dipped his head and crooned like a baby as Yara stroked his crest.

I didn't realize I was staring open-mouthed until Yara's lovely dark eyes caught mine. A wisp of a smile lit up her face and shuddered through me. I felt her studying me even as I bowed my head.

"He is still beautiful, even with his scars," Yara said.

I wondered if she was looking at me or at Vax.

Then she turned on her heel and left the way she'd come, just like that. Sweet Nasheira, how I wanted to follow her, but guilt held me back like a well-tethered vaiya.

I couldn't sleep that night. I felt every familiar bump of the Speaker's scar through my woven shirt. It seemed so foreign sometimes, like it wasn't even my body that I touched.

Out of nowhere, an unbidden thought leapt into my mind, a vision of Yara's small, white hands running over that scar and down my chest. Part of me warmed with desire, while another part flinched away under instant, hot shame. Clenching my fists, I rolled over, listened to the howling winter wind, and waited restlessly for sleep, waited for the wurm dream that always came more vividly when I was upset.

CHAPTER FOURTEEN

I didn't sleep well. Peeling myself from my bedroll, I pulled on my clothes and stumbled out into the predawn. I relieved myself behind my hut, listening to the bustle of the gatherers preparing for their daily outing. Other than firewood, there wasn't much to collect with snow on the ground, but it was a chance to stretch their legs before the afternoon tasks of mending and cooking. The enticing aroma of morning tea wafted to me, and I reasoned that it was still early enough to make my way to the cooking hearth without running into any of the daeson. *Coward.*

What I did not expect as I rounded the front of the shelter was Na-Jhalar. I nearly ran into the man before I realized it was him.

The Speaker stood barefoot and naked in the snow at the entrance of his hut. He looked like an animal who'd weathered a hard winter, gaunt beneath shrivelled flaps of excess skin. For a moment, his eyes focused on me, gaze flicking briefly to my chest, even though my Speaker's mark was covered. Raising his hand, he idly scratched his own scar.

My skin crawled. It felt like encountering the ghost of a

monster who terrified you as a child. I froze, as paralyzed now as I had ever been as a boy.

Na-Jhalar rarely came out of his hut anymore, and he certainly didn't interact with people or stare at them like this. His lips quivered as if excited by the prospect of speech, but nothing, save a string of gifen-stained saliva, came out of his mouth.

As I swallowed dryly and stepped back, it seemed that Na-Jhalar's eyes no longer stared at me, just through me, his gaze hollow and hard.

Mother of Yurrii, I could have sworn he was looking at me.

"He'll freeze."

Startled, I spun and saw Yara. She clasped a clay teacup in her hands. Her face was caught in an uncomfortable frown. "We should take him inside."

I glanced back at Na-Jhalar. I hadn't noticed the goose-bumps, the waxiness of his skin and the blue tinge of his lips and fingernails. "I'll get Fraesh."

That milky gaze tracked Yara, and I felt an overwhelming urge to lunge ahead and yank her out of its path.

"Delani," Na-Jhalar rasped and blinked at Yara.

"Come with me," I blurted. "Do not stay here with him."

Something about the strangled tone of my voice earned instant obedience from Yara. Only after we retreated down the snowy path toward the comforting sight of Fraesh and Iva's hut did she ask breathlessly, "Why?"

Shaking my head, mostly at memories of chani screaming, I answered, "He's... not right."

I stopped so abruptly that Yara nearly crashed into me. Swinging around, I forced myself to look directly at this girl who I didn't even know, whose delightful smile had haunted my lonely mind. Licking my lips, I croaked, "Yara, promise me you'll never be alone with him."

"Are you my keeper?" she snapped, drawing herself up.

I balked from the sudden hardness in her eyes. "I-I didn't mean..." My cheeks mottled and I swallowed the rest of my sentence and started over. "He hurts people."

She was quiet for a moment, but didn't look surprised at this as I led the way to Fraesh and Iva's hut. Both of us waited awkwardly outside while the healer got dressed. As we stood, I couldn't shake the eerie, repellent image of Na-Jhalar and his dead eyes coming to life as he saw Yara.

Mother of Yurrii, those eyes.

Perhaps Yara felt chilled by her encounter with the Speaker too, or maybe it was her encounter with me, but she spoke with a forced brightness that interrupted my dark thoughts. "That's your hut?" Standing on her toes, she pointed to the dwelling behind Fraesh and Iva's.

I nodded.

"It's well built," she said, and shifted uncomfortably when I didn't answer. "How is your bird?"

"Vax? He's good."

"Have you taught him anything new?"

I looked up at the wry undertone of Yara's voice and caught that angelic, fleeting smile, just before it faded.

"Manners," I answered, with my eyes down. My heart savoured the sweet laugh that followed. I hoped Yara would keep smiling if I didn't look up.

Then she said it, just broached the subject out of nowhere. "Were you custodian of the flock when you were a daeson as well?"

My mouth clamped shut, and I stiffened. At the same moment, Fraesh pushed out of his hut and nodded to us before heading briskly down the path.

"I'm sorry," Yara whispered, "I shouldn't have asked."

And she followed Fraesh away, leaving me standing in stupid paralysis.

It took several moments to shuffle to the privacy of my

hut. Guides, I had not thought that old title would jerk such a reaction out of me. Flopping on my bedroll, I blinked at my ceiling. I knew that Yara had heard of my past. Of course, she'd be as curious as the rest. Why should I be so blindsided by her harmless question?

Sighing, I pressed my hands to my temples.

Because she can see right through your sad, little disguise, like everyone else. And you had hoped her interest had been in the normal man you wished you were.

Shaking my head, I stood. I needed to get out of there, needed to get away from this camp and these people so I could paste myself back together again.

Swallowing painfully, I decided I would take Vax out. I would take my old friend for a ride. Everything became simpler from the back of a vaiya. And it was exceedingly difficult to take yourself seriously when subjected to the comical monologue of a happy bird. We would go, and everything would seem better when we got back.

Everything would be normal.

VAX and I spent the afternoon lounging by a sun-dappled, exposed stretch of riverbank. Icy water lapped at its frosty banks and familiar round, polished rocks poked through the snow. They were regurgitated gullet stones of vaiyas who'd passed this way before us. I wondered, as I sifted idly through them with booted feet, where those vaiyas were now. Had they been tied to camps, or were they wild, unfettered creatures?

Wild vaiyas didn't speak. Without human contact, how would the birds learn our words? Even vaiyas snatched from camps by wild males eventually lost their vocabulary.

Had I no one to talk to, not even Vax, would I forget how to speak?

Aimless thoughts meandered through my mind all afternoon. By the time I returned home, I felt pleasantly distracted from the anxiety of the morning, and I didn't think anything of the inviting bowl of food waiting for me. In fact, I was halfway through munching the first slab of tender harek meat wrapped in flatbread with dried berries when I noticed the bowl itself.

It was a pretty, well-made dish of dark clay with a striking blue stripe along the rim.

Iva makes the best flatbread. Nasheira only knew what I'd done to deserve it.

But when I returned the clay dish to my neighbours' hut with a knowing smile on my face, Iva said it was not theirs.

"What?" I frowned.

"It's not my bowl." Iva glanced up from repairing a net. "Where did you find it?"

"In my hut. You didn't make the rolls?"

This time Iva smiled wryly and said, "Ha! Make you rolls and send them in our finest bowl? I'm not *that* taken with you, Akrist!" *But someone certainly is*, her crisp tone implied.

Yara.

An unbidden image of curls and creamy skin fluttered through my mind. The thought of her sent a delicious shiver through me that I clung to desperately even as breakers of stagnant guilt followed in its wake.

Yara had left the food. She still wanted to see me after the fool I'd made of myself this morning.

"Aw, Iva," I spoke slowly. "I'm heartbroken. I thought we had something special, you and I."

The storyteller grinned widely before pinning me with a glance as penetrating as the needle she held. "Are you going to run from her?"

I fingered the bowl nervously and fought the paralyzing silence that sometimes still crippled me when speaking to a woman.

"She doesn't even know me," I mumbled.

"How can she if you will not let her?" she snorted.

Instead of answering, I pursed my lips, nodded dumbly, and ducked out of the hut before the storyteller could ask anything else. In the cold night air, I felt the prickling flush of anger burning my cheeks.

Had she heard my embarrassing encounter with Yara? We'd been right outside her hut. *What did Iva expect of me?* I was not the sort of man that women desired. Not as Iva was thinking, not as a mate.

True, the prospect of bedding an unheard of, exotic mixture of daeson and Speaker appealed to some, but the mystery was short-lived. No one wanted to commit to a Speaker who would not lead, a daeson who'd not been sacrificed, or the sad scrap of a man who pretended to be neither.

Yara's interest in me would fade like all the rest. So why was I encouraging it?

Because Yara was the sun, and as far beyond my reach as she was, I yearned for the warmth of that solitary smile. My life was beginning to feel cold and small without it.

I knew the borrowed bowl had been left as an invitation to meet again, but as I stood outside the hut Yara shared with her mother, my bravery fled. I left the dish beside the door without disturbing them.

Familiar reins of guilt guided me back to my bed, where the only company I expected was the wurm dream. I felt as inhuman now as I had this morning before my escape on Vax.

"Akrist?"

I jumped at the sound of my name spoken softly but distinctly on the other side of my door flap.

"Yes?" I answered too loudly.

"It's Yara. May I come in?"

Blessed Nasheira, what is she doing here? I couldn't speak. My heart drumming in my head nearly blotted out her next tentative words.

"I can go if it's not a good time..."

"Just give me a moment!"

Wrestling on my shirt, I stumbled in the dark to pull the pegs holding my door snugly shut. Cold air hit me nearly as hard as the sight of Yara in sputtering lamplight and swirling snow. I remembered the first time I saw her over the hearth fire. It was not that radiant woman who stood here now, it was the plain girl with curls. But even now, I detected that enchanting smile swimming in the depths of her dark eyes. *Oh, Nasheira,* I groaned inwardly. I wanted to take her in my arms.

"Is something wrong?" I blocked my own rampant thoughts before the guilt rode in to crush them. *Tell her to go.*

She held out what she'd been clasping to her chest.

The blue-rimmed bowl I'd returned earlier.

"I meant it to be a gift," she said breathlessly. "You didn't have to return it."

My gaze slid back to her face, taking in the way the wind tossed curls across her cheek, her slender outstretched arm.

Say something, idiot.

"Thank you." I nodded as I took the gift. I couldn't think of anything else to say, and it seemed safer to stare at the bowl in my hands instead of its giver. *Guides, how could this feel so awkward and amazing at the same time?*

I counted four more beats of my heart before hearing the words slip out of my mouth. "Do you want to come in?"

Guilt choked me as soon as I said it, clamping down with surprising malice. *She should not be here. You don't deserve her company, wurm!*

Yara had already nodded, and I'd already stepped aside to let her enter.

A lock of downy hair brushed my shoulder as Yara passed. She smelled like earth and cinnamon.

Yara waited, cupping her lamp against the wind as I re-pinned the door. When I turned, she spoke with downcast eyes.

"I want to apologize for this morning. I didn't mean to pry. Sometimes, my curiosity overcomes my courtesy."

"No, no." I swallowed, turning the blue bowl in my hands. "I owe the apology. I acted like a fool. That's nothing new for me." Exhaling slowly, I made myself say the next part even though it felt like exposing a soft spot to a stranger. "I'm not good at conversation, especially with women, and my past is hurtful to remember, but that's no fault of yours." Pausing, I waited until Yara's eyes found mine.

"You know, it's the strangest thing." Yara squinted as she spoke, then shook her head dismissively, that innocent blush still warming her face. "I feel *safe* with you, Akrist," she said, "as if I've always known you."

Do not feel safe, my mind retorted sharply. "I'm glad," I answered faintly.

"Is your Speaker safe?" Yara asked.

"What?" My daydreaming mind tripped at the change of subject.

"You said today that he hurts people." Yara pressed her hands against her cheeks. "He beats his chani, I presume?" Her voice wobbled.

"H-he used to." I floundered. "Why do you ask?"

She shrugged. "You seemed... angry... with him."

"Na-Jhalar maimed Vax," I rasped. "Crushed his skull. *That's* what happened to his eye. He's beaten his chani ever since I was a child because he likes the sound of them crying."

"Did he kill that woman? Delani?"

"No. She got sick."

"He kept shouting her name after you left. I helped Fraesh get him into his hut. He seemed to calm down with me there."

"I'm sorry," I blurted, hands balling into fists. "I should have stayed to help. You shouldn't have had to... you should stay away from him. I could protect you. If he tries to hurt you, you can come to me."

"I've already told you, I don't need a keeper." The spark in her eyes softened. "But I wouldn't mind a friend."

I probably should have said something, but I didn't know what.

"I—I'd like that," I choked out.

She smiled, stood, unpinned my door flap and left me there with warmth and dread both warring in my belly. I curled over and breathed through the nausea. I felt tangled by our whole conversation. *A friend.* But something about Yara's other probing questions still unsettled me. I felt used, somehow, and I couldn't pin down why.

CHAPTER FIFTEEN

Yara visited me at my hearth most nights after that. She steered clear of Na-Jhalar, and the Speaker seemed to forget her.

"Am I so forgettable?" she lamented jokingly.

I grinned at her over the flames. "You are most memorable to me."

"Truly?" She raised her eyebrows and dropped the beadwork she was stitching in her lap. "Tell me, who was your last *most memorable*, Akrist?"

My smile faltered. "I prefer to keep company with vaiyas, so I suppose it would be Vax."

She laughed out loud, and I swam in the sound of it. "Well, I can't compete with him. Vax is a true friend."

"You're considerably more well-spoken, and you don't bite... do you?" I frowned with mock concern and Yara giggled again.

We grew closer over that cold, idle winter, and that closeness both scared and delighted me.

Our friendship offended a number of people in our camp. I'd predicted as much, had even guessed whose feathers might be ruffled. I did not, however, anticipate Aella being one of them, until Yara disclosed one evening that my mother had taken her aside on more than one occasion with urgent, even threatening counsel against keeping my company.

"She said," Yara exhaled with puffed cheeks and blurted, "she said, 'Stay away from it.' Like you were a rock or a tree—"

"Or a daeson," I interrupted.

"She is horrible!" Yara burst out. "I mean… I'm sorry. She's your mother."

I shrugged. "She's always been that way."

"It's not right, how she treats you. How they treat all of these daeson."

Her sharp words gripped me like a stitch in my side. When was the last time I spared a thought for those boys? I hadn't. Not for as long as I could remember. I avoided our daeson more steadfastly than their own mothers did. What had I become? *A selfish wurm. You promised to save them once, but you don't have the stones, just like Hasev didn't.* Guilt curdled in my throat as I straightened and scanned around us to ensure no one stood within hearing distance. *Is she testing you?* I answered in a low voice. "The Speaker feels otherwise, and so does most of the world. Those are dangerous thoughts to think aloud, Yara."

She raised her eyebrows and jutted out her chin, eyes flashing over the flames between us. "I speak as I wish."

I smiled at her fierceness. "Indeed. You'd make a better Speaker than I."

❧

DURING MID-WINTER, an unseasonably warm wind blew through camp for a week, scrubbing away at our white-stained world. It was memorable because it was like a breath of summer in the midst of the cold, and it warmed my blood. Perhaps too much.

Lately, whenever Yara was near, I found myself wanting to stroke her hand or breathe in the cinnamon scent of her hair. We'd shared several meals this past week, and the comfort of her cutting vegetables beside me was exhilarating and terrifying at the same time. I was frightened I might slip and destroy the tenuous friendship we'd built, and I couldn't risk ruining it.

Before winter, I'd found a dip in the even plains where a stream crept through like a silver snake. Beside it, a massive white boulder, nearly as tall as a vaiya. It was a lonely sentinel in a lake of crackling yellow grass, a cold island towering over the passive, bobbing seadheads surrounding. It had quickly become my favourite spot away from camp.

Last fall, I'd regularly sprawled on the top of the white rock and baked every thought from my head while my vaiyas gurgled in the water and stalked mice in the grass. But it had been too cold to return for a visit until the warm wind blew through. And my blood warmed with it.

This morning, we'd hunted early, crunching through the frost of a grey dawn, and I had thought of nothing except how soft Yara's neck might feel under my hand. By the time the sun chugged over the horizon, our kills were gutted, skinned, and portioned into strips to sizzle dry in temporary smoke houses over hearth fires. There were shifts posted to turn the meat and, upon completing mine, I came to the rock before Yara returned with the gatherers. I didn't trust myself in her company today. Last night, I'd nearly reached over to tuck her hair behind her ear while she mended a basket. She'd been speaking animatedly about how she'd taught one of the vaiyas to peal tree bark off in long strips, and how it had halved her basket weaving time when my hand just reached out of its own accord. I'd barely snatched it back in time. No, I couldn't be trusted today.

After scrubbing dried blood from the backs of Voti, Vust, and Vuna in the icy waters of the creek, I settled onto the big rock. It already radiated heat. I pressed my hands against the stone, and they quickly warmed. As the sun crept overhead, I actually started sweating. *Incredible. When will you have the chance again to sunbathe in the middle of winter?* Stripping off my coat and shirt to use as a pillow, I inhaled the sweet, settling scent of vaiyas and melting ice. Although the air was still cold, the rock radiated heat against my bare back and I dozed.

"I think you're done on that side."

Struggling awake at the voice, I foggily realized that the sun had swung far overhead, and Yara stood ankle deep in melting snow.

I shivered and sat up. She knew of the place, of course. I'd told her about it the day after I discovered it, but she'd never visited me here. "Is there room for two?" she asked.

"There is." I smiled weakly.

She groaned as she hoisted herself up onto the rock beside me. Her scent filled my senses. Despite the chill, she gathered up her skirt with girlish abandon and flexed her legs to kick off her winter boots.

Mother of Yurrii! I thought, gazing at the round of her calves. Swallowing, I said, "How is your mother?" Enna had been ill.

"Better this morning." She stared at my chest instead of my face. "But I'm not here to talk about my mother."

I don't have my shirt on, I realized.

Before I could think anything else, Yara placed her small hand directly over the scar, as had happened so many times in my dreams.

An eager response arced through me, an awakening of

every part of my body. At the same time, the daeson part of me recoiled, and I flinched violently, but Yara didn't move her hand.

Stop her, Guides, before you do anything stupid.

I reached up to pull her hand away, but found I couldn't let go once I held her wrist. Breathing like a cornered animal, I felt Yara's pulse beneath my fingers, steady and even. *How can she be so composed?*

"What's wrong?" she asked.

"N-Nobody ever..." *Oh for Nasheira's sake, stop stuttering.* "I-I'm not used to being touched."

"How does it feel?"

Like the purest comfort and the dirtiest sin combined.

I couldn't answer her. I could barely think with her fingers brushing over the edges of my Speaker's scar, and the softness of her thin wrist under my thumb.

"Did it hurt?" she asked with careful casualness.

"No," I clenched my teeth.

"Liar," she drawled. She leaned toward me.

"Yara, we shouldn't." I counted my breaths. *Oh, Guides, I want her to. I want to taste her lips.*

"There's nobody watching us. When will I ever get a chance to see you shirtless again?" she smiled playfully.

Stop this while you still can, you fool. But I couldn't break from her touch.

She slipped her hand over mine and pulled it toward her face, and I could do nothing but shiver against the wave of emotions it triggered. I felt my fingers brush against her cheek, the delicate line of her jaw. *Oh, Guides.* I couldn't stifle the heavy, heady breath that escaped me when she slid my hand to her neck, and I lost myself in the softness of curls and warm skin and cinnamon.

"Yara," I moaned.

Stop this.

She parted her lips breathlessly and leaned towards me.

A sickening crest of emotions crashed into me like a physical blow from behind. I jerked away.

Vax hissed at the sudden movement, and we both jumped at the sound.

"I can't." My voice cracked, and I crumbled into myself. My thoughts clattered around me like broken clay.

She frowned. "I've seen the way you look at me. I'd be a fool to miss it. You want more for us, and so do I." She leaned toward me, rolled up her sleeves, and exposed the insides of her wrists.

At first, I couldn't grasp the meaning of the odd motion, but then it hit me. Jin had told me once how women flashed their daeson's tattoos at men they wished to bed. It was supposed to be alluring, the opportunity to share each other without the worry of conceiving a cursed daeson. Most men found a daeson-tattooed woman nearly as alluring as a Speaker.

Yara's wrists were unmarked.

So she's telling you she wants to lay with you, and she hasn't borne a daeson yet. Both parts of that thought utterly terrified me.

As if I wasn't already having enough trouble with accepting physical touch, the potential to father a firstborn son froze my breath in my throat.

"I can't be with you like that, Yara," I gulped. I didn't have the words to explain how broken I was.

Yara pulled her hands back, yanking her sleeves back over her wrists.

"I see," she said, all emotion drained from her voice. "I thought you, of all people, might be more understanding."

"Yara, please..." I exhaled, trying to snag the right words and coming up empty. "This is too much, too fast for me."

She turned away, her curls a veil. "Some of us are running out of time, Akrist," she snapped.

I gaped at her as she jammed her boots on, slid off the rock, and walked away from me through the vaiya flock.

"What do you mean?" I shouted after her. But she didn't answer me. She didn't even turn.

After that day at the rock, Yara didn't come to my hearth. She missed evening prayers for the next two nights, and on the third night, a rare occasion where Na-Jhalar was sober enough to speak lucidly, he announced that he'd taken on a new chani. Ice settled in my core as Yara stood and stepped toward the Speaker's hut.

Guides, no. My throat ached. I stood without realizing it. My fingers tingled. I was stumbling, taking wooden steps toward Yara, heedless of everyone else at the main hearth. *Look at me. Don't do this, Yara.* I froze as she turned and her eyes met mine. Resolute, but full of fear.

Then she ducked into Na-Jhalar's hut.

Mother of Yurrii, what have I done?

CHAPTER SIXTEEN

I n the days that followed, I vacillated between guilt, fear, and rage. *What was she thinking? One spurned kiss, one request to take things slowly, and she runs to him.* I couldn't speak to her. As chani, she wasn't allowed to be alone in the company of others, so it was easy to avoid her and let the anger fester. I shut her out. I nursed my shattered pride, and I didn't speak to Yara for two months.

When spring came, our camp moved further out onto the prairies, following the gazelle herds. More and more frequently at night, the wurm dream clutched at me and wouldn't let me go. I hadn't dreamed it for months. It came less often than it had when I was a child, but some nights it still ambushed me with a ferocity that froze my breath in my chest. Sleep became my enemy, but whenever I lay awake, thoughts of Yara lying beneath Na-Jhalar ate me alive.

A SCUFFING NOISE jolted me out of restless sleep. Whipping my blanket aside, I swung up; my fingers curled into claws and a scream perched on my lips, ready to fight the wurm outside my door.

Sunlight streamed through the thin crack. As I watched, twin bars of shadow shifted across the ground, followed by swirling motes of dust.

"Akrist, you in there?"

Jin. It's just Jin.

Stale breath puffed past my lips. I leaned over to pull the pegs from my door flap. "What do you want?" I croaked as I swatted the heavy curtain aside. Jin's silhouette straightened in the sunlight.

"Guides, I've awakened a bull."

Squinting, I raised a hand to block the bright, assaulting sun. "What time is it?"

"You've missed breakfast, and Darvie made flatbread." Jin slapped his belly and flashed a wide grin before sobering. "Are you unwell?" He leaned closer. "Find the bottom of a gifen bowl last night?"

"No, I'm fine." I scrubbed at my eyes.

"I can't believe you'd hold out on me, brother. You look like shit."

"You woke me," I snapped back, sharper than I intended.

Jin ducked his head between his shoulders and hissed, "Not so loud! Do you want the whole camp to hear?" Arching up to glance behind him, he wiped his nose and added, "Aaron turns as cold as ice when he knows I've been talking to you. Is that the thanks I get for being a good brother?"

Jin's mate was a gatherer, *thank the Guides,* otherwise Jin and I wouldn't even get to hunt together.

"Sorry."

"Well are you hunting then, or are you confined to your bedroll?"

"I'm coming." Pushing to my feet, I steadied myself against the doorframe. Anger and emptiness clawed at my stomach. Since Yara had become a chani, those seemed to be the only feelings I had. *I need to run.* "Which trail do we take?"

"The west one with the fallen ula across the gully."

"I'll catch up."

Jin nodded, and as he turned, I mumbled, "Thank you."

With strands of dark hair falling over his eyes, he offered another crooked smile, waved over his shoulder, and sauntered away with his spear cradled in one arm. I stared after him as he left.

Jin's walk utterly revealed him; his stride was a manifestation of everything that made up the man. Easy and open, strong and unshakable, he studied every path with careful consideration and was not easily pushed from the one he chose. *He's a good man, a good brother. I could speak to him about Yara, and he would listen.*

I let the flap swing shut and leaned back against the inside wall as darkness enveloped me once more. *And he will ask you why she chose him instead of you, why you pushed her away. No, you're alone now, and so is she.*

Shoving off from the wall with enough force to make the whole hut shudder, I dressed and shouldered my spear.

I need to run.

No one crossed my path as I strode toward the western boundary of huts. Plunging into the blessed quiet of crocus dappled grasslands, I stopped at a secluded copse of trees to relieve myself and to wash my face in the icy waters of the nearby stream. I slurped a few handfuls of water so cold my teeth ached. Then I stood, wiped my chin, and pushed my spear off my shoulder into my hand. Breaking into an easy run, I loped toward the western trap line.

Running eased the tension in my legs. Anger bled from me with each breath I took. Occasionally, anxious thoughts swarmed my mind like choking clouds of insects, but I sped up and left them behind, concentrating instead on the reliable thrust of well-trained muscle and measured exhalations of spent air. *Incredible that every fibre in my body knows exactly what to do, all working to move me. I could run for hours. I could never go back...*

I caught up with the other hunters too soon. They were on the trail of a black ox, very large. Spatters of blood marked the trail, and the dragging hoof print suggested he limped.

It seemed like a gift from Nasheira herself. Black oxen were maliciously intelligent and unpredictable. They often circled back on their own trails to ambush pursuers. Although the meat from one animal could feed us for months, it was extremely risky to tangle with a healthy bull. While an injured animal was still dangerous, we could follow it until it dropped.

Jin and Iva looked at me with raised eyebrows, but said nothing. We were potentially too close to the animal to speak. Falling into position, I stalked as silently as the rest, but felt netted by the painfully slow pace. Every anxious worry I'd left behind on my run returned to roost now on my shoulders.

Are you really so vile that Na-Jhalar seemed the better choice for her?

Swallowing, I bent my concentration toward the foot-prints before me.

She saw you for what you are. A coward. A pretender. Broken.

I bit my tongue and walked faster, but couldn't escape my swarming thoughts.

We tracked the wounded ox well into the afternoon. Toward evening, it led us to a shallow stream, moving fast between its bordering banks of shale. Our group split to scan the shore for signs of our bull's exit.

Jin and I reconnoitred north on opposite banks. We soon found that many points of the shale shoreline expanded into flat, cracked ledges so that, when we searched along the softer ground further inland, we walked nearly out of earshot from each other.

As I examined the ground before me, still lost in my fraying thoughts, footsteps thudded behind me—too heavy to be Jin's.

I turned. Time thickened like sap. My whole body swam in sluggishness, gripped by frost creeping up my spine. My eyes swung upward. And I faced the bull.

He stood less than five paces away. Enormous, his flanks slick with sweat and heaving with every hollow breath. Blood caked and dribbled down his right foreleg from a gaping wound at his chest. The bull dipped his head, flattened his ears, and brandished the wickedly wide arc of his ancient horns.

Mother of Yurrii, this isn't happening to me.

Slowly, I raised my spear to my shoulder.

The bull's eyes rolled back. A wet call rattled up his throat, and he charged.

"Jin!" My yell pinched off, choked and feeble. This was no feint. I knew it as I stumbled backwards, slipping on shale and into shallow water. I had one rapidly dwindling chance.

But I didn't even remember throwing the spear, just seeing it strike and skitter uselessly off the bull's back.

And then he hit.

I heard the distinct crunch of ribs breaking. A gurgling, short explosion of air punched past my lips. Then there was sky, nothing but cold, aloof clouds as everything tilted, and I landed brokenly in the stream.

White, churning water splashed around me. I heard clattering rocks and choking. Helplessly, I watched as the ox broke through the shredding spray, a bloody, black eclipse of hooves and horns.

As I tried to sit up, the bull stepped on me. A heavy hoof

drove into my right leg. Screaming, I felt mashed muscle and a sickening, wet thunk. A broad, wrinkled brow slammed into my chest. My head ricocheted off the submerged rocks. Icy water soaked all around me and I thought of Yara, but nothing after that.

CHAPTER SEVENTEEN

I stand in the midst of a vast storm. The air smells like static, and a powerful wind whips my hair against my cheeks. Rain drives down in sheets, spattering mud up the walls of the huts around me. Lightning flares, fracturing the sky like cracking ice, I realize I'm at the north end of camp because I recognize the four, stunted daeson huts. From within, I can hear crying, high and desperate, like the sounds daeson Sivi made days before he died.

You're too late, I think. The camp is already taking them to sacrifice. I lean against the wind with a hand over my face to block the stinging rain, and I scramble toward the daeson. I'm almost upon them when I see skirts flapping against bare legs. A woman with curly hair plastered to her face.

Yara.

I want to run to her and apologize, take her in my arms and kiss her, but when I yell, she doesn't hear me. The wind swells and screams past my ears. I can't reach her. I keep slipping.

She's carrying the daeson and they're howling in her arms, fighting her, biting and kicking, and I'm desperate to help, but the wind won't let me. I keep screaming as the storm swallows them *whole. The daeson, Yara, my whole camp, we all disintegrate under its force.*

✧

PAIN POURED in to fill the void. My head felt like someone was standing on it, but the sensation was nothing compared to the undiluted torture that tore through my chest.

"Yara?" The name sounded raspy and forced. Speaking it sent fiery, white spots darting across my vision.

I'm going to be sick.

The world tilted, and I tried to roll over as heavy churning rippled my insides. Heaving brought the pain down like falling rocks. I gagged, cried out in agony. I think I started to sob.

There were hands holding me down.

After a moment, with my head swimming savagely, I realized that I'd been drugged. The nausea, the fuzzy confusion, was not all the product of pain. A slow, sick current of gifen oozed like curdled milk through my veins, slowing my movements and inhibiting my torture.

Mother of Yurrii, I wondered, as foreign hands pressed against me and the walls around me continued to pitch and roll. *How much did they give me?*

Swallowing against the cresting sickness, I tried again, "Yara?"

"She's outside, Akrist." A voice. It sounded oddly distant and muffled and I couldn't place it.

"Yara!" I yelped and heard the answering echo of something screeching outside.

"Sit still!" Fraesh barked, but his voice softened at my flinch. "She'll be right back."

"I have to talk to her." My words ran together. I frowned at the clumsy mutiny of my own tongue.

"She'll be right back," Fraesh repeated evenly. Something about his calm, impenetrable manner infuriated me.

She won't be back. In the vision, she leaves. Takes the daeson. Dies in the storm. "I have to talk to Yara," I slurred. "Now!"

Fraesh sighed. I saw his portly outline over me now. His were the hands holding me down. "Lay down and stop yelling, and I'll go get her."

Nodding dumbly, I winced at the angry pain lancing through my skull. Fraesh's form receded like a ghost, and feeble lamplight followed him.

I lay alone in the dark with the sharp, cloying smell of junab, sweat, and smoke all around me. With no distraction, the pain and the effects of the gifen intensified, settling into my bones like vigorous, smouldering coals until it seemed that the smell of smoke had not come from my oil lamp at all, but was creeping, acrid and black, out of my wounds.

I dared not look down. Compromised by gifen, it was entirely possible that my eyes would be greeted by the macabre vision of my own body sizzling in flames, a hallucination of course, but one I had no wish to see. I shut my eyes and listened for Yara.

"Akrist?" A soft shaft of lamplight cut into the room at the same time I opened my eyes to see Yara with Fraesh standing behind her.

"Oh, Yara…" I gulped, reduced to sudden and surprising tears as relief and embarrassment overcame me all at once. *She hasn't left.*

"I'm here, Akrist," she said, sitting down. "What is it?"

I couldn't speak. Sobs choked me. I wanted to reach my hand out to her, but nothing was working right. I didn't have the coordination.

Snap out of it.

"Don't go," I blurted.

"I'm right here. I'm not going anywhere." Yara's assurance

sounded matronly and absent-minded. The chani often helped Fraesh with wounded hunters when Na-Jhalar allowed it. Two of them were the healer's daughters after all, and that was how Yara spoke to me now, like I was an invalid and a stranger.

How else would she talk to you with Fraesh standing right there? You haven't spoken to her in two months. You are a stranger.

"Don't leave." I struggled to form the words. "I *meant* don't leave without me. Don't take them. I want to come."

Yara glanced back at Fraesh uneasily, but the healer nodded and spoke in a low voice. "Go on. Comfort the fool, if you must. He's delusional, and you're safe in my hut. I won't tell a soul, and neither will my girls."

Hesitantly, Yara slipped her hand into mine. It was small and trembling. "I thought you were dead," her voice cracked.

A combined wave of warmth and wrongness washed over me, making me clench my teeth. It was too much, the gifen, the pain, and her touch. "Promise you won't leave," I gulped.

"I promise," she said.

I didn't believe her, and I gripped her hand as I slipped away.

THE FOLLOWING weeks of recovery were excruciating. Iva moved her bedroll to my hut so that Fraesh could attend to me in their hut day or night. Yara, Baline, or Celi often assisted him. The chani changed bandages and bedding and even helped me shave. Mercifully, they were thoughtful enough to turn their backs when the healer's ministrations turned to washing me, and the exceedingly embarrassing process of helping me relieve myself. Weak with fever and gifen, afflicted with a concussion, a broken leg, and any number of cracked ribs, I was wholly helpless.

I can't convey the pain and humiliation a grown man feels at having to be propped on his side so he can pee in a pot. And there is nothing—*nothing*—to describe how a daeson feels about it. I had never felt so damned incapable, so exposed.

Yara won't stay. If the dream is a vision, she'll take the daeson without you.

But she did stay. When Yara wasn't with the Speaker, she sat with me, keeping Baline or Celi or Fraesh as her escort. Her face had softened and rounded out. A winter of chani shares had given her curves, and the sound of her voice was the most beautiful thing I'd ever heard.

She told me that Jin had saved me. He'd hurled his spear from across the river and felled the ox with a fatal blow. He'd pulled me from the water, away from the thrashing animal. Holding me in his arms, my brother screamed for help until the others came. When we arrived in camp, it had been Jin who found Yara.

Vax was inconsolable. When they first brought me in, Yara barely kept the hysterical vaiya from charging into Fraesh's hut. They resorted to keeping the door flap pinned open so that he could at least see me. He'd kept faithful vigil outside Fraesh's door ever since. Yara had been comforting him that first night when I'd awakened and called for her.

In a matter of days, I could sit up without feeling like my head might split and pour my brains out over my chest, but the ever-present agony of broken ribs kept me from doing much else. *Mother of Yurrii*, they hurt so much worse than when Arsu had broken them. I couldn't breathe without being stalked by pain. It was uncomfortable to lie down and exceedingly difficult to sleep. Gifen helped a little, but the drug made me nauseated, and the vomiting—*sweet Nasheira above*—vomiting with broken ribs was easily the worst pain I'd ever known.

Fraesh suggested cutting my dosage. He feared I'd become attached to the medicine. Shuddering, I imagined myself sucked toward the same sickly path as Na-Jhalar.

I complied with the healer's instructions, and weaned off the gifen. The ever-present pain dipped its fingers a little deeper, and I became more aware of the deep throbbing of my splinted leg, but *thank Nasheira*, the vomiting stopped.

I stabilized enough that Fraesh allowed my transfer back to my own hut. Yara's chani escort still accompanied her when she visited me, and Guides, how I longed to ask her about the daeson, but I couldn't. We were supervised every moment we shared.

ONE COLD NIGHT, three weeks into my recovery, I woke in the dark to the sound of fabric rustling. A gentle weight settled next to my hip and the smell of cinnamon brought me fully alert. "Yara?" I croaked, disoriented. "Guides. What are you doing?"

"Shh." She lay beside me close enough that her curls tickled my cheek. "I missed you." Her voice sounded small, but her proximity pounded through me like a wave. As I struggled to swim to its surface, Yara slipped under my blanket, curled onto her side and pressed her back against me.

"You can't be here," I shivered.

"I'm stepping down," she murmured.

"As chani?" I frowned, feeling each one of her inhales as they expanded against my ribs. "Why? Are you all right?"

"I'm fine," she said.

I rolled awkwardly toward her, groaning at the pain it induced and speaking into her hair. "Did he do something to you?" I tried to keep the hardness out of my question and failed.

"No."

Would she tell you if he did?

Silence swallowed us both.

My jaw clenched and my nostrils burned. *Ask it. Just ask or it will sour every other word you share with her.*

"Why did you go to him?" my voice cracked. "*Right* after you offered yourself to me. Why did you want to be his chani?"

"Nobody *wants* to be a chani, Akrist." Her voice was dangerously low. "You left me little choice."

"*I* left you little choice?" I hissed. "I don't recall pressing you through his door."

"You didn't want me. Enna was sick. I *told* you that. I traded most of our food to the aeni when they came through. They had a tea Fraesh doesn't stock. It's helped Enna recover in the past, but I was alone, and I was hungry, and I needed the shares."

"You could have asked *me*, Yara. I wouldn't have let you starve."

She rolled toward me, mouth tight, and eyes hard. "Do you really think your Speaker would have let me stay in this camp if he asked for me as chani and I—an *unbonded* woman, a newcomer with no other ties—outright refused him? Baline says he prefers choosing girls that no one else in his camp has bedded yet. I thought perhaps I had a chance to dissuade him if I found a mate in time, but you made it abundantly clear you didn't want me. I was *alone*, Akrist, and I've been there before. I've counted my ribs out there in the wastelands. I've starved to feed my mother. Chani shares ensured I wouldn't have to do it again." She blinked rapidly.

An apology was on my lips when the cold realization hit me. *That's one of her tells. The blinking.*

I licked my lips. "Who else were the chani shares for, Yara?"

Her brow furrowed. "I just told you, for Enna. To keep us from starving. To—to secure my position." She blinked again.

I waited for her to elaborate, but she didn't. It all made sense now. I hadn't spoken to her these past months, but I'd watched. Tea wasn't the only thing she traded the aeni for. I'd seen her exchange fresh chani shares for preserved goods, the same sort of supplies Tanar and I had stashed so many years ago.

A stockpile. *That's what she's hiding, why she wanted your support. The dream was a vision. She plans to run.*

Rolling onto my back, stunned, I stared at my hut ceiling. "You're caching to save the daeson. That's why you needed chani shares. But why? Why would you try to save them?"

She froze and held her breath for so long, I didn't need her to answer to know I was right.

"Who told you?" her voice trembled with fear. "I haven't told anyone."

"Not the daeson?"

"No. Nobody. How do you know?" Yara's eyes were wide with fear, and suddenly I wanted to take her into my arms and comfort her, but she was still staring at me with shock pinching her face.

"I dreamed about it after the ox hit me, and you are a terrible liar."

Yara exhaled shakily. "You Speakers and your damned visions. You saw it? I took the daeson?"

I nodded slowly.

"In a dream?"

"Yes."

"Yet you didn't see an ox coming to knock the life out of you?"

"No," I chuckled softly. "That I missed."

She fell silent.

The clean smell of rain wafted under the door flap. Vax shifted outside, claws scraping against dirt.

"When you first woke up," she said slowly, like she was tasting each word on the way out. "You might not remember it. You were full of gifen and babbling... but you asked me not to leave without you, not to take *them*."

"I remember it." I sighed. *I was a fool. Fraesh was standing right there.*

"You knew then."

"I couldn't ask you. We haven't been alone."

"It's my birthday today."

Mother of Yurrii, I couldn't keep up with her, but I didn't dare break this moment.

"I share it with a brother." She spoke her next words hastily. "His name was daeson Jedas."

I flinched at the ugly title, but the rest didn't register.

"I was born only minutes after him."

Oh, Guides.

"With his birthing cord wrapped around my neck."

Sweet Nasheira. Twins with a daeson. Like Xen and his tainted brother.

"My mother thought I was dead until I started crying. I was touched by a daeson in the womb, nearly killed by him. No one would ever want me. My parents would have killed Jedas right there to save my honour, but our healer had seen the whole thing. She announced both births to our camp, and there was no way my parents could save my name after that."

Yara's lips twisted. She looked at me, but her gaze was in the past. "Jedas and I were close, even as babies. When he slept, I slept. When my father neglected to feed him, I'd cry in hunger. I think Father wished us both dead, but he craved the approval of our camp more. He couldn't afford the cut in food shares neglecting a daeson would cost him, and Mother was so attached to me. She'd tried for so many years to birth. I think she knew I would be her only daughter.

"And so my father reluctantly raised Jedas, and my mother raised me, and, despite their best efforts, neither could keep us apart. We were inseparable."

Yara's heartless, hushed laugh raised fresh goosebumps on my arms. "The beatings we got for playing together... Jedas's were always much worse than mine, but it never stopped us, not once.

"Our camp was livid that my parents kept failing to keep Jedas and I apart. Father couldn't stand the estrangement from everyone else. He left my mother when I was five. She last saw him in the embrace of an ani just before they left our camp.

"Alone, Mother doted on me during the moments I spent with her and lashed out like a savage when I cared for my orphaned brother. I wouldn't let Jedas starve. We were like two halves of one person, and I was sure that if Jedas died, I would too." Yara's voice broke. She turned her face from me and shivered.

A brisk wind ruffled the door flap and Vax clucked nervously outside.

"I was wrong," she croaked. "When we were eight years old, Pau and Yurrii touched, and all of the sway I held over my mother didn't stop her from sacrificing Jedas."

Yara's words stabbed through me and lodged in my chest, dragging me back to the night of my own sacrifice years ago.

"She thought I'd turn to her after to find solace." Her face twisted. "I didn't. I grew into a young woman alone, repulsed by the sudden attention from the men in our camp, men who knew me as cursed, touched by a daeson. Although none of them would consider me for a mate, they still wanted me for their beds." Yara shrugged. "I learned to hide my body, to shed attention like one sheds clothing. I got very good at it, and when it wasn't enough, when Enna began pressing the interest of young men on me, I left.

"I ran on the night of my fourteenth birthday and found my first aeni tribe shortly after. I couldn't..." Yara stopped. Words caught in her throat as she wiped her eyes and sucked in a jagged breath. "I had nothing left to trade, and I was so hungry." Her gaze flashed to mine, brimming with hollow pain. "I traded myself for food."

"Oh, Yara," I breathed.

"So this is not the first time." Yara pinned me with a pleading gaze. "At first, I became Na-Jhalar's chani because it was the best way to survive and stay in this camp where I've made... friends..." The long look she gave me took my breath away. "But I can't just sit by and let the daeson be sacrificed in six months." Tears rolled down her white face. "He would have been twenty today. You remind me of him in a lot of ways."

I swallowed against an awful ache in my throat. "I'm sorry Yara. I'm sorry I left you alone and pushed you away. I *did* want us to be more." *Say it. Just say it, for Nasheira's sake.* "I've never learned how to be *close* to anyone. They beat it out of us when we're young, and I felt like I'd break what we had. I was scared of losing you before we even started." *You are scared of fathering a daeson of your own and you've ruined it all. You could have left together. Look what you've done to her now.*

Any camp or aeni that caught Yara with four uncut daeson would brand all of them. Every time she traded, even if she hid the boys, she'd risk exposing them all. She needed a hunter, someone who could provide for her and those boys so that they wouldn't have to trade for meat.

That's what she wanted from you, Akrist. Not your heart. Just your spear and now you're a cripple she has to leave behind.

"Did you mean it? What you asked me when you first

woke?" Her voice was so small. "You said you wanted to come with me."

Tears filled my eyes. "I do want to come, Yara, but it's going to take months for me to heal now. I don't know if you can afford to wait that long. With sacrifice six months away, they'll start guarding the daeson soon—"

"I don't care. I'll wait for you," she whispered. "We'll go together."

And I cried. I couldn't stop crying. Not when my broken ribs screamed, and my head pounded.

Yara slipped her hand into mine and lay beside me until I could breathe again. She slept after that. I couldn't possibly, not with her against me, so when I was certain I wouldn't wake her, I eased away from Yara, tucked my blanket around her, and settled at the edge of my bedroll. A thousand thoughts poured through my head. My body felt heavy and drained, my broken ribs and leg throbbed, but I'd never felt so alive.

I SCREAMED. I couldn't stop screaming.

"Akrist!"

Oh, Nasheira. Not like this!

"Akrist!"

It felt like I was plunging backwards into black water, thrashing, panicking. Something pressed against my scar, but it was not the wurm. A gulping animal cry burst out of me as I swatted at the pressure on my chest and scrambled to my feet. My splinted leg screamed, unused to bearing any weight.

"Akrist, you're dreaming!"

Don't touch me. Don't touch me!

Yara's hand slid off my chest. "You were dreaming."

I panted, clawed at my chest and stomach. Blinking, I focused on Yara standing before me.

"You were dreaming," she said. "Akrist? It was just a dream."

Holding my breath, I swayed a little before uttering a pathetic, keening wail, and clutching Yara to me tightly. Over her shoulder, I saw the crack in the door flap. Rain streamed outside, backlit by the shivering, fractal lightning.

I stiffened. *Something was there.* Blinking, I refocused.

It was Vax, just Vax. He peered under the fabric, beak dripping, crooning anxiously.

"Akrist?"

Closing my eyes, I drew long, deep breaths of damp air, and slumped against the overwhelming aftershock of the dream paired with the potent sensation of Yara's arms cautiously encircling me.

"You all right?" she whispered.

"Oh, Guides, it was real." I buried my face in her hair. My ribs throbbed. Sweat rolled down my sides. Under my shirt, the scar on my chest still stung.

"The wurm dream?"

"Worse this time," I croaked. "You were there and—and it was coming in. Guides, I could smell it, and I couldn't stop it. I can never stop it."

"I'm here."

"I'm sorry."

There was a long pause before Yara spoke softly. "Why? Did you let it eat me?"

"What?" A short laugh escaped me. Wincing at the pain in my ribs, I pressed back to look into her eyes. "No." I smiled, shaking my head.

"Awake now?" she whispered.

"Very."

Yara's bright laughter bounced through my hut. Rain chattered outside swallowing every other sound.

My broken leg pounded in time with my heart, but I felt steadier standing than I had in a long time. Still coming down from the adrenaline-washed dream, I was surprised at the shift from alarm to arousal. The way Yara's hair tumbled in tousled curls against her neck, the curve of her collarbone glimpsed only in pale flashes of light. It was intoxicating.

Slowly, she brought her hand up again, reaching toward my temple, then curling her fingers in hesitation.

"Can I?" she whispered.

I swallowed, nodded.

Yara ran her hand down the side of my face along my jawline, and the swelling rush of warmth and shame felt as staggering and discordant as ever.

I ignored the guilt. I didn't want this to stop. I wanted Yara to keep going, felt my breathing hitch, and my spine tingle as she slid her hand down my neck, stopping where my shirt had come unlaced.

Closing my eyes, I remembered with delicious clarity the first time Yara had touched me, that light caress of cool fingers over my scar. I recalled what it felt like before the shame hit. Holding onto that, I placed my hand over Yara's and guided it slowly downward over the familiar lines and ridges of Nasheira's mark. I pressed her palm against my tripping heart.

"See what you do to me?"

Yara's answering laugh was low and seductive. Her lips parted, and her eyes fluttered closed as I slid my hand around the side of her neck, and stroked her cheek with my thumb.

I waited until she opened her eyes again and exhaled at the soft invitation I saw there.

"Can I... kiss you?" she asked.

"No," I answered. Before Yara could shrink away, I pressed her hand more firmly against my chest, drew her closer, and said, "I want to kiss you."

I bent, slid my hand along her jawline, and found her lips, traced the elegant curve of her neck, sampled the sweet taste of her tongue, and lost myself in her. I expected the guilt to crest, waited for it to bloom in my brain like black poison. It had always done so before, but this time it faltered.

Yara's fingers slid down my back, stirring ripples of warm shivers in their wake. My heart fluttered and lower down I felt the tugging stir of urgent desire.

She felt it too, slid her leg between mine, and pressed her hip against my groin.

"Yara," I groaned. My head rolled back as I breathed her name. Heat rolled through me, and I clenched my teeth to hold back the guilt. One of Yara's hands slipped under my shirt while the other tugged at the laces at my neck. I couldn't lift my arms without my healing ribs flaring with pain, so I let her undress me.

She explored me with innocent curiosity, her hands running over my shoulders and down my arms.

I smiled as she pressed her ear to my chest and listened to my heart. *Guides, she feels good against bare skin.*

Yara straightened and leaned back. The long muscles of her slender back corded under my hand. She unlaced her shirt revealing a thin chest scar, and my breath caught when she slid my hand beneath those laces.

The warm fullness of her breast overwhelmed me. I sucked in a short, ragged breath.

Yara's eyes fluttered closed, and she arched against me.

"Akrist."

At first, I barely heard my name through the hungry wash of lust. Guilt swam far below me, a dark predator circling in the deep.

"Akrist, lay with me," Yara whispered. Her hot kisses trailed down my neck.

We grinned as I settled awkwardly on my bedroll, my splinted leg jutting out like a stork's. Yara straddled me gently, her skirt flared over her thighs.

"I'm not hurting you, am I?" she asked.

"You're not," I rasped, leaning into her kisses, hungry for the salty taste of her. I was losing track of the guilt. It slid through my mind like a tunnelling wurm, but I was too stimulated to follow it. Yara's cool hands felt like rain on my skin, gliding down my chest, over my hips, and across my belly. I did not see the guilt pounce, but I felt it slam into me as she brushed over the hardness at my groin.

A malicious memory flashed through my mind from earlier tonight, before we'd slept. *I traded myself for food.*

"Yara, wait," I choked, and she froze above me. *Na-Jhalar used her too. Took her. Hurt her.*

"I'm hurting you." She glanced at my leg.

"No. I've never..." The remaining words of my admission stuck like cobwebs in my throat.

"I know."

"What if—" I swallowed and broke away from her searching gaze. "What if I do it wrong? What if I hurt you?"

"Do you love me, Akrist?"

"More than anything." My voice cracked.

"Then we'll learn together. We have a lifetime to explore each other." She leaned down to kiss me, whispering her next words against my flushed cheek. "I love you. Let me show you how I love you."

I was utterly clumsy. Yara jarred my healing leg several times, and I winced while she froze and apologized. We were not perfect that night in my hut, but we were honest, and we were one.

CHAPTER EIGHTEEN

Vax hissed as my door flap whipped aside. Shadows ribboned across the harsh morning light and I flinched as a booted foot scuffed to a stop inches from my head. Something jabbed my chest. I blinked stupidly down at the honed tip of a hunting spear pressed beneath my ribs.

"She's here," a clipped voice announced.

Another set of boots crunched past, straddling me to reach Yara.

Yara. Oh Guides, protect her!

I grabbed the spear shaft and wrenched it aside. Its tip snagged and carved a groove across my stomach as it went. Clenching my teeth, I swept my good leg under the feet of the body standing over me, but they kicked my splinted leg.

White pain hammered up my thigh and I bellowed, curled like a caterpillar, and struggled to draw my next breath.

A fist gripped Yara by the hair and yanked.

She screamed and twisted to grip the hand that held her, stumbling over me as the intruder hauled her ruthlessly toward the door.

"No!" I gasped and rolled toward them, but the spear

jammed against my sternum, pinning me while Yara's bare feet slipped in the mud outside.

She went down hard on her side, breath pounding out of her.

"Stay down!" The spear holder hissed and I blinked up at my little brother.

"Dero?" I coughed.

Mud caked Yara's skirt and her bare ribs as she scrambled to stand. Arsu yanked her to her feet, still holding her by her hair. Yara wheezed breathlessly, mouth wide and eyes bulging, both hands gripping her captor's wrist.

"Vax!" I yelled.

The vaiya hissed and crashed into my hut. Mud spattered as Dero spun to face the charging bird. Vax caught him under the armpit and tossed him sideways. My brother tumbled into the woven wall, and I scrambled for his spear, hoisting myself to a stand and ducking under Vax's whipping tail. "Stop." I limped toward Arsu, pain lancing up my leg. "Let her go!"

Several people streamed out of their huts around us, drawn by the noise.

Arsu ignored me, hauling Yara away even as she struggled to keep pace. Her sharp, shuddering wails, the ugly contrast of dark mud spattering her goosefleshed skin, Arsu's damned fist clenched in her hair, all of it undid me.

Vax hissed behind me, and my little brother swore. I glanced back to see my bird herding him away from me. *If you send Vax after them, Dero will take you from behind.*

Arsu dragged Yara further from me.

Holding my breath against the pain pounding up my leg, I lunged toward them too slowly. "Stop," I gasped, my breath streaming out in fog. Blood pounded behind my eyes. This time, when Arsu didn't turn, I set my teeth, hefted Dero's spear and pinpointed my target. Tuning out the startled screams from the crowd around me, I threw. The spear whistled past Yara's skirt and thudded into the ground ahead of Arsu's feet, freezing the pair of them in place.

"What in Nasheira's name!" A voice boomed from my right. Iva shouldered past several wide-eyed onlookers, shifting focus between me and the spear still wobbling in front of a gaping Arsu. "Akrist?"

"She's hurting Yara!" I roared.

"Let her go, Arsu." Iva demanded.

Arsu bared her teeth but complied, shoving Yara away from her so hard that she stumbled into her mother's arms.

I hadn't seen Enna lurking just beyond Arsu. Her face twisted and she hissed into Yara's ear even as her daughter covered her breasts with her hands.

"For Nasheira's sake, let them cover themselves." Iva scowled and spoke over her shoulder. "Fraesh, bring blankets."

I glanced down at my blood-smeared belly and realized for the first time that I stood naked and panting before half of the camp.

Vax squealed and stamped his feet at the tension settling like morning frost around us.

"Call off your bird, Akrist," Iva ordered. "And tell me what this is about."

"Vax, enough," I gulped, fingers tingling.

My vaiya stamped, but backed away from Dero, keeping his bulk directly between my brother and me.

I turned back to Iva, but Arsu's sharp voice cut in, clipped yet calm.

"I think we'd all like to know what this is about, storyteller." She pointed toward the centre of camp. "Do you hear that?"

From the Speaker's hut came a low, gurgling yell, like the call of a rutting bull.

Guides, I couldn't believe I'd missed it until now.

Iva's brow wrinkled.

"Not to worry, storyteller. With the storm last night, it's understandable that his caretakers wouldn't hear him." Arsu's mouth twisted into a humourless smile and she spread her hand over her chest. "But I am the Speaker's own blood and his anguish woke me early this morning."

I flinched as Fraesh dropped a blanket over my shoulders before approaching Yara with pursed lips.

"Na-Jhalar was calling for Delani, so I knew which chani he wanted." Arsu gestured at Yara with a curled lip. "I asked after the girl at her mother's hut, but the poor woman said she hadn't seen her daughter." Her voice turned venomous.

Yara wrapped her blanket around herself, sobbing and shrugging out of her mother's clutching grasp.

"With our Speaker frantic, and this fine woman worried for her child's welfare, I wasted no time." Arsu pinned me with a cold, hard gaze and licked her thin lips. "I had a fair idea of where we might find the girl, so I woke Dero to come with me, hoping that a familiar face might defuse the situation."

"She stepped down," I shouted.

"Did she?" Arsu arched her eyebrows even higher. "I don't recall hearing her announce anything at evening prayers, do you, storyteller?"

Iva stared at Yara as her shoulders slumped and her knuckles whitened. "She said nothing."

"Yara?" Something cold clamped my throat as I tried to catch her eye and she wouldn't look up at me. She had told me she'd stepped down, hadn't she? My memory was muddy with desire. Had I only heard what I'd wanted to hear?

"I was going to," she wailed, chin tucked to her chest.

Mother of Yurrii. Fear gripped me, wringing air from my chest. *What have I done?*

Arsu shrugged. "I was merely returning a wayward chani to a Speaker who's asking for her service."

Na-Jhalar's enraged bellow sang across camp.

"He hurt her, Iva," I urged.

"Do you think he's in any position to bargain, really?" Arsu drawled and she gestured to the spear skewering the ground nearby. "This man aimed to spear me from behind as I tried to serve my Speaker. You saw it as clearly as I did, Iva."

"If I'd aimed to spear her," my words boiled out of me, "she'd be pinned right now."

Iva took a deep breath and sighed, quieting both of us with her gaze. "Yara broke the chani vows," she stated.

"Iva, no," I breathed. *This can't be happening.* I limped toward her, "Listen to me—"

"You didn't think of the consequences!" Iva cut me off with a chop of her hand. Her gaze found mine, angry and injured. "Either of you. She knowingly broke her vows and you used your weapon against a fellow hunter."

Na-Jhalar howled from his hut, and the sound grated through my skull. *Stop this. Make her understand.* "Iva—"

"Restrain him." She turned from me, her clipped voice raw and agonizingly resigned.

"No." The word fell from my lips.

When no one moved, the storyteller raised her arm and her voice. "Dero! Hasev! Take him back to his hut."

"No!" I lunged toward Yara even as she crumpled like a dying fire. Feet squelched through the mud around me and strong arms clamped mine, hauling me back toward my hut even as I thrashed. "Don't do this," I hissed.

"Easy boy," Hasev whispered into my ear.

"Don't do this!"

"Post a guard and see that he stays there," Iva spoke over me.

"No hurt!" Vax squealed and snapped at Dero.

"Akrist. Control your bird if you don't want it speared!" Iva bellowed.

"Vax!" I snapped. "No. Stop."

And then we were plunged back into the stale dimness of my hut. My father and brother held me there silently. I wanted to scream and thrash out against the rising panic in my belly, but I needed to hear what Iva was saying outside.

Her muffled voice pressed past the blood rushing between my ears. "Take her to the Speaker. She is to stay in his hut and will remain his chani for five days more to repay her lost loyalty. She can officially step down after that if she likes. Keep Akrist in his hut too. A week of meditation will do them both good."

A week. He'll kill her. Hysteria boiled over in me, burning away the pain in my leg. I dove toward my doorway, dragging Hasev and Dero with me. "Don't do this," I bellowed. "Iva, don't do this." I kept yelling as Dero and Hasev restrained me. I screamed and thrashed until my own father choked the air out of me, and black spots swarmed my vision, and Na-Jhalar quieted at the centre of our camp. *Sweet Nasheira, he'll kill her.*

Iva stood at my doorway that night, having volunteered for a shift of guarding me herself, just as she had for six months before the moons eclipsed.

I thought I knew you.

I lay facing away from her, hands bound behind my back, my broken leg swollen enough that the splint straps dug into my thigh. Smoke swirled around us thick enough to make my eyes smart. I couldn't feel anything else.

"Fraesh gave Na-Jhalar double his regular dose of gifen as

soon as he was able," Iva said. "He's sleeping now, and likely to be barely functional for the week."

As soon as he was able? My nostrils stung as I inhaled. *You let him take her first. While he was angry. The whole camp let it happen. Guides, I could hear it from here.*

"Yara is..." Iva cleared her throat. "She'll be fine. My daughters are with her. I wanted you to know she's not alone."

I didn't answer. How could I with rage clawing up my throat and choking me? Instead, I sucked in the sourness of smoke drifting in from outside and let the ache in my throat build until the storyteller let my door flap close and left me in darkness.

I smelled smoke the next morning too. My nostrils stung and my eyes ached at the intensity of it. When Fraesh came to check my splint, I wrinkled my nose at his placid face.

"What's burning?" I croaked.

"Hmmm?" Fraesh loosened a strap to tuck padding beneath it.

"Something's burning. Since last night. Can't you smell it?"

The healer sat back from me for a long moment before gripping my chin and examining both of my eyes one at a time. "Did you hit your head yesterday?"

"No."

I wanted to wipe my eyes, but my hands remained bound behind my back. Even though Fraesh had ordered Jin, my current guard, to loosen my bonds when he felt my fingers were cold, they remained secure enough to immobilize me.

"Get some rest, Akrist." Fraesh sighed. "I'll see what I can do about getting you untied."

Iva released me from my bonds that night when she brought my supper. "There'll still be a guard at your door, and if I hear about any attempts to escape, I'll double that girl's mandatory shift as chani, understand?"

I winced at her use of Yara as punishment, shaking out my wrists. "Is she well?"

"As well as can be expected." Iva sighed, shook her head cryptically and left me. Her answer haunted me.

During the fourth morning of my confinement, it happened again. The smoke. I scrambled through my hut, rustling blankets, searching the grass walls for a subtle glow or flicker of flame. Sitting defeated, with a cold, spark-less lamp in my hand, I asked the guard outside.

"Can you smell that smoke?"

"No." I recognized Darvie's voice.

"Are there fires nearby?" Iva and the council posted scouts during fire season, as well as ordering everyone to douse their hearth fires before retiring for the night. But we weren't even close to fire season. It was still spring. The area surrounding our camp bloomed lush, green and healthy, and bountiful snow blanketed the mountain range to the south.

"It rained last night," Darvie answered shortly. "No fires."

Mother of Yurrii, what is wrong with me? My mind felt disjointed and crumbly, like burning leaves. *Is Fraesh dosing me with gifen again?* But this didn't feel the same. I *had* smelled smoke and it continued throughout the day. I buried my head beneath my blanket in a vain attempt to ease my raw throat and aching eyes.

CHAPTER NINETEEN

"Akrist?" An urgent voice woke me from sleep. Beneath my door flap, Darvie's boots had been replaced by another set. *Past midnight then. That's when they change.* I coughed, rolled onto my back and blinked, only to squeeze my eyes shut again as smoke stung them.

"Akrist, are you awake?"

The boots shifted. I recognized Jin's voice. My brother hadn't spoken to me during his past shifts on guard duty. "What's wrong?" I choked.

"Smoke," he said.

I sat up, fully alert. "You smell it too?"

"We need to wake the camp. It's getting bad out here." Jin brushed aside my door flap and his form looked ghostly and muted. "I think it's getting closer. I'm going to wake Iva. Can you walk?"

My younger brother pinned me with a hard gaze and I knew the question he really meant to ask was, *Can you walk fast enough to reach her before anyone knows you're missing?*

"Lend me your spear and I can."

I grabbed my blanket as Jin handed me his weapon and

helped me to my feet before turning toward Fraesh and Iva's hut.

Smoke hung in layered, sinuous clouds, a sombre garland strung across camp as I limped toward the main hearth.

"Yara?" My voice sounded strange and muffled. As I closed in on the Speaker's hut, the world washed away, leaving nothing but grey, billowing slate. "Yara, are you awake?"

I stumbled toward the doorway and hesitated only a moment before pushing Na-Jhalar's door flap aside and crossing the threshold. Weak lamplight and the smell of wet decay hit me. I gagged and clapped a hand over my nose and mouth.

"Akrist?" a voice mumbled from the shadows.

"I'm here," I choked.

I heard scuffling steps, then the lamplight guttered and cold hands gripped my arms. "Out. Get out."

She pressed me back. I felt the heavy, slack caress of the door flap at my back and, as we stumbled backwards into the smoke, I saw him.

It was just for a second.

The lamp flared and light reached the back wall of the hut. Propped there was the splayed, naked body of Na-Jhalar. Baline and Celi sat on either side of him. His skin was the spongy, pale colour of mushrooms and his mouth hung slack, like someone had punched a hole in his soft, fungus-like face. Vomit ran down his chin and crusted on his chest. His eyes were just two black slashes.

Horrified, I wondered if I stared at a dead body until a tongue wriggled in Na-Jhalar's mouth and his hand moved mechanically to stuff a wad of gifen into his cheek. Then— thank the Guides—the door flap swung shut.

"Yara?" I choked.

She'd buried her face against my chest, shivering in a

dirty night shirt that barely reached her knees. I swung my blanket over her shoulders, held her away from me, and froze.

I didn't recognize the face that blinked up at me. Blood ran from a gash on her forehead, past a gruesomely swollen black eye and down one mottled cheek. Her lip was split and she wheezed as she breathed.

"Oh Guides." I wanted to gather her into my arms, but she was already pushing away from me.

"I'll be fine," she slurred.

"I'll kill him," I announced. Gripping Jin's spear, I side-stepped Yara, but she blocked me, grabbing my wrist with trembling hands.

"Don't. He's not worth it." She peered past my shoulder, coughing as smoke filled her lungs. "We need to go, Akrist. Please."

She was right. The skyline to the south glowed orange.

"Vax!" I hollered into the night.

"Fire!" We both jumped as Iva bellowed the short, sharp word.

Baline and Celi ducked out of Na-Jhalar's hut and trotted toward the sound of their mother's voice.

My vaiya rounded the corner of the Speaker's hut, his crest raised. "Hot. Don't touch." He whistled anxiously.

Our camp convulsed like a great beast shaken awake. Muffled shouts ricocheted and words fluttered everywhere like pale birds dashing themselves against the cold night.

I boosted Yara onto Vax and led him north, away from the Speaker's hut.

"Can he carry us all?" she asked.

"Who?" I winced, leaning against Jin's spear hard enough for the shaft to bow.

"Can Vax carry both of us and all the daeson?"

I stopped. Black grit and flakes of ash feathered into eddies

around us. *Not now, Yara. We can't steal them now. I'm broken.*
Vax wailed and rolled his eye. Turning from Yara, I patted his
crest and tried to answer in an even voice. "He can. We'll be in
no shape to run though." The thought of carrying the boys
made my skin crawl. *Stop it. They're just little boys, for Nasheira's
sake. No different than you were, and you've vowed to save them.*

"We don't need to run yet, Akrist. We're just saving them
from the fire."

Their fathers can do it. Less than six months until sacrifice,
they wouldn't risk losing their offerings so close to the
eclipse. I winced at the cold thought, and looked back at
Yara's bruised and bloody face. I knew perfectly well that the
daeson wouldn't be a priority during a fire.

To our south, vaiyas bawled and stomped at the grim-
faced shadows loading wide-eyed children and awkward
bundles onto the animals' backs. People rushed back and
forth through the smoke like lines of ants. There was a
frantic order to it all as Iva's commanding voice sounded like
a horn guiding us in the dark.

"You stay here. I'll pass you the youngest ones," I said. I
could only imagine how they'd scream in the grip of a
stranger. Even after all this time, an unexpected touch still
incited raw panic in me. Most daeson shared the same aver-
sion to touch.

Three tiny huts with gnarled roots materialized out of the
gloom. A boy with black hair plastered to his face stood
outside the first one, fidgeting with his breech cloth. He wore
no shirt, but instead had his birthing blanket wrapped
around his shoulders. His ribs pressed in and out as he
breathed.

"Where are the others, the babies?" My own breathing
ratcheted higher and I couldn't stop it.

His gaze flicked to the hut to my left and then back to me.

The hut was so small I had to double over and prop my splinted leg to the side to reach within. When I touched a bare leg, its owner cringed and howled, but I didn't have time for niceties. Holding my breath, I pulled one of the infants out and wrapped him tightly in his blanket as he started wailing.

"Do you have any carry bags?" I shouted to the black-haired boy and he nodded and plunged into his hut. When he emerged gripping a tattered sack, I took it from him and passed it to Yara as the daeson baby struggled in my arms.

"Can you use it as a sling?" I asked over the baby's shrill squeals.

Yara nodded and crossed the bag's strap over her shoulder before reaching down.

"Hold on tight. He's going to fight you." I pressed the frantic baby toward her, and when she secured him in the makeshift sling and held him to her chest, I returned to scoop up the baby still inside.

"Will they both fit?" I rasped. *Please Nasheira. This has to work. She can't hold onto them both while they're fighting her.*

"I think so. They're small." Yara gasped as a tiny hand with sharp nails raked down her bruised face. She tucked the flailing limb back into the sling and leaned down to grab the second child.

The smoke parted, and I glimpsed Fraesh leading Na-Jhalar south through the haze. The Speaker followed with the torpid stiffness of a cadaver, his curdled face set in rubbery resignation. No one was coming north for the daeson.

Shuddering, I turned away.

The blonde daeson raced out of his hut, face twisting at the babies' shredding cries, looking to the taller boy for reassurance.

I limped toward them slowly with my hands outspread, but they cowered away from me.

"Listen. There's a fire. I want to set you on that vaiya so you can escape it. That's all. But I have to lift you onto his back."

The blonde boy whimpered.

"We don't have much time. If you don't let me put you on his back," I pointed to Vax, "I'll have to carry you myself, and I'm injured. We won't be fast enough."

With his sharp chin tucked into his chest, the dark haired boy stepped forward. I boosted both him and the blonde one onto Vax's back behind Yara and they sat there, stiff as two tavi pieces balanced on end.

"If you don't hold on with your legs, you'll both fall off." I shook my head and limped to Vax's neck, bracing my arm over his shoulder and using Jin's spear to balance myself. "Let's go." I pressed Vax north.

Behind us, our caravan wrapped the final scraps of our lives into hasty bundles.

Fraesh coaxed Na-Jhalar onto the back of Voti. Smoke swirled. Vaiyas moved out, like silver birds on slack, grey water. Our entire camp surged northward behind us.

Vax bent to nip at the frayed strap of my leg splint. "Come. No walk."

With the daeson babies screaming and squirming in Yara's sling, I braced my good leg above his spur and hoisted myself onto his back behind the two boys.

We waded through breakers of fetid grey smoke. Trees looked like long fingers of point pointing at the sky. Ashes swarmed like flies, clinging to everything they touched, and the wind whipped at our backs with cold cruelty. Eventually the baby's cries dissolved into coughing whimpers. The boys in front of me sat rigidly and breathed like trapped rabbits.

As his vaiyas called from behind him, Vax grew more

agitated and slowed despite my urging him forward. *He wants to protect his flock. No one in your camp is going to stop you now with a fire on our heels.* So, to appease my anxious vaiya, I let the caravan catch us, wincing as other travellers threw Yara and I dark glances through the smoke.

I never wanted her to be an outcast. Yara had made enemies by pairing with me and would make even more associating with these daeson, but I couldn't change any of that now. *No one else moved to save them. I didn't think of them either, not until Yara asked.*

Vax's drawn-out wail snatched me from my thoughts. I barely had time to react as the vaiya tossed his head and side-stepped in blind fear.

"Hey!" I protested, squeezing my legs and reaching around Yara and the yelping boys to grip Vax's neck strap. Jin's spear tumbled out of my grasp and clattered to the ground behind us. "Vax," I breathed. "It's all right."

Glancing over my shoulder at the fallen spear, I caught a glimpse of the horizon, past the slashes of dark trees. A horrifying, quivering glow bathed the sky. The fire was coming.

Sharp cries stabbed through the caravan, and we surged ahead with fresh fear. Bright embers rode the wind, threading through tattered leaves to singe our clothes.

The vaiyas bunched around Vax, their eyes white with terror, their bawls deafening. A cascade of cold dread washed over me as I leaned into the panting daeson, sandwiching them between Yara and me to grip Vax's neck rope with both hands. "Hold on, Yara," I urged. "All of you hold on."

Those were our last words before the fire overtook us. As it advanced, sparks drove into our skin, burning our hair and driving us into frenzied retreat.

I jumped at the crack of branches behind me, turning my head to see a frantic gazelle thump past. Two more followed, oblivious to our presence as they scrambled by, sides heaving and tongues lolling.

Vax bellowed, bucked once, and we toppled from his back. My fingers jerked free of the rope. I twisted and landed hard. White pain blinded me. I couldn't breathe past the fire in my ribs and the agony jamming up my thigh. By the time my vision cleared and I rolled over, Vax was far beyond us, shying and careening through his fleeing flock.

"Vax," I gulped.

The flock scattered behind their leader. Children toppled off their backs as the pack animals crashed through trees, shearing off baggage and shattering baskets.

"Vax, stop." I scrambled to my feet and limped after the vaiyas. Pain hammered up my splinted leg. Yara yanked on my arm, jerking me backwards. Stumbling, I swung around and blinked at the angry orange glow silhouetting her stooped figure. Clutching her bulging sling, she bent and grasped at a crumpled figure on the ground. The blond daeson stood beside her, eyes wide and glassy with tears. I saw a small, bare foot in the leaves and stared stupidly for a moment before realizing that it was attached to the limp form of the dark-haired daeson.

Scooping up the thin body, I was shocked by how light and lifeless it was. I seized the blonde boy by the wrist.

Small, scurrying things darted between my feet. Pale flanks of larger animals flashed past on either side. Beneath the reverberating thunder of hooves, I caught the crackling, roaring advance of something hungry crawling through the treetops.

Sweet Nasheira. We cannot die like this.

A deafening, bugling call cut through the noise. Hot wind blasted down on us, followed by the deep gust of great wings pumping through the sky.

Craning my neck, I caught a flash of gold through the

skeletal canopy. Another otherworldly call sounded from somewhere behind us. The deep whistle of dragon wings churning above us overpowered everything else.

My heart soared with them for a moment, before crashing back through my rib cage and into my stomach. "No," I murmured.

The Guides were flying right over, fleeing like the rest of us.

A glowing coal burned my cheek. As I strained for a glimpse of blue sky, fire leapt through the treetops above us. The cloak of flames swept over the top of our caravan like a door flap swinging shut.

We are dead. Oh, Nasheira, we will burn alive.

My foot sunk into something soft. I pitched forward, barely able to twist enough to protect the child in my arms. We plunged into icy water. My shoulder slammed against a shallow, rocky riverbed, and I resurfaced choking and clutching the trembling body to my chest.

The entire world roared red above us. Red debris pelted around us, hissing as it hit the broad band of water. My face burned. The child's hair steamed and the blonde boy gripped my arm and howled.

"Yara!" I screamed, slogging into waist-high water, scanning the terrified faces jostling around me as the rest of the camp crammed into the water. The bundle at my chest coughed and started to cry. "Yara!"

"Akrist!" her voice cracked. "I'm here."

Floundering, I tripped as I turned and went under, swallowing a cold draught of sooty water. Both daeson and I popped back up thrashing and coughing. My mind registered nothing but the heat and the soft sight of curls bobbing around my face.

"Yara!" I choked, grabbing her sling and pulling her close.

"Don't let go," she gulped, clutching the sputtering babies to her chest. "The water is too deep. They're heavy."

The roar of the blaze was unbearable. Scalding smoke boiled and churned at the river's surface, sucking away our breath. The dark, frantic flash of Yara's eyes was the last thing I saw before my vision blurred.

"I love you," I gasped into Yara's ear. "Yara, I love you and I won't let go." I was certain she could not hear my defeated voice over the scream of the fire. Smoke crawled up my nostrils and down my throat, like attacking fire ants. Every time I opened my mouth, more swarmed in to eat at my insides. Dizziness swamped me, yet I still gripped Yara with one hand while the boys clutched the other.

Around us, heads bobbed. People screamed. The river steamed, lapped at our chins, and pulled our hair. Smoke rolled and dipped, caressing the boundary between fire and water.

My mind muddied, my whole world collapsing and folding in on itself. I felt unconsciousness dropping over me like a net. The river's current became a thousand cold fingers raking across my flesh.

Nasheira, No! I screamed inwardly. *I cannot.* My fingers slipped. I held onto Yara and the boys as tightly as I could and still they were slipping. *I cannot save them. Do not take her from me like this.*

Something shifted in the air. The wind churned, caught, and raced forward. Fire rolled hypnotically overhead before tumbling over itself to plunge on through the tree-tops. The blasting heat and restless smoke lifted enough for me to gulp in a few breaths of air. It felt like sucking in sand.

My unsplinted knee buckled and all of us plunged into a cold slurry of water and ash. I clawed through the cloudy water, searching for solid ground. As my feet thudded against the sandy bottom and my good leg flexed straight, we broke into the world of air again.

I plunged through the water until my splint hit a rock and I toppled forward with Yara and the children in tow.

We landed hard. I tripped, caught myself, and an explosive gurgle of air burst from one of the babies in Yara's arms. I turned to see him coughing up water.

Yara blinked down at him, wide-eyed. Behind us, a child started to cry, a high, jagged squeal that scraped across my raw mind.

I lay wheezing, my cheek pressed against cool rocks. My broken leg felt like it was burning from within. "Yara," I croaked. "Are they alive?"

Her eyes welled, her chin wrinkled and, with tears spilling down her face, Yara nodded. "They are," she said.

All four. Somehow we saved all four. I rolled onto my back, but my lungs felt like someone was pouring soot down my throat. Curling upward, I managed a wet, shallow breath before the coughing tore into me and Yara pressed against me.

Charred trees loomed over us, creaking and clicking in a strange language that sounded like teeth grinding and knuckles cracking. At our feet, the black artery of the river pulsed and churned. Our caravan littered its muddy banks.

Fraesh and a few others scurried amongst the wounded, distributing the healer's sparse stock of junab. Their movements were fettered, and they spoke in whispers. Even the moans seemed muted, rising through hot, sour air. Our caravan shuddered and crouched like mice, holding our breath, certain that the slightest sound would bring our predator barrelling back to finish us. We could still hear fire chewing into the heart of the forest.

Sweet Nasheira, we are alive. The shock, the crippling relief soaked in. *We were almost burned alive. Oh, Guides, the fire rolled right over us, and we were almost burned alive.* I tucked Yara a little closer to me, despite the irritation of her curls brushing against my burnt forehead.

That's when I looked across the water and saw Arsu, her narrow gaze locked on me with unbridled disgust. It was enough to freeze my stomach and rock me backwards. As I sat dumbfounded, Arsu's predatory eyes flicked toward the two daeson hunched to one side of me and the pair in Yara's sling. Then she turned away.

When everyone had recovered enough to stand, our caravan backtracked through grey trees littered with twisted bodies of the animals that had been unable to outrun the fire. Stiff carcasses clawed at the sky. Vaiyas, harek, gazelles, all of them regarded us with milky, vacant gazes as we passed. I was terrified that the next pale corpse might be one of our birds. *Sweet Nasheira*, I dreaded finding Vax dead. Images of his burnt, broken body sizzled through my mind until every corpse we passed assumed the form of a one-eyed vaiya.

Nobody broke the silence of the smouldering graveyard as we sliced meat from salvageable carcasses and stuffed our waistbands with warm, slimy leaf packets. The gatherers picked junab to chew and apply to untreated burns. Because the plant was a low-growing succulent, it survived the flash fire remarkably intact. The only sounds that leaked from our limping caravan were small, occasional whimpers and relentless fits of coughing.

We found our vaiyas back at the burnt-out remains of our camp. Staggering into the middle of the flock, I drank in the sight of them. They milled around me like watery spectres, but their breath felt warm and sweet. They were bloodied. Carry bags and ropes slapped loosely at their flanks, but they were whole, alive and whole, *thank the Guides.*

One bird broke from the excited flock to bump me in the chest.

"Late," Vax crowed.

"Yes," I laughed and abruptly regretted it. Seized by a coughing fit, it was all I could do to remain upright with one arm slung over the big vaiya's neck.

Vax curled around me and clucked with all the sternness of a mother, "Straight to bed."

That night, Yara stood before the charred main hearth and announced she was stepping down as chani. No one challenged her. Afterwards, we both collapsed under a borrowed blanket and a muted, charcoal sky. Fat flakes of ash still rained on us, so we kept our heads under the covers. Blinking in the dark, enveloped by the sweet, humid warmth of Yara's breath, I absorbed the sounds of a sleeping camp, gentle snores punctuated by muffled coughs. The soft swish of vaiyas' tails paired with the deep, even draw of Vax breathing behind us. Small sounds spun into a delicate lullaby, sounds I thought I'd never hear again. I couldn't sleep. My ribs and broken leg throbbed with an angry, swelling pain, but I could manage it if I concentrated on the small sounds around me instead. The sound of Yara breathing was all I needed.

CHAPTER TWENTY

"Fraesh told me you smelled smoke before anyone else did. Was it like this in your vision?" Vax shied at Iva's voice. I leaned forward to pat the bird's neck, but the vaiya would not be pacified. His tail flicked in restless tempo behind me, and I felt muscles bunching as he sank into a defensive stance.

How do you expect him to calm down if you cannot? I ran my tongue over my teeth, frowning at the bitter taste of ashes.

"It wasn't a vision, just the smell." *Sweet Nasheira, I couldn't imagine anything like this. I've never seen anything like it.*

The southern mountain range loomed before us in the gloom. Peaks that, days ago, had been crisp with snow looked grimy and barren now, charred red by the breath of Pau himself. Burnt trees stood like black stubble on a raw face. Rivers of cold slurry tracked down the valleys like muddy tears. The whole landscape reminded me of a skinned animal, stripped of its flesh and mangled beyond recognition.

The cause of the carnage loomed before us, dominating the bruised horizon. One mountain had crumbled, collapsing in on itself as if Nasheira had punched a hole through its brittle skull. Glowing red oozed from the gaping cavity like lifeblood and smoke gushed in an ever-expanding column, a black tumour gobbling up the sky.

"Your visions, are they often accompanied by smell?"

I remembered the oily smell of the wurm as it came into my hut while Yara slept. "Sometimes."

"You should have said something." She glared at me.

I gaped at her. Was she really *blaming* me? *She confines you alone to your hut, lets your Speaker rape Yara, and then chides you for not speaking up when no one would have listened anyway?*

"I am not your Speaker," I growled.

I swallowed against the sudden tightness in my throat, and Vax hissed, sensing my shift from edginess to anger.

Her eyes softened and I noticed the dark circles under them.

"Maybe you should be," she said quietly.

I laughed to cover the sudden onset of emotions at her words: anger, fear, anxiety, longing. "Don't let Arsu hear you say that."

Iva heaved a great sigh. "Your visions are valuable. They would help you lead—"

"Don't," I barked, raising a hand, shaking my head even as the scar on my chest tingled. "I was a daeson. I cannot be a Speaker. You said so yourself. When Nasheira marked me, it was only to erase my past, to make me a normal boy."

"I said that to protect you. Na-Jhalar wanted to kill you. You would have been sacrificed just like the other daeson, but there are people in camp who would support you now."

"Perhaps the Guide made a mistake."

Iva touched the daeson's tattoo on her wrist. "Guides don't make mistakes."

I snorted. "Have you seen the bruises on Yara? On your daughters?"

She seemed to crumble a little at those words, and I immediately regretted them. Her daughters had been as battered as Yara when they fled Na-Jhalar's hut last night and Iva had still rescued the man who'd beaten them. Weariness etched her face now, her proud shoulders slumping. She looked like she'd lost weight. *Sweet Nasheira, has she deteriorated so much as Na-Jhalar's replacement?* I tried to picture the vibrant, golden-haired storyteller of my youth, the one who hunted every day and swore that eating gazelle lungs were the key to staying young, but the image wouldn't solidify in my mind.

"Arsu spoke with me last night," she sighed. "She's concerned that I don't have her brother's best interests in mind."

"What?" I stammered. "Na-Jhalar's *only* interest is gifen. His brain is rotten."

"She said that Na-Jhalar has spoken to her while she sleeps." Iva raised her eyebrows. "In her *vision*, the Speaker asked to be released from the gifen trance I keep him under."

"She accused you of forcing the drug on the man?"

"She saw me do it when she brought Yara to the hut, but Arsu has a sly tongue. She wouldn't accuse me outright. She said she craved my advice and that the vision frightened her. She assured me she would relay any guidance Na-Jhalar passed on to her in future dreams."

My stomach clenched and my ribs ached. "Do you believe her, that she's having visions?" But Iva didn't answer. She stared at the oozing mountain, head cocked almost as if she were listening for something.

"I'm sorry, Akrist. About Yara. I thought we could dose Na-Jhalar with gifen before he hurt her." Iva's words trailed off, and silence settled between us like the stiff touch of a noose around our necks, as if our next words could snap it tight.

For a long time, we watched the pillar of smoke undulating through the sky like an oily black wurm.

I licked my lips, anxiety scouring the last of my anger away.

"What would you have me do? You had me bound and tied inside my own hut the last time I acted of my own accord."

She turned, raw and exposed. "I've made many mistakes, ones a leader cannot afford to make. And that is the problem. Nasheira never meant me to be a leader. I would ask you the same question, Na-Akrist. What would you have us do? I trust your counsel above all others."

Na-Akrist. My chest felt as if the ash-filled air had cemented in my lungs. I remembered the paralysis that clutched me on the day of my choosing and scanned the mottled sky for some sign of a golden Guide, but there was none. *They left us when the fire started.* Iva still stared at me, waiting for an answer.

"Don't call me that." I forced the words past my lips and steered Vax away from the storyteller.

As much as I longed to heal the rift between Iva and me, it became a wound that festered. The more I avoided the storyteller, the harder it became to even glance at her without anger consuming me. *How dare she ask my advice after condemning Yara and me as she had? She treated me like a child to be punished.* It was easier to ignore the woman, especially as we journeyed. I made sure my place in the caravan was the furthest from Na-Jhalar and Iva both.

Our camp journeyed for seven weeks before we saw the sun again. *Nearly two damned months of slogging through ash and cold to escape the fire mountain's plume,* but by the time we saw blue sky again. I could walk unaided and the damage to my lungs had been soothed by Fraesh's herbs.

Na-Jhalar forgot about Yara—Iva kept him well-stocked with gifen. Baline and Celi, having seen Yara step down with no repercussions, both resigned as chani too. They still helped Fraesh care for the Speaker, but they no longer shared Na-Jhalar's hut or his bed. For the first time in their adult lives, the two sisters were free to court anyone they pleased. Some members of our camp grumbled that it was wrong, a Speaker with no chani, but I didn't see any of them volunteering to fill the position themselves. Many more threw disapproving glances my way whenever they saw me near Yara. I didn't care.

We grew as close as any courting couple. I bought her a gift from an aeni tribe our caravan passed, a pair of hair combs carved from a black ox horn with intricate flowers etched along their spines. They reminded me of the bull that had nearly taken me from her and how lucky I was to be with her. Yara wore them every day. We shared a tent, a bed, and sometimes I even found myself falling asleep with my hand still wrapped around hers.

We settled into our camp in early summer. I wasn't yet healthy enough to hunt. Anything more than an awkward trot twinged my recently healed leg, so I volunteered to scout out a westerly string of trap lines on vaiyaback. It was exactly what I needed. With Pau and Yurrii closing on each other as they had in my youth, and only eleven weeks until the eclipse, anxiety was already digging deep roots into me. Alone and in charge of my own trap lines, I could cache far more food than I ever could with the hunters.

"YOU WERE RIGHT," Yara whispered. We lay in our hut well after dusk. Evening prayers had run long because of the full moon ceremony. It was late when Iva added a notch to the wooden calendar, marking a week since we made camp.

"Right about what?" I frowned.

"About the daeson. They cannot act like normal children. They don't know how."

I still flinched at the word, but this time, I stilled afterward and counted my breaths until I was able to exhale slowly. "Have you told them yet? What we're planning to do? My leg has healed. We need to go soon."

She shook her head. "No. We rarely speak. I can't get them to answer me. They just stare at their feet."

The words I wanted to say stuck in my throat for a long time before I coughed and forced them out. "I will speak with them." The second sentence came easier. "You cannot undo a lifetime of conditioning in an instant, Yara."

"I know."

"Do you? Do you know how difficult it is for me, even now, to lay still in your embrace? There is a part of me that curls away when our eyes meet, when we touch."

She stiffened and raised her head to peer at me, eyes intense. Without breaking eye contact, she pulled one of the ox horn combs from her hair and raked it through her curls before pinning them back from her face. "You find me so distasteful?"

"No." I folded my hand into hers and smiled. "No, I love your touch, but I am daeson, raised to be untouchable. I will always fight to control that part of me. I cannot erase it any more than those boys can."

"How can you even enjoy it, what we have, if it's a constant fight for you to touch me?"

I drew her into a kiss, met her gaze and held it. "Yara, you saved me. Before you, I was numb. Your touch is my connection, my rope. If I let go of you I'd fall, and Nasheira only knows what I'd be when I hit bottom."

She frowned. "What will we do with the daeson? You were right. Anyone who meets them will know what they are. They can't hide it. People will want to know how we recovered so many from sacrifice. What do we say?"

I had thought about this already, and had an idea. "Do you remember the sickness that drove you and Enna from your tribe?"

"The sores and coughing? It was awful. It killed so many."

"A similar sickness swept through our camp a few years after the sacrifice. It killed two, but infected nearly half of us." I rubbed my chin. "What if we paint the boys with sores, tell them to cough whenever we encounter outsiders. No one will venture close enough to know the ulcers aren't real. Nasheira binds Aeni tribes and camps alike to trade with those in need. They cannot deny us if we aren't branded. They'll trade with us from afar, with as little contact as possible. They won't ever know the daeson for what they are."

Her eyes darted, unfocused and bright as she thought. "It could work."

"It's the least of our worries." I squinted and pinched the bridge of my nose. "Guides, if only we had more time. They'll start guarding those boys soon. The trap lines are providing, but not enough to get all of us through a hard winter."

"We have three more months."

"We have ten *weeks*." My words snapped as sharp and hot as flint-struck sparks.

She blinked, expressionless at my interruption.

"I'm sorry." Sagging against the instant tension in my shoulders, I scrubbed at my face with one hand and blurted, "They're staring. Haven't you noticed it, how the whole damned camp looks at the daeson? I forgot how they stare so close to sacrifice, like they can't wait to cut us open and bleed us out. It makes my skin crawl."

"It's not your sacrifice, Akrist," she whispered.

"We've made this our sacrifice." I touched the scar on my chest.

"We won't let it happen this time. They can't touch us."

I shook my head and whispered my next words. "They can destroy us, Yara. One false step, one mistake and we are all branded." The thought of her smooth cheek mutilated by a raw S-shape brought bile to my throat.

"Come here." She clasped a cold hand around my neck and pulled me to her chest. The scent of cinnamon enveloped me. Her voice reverberated in my ear over the steady cadence of her heart. "We will find a way."

"We need food," I sighed. "We're walking into winter without enough food and I can't hunt yet."

"I've been hiding dry goods since before we made camp. The daeson have been helping."

"What?" I straightened. "Where?"

"In Gideous's hut. His father does not watch him like Henri's does, and Jule and Fey are too young."

My mind tripped at the unfamiliar names, groped to place them in context. *The daeson. You don't even know their names.* I pressed my thoughts to the back of my head and licked my lips, "Where have you been gathering? The daeson never leave with the others in the morning. I've watched them."

"I send them north."

"Yara…"

"Don't 'Yara' me." Her gaze flashed. "And don't tell me it's dangerous. I've taught them the trails. Your hunters are as loud as oxen when returning from a kill. They've plenty of time to avoid a chance meeting. The older boys know the warning markings of the new pit traps, and they never leave at the same time. One always stays in camp with the toddlers to ease the suspicions of the elders."

I rocked back from her, studying her pale face. "How are you explaining *your* absence to the gatherers?"

"I've been sick, Akrist."

I held her away from me, but she wouldn't meet my gaze. *Oh Guides.* "What do you mean, sick?" My thoughts flew to the illness we'd just spoken of, the one that killed Delani and Chan.

"Mostly in the mornings, after you've already left." Yara's dark eyes found mine and her neck corded.

"I'm pregnant, Akrist. I haven't bled for months."

Pregnant. The word didn't make sense in my head so I repeated it out loud.

She nodded, eyes welling up with tears.

"Oh, Yara, thank the Guides!" I clutched her to me, "I thought it was something bad, that you were ill. Pregnant. A baby?" I stroked her hair, relieved laughter bubbling past my lips as I held her. "How long..." My words trailed off.

"Iva guesses eleven weeks." Yara spoke over my shoulder. Her words were like glass, sharp and brittle.

Eleven weeks, my mind calculated sluggishly. "Our first time," I concluded.

Yara stiffened and shrugged out of my embrace, pressing away from me.

Or her last, with Na-Jhalar. My breath soured in my throat as I remembered the Speaker howling, my own father dragging me away, and Yara's beaten face.

Was the baby mine or his? Nausea swirled in my stomach. *Oh Guides, what if it's a daeson?*

Yara curled away from me, her face slack.

This isn't her fault. Say something, you idiot.

"I don't care," I croaked. When Yara turned back to me, I pulled her toward me and wiped her wet cheeks with my palm. "Do you hear me, Yara?" My voice shook, but I poured warmth into my words despite the horror gnawing coldly at my belly "I don't care. It will be our child. *Ours*. No matter what."

Please not a daeson.

CHAPTER TWENTY-ONE

I adjusted carry bags and tightened straps on Vax in preparation for our morning trek. My vaiya knelt obediently at my touch. Hefting my spear, I swung into place, settling into the warm hollow of the old vaiya's back. Breathing in the wholesome, musty scent of him, I whistled the command that signalled Vax to rise and start our journey west.

Icy wind streamed past my face, wringing tears from my eyes. I concentrated on the measured thud of Vax's widespread feet, the artful elongation and contraction of his body.

Stress release was simple for a vaiya. If something agitated them, they ran. That's what Nasheira built them to do: act on their nervousness, focus that tension, and use it to fuel basic, immediate motion.

"It never fails," Hasev had assured me as a boy. "If you want a vaiya to be still, let it run first."

It worked for people too. *Yara is pregnant, and we'll be risking her life to save the daeson soon, abandoning our camp with winter coming.* It made my gut ache, but I could forget it all, for a time, on the back of a vaiya.

I returned to camp with the late afternoon sun and had ample time to wash down Vax and prepare the carcasses before Yara arrived home with the gatherers.

Despite the cold, this afternoon had been a prosperous one. My trap line yielded two fat gazelles and a baby harek. Roasted harek was Yara's favourite, and this one was small enough to bake without removing its impenetrable plates. With dried onions and mushrooms sandwiched between the gaps in its armour, I had the makings of a delicacy by the time the gatherers returned. *I hope she's well enough to eat it.*

But it was the healer who approached my hearth fire instead of Yara.

My throat clenched. "Is something wrong?"

He puffed out his cheeks and groaned as he squatted beside me. As tired as he looked, I knew Fraesh's stamina rivalled my own. The panic I felt as I looked around for Yara must have shown. "She's told you, I presume?"

"Am I the last person in camp to know?" I muttered, cheeks reddening.

"Of course not," Fraesh huffed. "Only her mother and I know. Besides, I'm not here to speak of Yara. It's you I'm here for."

"Nothing to heal here." The words fell flat from my lips.

"Perhaps I'm not here as a healer, then." He smiled softly.

"What do you want?"

Fraesh's eyebrows arched at my disrespectful tone, but he said nothing. We sat a while in silence while I stirred the coals and Fraesh stared into them.

"Iva loves you."

I coughed at Fraesh's quiet announcement.

"She thinks of you as a son, you know, ever since Hasev asked us to watch over you, and she never did handle the silent treatment well. When the girls were younger, they tried it all the time. They knew they could get whatever they wanted from her just by clamming up." He snorted and shook his head. "Celi still does it."

Swallowing against the sudden tightness in my throat, I glanced at Fraesh and Iva's hut across camp. I'd built mine as far as I could from theirs.

"I don't think she can handle it from you, Akrist." Fraesh sighed.

"This isn't some childish grudge, Fraesh. She wants something from me I cannot give and she let the Speaker hurt Yara." *What if she carries his baby?* I shook the thought out of my head. "She'd still be letting him hurt your girls too if they hadn't stepped down."

Fraesh didn't rise to my bait. Sniffing, he replied "Yara wasn't a girl when she chose to be a chani or when she coupled with you. She knew the risk, and my daughters weren't girls either. Iva didn't choose their path. They did. In fact, that's the only reason Iva accepted a leadership role, to protect our daughters while they were chani. She never wanted to lead."

"Neither do I." I spoke through clenched teeth, eyes flitting back and forth.

"*You've* been chosen, Akrist."

"I'm not a Speaker. That was agreed upon *when* I was chosen." I hissed quietly.

"Then what about the visions? You have a great gift—"

Something unhinged inside me. I turned and gripped Fraesh's arm as rage pooled like boiling sap in my belly. "Don't call it that!" I spat, my words quivering with strangled emotion. "*Never* call it that, Fraesh! Do you think I like losing control of my senses? Do you think I enjoy seeing people die in my dreams while I stand helpless to save them? It is *not* a gift!"

"Fine." The healer regained his composure quickly, like a bird smoothing its ruffled feathers. "A responsibility, then, but yours to bear nonetheless. You cannot ignore it."

"*I* do not ignore it," I growled. "No one listens."

"You cannot ignore who you are, what Nasheira has called you to do."

"What would she have me do?" I gestured towards the Speaker's hut, dropping my next words to a whisper. "Knock Na-Jhalar off his pedestal and start prancing around with a dragon scale necklace, shouting orders?"

"Of course not." Fraesh clasped his hands together. "Don't be ridiculous. No one is asking you to do that."

"Then *what*, Fraesh?" My voice cracked as I leaned toward him with open hands. "What does Iva want of me?" *I need to know now, because I'm leaving her soon, and neither of you will ever forgive me after that.*

"She's tired. We both are." He swallowed, and for a moment, his tough-as-harek armour cracked.

I caught a glimpse of the frightened man beneath.

Pointing toward Na-Jhalar's hut, he rasped, "That man is sucking the life out of anyone who comes near him, and it is Iva who's trying to hold everything together. She cannot lead this camp alone anymore, Akrist. She needs the support of a true Speaker. She does not ask you to expose yourself, just speak with the woman, for Nasheira's sake. She wants your opinions, your thoughts." He sandwiched my hand between both of his. "Nasheira chose you to lead. Iva is asking you to do so quietly. A quiet Speaker. Can you not give her that?"

Chewing on my lip, I blinked at the flames. *She thinks of me as a son?* Something cautiously warm threaded through my ribs and squeezed. Not trusting myself to speak, I nodded instead.

"Good." Fraesh smiled and patted my hand. "Promise me you will go talk to her before she drives me crazy."

"All right," I croaked.

He nodded, releasing my hand and slapping his thighs before standing with a groan. "Give me a hug."

I knew better than to ignore an order from Fraesh and dutifully stood and stepped into his rough embrace.

They think of you as their son, and you're leaving them.

A selfish part of me hoped Iva would hold on to a grudge and save me from the pain of reconciling. But I should have known better. The storyteller threw me an anxious glance when I approached her one afternoon after hunting. I started a conversation about something entirely practical and trivial —as hunters do—and in the span of an hour, I'd mended my bridges with Iva. Fraesh was right. As soon as I started speaking to the woman again, she accepted me with bright relief. I hid my guilt well.

FORCING MY BREATHING TO SLOW, I watched the dusk sky. Feathery highlights of red bled away into muted grey, and the blushing horizon paled at the sight of Pau and Yurrii. The twin moons hung like sinister sickles, low in the northern sky. Below them squatted the four tiny, crude huts. The daeson sat around their fire, not yet aware of my presence.

Go to them. You promised Yara you would. I wanted to, and yet my toes curled in my boots, and an utterly familiar emotion bloomed in my stomach like black mould. *How could I be so foolish?* I'd resolved to help these boys. I'd sworn to save them and in doing so, naively assumed that it would erase every old feeling I'd harboured for them. *You cannot undo a lifetime of conditioning in an instant.* I snorted, and the noise carried across the still evening air to the four huddled boys under my observation.

Gideous and Henri craned their necks and blinked at me over the fire. Exhaling through my teeth, I scrubbed at my chest, inhaled so hard that it made a whistling noise, and walked toward them. Stepping into the circle of firelight felt like crossing a physical border. As I encroached their space, the solemn daeson ducked their heads and hunched their thin shoulders like birds ready to take flight.

Despite old panic gripping my chest, a grim smile tugged at my lips. *You do not know how much I want to do the same. Sweet Nasheira, it really is ingrained in us, to withdraw, to bow down. Even the two toddlers are doing it.* They'd grown so much since the fire. Jule and Fey frowned at the coals, legs splayed and pudgy fists opening and closing as they stole furtive glances in my direction. Fey rocked forward and back, moaning softly.

Squatting down, I snatched a twig from the hearth's edge and poked at the coals. "Are you afraid of me?" I asked. *Like I am of you?* Fey's eyes rolled, and he continued rocking. The rest of the daeson remained frozen, like cornered prey.

After a few moments, Gideous shook his head. I'd never noticed how startlingly blue the boy's eyes were. "Don't worry," he stated, eerie gaze flicking over me to settle on Fey. "He does that all the time."

"Many daeson do." I shrugged my shoulders to shed tension. "It is an escape."

"Are you a daeson?" The tow-headed, knobby-kneed Henri pursed his lips and reddened at the words that had just escaped him.

"I used to be."

"You are a Speaker now?" Gideous eyed my chest. My tunic covered the telltale scar, yet I still squirmed inside, just as I had as a boy, at the unwanted attention.

"Not exactly." I smiled to cover my anxiety, and drew smoke circles in the air with the glowing, smouldering stick. Fey kept rocking, but he and Jule both stared raptly at the quivering smoke trail. "I prefer to be just a man—not a

Speaker or a daeson." Blowing at the writhing halo above us, I purposefully kept my eyes unfocused as I asked, "Did you ever wish you weren't a daeson?"

Henri leaned forward, and Gideous studied me suspiciously over the fire.

"Did you ever wish you were just regular boys?" *Of course they did, Guides, we all did.*

"Impossible. Against the rules." Gideous kicked the crumbling fire with his foot, sending spatters of sparks swirling. Jule yelped and grabbed at his knee as an ember alighted there. One glowed on Fey's crumpled leggings as well, but no one reached out to brush it off. *They won't even touch each other.*

I leaned ahead, palm open, and Fey howled and cringed like a beaten vaiya as I flicked the spark away. "It's possible," I said. "I can take you all away from this camp. If you want to, we can leave, and when we're gone, you will be normal boys. You won't be daeson anymore."

"What about our parents?" Henri's words made my chest ache. I remembered how I'd pined for Aella's approval as a boy, how I still yearned for Hasev to laugh with me as he did with my brothers.

"They cannot come. It would only be Yara and me." I swallowed. My next words stuck in my throat, false and flat as they fell out of my mouth. "We could be your family." *Guides, will it be easier to say in time, easier to believe?* "You don't have to decide right now, but we're leaving soon." I jabbed the stick towards the twin moons. "Before Pau touches Yurrii, Yara and I are leaving and never coming back. You can come, or you can stay."

Silence settled over us, an uncomfortable prickling tension that made the boys rub their feet together. Fey whimpered again.

"Something bad happens when Pau touches Yurrii,

doesn't it?" Gideous's voice hung in the air like a sharp, brittle icicle.

I swallowed and nodded. "Yes, something very bad happens." *Guides,* they looked like any other children now, frightened, tired, clutching for safety and security. "You could die. But not if you come with us. Yara and I will keep you safe."

The skinny, blue-eyed boy brushed his dark hair away from his forehead and nodded once.

"Can all of you keep this a secret?"

Gideous and Henri nodded in solemn unison. "Don't worry," Henri added, glancing at Jule and Fey. "We won't tell."

"Good." I grinned, pushed up and slapped the dust off my knees. As I turned to retreat to my hut, their gaze followed me, and I did my best to smother the recoiling daeson part of me. *They will come. They have felt the whole camp stare at them with hungry eyes. They will come.*

That night in our bed, Yara's hands flew to mine like small birds. Eyes dilating, she bit her lip and guided my hands to her stomach, pressing my palms against its firmness.

"Do you feel it?" she squeaked.

We lay absolutely still for several moments, but I couldn't feel anything. "I wish I could," I whispered. "Tell me what it's like?"

"Like fluttering."

Yara beamed, curls bobbing. I kissed her forehead and stroked her stomach. "Hello, child of Yurrii, small warrior." Pride welled in my throat and something more sinister closed in behind. I tried to push it back, but it spilled past my joy, pooling and icy. If the child was a boy, he wouldn't grow up cursed; by the time he was born, Yara and I would be far away from here.

CHAPTER TWENTY-TWO

I stood and wiped the blood from my hands, scrubbing at my palms with a clump of dried kiro. The fragrant sweet grass did little to dispel the sharp scent in my nostrils. When my hands were reasonably clean, I wiped both sides of my blade and hoisted the gutted gazelle onto Voru's back. It was early enough that the sun's rays seemed weak as they sluiced across the wooded trail, our highest trap line. The pits hadn't flooded here yet. Other hunters worked in silence, resetting broken trap spikes and recovering the gaping maw that had so recently swallowed our latest kill.

I chewed a strip of dried meat, the remainder of my breakfast. We checked this easterly trap line every morning as we left camp. I couldn't remember the last time we'd found an animal in the very first pit. Exhaling, I watched my breath hang in the air and kept my teeth clamped against the meat strip to keep from shivering.

We were less than a month away from the moons eclipsing and winter peered over our shoulders on mornings like these. *We should have escaped by now.* The thought threaded through my mind incessantly, but I wanted to keep

Yara near a healer for as long as possible, and our cache never seemed big enough. And then there was that sliver of hope, that there was still time to convince Iva that we didn't have to sacrifice the daeson. She hadn't even assigned guards to them yet. But every time I hinted at changing those boy's fates, like she'd changed mine, Iva clammed up. I knew better than to push her.

Patting Voru's flank, I coaxed the complacent vaiya up the trail. We skirted the next two pit traps as they remained concealed under carefully placed brush and leaves, identifiable only by the warning markings slashed into the smooth trunks of neighbouring trees. Upon approaching the fourth pit, we found it open and exposed, its camouflage of sticks and leaves swallowed up by the deep hole beneath. A glacial wind gusted at my back, and something shuffled loudly in the pit as it caught my scent. Turning back to the others, I nodded once and shrugged my spear off my shoulder.

Sidling to the edge of the hole, I frowned at the sight of a tunnel erupting halfway up the inside of the far wall. At the same time, the scar at my chest prickled and a rotten, wet stench rolled over the rim of the pit. Something white and fleshy shot over the edge of the trench, sending sticks flying as it slammed into my shin. A wordless, shocked cry burst from my lips, and I fell backwards still clutching my spear. The vaiyas blasted a warning call behind me.

"Wurm!" I screamed, scrambling back. "Wurm!"

Stocky tentacles caressed the crumbling edge of the pit, and the hunters behind me jolted into action, grunting as they hurled their spears over me. The projectiles whistled past my ears. I couldn't move. My leg burned like fire. With wide eyes and shaking hands, I pulled at my leggings and groaned as blood oozed from three crescent shaped cuts below my knee. Congealing, cloudy venom coated the wound.

Hunters streamed past me to stab at the wurm as it bucked and reeled silently. It thudded against the soil walls, oily blood spraying from its wounds, but the entire scene seemed far away, muted and unreal. *Clean the wound off. You are poisoned!* Clenching my teeth, I wiped my shin with the torn fabric of my leggings and then forced myself to stand.

A few hunters grabbed at the hissing vaiyas, holding their heads and covering their eyes to stop the birds from bolting. Someone clutched my arm and pulled me away from the pit. The wind changed and soon everyone was backing away, gagging and covering their noses as the stench of wurm overcame them. They'd wait for it to die from a sufferable distance.

"You all right?" Jin gulped. He still gripped my arm.

"It bit me," I hissed. "Damned thing bit me."

"It bit you?" Both Jin and I jumped at the sound of our father's voice. Hasev glanced at my leg, his brow knotted as he studied the shallow wound.

I swallowed. Nausea clawed its way up my throat, but mostly I gulped against the nervousness of speaking to Hasev. My father did not trade words with me often. "I'm fine, just a bit unsteady, that's all."

"You're a terrible liar," Jin chided. "I think you should sit down."

I shook my head, alarmed at the dizziness the gesture induced. *If I sit down, I might not stand back up.* "I want to see it." Patting my brother on the shoulder, I pushed away from him and hobbled toward the pit. Even with my breath held, the stench made my eyes water so profusely I had to wipe them before peering over the edge.

The wurm lay with tentacles twitching, white body riddled with spears, a curled carcass twice as thick as a man and much longer. Beside it, a half-consumed harek hung impaled on one of the stout spikes lining the pit. *Guides, it ate it, armour and all. It would have done the same to me.* I pressed a hand against my stomach, memories of the wurm dream flooding my senses. My gaze flitted to the entrance tunnel in the wall opposite me, and an irrational fear gripped me as my mind imagined a white demon squeezing out of the hole to finish the job its predecessor had started.

I shuffled backwards, returning to Jin and Hasev, a cold sweat beading on my brow. "Have you ever heard of one attacking like that, attacking a human?"

Hasev shook his head solemnly.

"I think you should sit down," Jin repeated.

As if in answer, my leg muscles jittered and then cramped. Jin eased me to the ground.

"Get a vaiya over here!" Hasev bellowed over his shoulder.

"Is he all right?" someone asked. I didn't know who and couldn't seem to open my eyes.

"We need to get him back to camp."

Their voices mashed together, grinding at my nerves like broken flint. My head started to pound. *This is how they kill their prey, paralyze them and eat them as they lay. This is how I die in the dream.*

Vaiyas bawled above me while hunters milled around. Jin and Hasev's voices faded, and then... nothing but darkness.

"It's all right. He's awake. He's back." Someone slapped my cheek. "You with us, Akrist?"

My eyes fluttered open, and I frowned at the sharpening image of my brother. "What happened?" I croaked. Leaves rattled above me and the solid press of a tree trunk pinched between my shoulder blades.

"We lost you for a second there." He leaned closer and muttered in my ear. "You're scaring the shit out of me. Stop it, would you?"

"I can't feel my leg." Grasping at my tingling thigh, my hand bumped into something and I looked down to see one of the vaiya's reins wound around my leg, digging into the flesh.

"We're trying to slow down the poison. Don't move." He pressed a hand against my shoulder as I rolled to one side.

"The smell is making me sick, and it's driving the vaiyas crazy."

"I know." Jin glanced over his shoulder. "We're getting you out of here. Just breathe for a second all right? You're as white as that bloody wurm."

Dizziness eddied and pooled in my head, swamping my senses as I sat up. I squeezed my eyes shut, gripped by the peculiar sensation that something might spill out of me if I opened them. Sagging against my knees, I sucked slow breaths of air and counted my teeth with my tongue until the nausea passed. A slow, gathering pain oozed through my body, but my mind was clearing. Either the tourniquet was working, or the venom had already diluted.

My skin crawled with the awareness of several sets of eyes trained on me. *I wish Iva were here.* The thought flitted unbidden through my head, a forlorn child's wish. Since we'd re-united, the storyteller had been too occupied helping Fraesh care for Na-Jhalar and dealing with the day-to-day at the camp to join the daily hunt.

"I'll take Voti back to camp," I said.

"Of course." Hasev nodded.

"I'll come with you," Jin added.

"No, I'll go."

I raised my head to identify the volunteer, and my stomach twitched as I focused on Arsu. A few hunters shifted on their feet and tossed uneasy glances between her and me. I remembered her foot against my ribs as a boy, and her fist in Yara's hair.

"I'm not feeling well," she said into the awkward silence. "I was thinking of going back anyway."

"Fine. Wonderful. Let's go, then." I extended my hand to Jin, and as he helped me to my feet, he pinned me with a warning look.

Voti crouched before me and clucked with concern. With Jin's aid, I persuaded my shaky legs to walk and settled into place behind the draped gazelle. Arsu swung up onto Vust, and the animal squawked once and stamped his foot.

I clucked my tongue, and Voti rose and swung away from the hunters. Vust followed behind. With the dead wurm in its hole at our back, I couldn't shake the feeling that I stumbled toward a trap of another kind. Exhaustion settled on my shoulders, raw and heavy. Instinctively, I pressed my legs tighter against Voti's sides, even as I swayed in my seat. Scattered birdsong and the chatter of wind-tossed leaves drifted in to accompany the soft steps of our vaiyas. *Come on, Akrist. Stay awake.*

"You think you're quite smart, don't you?" Arsu stated flatly.

Oh Nasheira, here we go... I shook my head, but stopped as the movement aggravated the throbbing at my temples. "Not smart enough to avoid a wurm bite."

"You think no one knows what you are doing."

Her words hit me like ice. My chest constricted and I waited for Arsu to elaborate.

"I know. I'm no fool. You and that hen of a storyteller think you can take over our camp, overthrow the Speaker, and poison every mind in his power."

I sighed, privately relieved. "Arsu—"

"I won't let it happen."

My leg cramped again, contracting and twitching below the leather band. I bit the inside of my cheek, gripped my thigh and answered, "Arsu, I assure you, I want nothing to do with leading the camp."

"Don't lie to me, wurm!" she spat.

Voti hissed beneath me as answering rage rose in my belly, smothering fatigue and pain, burning up my throat. My teeth clicked shut, and I drew myself up to physically curb the guttural reaction. I turned, despite the dizziness, and locked gazes with the woman. "Let's not do this now."

Vust dipped his head and snapped at his rider's toes.

I smiled as Arsu flinched and snatched her foot back before composing herself with all the coldness of a crocodile. "Someday your stupid birds will not be here to save you."

It's been a pleasure chatting with you too. I turned, reigned in my emotions and steadied my mount with a pat on the neck. We did not speak for the rest of the ride, but I couldn't stop thinking, *if Iva and I did overthrow Na-Jhalar, the whole camp would follow us, Yara and I wouldn't need to escape. I could save these daeson and every other that came after them and Arsu would be powerless to stop us. She's nothing without her brother's power, nothing but empty threats.*

"Can you not keep yourself whole for one day, boy?" Fraesh ushered me into his hut. I tried to smile, but couldn't find the energy.

"When did it bite you?"

"Not long ago. An hour, maybe?" I leaned against his doorway, and the healer turned to appraise me with a curt glance. He shot a finger toward his tidy sleeping mat.

"Sit before you fall down. Let's take a look."

I obeyed, easing myself down and resting on my elbows as Fraesh rolled up my leggings to survey the damage. While the flesh around the shallow wound blushed an angry red, the rest of my leg looked pasty and blue. Fraesh dabbed at it with a damp cloth.

"Did you lose your senses, after it bit you?"

"For a few minutes, Jin said." I cringed as Fraesh smeared junab over the cuts. "Have you ever heard of a wurm attacking someone like this?"

Fraesh puckered his lips and shook his head. Wisps of grey hair floated around his face. "Not unprovoked. Years back, Darvie got scraped when he speared one of the ghastly things. The cut throbbed a bit, gave him a wicked headache, but it was his own fault for not staying out of the way. Let's get this tourniquet off. Wurm venom is quick acting, and I think you're past the worst of it."

I cupped a hand over my eyes and grunted as pins and needles fired up my leg in response to Fraesh loosening the leather band.

"I wish I had gifen to give you." He rubbed his palm across his forehead. The aeni charged a fortune for the narcotic plant since the fire on the mountain wiped out most of the stock. We could no longer afford to trade for it.

"I hate the stuff, anyway." I tried to grin, despite the image of a gifen-wasted Na-Jhalar festering in my head. It wasn't the bitter taste of the leaves that repulsed me, it was the fear that perhaps, deep down, I was as weak as our Speaker, as easily hollowed out by the numbing herb. I didn't want to find out.

Fraesh patted my hand and turned to rummage through his healer's bag.

A shadow eclipsed the doorway, a tow-headed boy with a tear-streaked face and a split lip. He fired me an uncertain glance before resting his gaze on Fraesh. I struggled to place the boy until he spoke.

"Apa," he whimpered.

Baline's boy. Galeed. What would he be? Nearly twelve now?

He'd join the hunters soon. I'd seen him wrestle boys nearly twice his size, but I'd never seen him cry.

"*Guides,* child! I thought you went gathering with your mother. What are you—" Fraesh stopped short, crossed the hut quickly and clutched the boy's chin. "What happened?"

Fresh tears rolled down Galeed's nose, and he grabbed Fraesh's wrist with both hands, his blue eyes damp and urgent. "Apa, you have to come. He's hurting her, and I tried to stop—"

"Who, Galeed?"

I sat up, a pang of premonition prickling my stomach.

"Jhalar is—"

"Use his title when you say the Speaker's name!" Fraesh interrupted with a hiss.

"But he's hitting Mom! He's hitting her!"

"Fraesh," I croaked, pushing to my feet.

"I tried to stop him, Apa." Galeed pulled away from the healer's grip and wiped his chin, his throat working frantically.

A strangled yell sounded from the centre of camp, but Fraesh didn't move.

"Fraesh, let's go." I grabbed his shoulders.

"Ama is fighting with him. I think she's going to kill him." Galeed spoke to me now, and I nodded once.

"Fraesh, let's go!" I barked, and the healer twitched and stumbled over his feet as I steered him out the door.

My eyes blurred as sunlight assaulted them. Swift pain stabbed through my head, spattering my vision with black spots. I swallowed against the circling dizziness and hobbled beside Fraesh.

Laughter. High pitched, hysterical laughter dipped down into low screams before relapsing into barking, hollow mirth. Iva's yells blasted frenetic and unintelligible, punctuated by the thick thud of fists slamming into flesh.

Fraesh gripped my elbow as we limped through the camp's interior huts, flanked the smoking main hearth, and burst through the doorway of the Speaker's hut.

Chaotic darkness greeted us, black as ink and infused with the putrid scent of feces and rotten teeth. My stomach lurched, and I clapped a hand over my nose. Na-Jhalar's insane, grating laughter lodged between my ears, ricocheting through the soft tissue of my brain.

I groped ahead tentatively and tripped over something solid. Breathing through my mouth, I used both hands to identify the obstacle. My fingers swept over flesh, hair and then something sticky. "Fraesh, let in some light!" I yelped.

The healer shuffled behind me, clutched at the door flap and yanked it aside. A bar of pale light swept across the hut's interior, flashing over the features of Fraesh and Iva's daughter, Baline. She lay crumpled and naked at my feet. Her blonde hair fanned in a dusty halo around her head, stained by streaks of dark blood. Ribbons of red oozed out of her nose, across her cheeks and into her ears. "Oh Guides," I gulped, kneeling despite my throbbing leg, and laying one hand over her chest scar while holding the other above her mouth.

The healer made a noise that sounded like someone had kicked him in the stomach. Ripping the door flap from its frame, he fell to his knees and crawled to my side, draping the hide over his exposed daughter.

"She breathes, Fraesh." I nodded once. "She breathes."

Pushing away from the pair, I stood and limped toward the back of the hut. Two figures lay entangled like sparring bucks.

"Iva," I called.

The storyteller straddled Na-Jhalar. Pinned and kicking sporadically, the Speaker exposed his bloody teeth like a hyena, giggling and rolling his eyes even as his head cracked from side to side under Iva's blows. He didn't hit back. His flaccid arms lay spread like a martyr's, and his face looked like minced meat.

"Iva!" I hollered and grabbed her arm to pull her back, but the woman's strength shocked me. Despite my effort, she continued to pound Na-Jhalar methodically like dough.

Squeezing words out between gritted teeth, she drove each word home with another punch. "Never-Touch-Her-Again-Never-Touch-Her-Again!"

"Iva. Enough!" I clamped my arm around her neck and heaved backward. Hands clawed at my forearm, at my face.

"Stop!" Galeed pushed at his Ama's chest.

I hauled back harder.

Iva's body tensed beneath my arms and, for a horrified moment, I thought she'd hit Galeed.

"Stop it," the boy pleaded again.

"It's over, Iva," I added and just like that, it was. The storyteller sagged, and Galeed ducked under her arms, sniffling as Iva looked down at him in bewilderment before returning the hug.

I let go and stepped around the two. Na-Jhalar's beady eyes trained toward the sobbing child, and I resisted the urge to kick the man as I moved to block his view.

He laughed again, high and horse-like.

Mother of Yurrii, he is inhuman. A shiver trickled down my spine, and adrenaline leached out of me, leaving nothing behind but gravid exhaustion. *Do not fall down.*

For long moments the hut settled with the sound of Fraesh patting Baline's cheek and calling her name, Galeed murmuring to Iva, and Na-Jhalar's frothy breathing. We remained suspended like that for a while, floating in the cold aftermath of the incident, minds unreeling and thoughts smoothing out.

Then a shadow slipped through the doorway. Na-Jhalar's

face shifted from a smug sneer to astonishment and some-thing else, something darker. Longing. Lust.

"Delani," he murmured.

I turned to see a flash of dark hair combs and honey brown curls, the curved figure of Yara frozen in the entryway.

"Do not speak to her!" I spat, stomach recoiling at the carnal spark in Na-Jhalar's eyes as he licked his thick lips. Leaping over Fraesh and Baline, I grabbed Yara's elbow and pulled her outside.

"Akrist?" she puffed.

"What are you doing?" I fought to keep my voice low.

"They told me to come—"

"Who told you to come?"

Yara clammed up defensively under my interrogating stare.

"Who, Yara?" I shook her arm, immediately regretted it.

"Arsu did," she offered.

I pulled her to me fiercely, and she stood in my embrace rigid and unresponsive until I kissed her forehead and exhaled a hollow, shaking breath.

Dark, searching eyes found mine. "What's wrong?"

"Stay away from Arsu."

She stiffened at the order.

"Please, promise me, Yara."

"I promise."

But you cannot promise what is beyond your control.

CHAPTER TWENTY-THREE

The next morning, as I lay crippled by a persistent and painful headache, Iva came to sit with me. No doubt Fraesh had sent her to covertly check on his patient. For a long while, we lingered in silence before the storyteller finally scratched her nose and spoke.

"It is a bad omen, a wurm attacking like that."

I nodded.

"Perhaps it was what your wurm dream has been warning you about?"

"No," I croaked, and my lips twitched into a humourless smile. "I dreamt of the damned thing last night, same as always. I think it warns me of something greater than a bite on the leg and a headache."

It's how I die, Iva. I'm sure of it.

The macabre words slithered through my thoughts but not past my lips. Nothing passed between us except the measured sound of breathing. I turned an empty clay cup in my hands, unable to meet Iva's examining brown eyes. Instead, I fixed my gaze on her hands. They looked older than the rest of her, like gnarled tree roots wrapped in thin, blotched skin. Her knuckles were swollen and she picked at the fresh scabs. She was lucky not to have broken any fingers on Na-Jhalar's face. *This is not the woman I remember from my youth, full of vigor, a natural leader. Look at how much our Speaker has taken from her.*

As if reading my thoughts, Iva spoke. "I shouldn't have let Baline and Celi help care for him, after they stepped down. I —I thought he was too far gone to hurt anyone again. He forgot Baline wasn't his chani anymore. That's what she told me when she woke up. When she resisted him, he started hitting her." Her eyes hardened. "This isn't how it's supposed to be. Nasheira is *supposed* to pick just leaders." She shook her head, her shaky exhalations filling the space between us several times before she murmured "I would have killed him if you hadn't stopped me."

I would have let you if Galeed hadn't been there. The dark thought crawled through my aching mind despite my efforts to ignore it. Instead, I said, "He is not a man. He hasn't been for a long time."

"I thought he'd be dead by now." Iva's voice cracked.

The sound of it made my stomach drop. Our storyteller was a rock. I'd never seen her lose control, not until yesterday, and somehow this small sign of weakness felt like the first fracture of an avalanche.

Raking her hands through her hair, she licked her lips and blinked at the floor. "Nasheira help me for wishing it, but I thought he'd be long dead. I didn't think we'd have to take care of him for this long. When the fire came, we ran out of gifen for weeks and I was certain he would die. He had fits as it bled from his system. Did Fraesh tell you that? He'd shake and foam at the mouth, and I'd count every breath, hoping that the next would be his last. I *wished* for it."

"We have all wished for his death, Iva. Guides only knows how the man keeps hanging on." I swallowed. "Whether we are willing to admit it or not, none of us would grieve his passing. Do not punish yourself so."

"I question the Guides. I deserve punishment!" she said, and her gaze met mine. The absolute anguish I saw there rendered her momentarily unrecognizable. Raw fear peeked out from the husk of Iva's body, rattling through hollow spaces that had always before been filled with her liberal laughter.

I leaned forward and gripped Iva's arm. My headache responded fiercely to the movement, pounding against the back of my eyes. Scraping at my last reserves of strength, I pasted a reassuring smile on my lips and spoke with a conviction I did not feel. "Maybe that's why Nasheira sent me—to set you on the path as leader. Maybe Na-Jhalar's time is over."

My stomach coiled at the hopeful look on her face. I was playing a dangerous game. But I wanted Iva and the camp to thrive after I left.

"Arsu has been pestering me," Iva said. "She wishes to take over her brother's care, says it is 'her path.'"

Oh does she now? I recalled Arsu's wicked grin on the uncomfortable trip home yesterday. Saliva filled my mouth, and dizziness swamped me. *Breathe. Think. Ignore the headache. Something important is happening and you're not grasping it.* "She wishes she was Speaker. She always has, hasn't she?" I clicked the clay cup against my teeth despite the shivers it sent up my skull.

Iva shrugged and nodded. Her gaze flitted to my chest. "One cannot be Speaker unless they've been marked."

"One can lead though, using the Speaker as their puppet, and that is what Arsu wishes to do." *That is what she's accused us of doing.*

"Does she have followers?" Iva almost sounded frightened.

I swallowed and forced my sluggish mind to chug through memories like small stones under the current of my headache. "My little brother hangs on her every word. I don't know who else. I am not the one with my finger on the pulse of our people. That's always been you, Iva."

She shook her head. "My whole family hasn't been out of that bloody Speaker's hut for weeks. Pau and Yurrii could fall from the sky and we would not know it."

Something like ice slid down my spine as I spoke my next words. "So let Arsu do it." *Shit. What did you just say?*

Iva's head shot up. "What?"

"Let Arsu care for Na-Jhalar. She has no idea what she's in for. And you need to be free of him. When Na-Jhalar dies, our people will have to choose between Arsu and you. And the smart ones, they'll follow you. They respect you."

The storyteller sighed and scrubbed at the wrinkles on her forehead. "Arsu's tongue is as venomous as a wurm. If we give her this, she can persuade the camp's majority to believe anything she says is the word of Nasheira."

"Unless you and I lead together. A storyteller and a younger Speaker." The words came out of my mouth before I could stop them, and hope rose in my chest, filling it. I could convince Iva to stop the sacrifices. I was sure of it. "Look at the energy your *entire* family has poured into caring for the Speaker. It's not a one-person job, and it's eating you all alive, Iva. Arsu has no idea. She thinks she can lead Na-Jhalar around as easily as a hobbled vaiya, and that the world will bend their ear to her and ask her guidance. Give her what she asks, let her take the burden, and Na-Jhalar will be like a stone tied around her foot. He'll pull her under." *He's nearly pulled all of us under and it's time to come up for air. The people need you back, as a hunter, as a leader.*

I watched my friend, my *mentor* as she chewed on her lower lip and scowled at the wall, weighing her options.

"You can't do this anymore, Iva. You can't make Fraesh do this anymore, or your *daughters*."

Iva crumpled. Her brown eyes welled up and spilled tears in tracks down her tanned, taut face, like a rush of rainwater trickling across cracked earth. I could not tell if they were tears of defeat or release.

It's done now. Whatever I've set into motion here, I can't take it back.

Iva left without another word and, as she shuffled out of my hut, exhaustion rushed in to replace the void. My thoughts turned to sap, and I couldn't even consider the course I had just set. Sleep robbed my senses. Even my fear of the ever-occurring wurm dream piqued by yesterday's attack was not enough to keep me awake.

CHAPTER TWENTY-FOUR

"You told Iva to let Arsu have Na-Jhalar?" I could barely see Yara in the darkness, could not read her face. We'd walked to the northern boundary of camp, trying to clear my headache with fresh air. Clouds obscured the brother moons and wrapped us in darkness.

"Yes." I stared back, gauging her reaction in the thickening dark.

Yara remained still and composed as marble as she asked, "Why?"

"I think I can convince her, Yara," I whispered. "To save the daeson. We wouldn't have to leave. We could stop the sacrifice. Arsu can have Na-Jhalar. She'll think she has the power but everyone loves Iva. They'll follow her, and if I'm at her side." I shrugged. "They'll follow me, too. We could save all the daeson."

"Or kill us all." Yara shook her head, blinking rapidly. "Has Iva agreed to any of this? You've spoken to her?"

I sagged at the weight of her words. "I will."

"When?" her voice cracked. "Sacrifice is in three weeks. What are you waiting for, Akrist?"

Silence swirled like the wind of an oncoming storm between us. Neither of us spoke as inevitability crackled like static between us. *It would be safer to leave. Take the certainty of saving four boys over the idea of saving them all. You can't change the world, Akrist. You've always been invisible.*

Yara spoke again, her voice small and careful like she was creeping onto a slab of ice. "I need to know."

The realness of it all gripped me by the throat and shook me. "I'll talk to Iva tomorrow. If she won't see reason. We'll leave on the eve of the new moons. Iva may not agree with me, but she won't betray me either. I'm sure of that."

"That's five nights from now." Yara's voice sounded soft, pensive.

The wind crawled up our backs from the north, as dry and brittle as the leaves that blew before it. Soft curls tickled my face, and I felt the cool hardness of one of Yara's combs pressing into my cheek as she leaned into me and shivered. Blankets of clouds above us churned and parted. Moonlight spilled down the valley and camp below. Huts, smokehouses and hanging racks emerged pale and skeletal, marbled and wavering like underwater mirages. I blinked up at the cold faces of Pau and Yurrii—so damned close together.

"I hope you know what you're doing, Na-Akrist." Yara whispered.

THE NEXT EVENING, Iva led us in evening prayer. Arsu stood beside Na-Jhalar, and I clamped my teeth at the ever-present half sneer splitting her narrow face. Blessedly, halfway through Iva's storytelling, Na-Jhalar projectile vomited onto his sister's tunic. Arsu, choking on rage, hauled our incapacitated Speaker back into his hut as the rest of us ducked our heads and choked on laughter.

"You were right," Iva confided later, in her hut. I'd pulled her aside on the pretense of resetting a spearhead. Fraesh bustled out the door wordlessly as soon as I came in, but not without squeezing my arm as he went by.

"I have my mate and my daughters back," Iva said. "Better he drags down Arsu than us, and he's doing a fine job of it already."

My stomach clenched and I could barely breathe as I looked up from rewinding the spearhead, but Iva didn't notice, her face bunched by laugh lines and her teeth flashing in the lamplight. "Ah Guides!" she whooped and then guffawed so loudly that she snorted.

"What?" I gulped. *I can't do this. I can't ask her to change the world for me.*

The storyteller grabbed my forearm and leaned in to confide in a gulping whisper. "Last night Arsu came in here asking for help because the mighty Speaker..." Iva chortled. "...had shit himself."

Nervous laughter gripped me. It felt wrong to laugh, but we dissolved into helpless giggles until we caught our breath. "What did you tell her?" I finally gasped.

"I said: 'Did Nasheira not send you a vision about that?' You should have seen her face! Guides, she looked like a fish swallowing air. Fraesh choked on his stew when he heard."

"You didn't go with her?"

Iva waved her hand dismissively. "No, she wanted the job. Let her have it. Let her have it all. It feels good to be rid of the pair of them." She clamped a hand on my shoulder and studied me with animated brown eyes. "I should have done it long ago. Thank you, Akrist. I feel ten years younger."

Her gaze flicked to my chest and her eyes grew interrogative. The blessed lightness that had alighted in my chest fled like a flushed bird. *It's time. Tell her now. She'll back you. She'll save them.*

"And you look ten years older," she sighed as I grappled with my words. "How are you doing?"

"The wurm bite was shallow. The poison passed quickly." *Coward. Damn it. Just tell her.*

"You know that's not what I meant."

I bit down, surprised at the hot tongues of rage curling in my gut. When I could unclench my jaw, I answered her in a whisper. "You meant to ask how I am dealing with the coming butchery of four boys? Because that's what I've come to talk to you about."

Iva's hand slid from my shoulder. She broke her gaze, looked at the doorway behind me before murmuring, "You know I can do nothing to stop it."

My stomach clenched. "*Any* of us could stop it, Iva." I raised my voice and the storyteller's shoulders hunched as she winced. "Any one of us. Our people will listen to you. They'll stop this madness if we ask them to."

"They won't. They would see it as defying Nasheira's will."

"They are just boys, just little boys." Sinew cut into my hand as I lashed the spearhead to the shaft. "You said you valued my advice. You said people would follow me. If you really do think I am a Speaker, *listen to me.*"

Clammy silence descended between us. Out of the corner of my eye, I saw Iva staring down at her wrist, thumb rubbing over the blue circle tattoo and embedded pebble within. *How dare she balk now?* I twisted the lashing hard enough to whiten my knuckles and measured my breathing in the silence.

"Do you remember when I taught you to play tavi as a boy?"

Through the bars of a cage before sacrifice. How could I forget it?

"You asked me if I had a daeson. And I said yes," the storyteller whispered. "Besheck." She swallowed. "My son, my first son. We loved him."

"Don't." I swung my gaze back up to Iva, not trusting myself with more than a single word, but the storyteller looked through me, oblivious.

"What was not to love?" She shrugged. "He was a beautiful baby. Healthy, all fat and dimples and grinning like he owned the world." Iva spread her hands, cradling the ghost of the image in his arms. Her expression soured. "Baline was not even two. Do you know how hard it is to tell your two-year-old daughter she is not allowed to touch her baby brother? Do you know how difficult it was for me, forbidden to hold my own child in my arms?"

"Don't speak to me of difficult," I hissed.

She flushed and bowed her head. "We were young, younger than Darvie and Elba and Mira. Besheck was born eight—" Iva choked, cleared her throat and continued. "Eight months before the sacrifice. We spoke, Fraesh and I. We tried to find a way to save him, but if we failed, Guides, even if we succeeded, where would it have left Baline? Hasev had not yet met Aella, and he was wild and untamed in those days. We could not rely on him to care for her if we were banished." His eyebrows raised. "In all likelihood, they would have branded Hasev and Baline as well. Even if they didn't, our girl would be shunned, parentless, an outcast. No better than a daeson."

"So you chose her over him."

Iva's gaze met mine, pleading, desperate. "I'm not an evil woman, Akrist. I loved my son. I thought we could save him. I wanted Fraesh to desert with me. Baline was young, but I was cocky, certain of my ability to provide for my family in the wild." She paused and pursed her lips. "The weather turned early that year," she rasped. "And the fall hunt was bad. It was *so* cold. Baline would never have survived if we left. None of us would have. So, I paid an Ani. Fraesh gave him his rarest medicine, and I gave him a dragon scale." A deep frown creased Iva's face. "I'd found it, and we had no Speaker yet, and the Aeni, they will trade their teeth for them. We paid her, and we told her where our sacrifice would take place. She promised us she would take blankets and food to the daeson, and after the two days had passed, we would desert our camp and return for them. With all the camps on the move, we'd be able to join another. They couldn't turn away daeson that survived. They couldn't turn us away if we made it past the two days."

My throat ached. Iva's eyes were bright with tears, and I wanted to tell her to stop, that I didn't want to hear the rest, but the words swelled and tangled in my throat.

"On the eve of the eclipse, we took Besheck and all the others to the north. He was crying. It was so cold."

Stop it. I raked my hands through my hair. *Please Iva, stop it.*

"Fraesh was shaking just as hard as I was. I didn't know if I could do it—make the cut. But I knew if I didn't, someone else would. Fraesh had given me a rust-coloured powder to put on the wound to stop the bleeding. I coated my hands with it and, when the time came, I just gave him a little prick, enough to make him howl and bleed a little. I thought we could get away with that." She shook her head, trying to clear the memory. "There was an elder, she inspected them all after and stopped at Besheck. She told me if I didn't do it right, she'd cut him for me. I couldn't move until the elder stepped toward Besheck with a knife. I pushed her aside and did it myself. Then I picked him up while he was still screaming and hugged him, rubbing the powder into the wound so no one could see. They had to peel him out of my arms as both of us screamed."

"Iva," I begged.

"I left him there. I left my *baby* there in the cold. And I didn't even look back because I was sure the Ani would come. My hands were stained—how much was from the powder and how much was from his blood, I don't know."

Iva stared at her hands as though they were still coated in blood. We stood frozen, facing each other as the storyteller bit her lip.

"What happened?" I cursed myself for asking.

Tears spilled down Iva's cheeks and her face twisted into a grimace. "When we returned—" A deep, sob choked her. "There was so much blood, and there were wurm tracks everywhere. No blankets, no anything. They were gone. They were all gone. The Ani never came. Or if she did, it was too late."

I let the woman cry. I gripped the spear and swallowed and tried, unsuccessfully to hold back the tears that spilled from my own eyes. When she finished, when she lifted her raw gaze back to me, I spoke.

"What are you telling me, Iva?"

She gripped my free hand even as I flinched. "I'm telling you that you're right. I've never believed these sacrifices to be Nasheira's will. She's a mother too." She sagged. "But I can't do it again, Akrist. I've already lost a son. I'm not strong enough to lose my daughters or Fraesh by defying our laws, and I don't want to lose you either. Don't ask me to do this. I can't."

"You know the choice you leave me with then?" I rasped.

"Don't tell me. I'll say I never knew, and it will be the truth." Her eyes shone with tears and she gripped me in a fierce hug.

I clung to her because it was the last time I'd ever hold Iva. Then, I straightened, turned from Iva and left. When I flipped open the door flap, Arsu crashed into me.

"Iva." She bared her teeth and looked past me. "I need Iva. Is she in there?"

I kept walking.

I swore I wouldn't sleep that night. I paced the western hillside like a prowling vaiya, threading between the smokehouses, startling the fire tenders drowsing at their posts. Finally, when an icy rain pushed in from the north, and my nostrils stung from acrid smoke mingled with winter wind, I retreated to my hut where Yara already slept. Rain drummed against the woven roof, dripped through and patted insistently at my shoulder. I shifted on my bedroll, pulled the blanket over Yara, and closed my eyes.

When the wurm dream found me that night, as the foul creature crossed my threshold, its bulges gleaming in the watery moonlight, I heard a baby crying. My eyes watered from the stench of wurm and I lay paralyzed as always, unable to move as the thing chuffed across my floor, feelers wriggling. But the crying pulled at me, jagged and urgent. I knew it was Besheck, Fraesh and Iva's daeson. He sounded so helpless, so small. *He's just outside,* I thought. And as the wurm came for me, as the first feeler feathered over my stomach and latched on, I lunged for the door.

I DIDN'T HUNT the next day. I mumbled something about a sick stomach and ducked back into my hut with my morning tea as the other hunters filed northward and Yara left with the gatherers. In truth, I doubted my capacity to feign normalcy. I strode through camp edgy and off centre, still stalked by Iva's abandonment and last night's dream, and the cold anxiety of slipping and giving something away. *Don't wait for the new moons. Leave now. Tonight. You've made enough*

mistakes. Stay out of sight today. Tell Yara when she returns. Leave as soon as the camp sleeps.

I checked our caches one last time. Then I took Vax east, delved deep into the damp, mossy old forest, where the woods pressed close as a womb and it was easy to assume that no one had touched the place since Nasheira made it. Surely then, no one could touch me here either.

Dismounting, I sank up to my ankles in spongy moss and breathed deeply of the place. The earthy, dark smell filled my nostrils, a clean incense. Sparse sunlight leaked through the canopy, dappling the forest floor in wedges of green. I soaked in the quiet. No bird song, only the muted creaks, and shifts of small, careful creatures. Even Vax kept stoutly silent at my back, shifting, breathing, but unusually still. I slowed my breathing to match his, dropped my shoulders and tried to clear my mind. Nasheira knows how long we stood like that until my legs ached and my feet curled like they were sprouting roots into the verdant moss.

Without speaking, the old bird nudged his beak under my arm and pressed his big head against my ribs. I smoothed his crest absently and whispered into the sacred silence. "I can't do this."

"Play." Vax's simple, one-word answer brought a smile to my lips.

"I don't want to play, not right now."

"No." He straightened and fixed his gaze on me. "Prrraaay."

"Pray?" Swallowing, I frowned at Vax, but he pulled away from me to pick at his foot. I watched him preen, waited for an explanation, but soon my eyes ached from staring, and my bird offered no further answer. "Pray," I repeated with a sigh.

So I spent my afternoon with my knees pillowed by the carpet of moss and my intentions emptied into the silence. It was a good silence, the considerate calm of a listening friend.

When Vax and I finally pulled ourselves from the place, a certainty filled me. I'd done my best to protect Iva and Fraesh, it was time to protect my own family. We'd leave it all behind tonight.

❧

EXCEPT WE DIDN'T LEAVE that night. Sweet Nasheira, how different our lives might have been if we had, but Yara returned from gathering, pasty and ill. She spent the evening hours vomiting behind our hut on her hands and knees. I bit my tongue and boiled mint tea. *Tomorrow. She'll feel better tomorrow.* I convinced myself. I wiped her forehead with a damp cloth, and eventually we slept.

"Wake up!" The harsh hiss paired with a shake hard enough to click my teeth brought me instantly awake. *Protect Yara.* Jamming my heels against the floor, I rolled toward the arm that held me and drove my opposite shoulder up into my assailant. The shadow staggered, grunted and I twisted out of her grip, grasped under my bedroll and came up with a spearhead clutched in my fist. The lamplight guttered and jerked. As the pile on the floor scrambled back, I saw teeth bared, lips curled into a viperous sneer.

Yara is gone.

"Arsu," I breathed. *Snake.* "Where's Yara?"

"Guides!" she spat. "You sleep like a bloody corpse! I've already sent her to get Fraesh." As sleep cleared from my eyes, I noticed sweat beading her temple.

"Why?" I kept the spearhead raised. *Yara's sick. Arsu's lying.*

"It's Iva," she rasped. "You have to come."

I need to find Yara. "The Speaker is your job—"

"Please come!" Arsu squeaked in interruption, slunk toward me like a rat hedging for scraps. Mild disgust kept me from using the spearhead as her gaze slid to my chest.

The lamplight flared across her face. For a second I thought I glimpsed a twitching sneer, but it was gone so fast, and the light jumped now, throwing shadows across Arsu's face.

"There's no time," she said. "She's going to kill him. Please, I can't stop them. Help me."

Dropping the spearhead, I thrust my feet into boots and lunged out of my hut behind Arsu. The night cut into us, so cold my bare skin prickled and our boots crunched as we loped through camp. I hugged my chest and gritted my teeth as Arsu scuttled ahead of me, constantly turning back to check that I was following.

I half expected the woman to backtrack and tow me by the arm like an errant toddler, but then we closed on the hulking hut, and I heard it, the grunting punctuated by muffled, wet thuds, the low, keening cry.

A picture of Na-Jhalar's doughy face shredded to mincemeat soured in my mind. *Iva, this is not you. Do not kill him, not when you've just freed your family from him.* As we rounded to the entrance of the hut with its idly fluttering door flap, I remembered how Iva wore her bruises from the last time she'd lost her temper as a penance, when most would have worn them as a badge.

Arsu pulled back the door flap, held her lantern over her head and nodded at me. I shouldered forward, braced myself for the stench of rotten teeth and feces.

Blood, it smelled like blood.

"Iva!" I squinted and stumbled toward the silhouetted bodies grappling on the floor. "Iva, stop." I grabbed an arm and hauled back hard, expecting the rigid resistance of a woman wrapped in rage, but this body peeled back like a bloated leech. Unbalanced, I gripped the arm, stepped to brace myself and slipped in something slimy. The hut filled with a hollow, gurgling groan, and the body whose arm I held twisted toward me, teetered and swatted lazily at my right thigh.

I hissed at the unexpected jolting stab of pain, and then I saw the knife, bloody in Na-Jhalar's hand. Everything snapped into nauseating focus. Na-Jhalar, the man I held, not Iva. Na-Jhalar grinning, a macabre, dripping blade in one fist, and a gleaming, slack rope of sausage twisted and trailing from the other. My mind swung to the smoke huts and deft fingers stuffing sausage meat into casings, but the Speaker's gaze settling on mine snipped off the thought. Na-Jhalar's eyes were sharp and clear, completely unclouded by gifen. My gaze slid to his fingers fondling the kinked coils nested in his hand and then slowly, he pulled and the entrails draping behind him tightened. The room exploded into a raw, bubbling scream.

Iva lay curled on the ground, in the dust, writhing in the same dark, sticky pool I'd slipped in. Blood was everywhere. Her insides spilled out of her like a ball of wurms, Na-Jhalar pulling on her like a puppet.

"Iva!" I screamed. "Oh Guides, Iva!" I lunged forward on wooden limbs and Na-Jhalar, triggered by my movement, rolled back to Iva and planted the knife deep in her belly. Carelessly. Like he was claiming a slab of cheese.

"No!" I howled, slammed my elbow into his face. Teeth crumbled and broke off in my flesh. Iva's brown eyes locked onto mine as she gurgled and fumbled with the knife in her gut. I skidded to my knees, and grabbed her bloody hands. "No, don't touch it. Oh, Guides." Her fingers slid out of mine, pressed at her intestines, trying to put herself back together. *Oh, Guides.* Below her rib cage was all unravelling chaos, red and pooling, but above was Iva, my mentor, face chalky, gaze pinned to mine.

"Fraesh!" I shrieked. "Help. Yara!" Something smashed into the back of my head. Sparks swirled and settled around me. I was on the ground, my cheek at Iva's shoulder. "Yara," I blubbered, and a second crushing blow came. White dots swarmed my vision like fireflies. I smelled burnt hair, saw Arsu's lamp roll in between the storyteller and me. Then the snake's voice rasped at my ear.

"You're mine now, wurm. You, and those daeson, and your ripe little bitch are mine." My vision contracted. Arsu pressed something into my hand, and before the blackness swallowed me, I realized it was the knife.

CHAPTER TWENTY-FIVE

A soft, vibrating hum expanded, yawning into a louder, insistent pitch and scraping like cold stone against the insides of my skull, hauling me back to consciousness. I swallowed, tasted something bitter draining down the back of my throat. A weak whimper wound through my skull, grating against the ringing and striking sparks of discord as it went.

My shoulders felt oddly tight. Blinking, I tried to focus, but the sound, that shrill, aching sound, made everything fuzzy. I couldn't see past it. Licking my lips, I frowned at the gritty taste of caked dust. *Roll over. You're lying on the ground.*

Gathering myself, like a toddler bracing for his first step, I pushed, and white pain knifed through my eyes and thudded against the back of my head. I think I screamed, but the pain was louder, so much louder. *Something is wrong with me.* My skull felt like a cracked eggshell and my brains were the yolk.

Something's wrong. The thought clung, spread like mould. "Fraesh?" I croaked. *Why did I say Fraesh? Who is Fraesh? The* word lingered like a song on my lips, something that had been replaying in my mind, familiar, but elusive.

"Fraesh," I said it again, slowly. Testing it. *Where am I? Does he know?* "Fraesh." *Fraesh is a healer.* The thought leaked through the cracks of the humming in my head. *Fraesh is Iva's mate.* My chest tightened. *Iva. Iva is the storyteller. Iva is my friend, like a mother.* My throat closed. I swallowed and gulped small breaths of air.

The ringing in my head ceased. In the cold emptiness that followed, memories careened and split and roared down like an avalanche. "Iva!" I screamed, kicked my legs and flopped over onto my knees, biting my tongue against the sizzling pain.

"Iva!" I howled, fingers digging through the dirt, searching for the knife. If I could find it, I could stop Arsu, protect Iva, but my hands were tied behind my back.

This is the wrong hut. Iva isn't here.

Arsu had pressed the knife into my hand. *You're mine now, wurm. You and those daeson and your ripe little bitch...*

"Yara." I choked. *Oh Guides.* "Yara," I called again louder. Panic ignited in my sore head. *Vax.* If the vaiya heard me, he could push past the guard. I licked my lips, pressed my throbbing temple against the cold ground and shouted "Vax!"

Immediately, feet scuffed outside. The door flap flung open and light scoured the hut. I curled into a ball, squinting as my sentry grasped my hair. He shook me once, gently like you'd correct an errant child, but the jolt was enough to send me spiralling into semi-consciousness.

Only the voice, sharp with hatred, kept me pinned to the here and now. Quiet, yet still easily recognizable and articulate enough for a brow beaten prisoner to understand. "You call for that bird one more time, and I'll bury a spear in its belly, understand?"

Dero, my youngest brother.

"Understand?" he whispered, jerked my head back farther.

"Uh-huh," I slurred.

Dero dropped my head, and I lay reeling in the dirt, my eyes wide, my lips pursed, drowning in silence.

At sunset, when the bar of sunlight snuffed out from under my door, the vaiyas started calling. The wailing of the flock was unmistakable, that forlorn crescendo breathing into the crushed night sky. Their mourning cry echoed eerily through our hushed camp. The vaiyas could always sense it, that tremulous passing of a soul between our world and Nasheira's.

Iva is dead.

A howling, animal sob pressed past my lips, pulled everything out of me with it. I tried to hold it in, whatever the scream was spooling out, something that would be impossible to put back together again, but I couldn't. Couldn't stop it. Couldn't breathe. Rolling onto my stomach, I banged my head repeatedly against the cold ground, but it still took an excruciatingly long time for the darkness to close in and steal me from there.

DERO WOKE me with a kick to the ribs. I deflated with one eruptive wheeze. Curled up and coughing, I took several moments to differentiate the white maggot of my nightmares from my grinning wurm of a brother. When had that malicious, icy look set into his eyes? Dero took after our mother, Aella. He'd never held any fondness for me, but this, this unbridled hatred, when had it bloomed? How long ago had Arsu planted and tended this seed with venomous words and fertile lies?

My little brother hoisted me to my feet. As we exited the hut, he shoved me hard enough to make me stumble.

A large form closed from my left side. I turned and recognized Gideous's father by his blue eyes and his calm demeanour. Barth, his name was. Solid hunter. Quiet feet. Good man. If you didn't consider that he was going to let his first-born son be killed, that is.

At our approach, the small crowd clogged around the hearth fire parted like a vaiya flock with the scent of wurm in their nostrils. Hunter and gatherer alike pressed away from me, some avoiding my gaze and others meeting it with loathing.

I caught a glimpse of my father's face and shoulders above the crowd and swallowed hard. He made a move toward me but was held back by Arsu's supporters. His eyes mirrored my churning emotions, raw and red, brimming with helpless loss. I knew instantly that he did not believe I was a murderer. My legs jellied with relief. As I tripped and lost sight of Hasev, Dero spat and kicked the back of my thigh. "Move, wurm shit," he hissed.

I did. I limped past a deathly silent audience and into the dusty circle of the Speaker's hearth. Dero dug his fingers into my shoulder to stop me and I straightened to face Na-Jhalar, who was naked except for his dragon scale necklace. Arsu stood, hunched, half a step behind and at her brother's right ear, exactly where a serpent should be.

This is my hearing, I comprehended, taking in the gifen-stained spittle running down the Speaker's scarred chest and his comfortably clouded gaze. Arsu slunk forward, lips like stretched earthworms over her teeth and eyes hard with hunger. *And this is my judge.* Dread pooled in the pit of my stomach.

"Why is it tied?" Arsu asked Dero calmly.

It. My insides coiled. *Just like Aella calls me.*

"I told you to bind it," Arsu waved her hands in dismissal as if she could erase the red-faced stuttering boy before her, "so it wouldn't hurt itself. It can't harm itself here. What are we, animals?" She crossed behind me in one stride and started picking at the lashing around my wrists.

My neck prickled warily with the serpent at my exposed back, and Na-Jhalar at my front. I fought the urge to glance over my shoulder, struggled to avoid the wall of flesh in front of me, and instead set my skittish gaze over the heads of the crowd behind the Speaker.

"None of them are here. Your friends." Arsu's whisper rasped, barely audible over my breathing.

"What did you do to them?" I demanded through a clenched jaw. "Where's Yara?"

Arsu smiled. "She should be a juicy bit of chani again once we pop that pregnant belly of hers."

The bindings unravelled around my clenched hands.

Arsu leaned over my shoulder like a roosting raven and hissed into my ear with quick and perfect clarity. "Na-Jhalar would like to take her using the knife, I think. Cut her up like a sweet apple and—"

A red roaring in my ears washed out whatever came next.

I pivoted, my entire body's momentum driving my blow. The raw pain of my fist cracking into the side of Arsu's face was surprisingly satisfying, and her head snapped sideways before she pirouetted to the ground.

As I followed her down, I howled and punched the side of her head twice more before hands grappled me away. Words surfaced through the rapid current of noise seething past my lips.

"I'll kill you. I'll *kill* you! I swear it!" I raged against my captors, but they held me fast. I tried to ram my entire body into Arsu but they pinned me to the ground. I writhed and squirmed and fought, biting hands and kicking shins until someone's weight pressed against my neck so I couldn't breathe, and they only let up when my vision started to swim. My gasping, breathless words became a chant, a prayer, a promise. "I'll kill you."

Arsu's followers shook their heads at me, whispering among themselves, appalled at the savage before them. Then the yelling began. Shouts of "Wurm shit!" and "Kill it!" pattered around us, growing in intensity and volume.

"Enough." Barth's voice sounded muffled with my ear mashed against the ground. I gulped for air in the silence that followed.

Arsu stood to address the crowd. When she spoke, hot pain darted across her eyes, but she carefully enunciated every word. "It seems I made a mistake by unbinding this *thing*, by treating it as human.

"We all saw what it did when released. What any wurm would do. This is not a man. This is a Son of Pau, meant to be sacrificed long ago. This is a daeson who's hidden as a man among us only to strike at our heart, murdering our beloved storyteller." She paused for effect as people bowed their heads in sorrow. "This is Nasheira punishing us for stealing a sacrifice that was rightfully her due."

Arsu closed the distance between us until I could smell blood on her breath. My stomach squirmed at the scent. It flooded me with memories of the sharp, coppery smell from Na-Jhalar's hut that night, of my mentor laying broken, and I struggled to keep my eyes locked on Arsu's, attempted to coolly examine the dark flecks stamped into pale flinty irises, but the daeson in me choked. I broke from her gaze.

"Iva," she breathed. Her voice broke expertly. That she could speak *that* name, that she could rouse any semblance of sympathy for the woman whose death she orchestrated and summon false tears to those flat eyes, was abhorrent.

Heat rose to my face and my throat worked noiselessly.

Arsu continued with a slight smile that would have appeared sadly wistful to anyone else.

"Iva believed Nasheira marked this chest to balance the scales of its past. And look what happened to her." She shook her head dramatically. "We made a mistake, letting it live. This is not a man, never was. This is a daeson.

"We have let it live as a man. *Guides,* we have let it live as a *Speaker,* counselling our dear storyteller, leading amongst our hunters, revelling in a life without responsibility or submission to anyone. And look at how it has repaid our grace!" Arsu's arm swung like a stone ax back toward me, and the collective gaze of my camp settled on me as hungrily as they had last time the moons meshed. "Murderer!" Arsu hissed, and the mob pressed towards us, surging with shouts of "Kill it! Kill it!"

Somehow, I caught Aella's angular face at the back of the crowd, her long, lean body buffeted by elbows and arms around her, her eyes, as always, averted from mine.

Is this how she wanted to see me die? I wondered.

"Ah, but we are not murderers," Arsu crooned, and I wanted so badly to spit on her, but my mouth was dry. "We are children of Nasheira, and we obey her righteous law. It is not our duty to kill a man for his sins."

"Banish him!" someone else hollered.

"Yes. It must be banished, to be sure," Arsu replied. "It must be branded, so the rest of the world knows the gravity of its sin."

"Brand it!" This voice sounded like a carrion bird calling for blood. "Brand it, Arsu!"

For the first time, my gaze slid to the hearth fire. Smothered by mounds of cold, swirling ashes, no hot coals, no spearhead licked by flames and ready to carve a deep, smouldering "S" into my flesh. I frowned and felt suddenly fettered.

Arsu shook her head. "Yes, it should be branded for its sin. But not yet. Nasheira requires something more from a daeson," she said.

"No," I whispered as I finally realized her plan.

"For now, we feed it, shelter it, and keep it alive. We persevere until the moons eclipse, and we can offer Nasheira the sacrifice she has wanted for so long. We have let it live as a Speaker, now we let it die as a daeson. We will sacrifice it with the others."

"No!" I shouted as the crowd's crowing cries choked me out. My father's pale face turned away, and Arsu's dead eyes drank me in. Aella stood still as a stork in the roaring throng, huddled in on herself, her face upturned to the sky. She prayed, and even from a distance, I swore I saw cold dread swimming in her eyes.

CHAPTER TWENTY-SIX

I lost my grip on time and reason. I found myself back in my prison hut with no recollection of being escorted there. My right hand swelled. I couldn't move two of my fingers and suspected I'd broken them striking Arsu.

Faceless guards pushed cold, congealing plates of food across my floor. I don't know how many, or what the meals were. Sometimes I ate like an animal, shovelling food into my mouth with my left hand, aware only of the sharp tingling in my shoulders and the air licking my raw, recently untied wrists. Sometimes, the guards would leave the food and forget to untie me. I would sit and stare at the lumpy hills and valleys piled in the clay dish like it was a terrain I needed to memorize and map out in my head. I'd almost grasp the pattern of it before the door flap flicked open and the plate was whisked away.

Not all of my guards let me out of the hut to relieve myself. The ones who kicked plates of food under the door flap without untying me were the same who ignored my humiliated pleas for escort outside.

I tried to be as clean as the tiny hut allowed. Scooting my

back against the woven walls, I dug a hollow, and I buried my waste when I'd finished. But it had been days with no outer excursions. I had not bathed.

My head felt packed full of seed fluff, light, but somehow dense at the same time. The circle of my world became bound by grass walls and muted by a muffled buzzing between my ears.

The guards didn't touch me unless I tried to escape. I thought Arsu, or at least Dero, would come in to beat me. But Arsu didn't show her face at all, and Dero stayed outside when he was on guard duty. Arsu must have instructed him to leave me alone, and on the fifth day of isolation, I realized why.

Arsu wanted the camp to treat me as if I were already dead. You didn't beat a dead man. You kept his body safe until the funeral or, in my case, the sacrifice. If my captors had come in to hurt me, at least I would have felt *something*. As it was, the loneliness and despair suffocated me.

Arsu had ripped my tether from me like a fisherman carelessly tearing out a hook. My hope of saving the daeson, of returning to rescue Yara, floated out of my grasp now. I understood the resignation a drowning person must feel in those last seconds, but my seconds stretched into hours, and days. I couldn't find a way out.

There is no way out.

No matter how my mind crawled over the matter, no matter what angle I approached it from, I couldn't find an escape. I would be cut with the other daeson and branded. Even if I managed to somehow survive two days without bleeding out, without being gutted by wurms, I would be wounded, outcast, unclothed and weaponless. I would die, leaving Yara and our baby here. Dero, Arsu, and Na-Jhalar would hurt her because she loved me, because they itched to destroy everything connected to me.

The only thing keeping me going was knowing Yara would not want me to give up, not if there was the smallest chance I would survive.

One moonless night, my brother stood outside my tent, a shadowed silhouette.

"Dero?" A man's voice wafted through the door flap. "Arsu needs you at our hut. She said to wait outside until she calls you."

Gevi. The name clicked in my mind. It was Gevi, Arsu's mate.

Dero sniffed. "Watch *it* while I'm gone."

His boots crunched away from us.

Gevi held his breath until the sound of Dero's footsteps faded and then let it out in one wet, shaking sigh.

"We don't have much time," he said.

I frowned in the darkness. *Time for what? Is he talking to me?* The door flap brushed aside, and a swath of lamp light danced up the grass walls. I forced my breath out in even exhalations and kept my back to the entry, determined to feign unconsciousness. Then a small hand gripped my shoulder, and the scent of earthy cinnamon filled the room. Tears pricked my eyes as I breathed it in.

"Yara," I croaked.

"Akrist." Her voice wrapped around me low and smooth, yet snagging like someone had plucked a thread of it and wouldn't stop pulling. It carried every one of my aches and pains away with it.

I pushed up to my knees and twisted to face her, heard a small strangling sound catch in her throat.

Her pale face dropped.

Yara... My arms strained at their bonds. *Guides*, I wanted to hold her, wrap my arms around her and show her there was still some strength left in them. But all I could do was lean in, lose myself in her hair and cup my chin over her shoulder in an awkward embrace.

One of her hair combs scraped against my cheek. Over her shoulder, movement caught my gaze.

Gevi stood gripping a guttering stone lantern in one hand. The other hand clamped over his wrinkled nose and mouth.

I knew how I must look, how I must smell. *Oh Yara, I didn't want you to see this, to leave this as your last memory of me.*

"It's all right," I rasped. As I knelt, lost in her scent, Yara collapsed against me, her growing belly like an egg between us, and the rest of her as slight and frail as bird bones. I made sure she did not see the tears slip from my eyes as I forced my breathing to slow. I pressed my cheeks against her hair before she could lean back, but Gevi saw.

His hand dropped from his face. His lips pursed and he returned my nod with a small one of his own, before crouching to set the stone lamp on the floor inside the entry. Even as he pressed against his knees and straightened, Gevi's gaze held mine until the door flap closed between us.

Your enemy's mate. What is he doing?

"Let me untie you." Yara's shaking fingers ran over the bonds at my wrists.

I shook my head. "No. No time." I licked my lips, longed to kiss away the furrows on her forehead. "How long before Dero comes back?"

"We should have a few more minutes. Gevi put Arsu to sleep." Yara blinked at the ceiling and swiped fresh tears from her cheeks with her wrist.

"He never forgot." Yara's obsidian gaze flicked back to mine, and her fingers fluttered over her ripe stomach. "Gevi said he never forgot how you saved his baby."

My tired mind sifted through memories of sand. The

desert. Gevi and the bundle at his chest pinned under a broken-legged Vir. A lifetime ago.

"I've been trying—" Yara's hands pressed harder against her stomach, and she sagged forward, her eyes frantic. "I wanted to get to you. Jin and Hasev tried too, but Arsu has eyes on you all the time. None of them would let us pass."

"Yara..." *You shouldn't have come...* But I had wanted her to. "I love you."

She nestled into me again, wrapped her arms around my neck and clung there, swallowing sobs. "I love you, too," she choked.

"They will use that against both of us," I whispered into her ear, injected as much compassion as I could into the words so that she would listen. "They want to hurt me, understand? Long after I am dead, they want to hurt me, and they'll use you to do it. You have to get away."

Cold fingers pressed against my lips. Yara sat back and gulped, "I know." Even through the tears, her eyes flashed with determination.

"I cannot come." I choked on the sharpness of the words. They stabbed me as I tried to swallow them. Even if I made it out of camp now while Dero was gone, in my state, weak from hunger and captivity, I wouldn't make it far. "Maybe after..." I trailed off, unable to finish, unable to face it.

Yara kept nodding; her face pulled into a strained smile as she brushed my hair away from my forehead. "I know," she whispered.

And I realized she really did know. She knew I was going to die. This wasn't a rescue. It was farewell.

I shuffled towards her on my knees until her belly rested on my thighs, tucked her against my shoulder with my chin and lifted my elbows as she looped her arms around my rib cage. This time, when she slipped her small hands behind my back, I caught them both. *Oh Sweet Nasheira, how will you ever let her go?*

I kissed her eyelids, found her lips and drank her in desperately. We clung together, fusing, melting into each other's memorized spots and hiding from fate there. For a long time, I pressed my lips against the pulse at her neck and let tears run unchecked down my face. When our breathing finally synced and settled, when our chests rose and fell like waves on a lake, I felt the baby kick.

"You won't ever be without me, Yara," I spoke the words reverently, like a prayer.

She pressed her forehead to mine. We stayed like that, silent, feeling our unborn child fidgeting between us for several moments.

"I didn't do it." I winced as my clumsy words broke the perfect silence.

"I know." Yara's voice resonated, deep and hollow and already far away.

"You will tell our child I didn't do it?"

"I will tell stories of how brave, strong, and loving you were. Our child will know you."

I ducked my head and blinked rapidly. "Fraesh..."

"He sent you this." Yara's hands peeled away from mine. She reached into the front of her blouse, flipped her fist open in her lap and stared down at a small pouch rolling in her palm. "He said it will stop the bleeding and..." I watched her wrestle for composure. "It's small enough to hide in your palm when they come for you tomorrow night."

"Tomorrow night?" I repeated dumbly.

We both jumped as Gevi's boots crunched outside and he hissed, "He's coming. I can hear him mumbling halfway across camp."

"It's tomorrow, Akrist." Yara's expression mirrored a downed prey begging for a finishing strike.

"Hurry up," Gevi urged hoarsely, pressing backwards against the door flap.

"The sacrifice?" *Tomorrow.*

Yara nodded once. Gevi burst into the hut, eyes wide, lamp forgotten. His foot sent the dished stone skidding across the dirt before it tipped and its contents snuffed out.

"Yara, it's time!"

But Yara had crashed against me again, so hard she nearly tipped us both over. "I love you. I love you, Akrist."

Gevi yanked Yara away from me. I grunted in the dark and arched against my bonds striving to reclaim her, to hold her, to never let her go. At the same time, thankful that Gevi pulled her away, that she wouldn't be punished. The faint scrape of Gevi scooping the lantern off the floor roared like thunder in my ears and the door flap brushing my cheek stung like a cold slap to the face.

She was gone, and I had nothing left to hold onto except the fading scent of cinnamon and the small, firm pouch planted in my left hand.

You'll never see her again.

PART THREE
"OUTCAST"

CHAPTER TWENTY-SEVEN

On the night of the sacrifice, Hasev came to take me to my death. Again.

My gaze swung to the objects fluttering in his hands; a leather strip tied with a twisted, knuckled chunk of root. The wurm necklace, my ceremonial garb for this evening. Bunched around it, a worn and faded length of fabric, with careful stitching and scalloped edges.

He'd kept my birthing blanket. All these years. I swallowed. A vivid memory pressed into my mind, like the after-image of the sun; this night, twelve years ago, the boy version of myself fastidiously folding and stacking my clothes in the midst of a frenzied vaiya herd. The memory, the act of it, seemed ludicrous now. Tonight, I shrugged out of my filthy garb like a wurm shedding its skin and left it strewn behind me.

Hasev thrust the threadbare blanket toward me.

It wasn't long enough to knot at my waist, so I used the wurm necklace to bind two corners together at my hip. Arsu would hate it, as she hated anything out of order.

As we left the hut, a muffled growl tumbled through the

skies far above us, pulling my gaze upward. *A Guide! An angel!* My sore heart leapt, but above us hung nothing but low, churning clouds. An early snow waited to soak into our bones, but something else, something alive and curling through the ribs of those clouds waited as well. And it was no dragon Guide.

As I watched, a skeletal white light ricocheted through the cloud body followed by thunder. Thunder in the midst of a snowstorm. Never in my days had I witnessed the two together. It sounded surreal, like an underwater explosion, powerful yet muffled, something wild within struggling to escape.

Goosebumps raised on my arms as an icy wind threaded gleefully around my bare ribs. *Sweet Nasheira, how will you possibly survive this?*

A flat, succinct voice in my head answered, *you won't.*

As if the thunder had been a cue, Arsu's reedy voice floated out of the darkness from the centre of camp. "Come! Gather! It is time!"

A few vaiyas bawled nervous rejoinders in the darkness. Torchlight shifted, flames snapping like banners, and, from behind hulking huts, the mothers came first in their white beaded dresses.

One stood above the rest, still looking graceful even with shoulders hunched. My mother, her raven hair touched with silver—*How have you not noticed that before?*—still radiated cold beauty.

She has been waiting twenty-four years for this night.

"Gather!" Arsu's voice sliced through the crowd again, closer now.

Men in crusting face paint shifted on their feet, scratched at feather armbands and shadowed the women like ethereal guards. Finally, the crowd parted to reveal the Speaker's party.

Arsu came first, eyes slit against the torchlight. She led a vaiya, Vable. The poor bird had been muzzled and shivered with agitation as Arsu yanked his lead. An awkward load hung like a tumour from the animal's flank. Water bags balanced the load on the other side. I briefly eyed the wide clay pot, its top capped with bound leather. Water dribbled out a small hole at the bottom, leaving a dotted trail in Vable's wake. I'd never seen the water clock unpacked. Such an unassuming countdown to my death.

Na-Jhalar shuffled aimlessly behind his sister and the vaiya. As ritual dictated, he was unclothed, but someone had laced boots onto his feet, and he wore a heavy fur draped over his shoulders against the wet cold. Beneath that, the dragon scale necklace swung across his chest. Familiar brown stains tracked down the corners of his mouth. Even from this far, I saw he'd been heavily dosed with gifen. Arsu had let that mangled mind creep just close enough to the surface to use it as a weapon, but she'd keep Na-Jhalar perpetually dull now.

"Why is it untied?" Arsu snapped. "Dero!" My brother trotted obediently toward me. She kept her expression serious, but her eyes glinted with victory when she looked at me.

Guides, how she must be savouring this.

Her mouth twitched and her gaze flicked to the wurm necklace knotted at my waist.

"I'll tie him," Hasev announced. "He is my responsibility."

"Check the water level then, Dero," Arsu said calmly.

Vable balked as my brother snatched the bird's reins, peeled back the covering over the water clock, and beckoned for a torch.

"Down to the third notch," he reported, peering inside.

"Let's be on with it then." Arsu straightened.

I shrugged and turned north, toward the daeson's huts, and the snake's sibilant voice froze me in my tracks.

"We'll brand it now, while we still have a hot hearth fire nearby."

My throat clenched. I'd forgotten. *Sweet Nasheira, how could I have forgotten the brand?* My legs jellied, and Hasev's hand squeezed my elbow.

And so we turned, silent and single-file like ants beneath the clogged sky, not northward, but to the centre of camp and the Speaker's hearth. A stout green bough stood half-buried in a deep bed of coals. Ripples of red reflected the cold wind and washed a sickly heat across my face. Despite my efforts to control it, my breathing hitched, shortened and shallowed. I couldn't stop staring at the consuming whorls of orange while the crowd clotted around us and Arsu began to speak.

"With hunter and gatherer as my witness..."

Vable hissed and crowed. Two vaiyas howled in answer from the shadows.

"With the blessing of our most holy Speaker and the authority of Nasheira," Arsu drew the bough from the fire. My gaze pinned to the wicked flint, blackened and heavy with heat. *Nasheira help me.* I leaned back into Hasev.

"We condemn this daeson to be banished for the murder of Iva the Storyteller."

Hands clamped onto my arms, my shoulders. A choked grunt burst out of me as someone's arm locked around my neck and another's thumb dug into the flesh under my jaw. Together, they pressed me to my knees and held my head immobile, right cheek offered to Arsu. Pain spiked through my molars as my teeth ground together. My knees ached against the cold, hard ground. I could still see the woman approach through the spidery spread of fingers covering half my face.

She licked her lips and held the flint, which hovered close

enough to my face that its heat kissed my skin and the smell of hot stone filled my nostrils.

"May it be marked as forever invisible to camp and aeni alike." Hands clamped tighter, and bodies around me braced.

Forever wasn't very long when you were about to die.

Don't scream. Don't scream.

"May it be branded as the wurm it is," Arsu hissed, leaning in.

I closed my eyes.

Vaiya howls swung into shrill alarms, and someone screeched, "No!"

Before any of us could process it, heavy footfalls thudded against frosty ground and something crashed into the crowd at my right. Shocked screams dropped from the crowd and skidded aside. I opened my eyes to see the flint dipping inches away. Behind it, shimmering like a mirage through the heat waves, a tall, menacing shadow careened toward Arsu.

"No hurt!" the voice barked, and Arsu's beady gaze flicked lazily back to me before swinging the brand away to face her challenger.

"Vax, no!" I shouted, but my voice cracked. I swallowed and tried again. "Vax. Stop."

The big, one-eyed vaiya skidded and stamped his foot as he came to a stop, claws clicking. His crest flared, and his dark slit of an eye trained on Arsu. "Nooo. Hurt." He punctuated the words with a hiss.

Arsu flipped the flint-headed spear in her hand, hauled back and hurled it, burying it deep in Vax's chest. The thud sounded remarkably like thunder. My sweet vaiya didn't even make a sound. His trembling legs staggered. Then he toppled forward, beak smashing into the dust, his head folding under him as he twitched.

Vable's alarm call swung into a high-pitched mourning

cry, and the surrounding vaiya herd joined in, casting their cold, trembling howls to the turbulent sky.

"Vax!" I screeched, thrashing. Feet stumbled around me. "Vax! Oh Guides, Vax!" I broke free. Someone punched me in the temple, and I lost sight of the grey body curled in the dirt. Dizziness swamped me. The world spun and slid sideways. Several strong arms pinned me to the ground.

Arsu walked directly to the collapsed vaiya, pressing the quivering body sideways with one foot, and using it for leverage as she gripped both hands around the protruding spear.

"No!" I bawled.

Arsu hauled on the spear, and with each pull, Vax's bloody body rolled and jerked like a floundering boat.

"Vax, no!"

The spear sucked free and, as Arsu turned back toward me, she squared her shoulders and wiped her nose. No hint of a smile. No life at all in those eyes.

I sobbed and gagged as the serpent stalked back to the fire and jammed the sizzling spear deep into the hungry coals.

"Murderer!" I shrieked. "You are the murder—!" My cries were clipped as someone stepped on my broken hand, and I screamed.

Arsu's thin lips moved, but she said nothing.

As my eyes bulged and I panted in the cold dirt, I realized she was silently counting down. *Ten, nine, eight.* Mouthing the words and twisting the bloodied spear into the coals, *seven, six, five.*

The vaiyas' discordant howls buzzed through my skull. Vax's silver back slumped breathless beyond the hearth.

Four, Three. "I'll kill you! I'll ki—" A sharp kick to my head sent sparks snapping behind my eyes. Blackness strangled my vision. Without Arsu's lips to read, I ticked off the last two digits in my head. *Two, one.*

I didn't see the brand coming, but as it brushed the skin under my eye and then dug in, I screamed. I flopped like a fish and fought and shrieked, but all of it was scoured away by the brilliant white pain, a ringing in my ears, and the thick stench of scorched hair and skin.

CHAPTER TWENTY-EIGHT

They must have dragged me to the northern edge of camp because I held no recollection of arriving there under my own power. I only recall crumpled grass scrolling by underfoot. The boot marching beside me had an unravelling seam. *He should mend that.* I tried to reach out and pluck the loose thread, but I remembered my hands were tied.

They should untie me so I can put out the fire. For some reason, my neck wasn't working. The entire right side of my face kept curling toward my chest. Each heartbeat resounded like a hammer's blow. *My cheek. If I could just use my hands to bat out the flames...* I tried to catch the gaze of the man gripping my right elbow, but pain congealed like boiling sap under my skin, and my head was too heavy. *Can't he see I'm on fire?*

No, because now both he and the man at my left were busy propping me into a standing position. They kept jerking up on my arms and then planting me like a stick in the dirt. *I should tell them my knees aren't working either.*

A fat flake of snow settled onto my eyelashes and dissolved. Two more nested in the brown grass at my feet. It was less trampled here, so the flakes lay skewered high up on the blades, glowing orange in the torchlight.

Where are we? I winced at the haloed, harsh torches and the mass of faces around me. Four tiny huts formed a circle around my guards and me. The rest of the crowd shifted outside the boundary of the buildings, watching.

I stretched my jaw to counter the ringing in my ears. Someone spoke, and it seemed important, but I couldn't hear. *Who are they all here to see?* And then the wind puffed, and several snowflakes plastered my face and ribs. The piercing tone in my ears pinched off, and the world snapped back into sharp focus.

Vax. She killed Vax. Snow swarmed into my eyes, melting against the raw burn on my face. I remembered my fate and why I was there. I swung to find Arsu, the source of the voice, but instead, my gaze caught on a small form emerging from one of the huts: a boy with blue eyes, naked except for the filthy blanket he clutched around his bony shoulders. *Gideous.* His gaze met mine, and the incongruous hope in them broke me.

He still thinks I'm going to save him. Oh Guides, Gideous. I'm so sorry.

He turned, held open the door flap behind him, and ushered out the rest of the terrified daeson.

My throat closed. *They were together. They'd banded all together in one hut for comfort. Oh Yara, we could have healed them. They are still just children underneath it all.*

Henri came next, his red cheeks pasted with snot and tears, wisps of white-blond hair glued to it in patches. He didn't brush it away. Instead, his hands twisted the blanket he held into a tight cord, and his wet, brown gaze flicked to the clouds, then his bare feet, everywhere except the faces bunched around us.

Jule and Fey tottered out, shivering and blinking wide-eyed. Fey dropped his blanket, rose to the balls of his feet, and began rocking back and forth. Jule had been chewing on the end of the wurm necklace he wore. He spat it out to hiccup the single word, "Cold," and dissolved into gulping sobs.

They are so small. I blinked at the dimples on the backs of Jule's hands, and Fey's squat legs, folded in baby fat. *They're freezing already.* My legs tingled, and my arms pressed tightly to my ribs. A spongy feeling in the soles of my feet foretold of frostbite. Yes, I shivered against the gathering snow, but the daeson were blue-lipped, and they'd only just left their hut. *How long have they left them naked in there?* A tired rage pooled in my belly, but it did not have time to warm me.

Arsu spoke something final, and the crowd peeled away, leaving only the parents of the daeson, the Speaker, and Arsu herself. The ceremonial group pressed their firstborn sons out of camp and north. Snow bit at our heels, and that strange, muted thunder galloped through the skies far above us.

Unlike the ordered procession of my first sacrifice, where each daeson stumbled ahead of his sombre set of parents, we fell into a loose group behind Arsu, Na-Jhalar, and Vable. Our parents trailed behind us, Hasev's arm draped comfortingly around Aella's shoulders, as if the agony ahead was their own.

Na-Jhalar, in his incapacity, set a slow pace. At first, even Jule and Fey toddled easily among us, the cold momentarily forgotten as they stepped on each other's dragging blankets and poked at fat snowflakes.

But as we carried on marching, our silence broken only by the chattering of a snow transformed to dry, stinging pellets, and the incongruent muzzled sound of thunder far above, the toddlers started crying. They stopped walking and huddled on their blankets. Barth grabbed one under each arm even as they howled and snapped like wild vaiya chicks.

Occasionally Arsu halted Vable to check the water clock. By the time we stopped, darkness fully wrapped us in its embrace and I couldn't control my shivering.

My bare skin burned. My feet looked waxy. The other daeson stood silent and still, long past the point of shivering.

I peered at our dim, snow-scoured surroundings. Arsu had chosen a rounded hill where the forest thinned to sparse pechi trees. A deep, dry gully curled around the base of the knoll. *Our most easterly trap line.*

The first morning Iva had hunted with us again after I'd convinced her to hand care of Na-Jhalar to Arsu, she'd bagged a gazelle in the pit trap about a mile from here. We'd discovered two more, stags with locked horns, embroiled in an ula bush down this gully. We'd nearly missed them completely. Despite their nasal calls and thrashing attempts at escape, the gully effectively swallowed up the sounds of their struggle. Had we not been right on top of them, we would have walked right by without even knowing they were there.

That's why we're here. That's why she picked it. So no one will find us. Even if we somehow survived the two day period after our cutting, the likelihood of anyone discovering us in the gully was minuscule. I wondered who had told her of this place. My eyes scanned the crowd, and my gaze came to rest on my father.

Although he still held Aella's slender arm, it seemed my mother was doing the supporting now. Hasev stared into the void with rapidly blinking eyes and tight lips. Almost imperceptibly, he shook his head as he came to the same realization as me.

Dero. Had Arsu already turned my little brother against me back then? Who else would suggest the place? As I watched, Aella pulled away from Hasev, and he turned to regard her with a bewildered, lost look on his face.

Your part is over now, and Aella gets to step into a role she has rehearsed how many times?

Barth's squat mate shuffled forward as well, but Henri's young mother hung back, a look of detached disgust etched so deeply on her face, I couldn't help but wonder if it wasn't her natural expression. As I studied the three women, it occurred to me that there were no mothers here for Jule and Fey. *Yes, their fathers came to camp with them as babes, alone, remember? One of the other mothers has to cut them.*

A startling numbness bogged my chest, like clouded, icy water sloshing inside my rib cage. *It's all gone. Iva, Vax, Yara, your unborn child, you've lost them all. You haven't saved any of them, and you will watch these daeson die before you're gone too. It's happening now.*

Henri's father pressed his sullen mate forward with the others. She snorted and then obliged. Arsu held a torch over the open water clock on Vable's back, and then rounded the pack animal and unstrapped a coiled length of rope I hadn't noticed before. *It's happening.*

"Take them down while we pray." Arsu nodded to the daeson and flicked the rope toward Henri's father. "There's a group of trees down there that will work well." She pointed and turned away without a glance in my direction, like I was already dead to her.

We skidded down the steep ravine, Barth still carrying Jule and Fey ahead of us. Henri's father shoved the poor boy so hard, he tumbled past us and skidded into the frostbitten leaf litter at the channel's throat. Hasev kept a quiet grip on my arm, and somehow, we made it down without falling. On the floor, our feet sunk deep into drifts of leaves. Each one had been trapped down here, just as we would soon be. The sweet smell of earth filled our nostrils as we slogged a few steps into the sad spatter of trees ahead. Snow still fell, but it drifted quietly here. *We are already half buried.*

Gideous shifted beside me, his lips blue-black in the darkness as he watched Barth bend to deposit Jule and Fey in the crook of a tree. Henri's father was binding the boy to a nearby trunk. Sitting askew, with his legs spread-eagled and his arms pulled behind his back, Henri looked like a smashed doll. I knew he lived only by the quick rise and fall of his exposed ribs. Black mud and leaves smeared his white-blond hair and his bare backside too. *We cannot survive this. Even without the cold, it's too dirty down here. If the wurms do not get us, infection will.*

Gideous twitched as Barth accepted the remaining rope from Henri's father and turned toward us.

"It's all right," I whispered, and immediately wished I could take back the shallow reassurance.

"Hey!" Henri's father trotted behind Barth and pointed back to the toddlers. "What about them?"

My former guard halted, thumbing the rope in his hands as if he itched to strangle the man.

"Aren't you going to tie them?"

Barth glanced up at Arsu's back, leaned forward, and caught the young blond man by the chin before he could react. He jerked his head toward Jule and Fey. "Them?" he whispered gruffly, thumb curled into the crook of the man's jaw.

Henri's father swallowed several times, his gaze flitting between the two immobile, pale daeson and his captor.

"I don't think they're going anywhere." Barth shook the boy once like a rat before tossing him and turning back to us.

Gideous's father tied him down the same as Hasev did me, our naked haunches pressed to the cold earth, our shoulder blades and elbows scraping against the shredding bark of the pechi trees behind us, and our hands numb below their binding. Before Hasev retreated, he slipped his skinning knife beneath the wurm necklace at my hip. I flinched at the touch of the blade as he sliced the leather thong, but offered him a grateful nod when he left the blanket draped over my groin.

His blue-grey irises intensified as his eyes filled with tears, and he nodded back, but his focus latched on the mutilation on my right cheek instead of my eyes. And then he was gone, swallowed by the shadows of the gully as he backed away.

The men scrambled back up the ravine wall to assist their mates down the steep incline. Like storks at a swamp's edge, the trio of women in their formal white dresses inched down the crumbling bank with mincing steps. Arsu followed behind them, leaving Henri's father posted beside Vable and the water clock.

For the first time in my life, my mother marched steadfastly toward me. If the other women harboured any thoughts of balking before their daeson, they quashed them and followed suit.

I bit down on every boyish urge to drop my gaze as Aella closed the distance between us. It took all my strength to keep my eyes trained on her icy face. *Guides, control yourself. You're a grown man.* It certainly didn't feel that way, not from this vantage point, splayed gracelessly in the moist leaves as my towering mother stood over me like a marble statue. This was the closest she'd been to me since I'd found the dragon scale at eleven years old.

"Nasheira had two sons."

Arsu's voice jolted me from my memories, and for a moment I faltered, and my gaze slid to the knife in Aella's fist, the only part of her that moved. The thin sickle blade tapped against her thigh like Vax's claws had clicked against the ground before his death.

"She fashioned them herself, the first out of earth, and the second out of the sky. She named them Pau and Yurrii." Arsu's voice, garbled as it was from her ruined face, carried cleanly down the gully and back again.

This can't be happening. Not this fast. I bit the inside of my cheek until I tasted blood. *Control yourself. Keep your eyes on her, coward.*

"Pau of earth hated Yurrii of sky, who floated among the stars, while Pau lay like an earthworm in the dirt."

I ignored Arsu's recitation and made myself study Aella's face. *She knows you're watching her.* I could tell by the tightness in her jaw and the intensity in her eyes as they glared at the tree trunk above my head.

Henri began to whimper again. Arsu's beady gaze flicked up to the water clock and back. She licked her lips, glared unblinking at the crying daeson, and continued her recitation.

Henri's pitiful moans, his stupid cow of a mother hissing at him to shut up, threatened to undo me, so I concentrated on the beadwork at Aella's neckline. The pattern was far more complex than the simple, elegant string of beads that graced Yara's festival dress. *Oh, Yara.* My throat ached. *I failed you.*

"Pau grew a human woman from his soil, but when Yurrii came through her fingers into the ground—" Arsu paused, her teeth bared, her long-nailed fingers curling like spiders. "Pau killed him."

At those words, everyone standing pressed their index and middle finger to their forehead. The torch in Arsu's hand sputtered. Snow, sparks, and leaves eddied into the night as the wind skidded to a stop and then reversed.

I couldn't shake the horrible feeling that Arsu had orchestrated the whole thing as if the power of Pau truly did twist through the woman.

Out of the corner of my eye, to my left, I saw Gideous's knobby knee bouncing up and down.

Aella's gaze remained rooted to the tree above me as if something captivating had been carved there. *Guides, show something, some small emotion. Anything.*

Henri's keening wail swept through the valley and his mother kicked him in the ribs.

My breathing ratcheted faster, and I couldn't slow it, couldn't corral my fear. *Guides,* I hated my mother for her faultless control.

Somewhere far above us, blotted from our view, the giant moon Pau plowed to overtake Yurrii. At Vable's feet, the last drops patted out of the water clock, and Henri's father tipped the rim and stared inside. Shadows from his torch twisted his expression as he turned and nodded down at Arsu.

My heart slammed so loudly against the insides of my head; I could barely make out Arsu's last words.

"And she said to him, *'My first son, you shall never again grow the seed of life.'*"

Henri screamed as his mother dove towards him, knife extended. His heel caught her in the armpit, and the sickle blade sliced all the way up his inner thigh.

Mother of Yurrii. I turned from the black blood in the darkness, and Henri's excruciating squeals shot down the hollows of my spine.

Gideous's mother hesitated, gagged loudly, and then bent over her cowering son. I couldn't tell whether she meant to cut him or vomit.

"Wait!" Arsu barked, stabbing a finger at Hasev and Barth. "Hold his legs."

The men moved forward, frowning. Each wrapped a massive hand around Gideous's bony ankles while his mother blew wet breaths through puffed cheeks and tottered with her knife resting on her knee.

Further on, Henri thrashed and wailed in a widening puddle of his own blood.

"Do it," Barth snapped, and his mate blinked and then nodded. Strings of wet hair cast raked shadows across her face.

Gideous's blue eyes bulged as his mother leaned into him. He spasmed, his head cracking back against the tree and his legs drumming, almost jerking out of his captor's grip. A strange gurgling bubbled up his throat, but he did not cry as his mother castrated him. By the time she'd finished, his head hung against his chest, and he bobbed, half-conscious and drooling, his eyes fluttering beneath their lashes.

His mother straightened, and alternately wiped her palms down the wide front of her white dress, smearing ugly stains down the front.

I glanced at Gideous's wound. *Not as bad as Henri's. He could survive.*

Just then Aella moved. Still staring over my head, she swept towards me with a dancer's precision.

"Hasev!" Barth bellowed, and the two men dropped Gideous's limp feet. My father skirted Aella, and each man clamped onto my ankles and yanked my stiff legs apart. They kneeled, straddling my shins as if wrestling snakes, broad backs to me, hands locked on my legs just above the feet. And my mother, oblivious, side-stepped between them.

A strand of her hair slipped over her shoulder and brushed across the brand on my face as she bent and flipped back the blanket, exposing me.

I flinched.

Unfazed, she reached for me, and my stomach twisted.

"Aella," I spat through clenched teeth.

She froze, wicked knife hovering inches away from my crotch.

"For once in your life, look at your son."

The knife wavered. My mother's face hung only inches from mine. Slowly, those almond eyes upturned, that gaze locked on mine, and every fleck distended as her irises contracted.

I didn't kill your daughter. I didn't kill Tasie. I poured the thought into my stare.

Without breaking our gaze, in one deft movement Aella slipped her cold hand under my scrotum, cupped me, and pulled downward. The flat of the blade skimmed along the underside of my penis and, with a sharp jerk, it was done. Just a strange prick, a deep-rooted shock, and a wave of heat at my groin. That was it. For a moment. Then the pain shattered my body.

Fluidly, before the men at my feet could rise, Aella straightened, turned, and strode toward Jule and Fey. Halfway between us, she flicked my blood off the sickle blade with a snap of her wrist.

CHAPTER TWENTY-NINE

Pain sluiced through me as our blood-smeared parental party edged out of the gully without a backwards glance. A hot pulse stabbed from my crotch to my core as bobbing torches winked out over the bank's lip and the soily jaws of our shallow ravine clamped shut over us. Thick nausea took my breath away. I couldn't tell if absolute darkness was dropping over all of us, or if I was just losing my senses. Henri still howled, but a shrill tone blossomed between my ears and swelled to drown out my own shallow exhalations. The world tilted, and my head clogged with spider webs, but that faint crying tore through.

Concentrate. Do not faint.

I'd smuggled Fraesh's pouch here in my broken hand. After examining its contents in the hut—a chalky red powder, a sharp shard of clay pot, a bone needle and a long thread—I'd pressed it into my right palm and wound a bandage around my fist to conceal it and prevent me from dropping it if I lost consciousness. Now, I picked at the bandage knot with numb, trembling fingers. With my hands tied, I couldn't unravel it. Yanking at my bonds, I yelped as my broken hand screamed in protest. The cobwebs came rushing back in. Blinking in the dark, counting my breaths with my chin tucked against my chest, I waited for them to clear.

Breathe, and undo the knot. Pressing back against the tree, trying to ignore the pain between my legs, I hooked a finger under the knot, loosened it and unravelled the bandage from my right hand.

Fraesh's pouch fell from my hand, bounced off a tree root and rolled away from me into the leaf litter.

Shit. Shit. Shit. Now what? I couldn't reach it. *You're going to have to turn around.*

Gideous rustled beside me, his weak moan mingling with Henri's.

I braced myself, lifted my legs, and planted my heels. Lifting my rear, I shimmied over and flopped down like a fish, groin muscles trembling, crotch on fire. *Keep going.* I sobbed an exhale. *Don't stop. No time.* I clenched my teeth and repeated the maneuver, scooting around the pechi tree inch by inch until I was halfway around.

My fingers felt dead. Fanning over the wet ground, I searched for the round pouch amidst the slimy leaves and poking twigs.

Come on. It had to be right here. *Come on, damn it.*

Gideous's groan cut off, sucking into a ragged inhale. Something, probably his head, thudded against his tree trunk. Above us, the wind gusted, and a fresh stampede of leaves rattled over the edge of the gully.

Henri's screams broke into gulping sobs.

"Akrist?" A small voice reached for me in the dark, so shaken and tired, so *childlike*, it made my throat close.

"I'm here, Gideous," I croaked.

"They left us," he breathed.

Henri must have heard because his crying escalated again.

"It's all right." I raised my voice in response. *Guides, stop saying that. It is not all right. It's not.* "We're going to get out of this." My fingers groped across the ground behind me, clumsy, uncooperative. *Sweet Nasheira, please let me find it.*

"They cut us," Gideous squeaked. "I'm bleeding!"

Henri howled a panicked rejoinder.

"Me too." I kept my voice firm. "But I have medicine that will stop the bleeding. We just need to get untied, all right?"

A long pause.

"How?"

How indeed. "I brought something sharp, but I dropped it. Give me a minute to find it and I'll cut my ropes. Then I can free all of you." *Find it. Find it.* My shoulders cramped as I stretched my bound arms as far away from the trunk as I could, up to my wrists now in leaf litter. A deep, earnest throbbing reverberated through my pelvis. I sniffed and ignored the itching, oozing blood I sat in. *Hurry up. Guides.*

Above us, the storm paused and Henri hushed. For awhile, the only sound in the gully was the dry sift of my hands through leaves. *Nothing from Jule and Fey at all—*

A few times, in the prison hut, when I'd finally understood my inevitable end was near, a grisly preview of my fate scrolled through my softened brain, and I couldn't smother it. I'd lain there, and the sounds of the daesons' phantom screams as their mothers butchered them carved into the grey matter between my ears and left me scooped out. I had convinced myself that the screaming would be the worst part.

In reality, the silence now was so much worse.

"I have an idea," I blurted. "Can you move at all? Can you cover yourself in leaves, like a blanket, while you're waiting? You too, Henri. Use your legs and dig, just like a vaiya. We have to keep warm."

Leafs chuffed from Gideous's direction, but I couldn't tell

if Henri was doing it too. The noise effectively covered my search for long enough that the storm unravelled into stillness without me noticing. Long enough that when I finally stopped clawing at the ground behind me, the only sound in the entire gully, in the entire world, was the dry whisper of snow settling around us like a flock of waiting birds.

"Gideous?" I whispered.

"You can't find it, can you? The sharp thing you brought."

"No." The word burst out of me as a desperate half laugh, the swollen burn on my cheek pinched and hot pain burrowed into my cheekbone. I let my head fall back against the tree trunk. "I can't find it." The silence of Henri, the utter quietness of Jule and Fey, swallowed me whole. Tears pricked at my eyes, and my neck muscles corded. I blew a long breath before gulping. "I'm sorry."

"It's all right," Gideous offered.

The sky marbled into faint light. Clouds skidded by overhead, and then the world curtained into darkness again.

"Do you think they're dead?" He shifted beside me.

I swallowed, and my throat pulled tight. The needle, the clay shard and Fraesh's medicine, all of it lost. "I don't know," I answered.

Nasheira, just take us already. Dry pellets of snow scratched at my upturned face and settled in the burnt grooves of my branded cheek. I couldn't feel my feet at all, and my hands were stiff like stone. *What are you waiting for?* As if in answer, a faint but wretchedly familiar smell snaked into my nostrils. My stomach dropped. *Oh, Guides. Oh no...*

"Do you smell that?" Gideous's voice trembled, and I nodded in the dark even though I knew he couldn't see it.

"Wurms," I choked.

Cradled in the cold black of a cloudy night, we sat frozen with the putrid smell of wurm stinging our nostrils. My eyes ached to decipher shapes in the dark. Snowflakes clotted around us. Did I imagine it, somewhere in that faint clatter of branches shifting, the dry chuff of maggoty skin heaving across the ground?

We are as blind as they are.

I strained to listen over my galloping heartbeat. I counted my teeth with my tongue and measured my breathing, even when the oily stench began to burn my eyes.

Gideous cannot see you, but he can hear you breathe. Keep him calm.

Beside me, the boy did not move, but his breaths sawed, shallow and scraping through the dark. Even though we were tied, even though I knew that touch would not comfort a daeson child, I wished I could hold his hand.

This is it. The realization clobbered me like a boulder to the belly. *This is how it ends, the wurm dream. It's the middle of the night, you can't move, and they're coming to eat you alive.* An answering tingle crawled up the skin of my belly and over the scar on my chest. My breath left me in a harsh snort, and Gideous jumped at the noise. *My life has been a cruel joke. Give me the gift of prophecy, torture me with snippets of the future, and what in Nasheira's name was I supposed to do with it? If it ends here, what difference did it make? Why bother? Why choose me?*

Sound tumbled down the gully toward us, muffled by the snow, but unmistakable. A soft, burrowing churn of soil, the pop of tiny tree roots snapping, and the tang of upturned earth mingling with the oily smell of wurm. They came from my left, twisting out of the soft banks of our ravine, curling toward the smell of our fear, Pau's wurms coming to finish us.

Gideous's breath whistled in and out through his teeth, impossibly fast. His tree shuddered, leaves rattling as he railed against it.

The scratching of the wurms' approach stopped. I imagined all those stubby, wriggling feelers sampling in the dark, and then the sound avalanched toward us, eager and unstoppable.

You are the only thing standing between these boys and the monsters in the dark. You are the only hope they have.

Wrenching myself around the tree trunk to face the oncoming wurms, I bellowed, "Hey! Hey, over here!" *Oh, Guides.* Thick bodies raked through the leaves, coiling toward me. *You have to get all of them. You have to get them all away from the boys.* I slammed my heels against the ground, screamed again, "Hey!", and rammed into the tree behind me hard enough to make branches clatter.

And then they were on me. My next scream was wordless as the first wurm's meaty flank grazed my calf, spasmed and twisted around. Hundreds of stout feelers clamped onto my thigh and over my stomach, pressing, kneading me like dough. I opened my mouth to scream again, but the horrible smell poured down my throat and choked me. Teeth snagged on my stomach, slicing a shallow path upward. Feelers scrambled up my chest, over my shoulder, and the whole wurm shuddered as it brushed over my scar.

The teeth retracted. Every finger-like feeler clogged onto the scar, flattening against the bumps and ropey tissue, retracing the path of the dragon's tongue that had flayed me twelve years ago tonight. The weight of the wurm sandwiched me against the tree, and I couldn't breathe as it pressed into every pore of my Speaker's mark, hungrily examining its edges.

And then the weight lifted, and the stench vanished.

I inhaled, and my lungs filled with the scent of fresh earth. Something sweeter filled my chest, poured through my cold and hollow limbs, and saturated my bones. As I breathed, a presence lodged in my rib cage and breathed along with me. My reeling mind snagged, caught, and clicked into the consciousness of another. The overwhelming presence of a Guide pulled and threaded through my spine, weaving to fill every hole in the fabric of me. It rang with familiarity, reminiscent of the last sacrifice when I'd been pinned under the wings of the dragon who gave me my scar, when she'd dipped inside my head and we'd connected somehow. But *this...* this was more. This was intimate.

Oh Nasheira, I did not know how empty I was until this second.

Tears rolled down my cheeks. I absorbed the impossible fact that I wasn't *singular* anymore. The force of an angel folded in me, nascent, waiting.

Something else waited too. The wurm.

I blinked into the darkness before me and saw nothing, but knew, as easily as I knew where my hands lay, that it hovered inches away from my face. Somehow I knew that two others slithered around it, arcing toward Gideous, toward the rest of the boys. I focused on the sightless face that I knew squirmed inches away from mine, and thought: *Stop them. Do not let them eat those boys.*

An eager response spun through my mind, green and wriggling with excitement. The segmented body curled past my shoulder and heaved itself at the nearest wurm.

The scavengers scraped and thudded in the dark, wrapped and wrestling, while green enthusiasm in my brain darkened to maroon. Adrenalin cresting, I didn't pause to question how my mind suddenly registered foreign thoughts in colour. I didn't address the anomaly of an utterly lightless night and a foreign sense stepping in to let me know that there were three wurms, and then two, and then just one, the one I could feel. There wasn't time to analyze any of it.

Wet, sucking noises echoed down the gully, and I realized that the wurm who'd scrutinized me, who'd dispatched the other pair on command, now cannibalized its kills. My mind grimaced. "Stop," I said. And it stopped. *It's listening to you. Mother of Yurrii, what's happening?*

Red pangs of hunger swirled like crows in my mind, but the wurm stopped.

I squinted and leaned toward the white body as it reared up to face me in the dark. *Now, untie me.* Red wavered to pale peach in my mind, questioning, confused. I licked my lips and tried again. *I am tied to this tree. Cut me free. Bite the ropes around my hands.*

A happy, green spike of understanding and the wurm curled toward me. I added hastily, *don't bite my hands, just the rope.*

I was answered by a pink curl of irritation, and feelers feathered around my numb fingers. As they grazed my broken hand, I sucked in a sharp breath, and the wurm jerked back and curled in on itself. Orange anxiousness washed over me in waves.

"It's all right. It was already broken," I blurted. *The ropes.*

The wurm remained coiled like a caterpillar.

Please, just bite the ropes, I coaxed, and slowly, it uncoiled. Feelers slid up my left wrist and wrapped around my arm. I felt a slight, wet suction and the serrated edges of several shuddering teeth as a jawless mouth enveloped my frozen fist like a giant leech. I fought the urge to flinch as the lumbering wurm sliced my bonds with the precision of a healer snipping stitches.

My arms flopped to my sides. Clouded pain sluiced past my broken bonds with the force of floodwater. The world tilted, and I fell away from the tree, my forehead mashing into caked snow and leaves. Unconsciousness clutched me, dragged me deep into the undergrowth, down and away from the gully. *No! Not now. Please!* My mind thrashed, I broke free and surfaced, sensed the scavenger rounding the tree and then its coils pressed around me.

"Don't," I choked and was swamped by faint blue hurt as the wurm froze, feelers fretting about its featureless face.

My head began to pound. Nausea congealed in my stomach, and I pressed my hands to my knees, bobbed to a sitting position, and raked my hands through the leaves around me. The pouch had to be here somewhere. *Guides, what if the wurms swept it away as they fought?*

And then my fingers bumped into something amongst the litter, round, smooth, but lighter than a stone. I shuddered as my hand closed around Fraesh's pouch. *Oh, Thank Nasheira!* I nearly cried in relief. Peach tones of worry reached for me as I clutched the pouch in my hand. I shook my head.

Leave me be. Free the boy now. Cut his ropes.

Gideous didn't move or make a noise as the wurm slid behind his pechi tree, and I dragged myself after. I knew my feet followed me. I heard them dragging behind me like boulders tied to my ankles, but I couldn't feel them at all.

"Gideous." I pressed the back of my hand against his cheek and then brought the pouch to my mouth, unwinding the thread with my teeth. "Gideous, come on. Wake up," I mumbled.

A green-blue swirl of satisfaction bloomed from the wurm and Gideous's arms flopped forward. I cradled the open pouch carefully against my ribs with my forearm and pulled Gideous toward me. Leaning into his face, I waited for the puff of his breathing to tickle my cheek. "All right." I sniffed. "All right." Relief swirled into dizziness, and I remembered that I still bled.

I eased Gideous back against his tree and plucked the medicine pouch from the crook of my arm. Bracing myself, I pressed open my legs, and the angry wound at my groin sent a spasming, raw pain up my pelvis and into my hips. For a moment, I tottered and prayed once more that I wouldn't faint. Yellow-green bubbles of encouragement kept me afloat until the light-headedness passed. Gingerly setting the pouch on the ground between my knees, I flipped open the fabric edges and pinched Iva's red powder into my hand. I had to prop myself up on one hip to reach underneath my crotch.

One, two. I gritted my teeth and squeezed my eyes shut. *Three.* I pressed the flat of my hand into the wound and did my best to stifle the gurgling cry peeling out of me. Counting five more seconds, I waited until the warmth of blood leaked through the caked powder before re-applying a second layer. This time, already awash with pain, it was the incongruity of reaching for a familiar body part, and encountering nothing but air that threw me. I frowned as the stinging powder slowed the blood flow and couldn't shake the disjointed feeling until I let my hand fall away a second time.

"Gideous." I turned my attention to the boy again. "Gideous. Wake up."

Nothing.

Pursing my lips, I scooped red powder onto my palm and blindly fumbled for the boy's crotch in the dark. Swallowing sickness, I pressed the powder into his wound while Gideous stirred and whimpered in his sleep.

Now the other boys. I sighed and blinked in the forlorn dark. The silent world around the gully hunched under a muffling blanket of snow. *How many other daeson are dying right now? Hundreds? Thousands of us? Freezing, bleeding out while the world buries us alive in white as if it can't forget us soon enough.* There wasn't enough powder, not for Henri's wound, not for the silent Jule and Fey. *Only one length of thread, and too dark to put in stitches.*

"Doesn't matter," I whispered and tried to shake the thought out of my head, but a horrible, heavy weariness pulled at me now. As I sat naked in the snow next to Gideous, I knew I didn't have the energy to crawl to the other boys.

Bring them to me, the other boys. One more is tied, two smaller ones aren't. Bring them all here. I waited for the wurm to respond and was repulsed to detect a thread of red hunger beneath its green, obedient response.

Do not hurt them. When you pull them, don't use your teeth. Can you do that?

A swell of purple shame squelched the traces of red, and the wurm chuffed off in the dark.

I propped Gideous against my left side and swept cold layers of leaves over us as the wurm retrieved the other daeson, one by one, pressing them like offerings against my legs. They were cold. Their little bodies were so cold, and there weren't enough leaves in the world to warm them.

"No," I spoke through gritted teeth dragging my icy hands through swathes of leaf litter, fighting the creeping cold of exhaustion. When the wurm brushed against my back this time, sending anxious trills of orange through my failing mind, I swore I smelled the soft scent of vaiyas. Countless memories of sleeping against the strong warmth of Vax's back flooded my mind, and the forgotten leaves slipped from my fingers.

Vax.

I cried, powerless to stop the wurm as it curled around me, around all of us. I had no idea, until that moment, of the size of the thing, how it could encompass us completely. That was the last thing I was aware of, the sheer size of it, and the warmth. I pressed into Gideous, pulled the other boys onto my lap, and wrapped my arms around them, sobbing.

That is how we passed the first night of sacrifice, curled up in the coils of a hungry wurm, while I dreamed of Yara surrounded by snow and screaming, curled around the globe of her belly, birthing our child alone in the woods.

CHAPTER THIRTY

I remember crouching at the mouth of a V trap with Jin, waiting for the remainder of our hunters to funnel a herd of gazelle toward us, and realizing my foot was on fire. Swearing, clambering out of my crouch, I looked down in time to see a line of fire ants pouring over the rim of my boot. I'd badly wanted to wallop my brother as he clutched his ribs and snorted until tears rolled down his face, while I tore my boot off and hopped around like a heron, brushing away the angry, clinging line of soldiers.

Mother of Yurrii, the pain felt *so* disproportionate to the insect's size. Any thought, other than escaping their furious attack, fled my mind. Of course, I'd unwittingly chosen to stand directly over a nest of the damned things, and Jin—who had seen the whole thing coming—thought it was hysterical. We barely managed to compose ourselves before the startled gazelle herd stumbled toward us.

After that, I never failed to diligently study the ground beneath my feet before settling in. And I never forgot the surprising intensity of that pain.

At dawn, I awoke in agony, as if my feet had smashed through the crown of a fire ant nest and they were swarming me. My crotch burned. My cheek ached. I could barely suck in enough air to scream. The cries bursting out of me sounded like the choking calls of a drowning victim. *Oh Nasheira, oh Guides, my feet.* They felt flayed to the bone. Suffocating in that torture, I had no idea where I was, or what had happened. I drowned in that swelling, unbelievable pain. *Worse than the branding.* At least then, the agony had dulled once the flint burned deep enough. This showed no signs of relenting.

Only when light bleached the horizon did I realize I was outside. A small wedge of grey sky peeked through a misshapen hole about an arm's length above me. *Am I buried?* Panic rose in my throat and, at the same time, warm walls shifted around me, and an odd, uncertain memory seeped through my pain-soaked mind. *The wurm. You were controlling a wurm... Impossible.*

Alternating waves of muddy orange and blue lapped at the frayed edges of my mind. Worry, braided with despair. I knew with a deep certainty that it came from the wurm wrapped around me. *It happened, then. It actually happened.* The pain in my feet crested, shot up the hollows of my shin bones, and the patch of sky above shrunk as the wurm curled tighter around me.

"Stop!" I gasped between screams. "You're. Suffocating. Me." I thrashed an elbow out, struck a firm coil and it loosened. The two colours pooled into apology as the wurm released, and the world unwound around me.

Black stains of greasy blood fanned across the white snow between the pechi trees. The wurm bodies were gone. I scanned my mind, searching for that underlying thread of hollow red hunger. Unable to find it, I came to the sick realization that, sometime through the night, my wurm had left us to finish eating the other two. Blue despair swirled and sank in the back of my head, and I frowned at the incongruity of the emotion. *Why would it mourn something it had no problem eating?*

And then I saw the daeson. In the grey of dawn, dusted with snow, they looked like toppled statues. All four of them lay abandoned, Gideous curled in on himself like an egg, Henri face down, and Jule and Fey's pale, round faces scanning the sky, snow lacing their long eyelashes.

"No!" I lurched forward, punching past the fidgeting, faceless wurm and crawling toward the boys as my feet and groin screamed in protest. "No!" I clutched at Gideous's shoulder, and even my numb hand balked at the hardness, the wooden texture of his skin. *All of them.* They were all long gone.

"You left them!" I shrieked, rounding on the hunched wurm. "You left them to freeze!" It cowered, pale yellow wafting from it as it turtled in on itself. I dragged myself back to it and punched ineffectually at its coils, screaming, "You let them die!" Meaty flesh shuddered beneath my fist while my hot rage shoved aside the extended deep blue anguish. I kept punching, punctuating every wet word until my knuckles throbbed, and my breath left me in an aching wail, "Why?"

Riding a wave of blue misery in my mind, four small globes of green bobbed to the surface, faded and winked out.

I gathered them in my arms. You curled around all of us. I was holding them. Gideous was breathing!

Again, beneath the pale yellow fear, a blue lake and four pricks of green, flashing and then extinguishing. As the ache in my chest competed with the fire in my legs, I realized the wurm was trying to tell me the boys had died in the night.

When they were gone, it had shifted its coils and its efforts to shielding just me from the cold, and that is when my feet began to thaw.

"Guides!" The word tore out of me, rupturing into a wretched sob. I flopped back toward the boys, sat between Gideous and Henri and pulled the pair of stiff toddlers onto my lap. A mat of leaves had frozen to the back of Fey's head, and I curled over him and bawled as I tried to brush it off. My head swam with blue. The wind flickered over my skin like fire, and my feet smouldered. I would have given *anything* to pass that heat onto the small sleeping dolls in my arms, but it was too late. All of the sick heat gathering in my chest wasn't enough to bring them back. *You let them die.* The awful realization strangled me. The thought aimed inward this time, not at the wurm. *You told them you would save them, and you let them die.*

Sunlight pooled at the edge of the gully, garish in its peach tones. I bent over the boys, squeezed my eyes shut and rocked, raining useless tears on their cheeks, praying with all the stupid hope of a naive, lost child, that they would wake up—that *I* would wake up.

I screamed as feelers wrapped around my elbow and pulled me back, but the sound was muffled because the whole world folded into a muted mess. I tried to yank my arm from the grip of a jawless mouth that held me with all the gentle firmness of a mother vaiya moving her chick.

The wurm ignored my weak wriggling and pressed pale green assurances past the black in my mind as it dragged me up the gully floor. When it reared up, pulling me with it, my foggy world snapped back into painful focus.

"Hey!" I yelped, and the protest devolved into a garbled wail of pain as my half-frozen feet scrambled for purchase in the leaf litter. I looked down, certain I'd stumbled into the coals of some half-buried fire, but only saw snow and my yellow-grey toes. When my gaze swung up, the soft, crumbling bank of the gully rose before me. A cavernous hole, laced with tree roots, yawned at face level. My stomach coiled.

Wurm tunnel. This is where they broke through last night —and before I could finish the thought, hundreds of fat feelers began stuffing me in.

"No—" My open mouth filled with falling dirt. Clods of it plopped onto my shoulders as my head pressed past the fibrous roof. I squeezed my eyes shut, spat, and pinched my lips. *Stop! What are you doing?* But the wurm ignored me, industrious feelers tucking my limbs through the opening like sausage into casing. Exhaustion leached into my bones, and I couldn't protect all my various wounds from the jostling. Pain pounced from everywhere at once.

The wurm hauled itself into the hole after me, dirt sifting beneath its belly, segmented white sections sweeping my ribs and thighs. Only then did I realize how large the interior of the cavern was. "You cleared it? When?"

The wurm lifted its face. Backlit by watery morning light, I could only see shadows of its feelers fanning in waves and the vague darkness of its amorphous quivering mouth. I would have shuddered at the gruesome display if not for the accompanying green ring spinning through my head.

"Quite pleased with yourself?" I quipped.

It froze, and the happy ring warped and dissolved at my acidic thought.

I'm sorry. I swallowed. *You did well. It's much warmer here, and I couldn't have dug this alone.* A colder, more personal reflection prodded me. I'd already be dead if not for this wurm. I needed to watch my thoughts. I'd still be dead if it decided to leave.

Acerbic fear saturated my mind. The wurm's jawless mouth sucked shut and its blunt face pressed within inches of mine. Sour breath slid past its clamped feelers with a deep, shuddering whoosh. For some reason, I was struck with unbefitting wonder at the fact that it breathed. *And it hears your thoughts, even the ones you try to shield. What in Nasheira's name happened last night?* My heartbeat ratcheted faster, responding to the agitation rolling through my skull. *All right.* I held up both my hands. *All right, no talk of leaving.*

Soon after the wurm settled, the pounding in my feet and the pain between my legs flared again, and I could do nothing to tamp it. Cool buds of yellow-green billowed over me and the slow cadence of the wurm breathing pressed against my side. For a long while, I swam in hazy discomfort, decompressing. I poked at the shallow wound scraping up my stomach, amazed that it had not festered, and my head didn't yet pound from the wurm venom. *We are bonded somehow. Does that nullify the poison?*

Eager green spiked in my head.

"The scar?" I croaked. "It happened when you felt the Speaker's scar?" Vaiya chicks imprinted on the first face they saw after hatching. That's how we domesticated them. Wurms were sightless. It made sense that if they bonded similarly, they would do so by feel. *Would you have eaten me if you hadn't found the scar?*

A jaundiced curl of confusion.

Do you remember anything before the scar?

Red. Hunger, diluting to pale perplexity.

In the confined cavern, the warmth of the wurm grew smothering. My feet settled into a dull throb that synchronized with the wound at my groin and my fractured hand. My fingers tingled. Sleep pulled at me with an appeal only matched by the hunger prodding my brain. I couldn't tell if it was mine or the wurm's.

When was the last time I ate? My stomach pinched, recalling the untouched plate of sliced harek I'd turned aside on the morning of the sacrifice.

The wurm stretched, wistful feathers of red tickling my thoughts.

How are you *still hungry? Guides, you ate two bloody wurms earlier.* I glanced down at my pounding feet. My toes swelled like sausages. Bile stung my throat and I gagged. *You can't walk. Even if you had a weapon, you can't hunt. You're a dead man, Akrist.*

The wurm shuddered and swamped my mind with thick yellow terror. I struggled to resurface. Breath sawed out of me in sharp coughs. "How fast can you travel?" I blurted.

A frail sunrise of yellow and orange answered me.

I pressed forward the image of a pit trap, the one Fraesh had found the gazelle in, about a mile up the gully. In my head, I carefully detailed the gnarled ula tree nearby with the trunk I'd always thought resembled a sagging face. *Can you go there? There may be food, an animal trapped down a hole.*

Nothing but undiluted yellow now.

I tamped down the swelling panic in my mind, loosened my shoulders, and offered my palms. *Look, I'm not going anywhere. First get the blankets. There should be four or five, under the snow—*I faltered, blinking in the dark, and pressed my head back into the scratchy soil. *Under the snow, near the boys.* I pictured my scalloped birth blanket, and the wurm wriggled and squeezed out of the hole.

It took awhile, but after it fetched the blankets, I coerced it into leaving with the promise of food. As I folded the snow-crusted blankets around me, the wurm slinked past the frame of the tunnel entrance, past the boys, and I added: *If it is something with fur, bring it all back. Don't eat it until you bring it here.*

When the wurm had gone, and its tinted mental imprint

washed out to nearly nothing, my breathing accelerated again. I couldn't stop it. *What if something comes for the boys while it's gone? I have nothing, no weapon. I can't even crawl, for Nasheira's sake.* But nothing crept into the valley except sunlight. Birds trilled far overhead, one of them employing the same low whistle Jin liked to use to identify his position during a hunt. My stomach ached, and I shivered, but I stayed awake until colour bloomed in my mind again, and my wurm appeared in the entryway clutching a bloody half of a black ox yearling.

I said bring it all back if it had fur. I frowned, and the wurm presented the half carcass with a nudge and a satisfied trill of green.

I ate as many mouthfuls of raw meat as I could swallow, and then, while wiping my hands on my bare thighs, asked the wurm to find me dry bark, hairy moss, and a thin green bough. *And a pouch, by the boys. It had red powder in it, with a long thread nearby. Can you remember all that?* Despite its blindness, the wurm retrieved it all with expedient eagerness.

I dreaded the exertion of starting a fire. My bones felt waterlogged and my muscles flat. A small voice in my head struggled against the thickening web of lethargy. *Keep moving. You need fire. If it gets any colder, you won't survive with just the wurm's warmth. And if you lay down now, you won't ever wake up.*

I doubled up Iva's leather thread to build a fire bow and then leaned into the gruelling task of starting an ember bed on a wide chunk of bark at the lip of the tunnel. When my energy flagged, when the wound at my groin began oozing blood, warm tones of yellow-green bolstered me. With shaking arms and cold sweat clammy against my ribs, I offered fervent praise to Nasheira when the first curls of smoke twined around the fire stick.

The wurm balked at the embers. I remembered they hated fire. *It's all right. You don't have to stay. I need more wood. Dry. And the same hairy moss, lots of it.*

After noon, I basked in the glow of a hearty fire. I had the wurm pull off the haunch of the ox calf while I used a chunk of wood to scrape a crater in the coal bed large enough to bury and roast the leg. I undid the fire bow, picked the needle out from the pouch, and coped with the uncomfortable task of stitching the wound Aella had dealt me. I couldn't really see it. Just reaching it involved nearly folding in half, and I sorely missed the use of my right hand, so progress was slow and excruciating. Tugging the last knot tight, I deflated with a damp exhale and fell back against the tunnel entrance, my sweating, trembling fingers slick with blood. My vision blurred. *Climb inside. Do not fall asleep out here.*

My last shred of resolve plucked tight, twisted and frayed as I scrambled to scale the lip of the cavern alone. I couldn't bribe the wurm near enough to the fire to help. As soon as I rolled into the shelter, as my clumsy hands pulled tangled blankets over me, I pleaded with the pale form lurking far from the fire.

Please don't let it go out. Wake me if it's dying, all right? I can't light it again, and I need it, understand? I need it to live.

It arched, feelers sampling, and offered a green affirmative.

Don't eat the boys.

A sharp wince. Blue, indignant hurt shuddered through me, but I still sensed the undercurrent of red.

You can have the ox. Whatever is left that's not cooking. Can you peel off the skin? I licked my lips and tried to think clearly, but exhaustion gripped me. I tried again. *Do you think you can leave the fur behind?* Sweet Nasheira, I would need more than birthing blankets for clothing.

Pale green, wavering. I wasn't sure it understood, but my

body bore down in heavy connection with the ground beneath. Every part of me ached for sleep. I pushed off one last frantic thought.

Don't let anything eat the boys. Don't let anything near them.
And then I was gone.

CHAPTER THIRTY-ONE

Some time through the night, the wurm awakened me, as requested, when the fire subsided to a sleepy smoulder. I jumped at the touch of a single, soft feeler. A strange realization struck me as I straddled the blurry edge of awareness and blinked up at the monster who'd shadowed my nightmares since childhood. *I can't smell it*, I realized.

I inhaled deeply and frowned in mild surprise at the absence of the stench that had announced the presence of every wurm I'd ever encountered. I smelled burnt hair, smoke from the fire outside, and beneath all that, the rich syrupy scent of autumn bleaching the leaves above. *No smell of wurm, though. Because we imprinted?* I raised my eyebrows at the thought. True, it would be difficult to bond with something when the very whiff of it induced gagging. *Did it somehow shed its stench once it imprinted, or does it still carry an awful smell, and I am the only one unable to detect it?*

My wondering ceased as the wind changed, and a clump of black hair rode the fire smoke past the wurm toward me, settling on my lap. I leaned around the wurm and peered into the dark. Clots of dark fur swirled and scattered across the gully floor. Easing my sore body out of the hole in the bank, I shivered, leaned toward the fire and reached for the buried leg of calf. I'd left the hoof as a handle to pull it out of the coals. When my hand closed onto a slimy, jagged stump of bone, I recoiled, wiping my palm on my thigh. A clotting cramp gripped my stomach, and pink projected pain hinted that the ache I experienced was not my own. *Sympathy pains. For a wurm?*

"You ate the hoof?" I swung back to the wurm, a sharp snort of laughter escaping me as I took in the clumps of wet, black fur clotting its fidgeting feelers. An errant tuft rolled into the coals, flashed and then fizzled out. "And you left the fur." I smiled, despite myself. *I meant leave the hide. I needed the whole hide to wear. Clothing.*

The wurm, occupied with sweeping stubborn hair off its feelers, offered only distracted, yellow confusion, plaited with flushed distress.

I pressed a palm against my sympathetic stomach and groaned. "What else did you eat?"

The remainder of the ox carcass, save the roasting leg and the migrating mats of fur, had disappeared. My gaze shot over my right shoulder, and only when I squinted into the gloom could I discern four quiet bodies folded near the pechi trees.

The pechi trees! Silhouetted against the soft night sky, several of them stretched serenely to the stars, but at least two, Gideous' and mine, had been felled. Their sharp, splintered stumps jutted out of the gully floor like exposed ribs. Branches lay stripped bare and large gouges cratered the trunks.

You ate trees. I turned back to the wurm who still battled the barrage of fur clinging to its face. Wistful tendrils of hunger swirled through me. *You can't eat trees.* I reached forward, snagged a rather large wad of fur away from the wurm's face and shook my head at the insistent red clouding my mind. *It doesn't matter how hungry you are. No trees. No rocks. How has your kind even survived this long?*

I tucked the fur under my arm, plucked a handful of twigs from the leaf litter beside me, and then used both to stoke the fire. Orange light illuminated the gully, and I pulled a few dry chunks from my pile of wood to feed the flames. Grasping the footless haunch by its gnawed bone, I shook it out of the coals. The skin crackled, blackened and crisp. Grease burned my fingers as I peeled back charred hide and inhaled the incredible aroma of cooked meat. Sharp red spiked in my mind even as the wurm balked from the fire.

Go. Scavenge. I will be right here. Find an animal. Saliva filled my mouth, and I burned my tongue as I bit into the haunch. Hot juice rolled down my chin. I closed my eyes and grunted as I chewed. *I wonder if it feels hungry because I am hungry. Does the empathy flow both ways?* Guilt touched me as I watched the pale creature coiling, practically pacing the edge of the firelight's boundary. I paused mid-chew. *It won't be enough to fill you anyway. I've only had a few bites, and I can't hunt until I can walk. I need you to go to a stream or a river. Look for large pine trees. Gazelle sometimes sleep under the hollow, wild vaiyas too.* I concentrated on conveying both of the images clearly. *Bring what you find back, and I'll tell you which parts are safe to eat.*

Broadcasting a sullen stream of grey, the wurm slipped into the excavated tunnel behind me. Jagged anxiety rose in me, as the wurm's presence curled away, tracing a subterranean course from the gully. While it was gone, I devoured the charred leg of meat, banked the fire and gathered as much ox fur as I could. *Don't look at the boys.* Tears stung my eyes as I plucked tufts of fur from the leaves. *Do not break down.* I bit my tongue. *You don't have the strength to put yourself together if you break down.* I curled back into the cavern mouth, into the nest of birthing blankets, and examined my feet in the orange glow.

Fluid-filled blisters bulged beneath taut skin. The three smallest toes on my left foot boasted ugly half moons of maroon under their nails. *Frostbite.* I'd seen its grizzly effects before, following the devastating snow at the lake camp, and several times since. *Mother of Yurrii, I cannot lose toes to this, and I don't have junab leaves to fight infection.* Even if I knew where to find it, the low-lying succulent was almost inaccessible in winter, shrivelled and buried beneath deep blankets of snow. Wincing, I tucked the wadded ox hair around my wounded feet and wrapped the smallest blanket around them. Then I curled under the rest of the layers and let sleep pull me into numbness until the wurm returned.

Grass green spikes of cheer heralded the wurm's discovery of food long before it emerged from the back of the tunnel. The fire at the entrance had shrunk to a lightless smoulder, and I couldn't identify the carcasses it dragged, but there were three of them. "What did you find?" I asked from under the blankets.

The bounding green in my head smoothed to a solid background, silhouetted clearly in the centre, a ridged and tapered twist. I frowned. The wurm pushed the still warm carcasses against my leg, and I stroked the pelts while the image repeated in my head, this time mirrored. Ah! The slight spirals were horns. *Gazelle? You found gazelle?* No response until I concentrated on the image of a plump, young buck, and then, a bright green bubble of affirmation.

"Good." I grinned, reached forward and patted the wurm. Relief and exhaustion simultaneously pooled in my belly. I had my hides, but no knife, and no energy to skin them. Even if I managed to somehow dress the carcasses, it would take days of scraping, soaking and stitching to make a decent overcoat, and I needed clothes now. I lost every shred of warmth the wurm provided me the moment it left to hunt for us. I couldn't last like this.

Feel this. I pulled a blanket off my chest and pressed it toward the wurm's feelers. As it examined it, I explained. *It is the skin of an animal, taken off all in one piece. I need the skin of these animals for me, or I'll freeze. I'll die.* Pallid horror swamped me as the wurm dropped the soft blanket and shuddered. *I have no knife. You have teeth. I can show you how to take the skin and the fur off, all in one piece like this blanket. If you do well, you can eat all of the gazelles after, everything but the bones and heads.*

I slid out of the cave and waited until the wurm obeyed my command to pull the trio of gazelles to the far side of the coals. Refuelling the fire, I hauled myself back into the cavern mouth, re-packed my feet and burrowed, shivering, back under the blankets. *All right, here we go.* Closing my eyes, I pictured the gazelle splayed on its back with a shallow cut tracing from under its chin to its tail, branching at the legs. Under my meticulous instruction, my loyal wurm skinned all three carcasses, gorged on its reward, and moved a substantial pile of wood next to the boys.

At dawn, I set the pyre and cremated the daeson.

I squinted up at the oily column of smoke writhing skyward before tracing it down to the pyre and the four bodies engulfed within. The soft smell of burning kiro grass soothed my insides, and I thanked the wurm again for gathering it. Its consciousness reached for mine like a small hand requesting reassurance. I projected thoughts of warmth and safety down and around the far bend in the gully where I sensed it waiting, too terrified of the funeral fire to venture closer.

They are the first, I realized. *The first eldest sons to be sent to Nasheira in smoke, instead of left to rot for Pau. They are free.* Blinking at the sunrise through the smoke, eyes stinging with tears, I swallowed at the earthy tones of consoling green the wurm sent from afar. *Tonight will mark two days since the sacrifice.* That meant any daeson out there still alive could be rescued after sunset. Aeni often scoured sacrifice sites because, once healed, daeson made fantastic servants, ones who owed their masters their very lives. They wouldn't touch me, though, even if they found me. I was a branded man.

Brushing a finger over the tender scab on my cheek, I wondered where Yara was. I ached for her. *Mother of Yurrii.* I gulped. *Please protect her. Keep her safe.* That short prayer was all I could allow her. If I didn't move to deflect them, thoughts of Yara thudded through me like well-aimed spears. "Don't," I gasped. *Don't think about her. It's pulling you under. You want to save her? You focus on staying alive first.*

The wurm hunted while I worked. As it left, I pressed a bright map of the entire trap line branching past our gully into its mind and followed with an earnest warning. *Stay away from other people. Stay far away from them, their food and their vaiyas. They'll kill you if they can.* I feared losing the wurm. The thought seemed ridiculous; I feared losing a *wurm,* a wretched scavenger, the wicked icon of Pau, white trespasser of my nightmares. Yet this one was different. Some sentient switch had flicked on when those feelers found my Speaker's scar. I couldn't pinpoint whether the awakening occurred in me, or in the wurm, but I felt certain now, had I been a bare-chested boy, it would have devoured me.

It eats trees, for Nasheira's sake. I snorted as I ran my fingers over the deep gouges in the felled pechi trees. My fingers closed on a hard, half-buried slice of white. I jiggled it free and held the wurm tooth up to the light to examine its edge. Razor sharp.

"Good," I murmured and crawled back to the cover of my

cavern. The heat from the blazing pyre pressed against my bare back as I went. *Naked. You've survived a snowstorm, a sacrifice, and two nights exposed to the elements naked, frostbitten and wounded. Without the wurm, how many times would you have died by now?*

I reached for the colourful comfort of its presence, unaware I'd done so until cold anxiety washed through me. *Too far. It's too far for you to sense.* I swallowed. *It's doing its job. Get on with yours.* Crawling past my hearth fire on bruised knees, I rotated the three blackened gazelle skulls skirting the coals and pulled myself with a groan into the gully wall, wurm tooth clenched in a fist. My feet stung as I pillowed them on the pile of ox hair and spread the five small birthing blankets across my lap. *Thank Nasheira, there are five.* I'd sworn I'd seen Henri drop his. The toddlers had too, at numerous points in our gruesome procession.

I'd not appreciated the essential symbolism of the blankets until now. Each daeson parent apparently had, though, because they were all here; each blanket had been hand-stitched by a father, token symbols of sanctuary against the elements. In the end, it was all that delineated sacrifice from murder, the fact that they left you a damned blanket. So, yes, all five had been carefully accounted for and left behind. I fingered the scalloped edge of Hasev's handiwork. Funny that this faded cloth, kept all these years as a representation of refuge, would become under-clothing for me now.

I smoothed the smallest blanket over my knees and scored a line down the edge of it with the wurm's tooth. Once I'd cut eleven arm-lengths of leather thread, I sawed duplicate rough forms of a tunic with the two largest blankets, and cut the smaller one into leggings. The leftover cloth made a simple breechcloth and belt.

My fingers were nicked and bleeding from gripping the wurm's tooth and, despite my nudity, sweat rolled down my ribs as I crouched in the cavern. Stretching, blinking at my hearth fire, I stopped only long enough to bank the coals, turn the gazelle skulls and scoop a few handfuls of melted snow into my mouth.

With my thirst quenched, I scraped up the last patches of snow I could find and funnelled it, sizzling, into the fractured holes punched through the forehead of each skull. Returning on stiff knees to my shelter, I wrapped and secured the breechcloth over my hips. I used the wurm tooth to cut small slits parallel to the outer edges on what would be the front panel of my leggings. Once I'd done the same to the rear panel, I began sewing it all together, poking the thick thread through pre-cut holes using the needle as an awl. The delicate task emphasized a lingering numbness in my finger pads and a twinge in my wrists.

Before the wurm returned, I'd completed the leggings, shimmied into them and stuffed the breechcloth with a wad of ox hair padding. The fabric felt like fire against the stitched wound at my groin. *I need junab.* Gingerly, I clutched my belt and winced as my thumbnail caught on the shallow scab at my stomach where my wurm's tooth had grazed me. *Strange. Not infected. Not even red.* Recalling the angry, poisoned puncture at my leg from the wurm in the pit trap, how the wound had festered, the horrible, heavy headache it had induced, I frowned. *Am I immune to my own wurm's venom?* It seemed more than that. As I peered down at the scrape, the back of my neck tingled. *It's mended since yesterday, enough for you to notice. From poison to balm then?* My eyebrows rose at the thought. *Perhaps I don't need junab after all.*

Pink billowed amidst my grey thoughts, feathered and cloudy. I paused, needle still hanging in my hand, and smiled. Colour soaked into my blank mind. "Still hungry?" I squinted into the black tunnel but heard nothing.

Dull green muddied the pink frustration, and I took that as an affirmative.

"No luck? Did you find the trap line?"

A smudge of green again. Yes.

"What's wrong then? No food?"

Red hunger spun into the mix, and the whole palette muddled to brown. I caught a vague shape, long ears and a bunched back. It repeated once more before diving into the burrow of brown.

Rabbits? Two of them! Wonderful. One for me and one for you then. So what's wrong, hollow belly?

The ruined puddle of emotion expanded in my mind. Far in the throat of the tunnel, a soft sift of dirt announced the wurm's approach. I pressed a few more stitches through the sleeve of the shirt in my lap and waited. Sure enough, the flower of feelers squeezed through the hole, half of them pressing out against the widening cavern while the other half cradled a floppy, long carcass. Even in the half-light, I admired the white fur of a sizable jack rabbit.

So you ate the other one... I guessed as the huge wurm extruded out of the tunnel, segment by segment. *I expected as much. You brought one back one for me, that's good enough.*

The wurm dropped the rabbit. Half of the feelers flocked to the right side of its face where a few of the appendages hung limp. Its shapeless face twisted and tipped down. When it shook its head with a snap, the lifeless feelers flapped like wet cloths and rings of teeth in its mouth shuddered.

What's wrong? Frowning, I leaned toward the wurm and my throat compressed as an awful image of Vax's crushed eye socket gelled in my mind. The wurm in the shadows balked away from me just as the wounded vaiya of my childhood had done. I dropped the needle and pushed the crumpled fabric off my lap, scooting towards the wurm, heedless of the white coils that bulged taller than my torso. *What is it?*

Pressing a blue web of pain at me, the wurm arched away, and a few of its feelers jerked at something like desperate fingers picking at a knot.

"Let me see." My hoarse whisper sounded too loud, but the wurm didn't jerk, even as I pressed my hand against the side of its featureless face. *Come on, let me look.*

Some of the clutching feelers fell away from the right side, curled and flexed nervously. Then one of them twisted and pressed against the back of my hand as the wurm curled to expose its right side to me. Even in the near dark of the cave, my eyes perceived a familiar dark cord cutting deep into pale flesh.

"Ah, Guides!" A looped snare garrotted around two of the wurm's feelers tightly enough that they looked pinched off. Below the constriction they bulged grey and flaccid. Acid curled up my throat. "I showed you the signs! I told you to watch for the trees with five slashes!" As the hot accusation left me drowning in my wurm's purple shame, a sober realization broadsided it. Yes, I had passed the image of five horizontal slashes on a tree trunk that signalled a spring snare on our trap lines. I'd warned the wurm to skirt the signs if it came across them and an animal hadn't already sprung the trap. The wurm who couldn't *see*, who navigated entirely by feel and by sound. *Sweet Nasheira,* even if it scrutinized every tree trunk on the trail, it could have easily missed the visual clues. What in Yurrii's name had I been thinking?

"I'm sorry," I gulped. *I can get it off. Just stay still, all right?*

A trembling green assent drifted my way, but the whoosh of the wurm's breathing quickened as my hand slid off its cheek to reach for the snare. I thought I could loop a finger under the cord and slip it off, but as I pressed, the giant wurm quivered, and I couldn't get underneath the snare. "All right." I licked my lips, shifted and raised my right hand. My fingers curled protectively against my palm. Awkwardly, I hugged behind the injured feelers with my right forearm and tried to loosen the snare with my left. The feelers surrounding my right wrist looped to stroke my fingers. My fingertip wriggled beneath the cinched snare and eased it loose. Exhaling in victory, I flicked it aside. The wurm shuddered and laid its massive head over my knees like a vaiya.

"All right." I panted and patted its head. "You're right. Bad idea. No more trap lines."

It wasn't until later, as I skinned and dressed the rabbit to roast it, that a curious question rolled over in my mind. *If it can't see, how does it know the shape of a gazelle horn? How does it compose the image of a rabbit?* I turned to the wurm, aware that it had overheard, and waited for an answer.

It lifted its head but kept sucking on the pair of injured feelers as it flipped me the mental equivalent of a shrug.

Irresistible odours wafted into the cavern as the rabbit roasted. I gorged on hot, rich meat as the afternoon sky darkened and a misting rain blanketed the gully. Shivering, bare-chested, I licked the last morsels off my fingers before choosing a large half-crescent of fungus from the pile stacked near the wood. I'd instructed the wurm to gather it along with fuel for the fire. Fishing a branch from the wood pile, I pressed a hollow into the flat top of the fungus and then scooped a glowing coal into it. Pressing another slice of fungus on top, I ferried the ember bed, and the remaining half of the rabbit back to the cavern.

"Not much," I apologized as I leaned into the entryway.

The wurm lifted its head, gingerly touched the meat and recoiled.

It's cooked. I smiled. *Tastes better than trees, I assure you.*

I couldn't shake the feeling, as the wurm's shapeless mouth slowly took in the rabbit's head, that it ate the offering entirely out of politeness. Shrugging, I turned, reloaded the fire against the rain and then, after a moment of staring at the dampening wood pile, set to work transferring it to the tunnel entrance. By the time I settled back into the cavern with my sewing, exhaustion hung heavy in my limbs, and the pain of all of my wounds amplified. I held the half-sewn shirt in my lap only a moment before pulling it up to my chin, leaning back against the warmth of the wurm and closing my eyes. I drifted off, confident that the fungus-cradled coal near my feet would smoulder for around five hours. *If the sun has set, you are a free man by now. You've paid your debt. But if Pau's curse has been bled out of you, why does everything feel the same?*

CHAPTER THIRTY-TWO

I awoke shivering. Rain permeated the cavern as a clinging mist, beading the blanket covering me. The grey atmosphere offered no hint of the time of day. As I leaned away from the warmth of the wurm, my mind reached for its colourful consciousness and stumbled when it didn't find it. Startled, I turned in the half dark and realized it slept. Deep draughts of breath filled and drained from thick coils. Injured feelers remained tucked into its shapeless mouth. Other than the occasional twitch, the other feelers relaxed, motionless and half-curled. The sound of the wurm slumbering, the slow expansion and release of its pale flanks, eased me, as steadying as the waves of a lake. I would have watched it, fascinated, for much longer had I not remembered the fire.

I curled toward the stacked fungus on my left side, wincing at the stiff pain of cold limbs and aching injuries. As I twisted to grab the coal bed, my back cracked, and I groaned at the small release. I tipped up the top fungus plate and breathed glowing life back into the nested coal before adding a few curls of bark. My eyes stung with smoke, and the wurm shifted, restless in its sleep, but soon a tiny flame licked to life and bathed the grey cavern in wavering orange light. I leaned into it, hungry for warmth, swimming in the fog of my breath. *Guides,* I ached for a full fledged blaze, but the wurm would surely wake and bolt at the prospect of flames in such close proximity. I valued its steady warmth at my back more than the smoke-soured, half-starved fire that confinement was sure to produce. I fed my fire a few more morsels before capping it with the fungus top.

Rain fell outside in earnest now, and the wurm slept on. I sighed and picked up Fraesh's needle. *You have to finish the tunic today and start scraping the gazelle hides. You'll not pass another night half-clothed, not in this rain.* Even in this shelter, with the wurm to bolster me, the insidious creep of cold gnawed my bones. It would take me if I let it, just like it took the four daeson. *You won't finish in time. You'll freeze and some-day, someone will find you here half-naked, half-eaten by a wurm, needle still in hand.*

"No," I breathed, pressed the needle into the first hole and plucked the leather thread out the backside with resolve. *One stitch after the other. Don't think about the rest. Just one stitch.* Sweeping my mind clear, I fell into the methodical task, and at first, my mind eased as I busied with simple work. But my fractured right hand throbbed as I cradled it in my lap. My body screamed to stretch, to walk, despite my damaged feet, and soon my left hand cramped at its unfair workload. My mind refused to stay empty, swamped instead by images of Henri squirming in his own blood, Gideous's mottled, frozen face, and my mother flicking her bloodied blade. Whenever I paused to tend my lonely coal, the smoke smelled of yester-day's pyre.

They still lay out there, those boys, their remains, what-ever the rain had stolen from Nasheira when it snuffed out the pyre. I'd failed them in everything, even a proper crema-tion. The coward in me yearned to run from this place, from that fact. My frostbitten feet were retribution, intended to pin me right here, next to those four charred bodies outside.

My work swirled into a blotted mess in my hands. I pursed my lips against the tears, held the fabric closer to my face and blindly jammed the awl through its course. *Stop it! In and out, one stitch after the other, that's all. That's all there is.*

By the time the wurm woke, my hand trembled as I bound the last inseam on the tunic sleeve. Red blossomed in my mind, and the coil at my back shifted. I rocked forward as the wurm unravelled and sprang awake with unnerving ease. As it lifted its head and turned to me, the red expanded, a sharp and hollow itch crawling from my brain to my belly.

"Are you ever full?" A half grin pulled at the corners of my mouth even as my gut twinged sympathetically.

The wurm swung toward the back of the cave and then snapped its focus back to me, still sucking its bruised feelers.

First, let me see. I left the needle half pressed through a hole and shook out my hand before beckoning to the wurm.

Dirt rained down on us as the meaty body knotted itself and brushed against cavern walls. The wurm's face hung before mine, feelers threading through my fingers. *Spit them out so I can see them,* I ordered, and it obliged, sullenly. Two trembling feelers hung bruised and banded by the snare, a layer of clouded mucous coating them. I took them in my hand, prodded them gently and asked the wurm to press against my open palm. "All right." Satisfied that there appeared to be no serious damage, I nodded. Red threatened to suffocate all my other senses. *All right. Go, eat. No trap line. No people. No trees, for Nasheira's sake. Where will you look?*

A blue, serpentine band wove through the red landscape.

I nodded. *Rivers are good. Find a well-packed trail close to the edge and wait there. If you are quiet enough, something will come to you.*

As the wurm squeezed into the rear tunnel, I frowned

down at my slimy left hand. *Am I imagining it, or is the cramp easing?* Burrowing away from me, the wurm answered in bright green. I spread my fingers wide and wrinkled my nose at the gelatinous webbing arcing between them. Clenching my teeth, I smeared an experimental dab over the knuckles of my right hand and waited. It didn't take long. Shocking relief swam through me as the wurm saliva numbed the grating ache of my unhealed hand. *I was right before. It's like junab.* I wasted no time in applying it to my other injuries, although little remained for my feet.

No matter. I blinked down at my toes. Some of the blisters had broken and oozed freely. Fraesh would tell me not to drain the swollen ones that remained. It would only invite infection. With the skin stretched so taut over most of my toes that it shone, I didn't want to handle them more than necessary.

As the edges of my pain dulled, I plunged into my work. As soon as I finished the undershirt, I set it aside and crawled past my wood stack to the cavern mouth. My bladder sounded a sudden and urgent appeal. I hadn't pissed since Aella cut me, and I cringed to think of what she'd damaged down there, but I crawled out into the rain, and knelt in the soggy leaf litter. When it came, I winced in expectation of pain, but there was none, and everything seemed to function as it had before my mutilation. *Congratulations,* I thought sourly, *you can still piss.* I finished, gingerly tucked in, and hobbled to the fire pit where I'd buried the gazelle hides and the rabbit fur in excess ashes.

Wrapping the sopping mess over my shoulder, I crawled back to the cave, gripping a flat stone in my fist. Along with the food, firewood, kiro grass, and endless other life-saving errands, I'd remembered to ask the wurm to fetch me a flat rock. *Thank the Guides you do not have to search for one now.* I shivered at the rain rolling down my back and hauled myself to the muddy entryway. Then I repeated the trip with the scorched gazelle skulls.

Inside, I fed my coal, shrugged into my newly made undershirt and paused to trace the scalloped neckline of what had once been my birthing blanket. What a strange comfort, having Hasev's handiwork pressed against my chest. Blinking, I spread out the first soggy gazelle hide, flesh side up, and began scouring it with the stone.

The wurm returned when I was halfway through scraping the membranes off the third hide. I could tell by the tidal wave of red that it hadn't fed. Colour pierced me so intensely that my stomach clenched in reply.

When it squeezed into the cavern, it flooded the room with a sunset of hunger and anxiety. Its feelers froze, and its head shot up as it sampled the air. Then, with shocking speed, it lunged toward me and latched onto the fleshy gazelle hide. Teeth sliced across my knuckles as my left hand rose in defence.

"Hey," I bellowed. "Stop!"

The wurm jerked and lobbed a spike of red anger in my direction. The hide hung crumpled from its mouth. It did not chew, but it didn't release it either.

Drop it, now. I crammed the cold thought past the wash of red with slow authority. Blood beaded on my hand as I held it high. "Look what you've done." I flicked my wrist to show the wurm the shallow wound it had inflicted, then chastised myself. *It can't see.* I licked my lips. *You cut me. What's wrong with you?*

The pulsing red evaporated from the cavern, and the wurm deflated in the vacuum left in its wake. Its mouth slackened. It dropped the hide and plowed over it, head ducked and feelers trembling as it dabbed them over my hand. Feathered purple shame wisped over me, fringed with blue anguish.

I'd been unaware, until that moment, that I'd been grip-ping the flat rock in my left fist the whole time, that I still held it raised as a weapon. A stale exhalation spooled out of me, and I lowered my hand. "What are you doing?"

Pinched hunger galloped through my mind.

I know you're hungry, but there's no meat here if you didn't bring it. My teeth clacked shut as Fraesh's plump cheeks and crinkled eyes rose in my mind. The healer had offered Hasev that playful rebuke whenever the hunters returned long-faced and empty-handed to camp. The corner of my mouth twitched, and a suffocating band clamped around my chest, but I clenched my teeth, inhaled, and kept my gaze focused on the wurm. *Look, it's not my fault you didn't find anything, and coming back here to sulk isn't getting you any closer to food in your belly.*

The wurm snorted a short exhale.

Carefully I composed the image of a tree with rounded leaves and green pods that ripened and cracked to brown husks. *Cobnut tree. There are some near the trap line. The nuts are hidden under the leaves, usually in clusters of three or four. Only eat the nuts, not the trees, understand?*

The wurm's feelers fanned, and I cringed as it ground its teeth eagerly.

If you ever fill that belly, and there's any left for me, bring them back. I pieced together the particulars of the location as best as I could remember, and the wurm jerked out of the cavern, red and budding green ripening in its wake.

I finished scraping the gazelle hide, careful not to snag on the holes the wurm had punched through it, and then prepared the jackrabbit in the same way. They'd need to be thoroughly rinsed before the next step, more so than rain could provide. Luckily, the wurm knew where to find the river and, if it returned full, I hoped I could trust it to ferry the hides there, pin them under with large rocks and let them rinse overnight. Once rinsed, wrung and dried, I could start tanning the hides, but for the moment, until the rain stopped, I had nothing to occupy me save tending my fire starter.

I rolled the hides into tidy bundles and then, groaning against stiffening muscles, I slipped outside, cupped my hand and greedily drank rainwater from a hollow I'd grooved just past the cavern entry. With water sloshing in my belly and rain chilling my cheeks, I retreated into the cavern and fed the ember bed. Arranging my ruined feet on their ox hair bed, I shrugged down into the faint warmth of my newly sewn shirt, leaned back against the curved cavern wall and breathed. I listened to the rain, felt for the consciousness of the wurm, and when I'd confirmed that it was still too far to sense, I curled up and cried. Gut-wringing, ugly, lost child cries.

I let them choke everything else out of me.

CHAPTER THIRTY-THREE

I must have slept because I do not recall the wurm returning. As I blinked past foggy puffs of my breath in the gloom, small things registered, the velvet touch of dusk, an expanding warmth against my ribs, and the tender realization that the wurm had tucked against my side without waking me.

My throat ached, and I couldn't fight the aimless feeling of lightness in my limbs, like I was debris, scoured and washed clean, drifting in a soft, tangled clump. I felt separated from reality, from myself, from my own mottled feet, as if my earlier breakdown had peeled away layers of damage and left only my bleached essence floating above it all.

What if I don't get up? How long until I dissolve like foam on water, until the wurm devours me, and the cavern slumps in to swallow my remains? When does Yara's last memory of me unravel? At what point does she study our child's face and not find the ghost of my features there?

"Stop it," I hissed, and the wurm jerked in its sleep. "Keep moving."

When the wurm awoke in a familiar unfurling of red

hunger, I presented it with the rolled up hides. "Don't eat them, and don't lose them. Pin a big rock on top of them when you get them to deep water. Hunt if you like after that, but I'll be sending you back later to fetch the hides, so remember where you put them. Understand?"

The wurm answered in a pale green that fluttered into peach tones. I smiled and patted the side of its face. "I can't keep calling you 'it.' You aren't an it, are you? Do wurms even have a sex?"

The wurm reared up, huffing softly.

Are you a male, like me?

I was answered by a violet curl of distaste so immediate that I chuckled.

"A female?"

Green.

To the river then, my girl. Don't forget where you pin those hides.

I'd sharpened three dozen wooden pegs with the wurm tooth by the time she returned. Green wafts of contentment announced my wurm's arrival, punctuated by a shaft of anxious yellow when she didn't find me in the cavern.

"Out here." I blinked past the smoke into the moonless night until I made out her pale flank skirting the edge of the fire light. *You are happy. You must be full. What did you find?*

Green wisps flickered through my mind, whipping tails and blunt heads, darting in happy unison.

"Fish?" I blurted, eyebrows raised. *How did you catch fish?* Leaning forward, I added, *Can you swim?*

Beyond the firelight, the wurm wriggled excitedly as she projected a faint grey negative, followed by the strikingly clear image of a blue tree falling into a river.

I don't understand.

The image shifted to a top view of a winding river with one shallow bank partially barricaded by a blue obstacle.

Green ribbons funnelled into the mouth of the open V and accumulated there. One by one, they winked out.

"A log?" A wide smile broke across my face, and I winced as it pulled at the tender brand on my cheek. *A fallen log jutting out from the bank, and you herded them into the V, like a fish trap?*

A bouncing, green affirmative tossed through my mind like laughter as the wurm's sightless face bobbed in the darkness.

"How many did you catch?"

Green wisps dotted my mind like stars, and the wurm's head bobbed faster as waves of green-blue content rolled off her.

"Bellies-full, huh? Impossible. There isn't enough fish in the river to fill that hole—"

As I spoke, the wurm skirted the fire and deposited two fish in my lap. Deep-bodied, sizable carp. I hadn't seen them tucked behind her feelers.

Smooth rows of oval scales the size of fingernails gleamed orange in the firelight. I traced a finger down the flank of one fish and stuttered, "Th-thank you." I hadn't asked her this time, to bring me back food, and I'd assumed she wouldn't remember. Reaching up, I patted the side of the featureless face hovering before me in the dark. *So smart.*

Waves of giddy green bubbled over me as the wurm pressed into my hand, preening. Sentient. Intelligent. Even now, in the direct face of evidence, I struggled with the idea. Yet here she was, surprising me, saving my life on a daily basis.

We both went to bed with full bellies that night. The next morning, the clouds cleared, and the wurm fetched me my rinsed hides. I set up next to the tree stump I'd been tied to on the night of sacrifice. One by one, I looped each hide around the stump and then wrapped the ends around a stout branch. Twisting the branch allowed me to wring the hides thoroughly. Then I stretched and pegged them to the gully floor to dry. In the heat of summer, a hide could dry in hours. Today, after so much rain and with a weak pre-winter sun pale in the sky, I judged it would take all day.

Laying the second fish over hot coals, I settled near the fire. Thoughts of Yara circled like birds settling to roost. I rubbed at the tightness in my throat, and stared into the coals until I could swallow. A sharp crackle of wood made me jump and blink down at the fish. The whole flank of it had charred. I yanked it from the flames and inspected it with a frown. *Badly burnt.* Yet I only remembered staring into the coals for a breath or two. *Focus. You ruined a whole fish.* Shaking my head, I chewed on the overcooked scraps of meat and picked through the bones to find suitable needles.

As I worked, I pressed my mind blank and consciously kept the soggy remains of the daeson's pyre at my back. Paired with the smell of burned fish, the gravity of that crumbled mess threatened to squeeze the life out of me if I looked at it for too long. Instead, I nursed my bruised knees and flexed my toes. My kneecaps ached, wrapped in raw and mottled purple skin. *How much longer can you crawl around this gully like a wurm before you just lay down and...*

I clamped my teeth at the unfinished thought and inspected my toes. Less swollen today. Three of my left toenails had turned completely black. I was sure to lose those, but so far, no blackening of flesh. The wurm saliva, applied daily, seemed to be working. No infection. A mild fever perhaps, but everything seemed to be slowly healing.

Lose those toes, and it is over, you're a dead man.

Sighing, I consciously countered the darkness. *A few more days and I'll have proper clothes. I'll be healed enough to walk.* I allowed that thought to fill my empty chest. Escaping this subtle prison, beginning my search for Yara, maybe I could think of her then without drowning. Maybe I could close my eyes and see her face without it feeling like the gully was swallowing me.

My wurm returned that evening, irate and empty-bellied. She curled into her cloud of hunger like it was a blanket and abruptly fell asleep. I unpegged my brittle hides before fetching the gazelle skulls from the hearth fire. All three contained the warmed brain slurry I'd prepared before the rains came.

Pouring the oily mixture onto the hides, I spent the next few hours working it in. One-handed, the task took considerably longer than I remembered, but it was therapeutic, the hide softening and yielding under my hand as it absorbed the warm slurry. As I tanned all three of the gazelle hides and the rabbit, I imagined my own brain reduced to grey jelly, smoothing rough thoughts, soaking hard memory into softness. At one point, I swore I heard a working tune, one our camp women sang to pass the time when they tanned hides. It echoed as clear as if they sang right outside the cavern entrance. One of the singers sounded just like Yara. I flinched, not fast enough to catch the unravelling thread of pain. It was all I could do to hunch over the soggy hides, eyes screwed shut and breath pounding out of my lungs until the feeling rippled into stillness, and the song faded to ice. When I finished the last hide, I pressed them all into tight rolls, gathered them to my chest, and tipped sideways. I fell asleep like that, slurry-softened hands clutching my only chance of survival.

Before my wurm left to hunt the next day, she woke me. When I stared at her, unrecognizing, she pressed a gentle yellow query into the grey of my mind.

"What?" I mumbled. "What do you want?"

She kept asking, dropping small stones of yellow into my mind, like pebbles in a creek until the numbness of sleep receded, and I realized she was asking me what I wanted. I hadn't remembered until just then, that there was something I wanted from her. A tool.

I had her carve the pechi tree stump into a blunt tapering edge. She did a remarkable job of it in considerably less time than it would have taken me. Once she left, I straddled the tree stump scraper, stretching and buffing the hides, working them over the blunt wooden edge as they dried, and rubbing second coats of brain solution into the tough spots. Although sweat stung my eyes, and my fingers screamed in protest, I kept working and stretching the hides until they dried completely. By late afternoon, they were ready to smoke.

Using the fish bones, I pegged the hides into the rough shape of a sack, set a tripod of green sticks over my waning fire, and added a large chunk of wet, rotten wood to the coals before sliding the open end of my hide sack over the frame. Once properly smoked on both sides, my hides would be water repellent, washable, and wearable. Three gazelle hides would be enough to make an overcoat, a short one, but I could lengthen the hem and make sturdier leggings later on if Nasheira blessed me with good hunting. I had nothing to do now but wait for the hides to darken. An odd thought struck me as I dozed. *You are supposed to be long dead by now, branded, cut, unclothed and tied out for the scavengers to finish. You are a ghost. Arsu will never see you coming.*

I let that hard seed of vengeance root in my chest, perhaps because it coiled, colder and more manageable than the fire of emotion that engulfed me when I thought of finding Yara.

🗲

WEEKS PASSED BEFORE I WALKED, not days. Despite my careful prayers, my healing slowed just as surely as the sap in the trees around me did. We starved for days. Rain turned to snow. The wurm hunted and returned daily in a wash of forlorn red. I allowed her to return to the pit trap only after she pressed the image into my mind in desperation, and promised, as well as a wurm could with imagery and colour, to stay off the rest of the trap line. She returned that day with a skinny, half-devoured gazelle. I could tell by the accompanying purple wash of shame that she'd been the one who'd done the devouring, but I said nothing. She looked flaccid and grey, like a half-deflated water sack.

My stomach continued to cramp long after I'd filled it with gazelle meat. It wasn't until that night when my gut ache evolved to stabbing pain that I demanded, gasping, *What did you eat? Not just the gazelle, what else?*

She wouldn't tell me. A rock, a tree, something she shouldn't have, that much was certain. *Guides, let her eat it all next time. Your own hunger doesn't hurt as bad as these damned sympathy pains.*

My right hand had mostly mended. I couldn't straighten the last two fingers—they'd fused into a crooked, curled mess —but my forefinger and thumb gripped well now, so it didn't take as long to prepare and tan the gazelle hide. It provided just enough material for boots. I cut the soles roomy and lined them with white rabbit pelt. With a crutch tucked under my armpit, I paced the snowy gully floor, wincing, practising. Learning to walk again like a child, my sad, shuffling steps marred the world of fresh white around me. The frostbite didn't hurt anymore, but two black toenails had fallen from my left foot. The exposed nail beds felt raw despite the application of wurm saliva.

The next morning, perhaps a month after the moons eclipsed, I left the gully, limped over the lip of it like a newborn out of a dark womb.

In one hand, I gripped a fungus-capped coal bed and the

snare that had caught my wurm; in the other, a crude bone spear like a cane. My clothing hung heavy from my shoulders, grounding me as I blinked up at the treetops.

Shrivelled leaves rattled. Every restless thought that had threatened to drown me in the crevasse, every emotion I'd diverted, waited for me in those branches. I straightened as they dived. Images of Vax, Iva, Arsu, Yara, and my unborn child pelted me. My feet stumbled forward into soft, ankle-high snow.

I pressed away from the ledge and let it all fill me: my flocked emotions, the crisp bars of sun slanting through the open trees, vast swathes of snow-blanketed forest floor, still as held breath. I swallowed it all, swelling, held together only by the stiff seams of my multiple scars. I'd burst without them, the rest of my skin too weak, wrapped with roped tissue across my groin and my chest and my cheek.

I trudged further from the ravine, scrambling to steady myself against my spear. And the world still filled me up until it spilled from my mouth and purled past my lips, a steady current of words.

"I'm coming for you. I'm coming."

I'm coming.

CHAPTER THIRTY-FOUR

To avoid retracing the path we'd trod the night the moons eclipsed, I chose a different route south toward my old camp. As I threaded through the trees, an unsettled prickling roosted on my shoulders and pinned me in its grip. I couldn't place its source. At first, I guessed it was a fear of the wurm leaving me. She'd saved me in the gully. Our attachment had rooted in that hell of a hole. Would it wane as we left it behind? I reached for her like a child tugging at the corner of a blanket, and she answered from far ahead to my left with a content green trill. *No,* an instinctual knowledge threaded deep in my bones, *we are bonded. She could have left you hundreds of times already, but she stays. What, then?*

A branch snapped to my right. I sank against my spear, then fumbled to twist it from staff to weapon position. Breath snagged in my throat as the shaft slipped from my hand, and a small harek bolted out of the undergrowth, squealing, ears flapping like flags as she galloped away. *A half-grown sow. You, who once single-handedly brought down a black ox, tremble before a harek sow.* I flexed my half-healed hand, blinked down at the crooked fingers that refused to straighten, and bent to pick up the spear, relief pooling in my belly.

An orange, hopeful query pressed into my mind.

"Harek." I answered the wurm with a sigh. *No, I didn't get it.* "Mighty hunter." I murmured, and at the same moment realized the source of my fear. It wasn't any animal I feared crossing paths with. Guides, I wielded my own wurm. No, I feared humans, my own kind, what they'd do to me once they spied the brand on my cheek, how they'd butcher my wurm if they found her. Mostly I feared what a world freshly scrubbed clean of all daeson looked like. I'd seen it once before, and it had not changed me for the better.

There would be at least one daeson left if my child was a boy. And somehow, I knew he would be.

"He will never be daeson," I whispered under my breath, plunged the spear ahead into the rattling undergrowth, and tracked south. *I will save at least one damned son from his wretched fate.*

I needn't have worried, not about meeting a person, that is. A week and a half south of my abandoned ghost of a camp, my wurm scouted ahead of me, impatient at my wretched pace. I carried my spear now, but still limped as I trudged through a swath of crackling brown prairie. My frostbitten feet and the tight scar at my groin still announced themselves with each step I took. Older wounds haunted me too. The ugly brand on my cheek ached in the cold, and my right hand still wouldn't grip properly. I often dropped my spear.

Just the cold, I reasoned as I closed on a thick tree line. *You'll heal faster when it's warm.*

My wurm lobbed an urgent yellow warning, a silhouette of a man.

Where? I froze.

Using a green orb to mark my position, she placed the image of the yellow figure ahead of me, marred by blue trees.

Then she added a wriggling pale reproduction of herself, doubling back toward me.

Don't! She obeyed with a trembling shock of blue, just as a vaiya's warning call blasted through the clearing.

Vax! My heart bolted before my mind could reason with it. I shook my head. *Vax is dead. Arsu killed him. Snap out of it.*

"Ho there!" A bundled form waved from the tree line, foggy breath wreathing his head. "Nasheira's peace with you!"

I didn't return the expected reply of *May her Guides mark your skies.* My tongue wouldn't move. But the man still flashed a toothy grin and strode toward me. I saw, even from halfway across the clearing, that he was well wrapped in furs, and idly wondered if I could overpower him and steal them.

As if reading my thoughts, a dark vaiya, smaller and wirier than my Vax, hissed from behind my greeter. Another younger one sank into a defensive crouch. I couldn't be sure, but I thought I saw heads peeking over their silver backs, the ani's mates perhaps. I didn't have time to consider further, because the exuberant stranger waded through the grass toward me and shouted, "Perhaps you could settle a bet for us? I swore I smelled wurm just now. My vaiyas bawled, but my girls say they smell nothing and blame the warning call on you. You didn't happen to catch a whiff of one of the wretched things just now, did you?"

The ani stopped about ten feet before me and stretched his back, exposing a round belly. His gaze flicked over my shoddy overcoat and settled on the rough bone spear resting against my collarbone. Lips twitched as he opened his mouth to speak again, but before he could, I tilted my right cheek toward him and pointed to the S branded deeply there, the one that marked me as outcast.

His smile sagged. Breath whistled through his teeth before he spun and fell over himself in retreat. Scrambling away from me, the ani leapt onto the big vaiya and crashed into the woods, leaving his women and the smaller vaiya to trot after him. I squinted, heart pounding and breath held, but neither of the women looked anything like Yara.

When my wurm sent her orange question, it was braided with green, and my lips relaxed into a half smile as I understood her joke.

"No," I answered. "I didn't get him."

WEEKS PASSED. Wounds healed. I carved a spear so I could practice throwing. My crooked right hand fumbled less often. Numbness lingered in the pads of my thumbs. Sometimes all my fingers prickled like I'd shoved them into nettles, a permanent reminder of the weeks I'd been bound before sacrifice. As for the sacrificial cut, it had been a clean amputation, and it held well after I removed the stitches. Sometimes though, Nasheira forgive me, they *ached.* Even though they weren't there, my stones ached. Often I'd catch myself reaching to re-adjust down there, hand closing on nothing, itchy where I couldn't scratch.

Thick pink crescents of toenails crowned my misshapen toes. They froze so easily now. I wore twice the layers in my boots than I had in any previous winters, and still my feet often mottled white.

Occasional but fierce headaches plagued me, ghosts of blows delivered in the past. Sometimes my thoughts mashed and blurred together. Anger boiled up in me easier than it ever had, but I couldn't decide if that was a symptom of my injuries or just my circumstances.

Regardless of all that, I was whole enough to hunt. Snares weren't an option now that I moved as fast as the aeni. The wurm and I quickly adopted a routine in which she'd track ahead, locate potential prey, and drive them back toward me. I'd ambush and strike with the spear. It worked exceedingly well. She could sense the quietest things crouching in the undergrowth from miles away but was often not fast enough to catch them.

At first, I doubted her rapid growth, but there was no denying the stretch marks across her pale flanks. When she'd imprinted, she'd been twice my height. I stroked her stretched skin and frowned. *She must be twice the size she was then and as wide as you are tall. The slower she gets, the more voracious her appetite becomes.* It would outpace us soon. We'd done well hunting on the move, but lately, we spent more and more of our time pursuing food and less of it tracking south. My wurm would take down entire kills, sometimes multiple animals, and cry famine hours later, refusing my pleas to scan ahead for human life until I fed her more. I grew used to incessant hunger pains, a world awash with red, and the constant vigilance required to ensure she didn't ingest anything harmful.

In the coming weeks, I became the one who impatiently trekked ahead, crunching through tangled brush and pale prairies while my behemoth of a wurm trailed behind. When stomach cramps doubled me over and crashing waves of alternating orange and red hit me from behind, I hunted for my wurm. I apologized. I knelt before her as she sucked the bones of still steaming carcasses, and I pressed pictures of soft curls and the scent of cinnamon into my wurm's mind. I begged her to search for Yara, and she tried, she really did, but the sliver of blue sadness she returned to me as she scanned the vast landscape around us was quickly consumed by fiery red. Hunger ruled my wurm now.

Her skin itched and split. Junab salve would provide some relief, but the plant died back in the winter, and I couldn't recall any other remedies, even if I could find them amongst the frozen grass. When I rubbed down the flaking patches I could reach with grease drippings from our last kill, the smell drove her so mad I feared she'd bite herself.

One night, she boldly approached my evening fire. I watched her over the flames. When a log popped, lobbing a flock of sparks skyward, she reeled back, jawless mouth twitching, rows of teeth grinding, far above my head.

"Don't look at me like that," I mumbled past a mouthful of food and craned my neck to stare down her quivering, cavernous maw.

Hours ago, she'd sensed a black ox in our vicinity. From far behind me, she'd conveyed its location, and I'd crept up on it from the downwind side until I saw the cow, bedded down in the dusk. Only the wide arc of her horns and her small, flicking ears bobbed above the surface of the grassy plain between us. The evening breeze and I balanced in a frigid, formal dance. I'd wait for the next hesitant gust to rattle through the prairie toward me and only then would I edge forward through the snow-marbled grass, footfalls muffled.

As I crept close enough to hear the soft grind of the ox chewing her cud, raw hunger swelled and stabbed at my stomach. Red, acrid smoke clogged my mind, and I fought to hold it in check. One last sigh of wind skimmed the bobbing grass, and I slid into position.

Now, I ordered. Far upwind of the ox and I, branches clattered and snapped. The cow jerked, head tipped up, nostrils quivering. Although I couldn't smell it, I saw the exact moment the ox caught the scent of my wurm. Shuddering, she lunged away. I rose behind her and buried a spear between her ribs.

My wurm crashed through the brush like a slow motion avalanche. When she arrived, she swallowed the ox whole, just latched on and enveloped it. She didn't notice the missing foreleg.

"Don't," I repeated, chewing my mouthful of meat slowly. She swayed above me, red cascading off her like coals, belly still grotesquely distended and lumpy. *I get to eat too. Or would you have me starve and leave you all alone?*

Feelers jerked, and my gargantuan wurm shrank from my firm thought and flopped away from the fire. I exhaled. It took three swallows before the greasy lump of meat slid down my throat.

The next day, she couldn't move. "Your own fault," I sniffed and clutched at my own aching stomach. "Try chewing next time."

Only red answered me. That was the only colour she spoke with now.

Well if you want food, you have to follow. Takes too much time for me to track big game alone. You eat more than an entire camp.

More red.

"Guides!" I threw up my hands. "I am going. With or without you. I need to find her! *I* need to eat." I jabbed a finger at my chest. "And more than just a stringy leg of meat every three days!" Snatching my spear from the crook of a tree and kicking dirt over the cold coals, I turned from her and shook off the wisps of pale orange clinging to my wrists and ankles.

Mother of Yurrii, she kept me chained, circling her pit of hunger. *She saved you. You'd be dead without her. How many meals did she bring you as you wallowed in that gully?*

"I've repaid her tenfold, and I need to find Yara," I muttered as I trudged further from my wurm's reach. Red peeled in my mind, and I shouldered the spear and quickened my stride. It took a surprising amount of distance to outpace her connection. As she'd grown, so had her range of communication. I hadn't lost touch with her since the gully, and my wurm had almost tripled in size since then.

At first, I relished the hollow feeling in my head. I meandered down a game trail, poked at the caved-in remains of an old pit trap, knelt at a stream and washed without external thoughts ambushing my mind. Then I drank until my belly sloshed with icy water. *Mother of Yurrii,* how marvellous to feel full without that counterpoint of foreign hunger.

I stared at my reflection. Even blurred by soft eddies, my own face shocked me, the wild, black beard, gaunt cheeks and ropey serpentine scar. And, my eyes, as wounded as Hasev's, yet as cold as Aella's. *What have you become? You're not Akrist anymore. Will Yara even want you?*

My thoughts. Only my old daeson nemesis for company without the wurm to fill my mind. I left the stream and gathered some nuts from under the apron of a huge sagging tree, but couldn't bring myself to eat them. The emptiness in my brain itched. Some unidentified puncture pulled at my organs, sapping my strength. I tried to hunt but could manage little more than crouching by the game trail near the stream, and nothing came to drink.

When I finally stumbled back into the range of my wurm, her red greeting filled me like firelight. *I'm sorry.* My foot crunched over my half-buried hearth before I realized she'd moved. "Where are you?"

Orange, desperate, drowning and thick.

I couldn't find much without you. I clutched the edge of my overcoat against my chest. It bulged with stale nuts, a mere mouthful for my poor wurm. *But you can have it all, and together we'll bring down something bigger. You just need to come and find it with me.*

I circled the fire and picked up my abandoned carry sack. *Where are you?*

Red. A red egg, surrounded by brown.

Come on. Just come out. I said I'm sorry. I frowned at the lack of response. Stumbling farther from the hearth, I followed the wide wurm trail. Snapped saplings and scuffed snow led me west until the trees thinned, and a strange, knobbed mountain range stretched like the horizon's backbone. I came to a soft hillside topped by an ample, ancient-looking tree with skeletal branches. Lonely leaves clattered like beads in the breeze. The tang of fresh soil hung in my nostrils as I took in the crumbling hole chewed into the flank of the frozen hill, directly under the tree.

My feet slipped in crumbling soil as I scrambled up the lip of the tunnel and stumbled blindly inside. "What are you doing?" I flinched at the unexpected echo. *Are you eating dirt?*

The grinding screech of teeth and tumble of churned soil prickled the hair on the back of my neck. "Stop it. You'll get sick." Groping in the dark, I straightened, stretched tentatively for the ceiling of the fresh excavation and couldn't reach it. The frantic sounds of my wurm digging reverberated in my ears, and I tipped my head, comprehending the size of the cavern she carved by the odd echo of her efforts. Swallowing against the sudden picture of being crushed by the collapsing hillside, I licked my lips and edged ahead. Even in the pitch black, I could sense her, reach out a hand, and rest it on her shuddering flank. *Please stop and tell me what's happening.*

But she wouldn't. She ignored my pleas with the resolute intuition of a bird building a nest. She met my questions with a wall of red and a frenzy of digging. When I finally retreated to the lip of the cavern and sank onto an upturned rock, she didn't notice.

Blinking out at bleached daylight, I choked down a few of the stale nuts, then built a fire and roasted the rest of them, licking my fingers as I turned them on a flat rock near my hearth. The smell of leaf mould soon gave way to a warm and earthy aroma. I popped another nut into my mouth, crunched on it, and nodded. "Mmmh." I closed my eyes. *Better.* "I'm eating," I mumbled, leaning back toward the cave. "And you're missing it."

Nothing. Not even red from her now, just the grating of my wurm burrowing into the heart of the hill. I rubbed the back of my neck and scanned the vast afternoon skyline. Something flew in the distance. My heart sparked, and I squinted, hoping to catch a telltale flash of gold, but the silent flyers coasted too far off to gauge their size or identity. How many times in my childhood had I lain back in a field of kiro grass, breathed deeply of that sweet scent, and imagined I was flying away with dragon Guides? *And now you are bonded with a giant of a wurm, and she anchors you to this spot.* I winced at the thought, afraid she'd overheard, but the digging didn't stop. She kept at it until late in the afternoon, and then my wurm slept.

I gathered more firewood, discovered a small game trail leading back to the stream and set a few snares at the narrowest points. *Temporary,* I convinced myself. Just enough to bolster us before we moved on to find Yara. The wurm and I were both exhausted and hungry. Perhaps that's why she was digging this burrow to rest in, like she had at the gully. A day or two and we could start our search again, refreshed. I resettled near my fire, lost myself in the wavering eddies crossing the surface of the coals and wrapped my tired mind in images of Yara. *Please Nasheira, keep her safe. Take me to her.*

The next morning, the wurm wouldn't move. She lay curled in her vast burrow and stabbed me with hot, red lances of hunger.

"I'm going," I gasped, clutching at my stomach. *If you want an animal big enough for you to eat, you're going to have to find it for me.* As I thought it, her senses expanded and pressed past me in a wave, like fissures across collapsing ice. For a few moments that was it, just that cold, crackling search as far as my wurm could reach, and then a warm pinpoint of light, followed by another, and another, until I could count five bright spots in my head.

What are they? I scrambled toward my spear, hissing through my teeth at the hunger pains coiling in my belly. The silhouette of a stout body with short legs and a flat snout pressed into my mind. *Harek. I won't be able to get all of them.* Hard red trampled the rest of my thought. I pursed my lips, turned and trotted toward the unseen herd of armoured harek.

When I returned, sweating and puffing, dragging a sizeable old sow behind me, my wurm practically screamed in red. Her thrashing reverberated deep in the hillside as I jerked the carcass up the soft incline. *She's just hungry. A few good kills from your trap line will revive her and then we'll go.* I rolled the sow into the mouth of the cavern. It felt like offering a sacrifice to Pau, like feeding a demon. *Would she devour me?* I wondered, staggering and gulping for air. *If you lost your footing and fell in right now, would she eat you whole along with the harek?*

CHAPTER THIRTY-FIVE

M y wurm didn't revive after she burrowed. Instead, it seemed like she was chewing away at me. She'd wake me in the middle of the night, the hot pain of her hunger bringing tears to my eyes, taking my breath away, and it was all I could do to crawl away from her and track the next kill. I couldn't sleep. I set trap lines, built a stone fish trap in the creek. No matter how much I brought back for her, it was never enough.

This is how I die, then, I pondered one night, as she slept. I lay exhausted in the dirt, smoke from my fire smudging a starry sky. *I am consumed by a wurm, but it is my mind she eats first.* Tucking my hands into my armpits, I shivered against the cold and huddled closer to my weak fire. It hurt to lie down for too long. All of my bones jutted and bruised my skin.

I blinked at the sharp, indifferent stars, and my throat spasmed. *Just leave her. Just run. Find Yara.* But I couldn't, it was too late. *She's a parasite.* I realized. *Like Na-Jhalar was to Iva and Fraesh. She's sucked you dry, and you have nothing left, no energy to run.* It was true. Only the sheer, molten force of her hunger galvanized me to hunt. Without it, I crumbled like a broken puppet, discarded and splayed in the dirt until the next time my wurm called for food. I counted seven falling stars in the sky that night before she woke again.

Two mornings later, I found a yearling gazelle wheezing in one of my foot traps. It'd pulled half the stakes out of the hole, but not before the snare tightened on its leg. Heaving the small carcass, I lost count of how many times I collapsed hunched over on the trail, my own ragged breathing echoing that of the poor gazelle in its last moments. When I reached the hillside cave, I pushed the scrawny offering down the dark maw of the tunnel and licked my chapped lips. A bitter wind flanked the hillside and frosted my eyelashes together, but everything else was still. No movement in the cave. No blazing orange-red hunger.

She's sleeping, my mind sighed. I crumbled against the entryway, too tired to revive my fire, and slept sitting up. I awoke only when my legs launched a tingling protest. The sun had swung over the hillside, and the shadow of the ancient tree's branches dappled the snow like lace. A faraway call of a wild vaiya floated on the breeze, and then silence. I frowned and uncrossed my numb arms. *Silence. She can't still be sleeping...*

"Oh Guides," I rasped. I hadn't been in my wurm's burrow since the day she'd dug it, but I tumbled headlong into it now. *She's dead.* The horrible thought prodded me. *She's starved to death. Oh Guides, no.* Tree roots raked my cheeks and soil sifted from the ceiling as I lurched through the tunnel and slammed into something solid. I fell back stunned. *It caved in on her.* I swallowed, scrambled forward and pressed my hand against the obstruction, expecting to feel cold lumps of clay. Instead, my palm brushed against something warm with the rough texture of tree bark.

Pressing harder, I felt it stretch and then spring back, like fabric or netting. It reached all the way to the ceiling.

Trotting back out of the cave, I pressed a coal from my fire starter into my lamp and nursed a flame to life on the lard moss wick. Cupping the sputtering light, I edged back into the cave and gulped against squeezing panic. The gazelle carcass lay untouched against a white mass of webbing that clotted the entire cavern from bottom to top. Beyond it, I couldn't sense my wurm at all.

"Hey!" I shouted and slammed a fist against the thick, tangled mess. "Wake up!" *She left you, and she's blocked you from following.* "Wake up. This isn't funny." I punched a few more times, my breathing ratcheting higher and my chest pulling in on itself. *Don't do this to me. Please.* All this time I'd hunted for her. Fed her. Cared for her wounds. And I could have been searching for Yara instead of anchored to a wurm that sucked the marrow out of me until I was too weak to leave. *This can't have been for nothing.*

I slid down the wall and spread my throbbing hand flat against the foreign surface, and then it moved. Something rolled and pressed outward, stretching the thick webbing like the skin of a pregnant belly. I snatched my hand back, hissed and scuttled backwards. And that's when it bloomed in my mind. A tiny, sleepy thread of green. *Her.* My wurm.

"Oh thank Nasheira!" I blurted before a sudden sob caught in my throat. I spread my fingers, pressed my palm against the rough membrane, and she moved again, languid and massive.

Are you—Are you all right?

She answered in a settled emerald affirmative. A stupid grin pasted across my face. *Oh Guides, how I've missed green!* My own hiccuping laughter skittered through the cavern as I held up the lamp and ran my fingers over the pale, ropey surface. *A nest.* I shook my head. *You've made yourself a nest.*

The night after I discovered my wurm's nest, a bitter storm clambered over the western mountain range and swallowed our hillside retreat, pinning me in the cavern with my dormant wurm. The webbed, reinforced wall stretching to the ceiling offered slight comfort, but I couldn't shake the fear of being buried by earth or snow.

Where was Yara right now? Had she found shelter? My stomach sank. I'd pulled Yara in. Fell in love with her when I knew better. Ignored the voice in my head that had warned me away, let my inflated ego convince me that our plan, our escape, could work. *And now she's probably—*

I squeezed my eyes shut, clipped off the horrible thought, and leaned back against the warmth of my wurm's nest. Though the storm screamed overhead, pulling the smoke of my small cook fire out the snow-drifted entrance like an unravelling thread, I was warm. I was fed. I'd gorged on the half-cooked meat of the thin gazelle, gobbling it up so fast that I'd scrambled to the entrance, doubled-over and vomited into the blizzard with snowflakes stinging my face in rebuke. *Stupid.*

Now, despite the warmth, coldness consumed me. I felt empty, not just my stomach, the *whole* of me had hollowed. I was alone, for the first time since the sacrifice. *Did you do this to her?* The sudden question sprang to my mind. *You didn't feed her enough. You didn't hunt enough for her, and now you've ruined her too, just like Vax, just like Yara. This is your fault, isn't it? Your wurm's gone dormant because you couldn't feed her.*

"Maybe they all sleep in the winter." My lips cracked as I mumbled to myself in reply. But no, that was wrong. I shook my head. *You've seen wurms in winter time before.*

"Never as big as her."

Except in your vision.

These were the thoughts that followed me into unsettled

sleep. Only the soft green of my wurm purring through my broken brain kept me anchored there.

It struck me, some days later, how close I'd come to death, how emaciated I'd become, the translucent thinness of my skin, hair falling out of my head. Had my wurm not sealed herself in dormancy when she did, had rabid red not faded into green, her hunger would have killed me, and most likely her as well. For, after I was gone, what was to stop her from filling her empty belly with trees and rocks and Nasheira knows what else? Anything to ease the painful void. Was that why there weren't any wurms her size? Did the hunger just eventually consume them? *Mother of Yurrii, what an awful existence.*

I survived the next few bitterly cold weeks by collecting the odd kill from my short trap line and quickly retreating to the warmth of my wurm's cavern. Once again, she was saving me. If not for the furnace of her slowly shifting presence behind the webbed wall, I'd have died of exposure. I didn't have enough reserves to survive a cold snap alone. I couldn't keep myself warm, but I didn't shiver, and I felt exhausted all the time. I knew the signs of exposure well enough. I lived only because I slept against my wurm's warmth in a shelter of her making. I slept a lot. I healed, slowly.

At some point, I started to gain strength. I noticed that I could check my whole trap line and still find the energy to fish afterwards. Life returned to me in tiny increments. I found a flint formation exposed by the creek bed and practised making spearheads and honing edges sharp enough to shave with. I shaved. Sweet Nasheira, how strange to be bare-faced again.

At night, I cried for Yara. I swore that the next morning would be the one where I left the cavern and didn't come back, but I couldn't. I couldn't leave the wurm, I just didn't have the strength to do it.

One bright winter morning, as I checked my trap line, I stretched my neck and caught a flutter of movement in a ula bush to my right: birds, hundreds of them, with sleek olive bodies, flicked crests, and black masks around their eyes. They massed in huge flocks for a few specific weeks in late winter and then vanished with faultless timing every year. As a child, I'd often wondered where they went.

As I watched the jostling flock, my throat tightened and my breathing hitched. I blinked rapidly at the harsh sky overhead and counted the weeks in my head. Recounted. "Oh Guides," I moaned as the full force of it struck me and dropped me to my knees. Sagging in the snow, I ticked the weeks off in my head a third time with agonizing deliberation. *Thirteen. Oh Nasheira, it can't be!*

I sat back on my haunches as the world around me blurred behind a wash of sick heat. An awful, gagging noise tore past my closing throat, and I clapped my hand over my mouth. Hot tears pooled in the scar on my cheek. It was at least thirteen weeks—that was my best guess since many days blurred together—since the moons eclipsed. *That puts Yara at forty weeks. Full term. Your son is being born without you. If she ran, Yara is alone.*

On the way back to the cavern, every bird call sounded like the mewl of a newborn baby. Hunger pangs twisting in my gut, reminding me that Yara could not hunt. When I broke through hard crusted snow, wallowing in the drifting powder beneath, I imagined her trying to gather food in this, a babe clutched to her chest.

I have to go to her. I cannot stay here and wait anymore.

I strode purposely back to the cavern to pack my bag and abandon my wurm, but a set of tracks near the entrance froze me in place. Serpentine and scuffing through the snow, they skirted the hilltop under the ancient tree.

"Wurms," I gagged. Small ones, judging by the girth of their tracks, just human-sized, but I sprinted into the cavern regardless. An unbroken, white wall of webbing greeted me, along with serene green. "Thank Nasheira." I blurted as I ran a hand along the corded, bulging length of it. *They would eat her.* The thought stabbed at me. *Like maggots, just chew right into the side of her, her own kind.* I shuddered and swallowed. When I went back to the cavern entrance to study the tracks. I found something else among them. A footprint. A human footprint.

It wasn't mine, too narrow, and whoever made it had come before the wurms had. I found a few other partial prints nearly wiped away by the wurm tracks. Perhaps the traveler been scared off by them. *But someone knows you're here, and if they find your wurm, they'll kill her.* I shivered.

I kept my cook fire high after that day, postponing leaving once again.

I packed my food and supplies with me in the mornings when I left to hunt, and I didn't leave the cavern without a roaring blaze to stand sentinel in my wake. I couldn't leave my wurm undefended. I just couldn't. *She never left you to die. And she could have. Guides, how many opportunities did she have to just go and not come back?*

We stayed strange partners like that, this looming, gravid wall that whispered green promises of life like buds on tree branches, and I, her awkward guardian. I endured my first winter as a shunned man and watched the weak and watery sun bloom into the hesitant warmth of springtime. One morning at the edge of my game trail, I startled a wild vaiya, raised my spear to take her, but the angle was wrong. It was then I noticed movement at her heels: a row of three chicks bobbing behind her. I let them go.

THAT NIGHT, my sleep was interrupted by the stench of rotting teeth and the harsh rasp of someone breathing in my face. *Close. Too close.* I recoiled, bolting awake with a wordless yell and reaching for the skinning knife I always kept within reach, but it wasn't there. Its blade flashed toward my face, wielded by the man crouched over me.

I slammed his weapon arm aside and the blade plunged into the dirt beside my head. Gripping his wrist, I jammed it outward, unbalancing him.

He crashed into me. "Careful now." A reedy voice, coughing as I panted. "Can't have you carving yourself up before it's time."

Clamping my right arm around his neck, I dug my left thumb into the hollow between the bones of his wrist, praying he'd drop the knife, but he bit my hand, slipping out of my grip as I screamed.

Sitting on my stomach, he raised the blade for another strike.

I bucked my hips and his hand flew over my shoulder to brace himself. The knife stabbed wide again. I landed a punch under his ribs, heard the breath bark out of him and the knife clatter out of his hand. Twisting onto my hands and knees, I lunged for it.

Small things swam into startling focus as we grappled. Bony, scabbed knees, torn leggings, and a hooded aeni coat. Long fingernails gouged my arm as I reached the blade first, closed my right hand over it and rolled to attack. My malformed fingers cramped. *No!* I fumbled and the knife slipped out of my hand. *Guides, no!*

My attacker jammed his knee into the soft flesh of my left elbow, punched me in the head, and reclaimed the knife. Pinpoints of white swarmed my vision as he straddled my chest, pinned both my arms with his knees and pressed the blade to my throat.

I'm dead.

Green eyes studied me coolly as he panted and pressed a finger into the brand at my cheek before pointing to a deep s-shaped scar in the hollow of his. "We're twins, see?"

Branded. An Outcast. Like me. "What do you want?" I wheezed.

"Never been twins with a Speaker before." He sniffed and scratched at the freckles on his nose before leaning back from me. "S'pose they all taste the same, regardless."

You can still overpower him. I glanced at my dying fire paces away. *Roll him into the coals,* but I couldn't move with the knife pressed against my throat and his knees digging into my arms.

"Just tell me what you want," I gasped, unable to feel my fingers.

Yellow teeth flashed as he pulled his lips back into a cruel smirk. His nose whistled as he sucked in a long inhale. "Same as anyone wants, really." A log shifted in the fire. Sparks snapped and flames licked to life, bathing us in fresh orange light. "I want to eat."

Red hair. He has red hair. I gaped at the face grinning down at me. Freckles. Cold green eyes and red hair. I'd only seen it once before in my life.

"Tanar?" I blurted and he flinched, face twisting and knife digging into my neck hard enough to break skin. Sour yellow washed through my mind and the ground at my back shuddered softly. "Tanar, it's me," I gulped. Warmth trickled down the side of my neck.

He wrinkled his crooked nose and squinted at me through pale lashes. "I don't know any Speakers," he chanted in a high, sing-song voice.

"Akrist."

He flinched again.

It is him. Mother of Yurrii. "We knew each other as boys, as daeson. I was going to save Xen with you."

"Akrist wasn't a Speaker." Tanar's sunken face pinched, his green eyes wide and white-rimmed.

"Tanar, listen to me." I swallowed and the knife blade slid across my neck, slick with my own blood. "We were friends. I thought you were dead, but I have food if you're hungry. I can share it." Sweet Nasheira, how had we ever crossed paths again in a world so vast, after all this time?

Tanar shook as he crouched over me. I realized he was laughing only when his inhales shifted into short, hiccuping squeals. "Share it!" he sang, grinning again even as the tendons stood out on his neck. "Yes, share it," he chortled.

"We can eat right now if you put away the knife."

He ignored me. "Share it," he sighed, shaking his head and scrutinizing my face with a dissecting gaze.

He's unhinged. Clenching my teeth, I bucked upward. Tanar must have been half my weight, lighter than Yara, but he jammed his knobby knees into the hollow of my elbows until nerves pinched and I cried out in shock. Orange swam behind my eyes, and a low rumble sang in my ears like thunder.

Tanar cocked his head, wiry frame still curled over me. "Earthshake," he muttered. Then his focus swung back to me, green eyes hard as jade. "You can't have the knife. I'm using the knife right now."

Distract him. "What happened to Xen?"

"Say that name—" he choked, tears springing to his eyes. "Say that name again, and I'll gut you while you watch."

I licked my lips. "How did you find me, Tanar?"

"Never left." He gulped.

"You did. You stole my cache and you took the baby."

"My cache." He parroted, eyes focusing on my neck

instead of my face. "I'm a wurm. Wurms follow camps. Follow food."

"You followed our camp?" I frowned. "All this time?"

"Lost and found. Lost and found. Far behind." Tanar nodded, red hair glowing in the firelight.

"That's impossible," I whispered. "All these years? We would have seen you. Someone would have caught you."

"Someone did!" Tanar howled and pointed to his branded cheek. "Carved up the wurm. I lost the camp, but I found you. You. You had a bird." He slapped a palm over one eye. "A one-eyed bird. I remember him. Follow you back to camp, back to food, but you keep coming back here, and I want to eat."

"I don't know where my camp is, Tanar. They left me with the daeson."

"Lost and found. Lost and found. Far behind," he sang. "I want to eat."

I eyed the bag leaning against my wurm's wall of white to my right. "I have food in my pack. Take it."

"Liar." Tanar hissed. "I already looked. Food in your belly."

It was there. Dried meat. Nuts. I frowned and re-focused on Tanar. A long strip of smoked meat poked out of the pocket of his jacket.

"I'm not a liar. You took it already."

"Share it. You said you'd share it." He bared his teeth again.

"If you took it all, I don't have anything else to share."

"Yes you do," he chanted and leaned into the knife.

"Don't cut me," I gurgled. Blood ran freely down my neck and Tanar traced a finger through its path. *Oh Guides.* "Tanar, don't cut me. I don't have anything else. Please." Red roared through my mind. My vision dimmed and Tanar's outline muddied into a pulsing green silhouette.

"I'm a wurm who no one ever taught to hunt." Tanar

licked his bloodied finger and grinned. "Wurms eat anything, you know. People are easiest because they're slow and stupid. Never tasted a Speaker though. S'pose they all taste the same, regardless."

"No." I flailed beneath him, kicking my legs. *Oh Guides.* My eyes slammed shut and Tanar's silhouette remained, a searing green after-image in my mind.

The floor shuddered violently behind my back. A deafening roar filled the cavern and pulsed through my chest, and an utterly foreign voice poured into my head.

Do not move.

Tanar froze above me.

Open your eyes so I can see him.

My eyes flew open. Tanar still squatted on my chest with the knife pressing into my neck, but he was gaping at the wall of white beside us, and his silhouette swam with green.

The wall undulated. Its webbing bulged. Something huge tore through it, clobbering Tanar.

He flew off my chest, narrowly missing the fire and skidding onto his side several paces away. Dust coiled around him as the knife clattered out of his hand.

I rolled to reach for it.

I said, don't move! The voice in my mind pounded.

"Wh-who are you?" I winced.

A long shadow stretched over my head.

Tanar screamed.

I strained to focus past my fire.

A limb thicker than a man, glistening with pale gold, pinned Tanar's leg to the cavern floor as he squirmed to escape. The dark, tapered talon puncturing his thigh twitched and he howled and grabbed the knife, stabbing downward.

Before I could yell, the wicked claw convulsed back, and the blade skidded harmlessly across its hard crescent curve before jarring out of Tanar's hand. He scrambled away from it. Hands clutching his leg, he fled the cavern.

You let him go. The voice in my head was laced with sullen blue. It was familiar somehow.

I dove for the knife, grasping it in trembling hands. "Who are you?" I asked again, blinking at the golden limb that stretched almost to the entrance of the cave, damp wrinkled webbing, burnished scales, all unfolding before me.

It's me. Nardiri, the voice answered.

And I could not respond. I couldn't process it, what I heard, what I saw. That impossibly long limb, flexing rhythmically in the faint light, dainty claw scraping a pattern in the dust where Tanar had just lain.

A dragon's wing.

Nardiri was a dragon.

ACKNOWLEDGMENTS

First and foremost, thank you to my family for giving me so much time to play with words. To my Writer's Alliance crew, bless you for being the first to heroically wade through those words in their rough form. Essa Hansen, Sunyi Dean, Alia Hess, Jennifer Lane, Nanette 'Sammy' Geiger, Darby Harn, Ravaena Hart, C.J. Hart, and Alexandria Thompson, your help was immeasurable and immense. To my editors Igpy Kin, Michelle Heumann, and Allison Alexander, your incredible vision took my story from a watery idea to a poignant, vibrant tale in ways I could never have imagined on my own. Thank you to Yubo Su with Cornell Ask an Astronomer for your wonderful, in-depth correspondences on the intricacies of dual moon eclipses. Lastly, to everyone at Mythos and Ink Publishing, thank you for loving my story enough to take a chance on me. You've all made a lifelong dream come true.

GLOSSARY

Aeni: Smaller nomadic counterpart to the larger camps. They never settle in one area and are excellent mapmakers and scouts. Individuals never reveal their names, except to their closest kin. Individually, to strangers, they are all called ani.

Bury Bug: Parasite similar to a tick. It embeds itself between the scales of both vaiyas and dragons.

Chani: Concubine to a Speaker. Their families are well provided for. Chani are not allowed alone in another's company while they hold their title. Technically, they are allowed to step down from their role, but few do so for fear they will be cast out.

Daeson: Title of the eldest son in a family. It means 'damned son' in the old language.

Elder: An older member of a camp, chosen to act as one of several councillors to the Speaker. The position is not guaranteed to all older members of a camp. For example, if a man abandons care for his daeson, he revokes his future elder position as well as losing hunter shares.

Gifen: Narcotic plant. Leaves are chewed to release their bitter juice. Used for pleasure and also medically to dull pain.

Guides: Dragons. Nasheira's angels sent to guide her people out of the wastelands and toward hunting grounds. They choose leaders (Speakers) in Nasheira's name by marking chosen individuals with a complex scar across their chest.

Harek: A pig-like animal with plated armour, similar to that of an armadillo.

Healer: This camp member is skilled at midwifery, herbalism, undertaking, and tattooing. Healers preserve and pass on knowledge of medicinal plants, keep a history of daeson births in a camp, prepare bodies for cremation, and provide the rare blue ink used to tattoo a woman after she's born her eldest son.

Junab: A low growing succulent. Its leaves are crushed and used as an effective (but smelly) antibacterial ointment.

Kiro: A sweet-smelling grass used for incense and bedding.

Na: Prefix in front of a name that signifies that person is a Speaker (e.g. Na-Jhalar).

Nasheira: The Goddess. Her eldest son is Pau and her youngest is Yurrii.

Pau: Eldest son of Nasheira. The first daeson. Murderer of Yurrii. The greater moon is named after him and he is symbolically represented by a wurm.

Pechi: Type of deciduous tree, similar to a poplar.

Speaker: An individual marked by the guides to lead a camp. They frequently have prophetic visions and always have 'Na' added to their name to signify Nasheira has chosen them to speak for her people.

Storyteller: Keeper of a camp's history and legends. With no written language, history is passed on orally, through song and storytelling. Ideal storyteller apprentices must be well-spoken with excellent memories, and natural people skills as they are often emotional councillors as well. In camps with no Speakers, leadership often falls to the storyteller.

Tavi: A popular game played with two pieces—one dragon and one wurm—per player. Players take turns guessing which hand their opposition holds the dragon piece in and win a round if they guess correctly.

Ula: A tree that produces berries poisonous to humans, but irresistible to vaiyas.

Vaiya: Pack animal, like a large bird, but scaled instead of feathered. They are intelligent and can be taught to speak.

Wurm: Blind Subterranean predator and scavenger shaped like a maggot, but with teeth and face tentacles. Wurms are larger than men and are a symbol of Nasheira's eldest son, Pau, the first daeson.

Yurrii: Secondborn son of Nasheira. Murdered by his older brother, Pau. The lesser moon is named after him and he is represented by a dragon.

REVIEWS MAKE A DIFFERENCE

Did you know that one of the best ways you can support an author is to leave a book review? All it costs is a few minutes of your time! If you liked this book, please consider leaving a review on the website of your favourite bookseller.

ABOUT THE AUTHOR

At a young age, Shelly Campbell wanted to be an air show pilot or a pirate, possibly a dragon and definitely a writer and artist. She's piloted a Cessna 172 through spins and stalls, and sailed up the east coast on a tall ship barque—mostly without projectile vomiting. In the end, Shelly found writing fantasy and drawing dragons to be so much easier on the stomach.

Shelly's tales are speculative fiction, tending toward literary with dollops of oddity. She enjoys the challenge of exploring new techniques and subject matter, and strives to embed inspiring stories in her writing and art.

f facebook.com/shellycampbellauthorandart
🐦 twitter.com/ShellyCFineArt
📷 instagram.com/shellycampbellfineart

AN INTERVIEW WITH THE AUTHOR

WHAT INSPIRED YOU TO WRITE UNDER THE LESSER MOON?

The inspiration for the book stemmed from a fascination with ancient civilizations and what drove some of their more enduring practices. What motivated the Aztecs to believe that the sun would snuff out if they didn't feed their gods a human sacrifice when certain stars aligned? How did the Kapu system decide that bananas were forbidden for ancient Hawaiian women to eat? Why do many cultures still prefer sons over daughters? Where are the similarities and differences in our creation stories, and how do these core narratives shape who we are as a societies? I wanted to explore how harsh climates and declining populations could push people to the edge of their beliefs and beyond.

Since there's evidence of dragons in so many of Earth's old tales, I made them real and central to the religion of this complex, Stone Age world. By the time our main character, Akrist, is born, this religion has been broken for some time. The goddess Nasheira rarely chooses leaders among her people anymore. The dragon population is declining. They don't guide faithful followers to hunting grounds as they once did.

Overall, I hoped this story would highlight humanity, the good and bad of it, this common thread that ties us all together, whether we live on a modern Earth, or a vast stone-age world where dragons still soar in the skies.

WHAT WAS YOUR FAVOURITE (SPOILER FREE) SCENE TO WRITE IN THE BOOK?

Well darn, my favourite scenes are all spoilers. One fairly innocent one comes to mind though. It's when Akrist's love interest, Yara, first shows him kindness and he has absolutely no idea how to react to it. The poor man is so used to being scorned and betrayed. It was a treat to finally give him a few moments of kindness after putting him through the proverbial wringer for most of the book. It felt like I owed him that scene.

HOW DID YOU COME UP WITH UNDER THE LESSER MOON'S CREATION MYTH?

Societies are shaped by their creation myths, sometimes in profound ways, and sometimes more subtlety. The plot for *Under the Lesser Moon* came from a simple idea. Many of our world's foundational stories, and therefore many of our cultures, hold the firstborn son of a family as a revered and blessed position. What would a society entirely opposite of that look like, a culture built on the idea that firstborn sons are lowly and cursed? What subtle changes and ripple effects would that cause? What happens when a creation story gets twisted and misunderstood? Since I required a myth that included the dual moons eclipsing, dragons, wurms, and the idea that eldest boys are somehow cursed, I custom-built the creation story to suit. Mythos and Ink, my lovely publisher, created a video of *Under the Lesser Moon*'s creation myth and included my art, telling the story though cave drawings. I'd love for you to see it! You can find it by looking up "Mythos & Ink" on YouTube.

TELL US A BIT ABOUT YOU!

At a young age, I wanted to be an air show pilot or a pirate, possibly a dragon and definitely a writer and artist. I've piloted a Cessna 172 through spins and stalls, and sailed up the east coast on a tall ship barque—mostly without projectile vomiting. In the end, I've found writing speculative fiction and drawing dragons to be so much easier on the stomach.

I grew up in Sundre, Alberta, nestled against the Rocky Mountains, and surrounded by a big, wonderful extended family. I've been lucky to have a great career in the oilfield as a plant operator, and I haven't strayed far from that beautiful Alberta terrain and all those wonderful people. Cochrane, Alberta, is currently home, and I love exploring it with my wonderful hubby and two sweet boys.

WHY DID YOU DECIDE TO BECOME AN AUTHOR?

My head's been swimming with stories for as long as I can remember, you know the type. I decided to become an author because I've put so many years into some of these tales—let's not talk about how many years exactly— and after all the work, I thought some of these manuscripts deserved more than a disorganized folder on my personal computer. These stories stuck with me, so perhaps there are readers out there who might get excited about them too. Fingers crossed.

WHAT'S YOUR BIGGEST FANDOM?

Do dinosaurs count as a fandom? I mean, technically, every four-year-old kid out there is with me on this, right? And it's got to be one of the oldest fandoms out there. I also enjoy Star Wars, the Marvel Universe, Harry Potter, and The Hunger Games, not all in the same room though. That'd be crowded and messy.

WHAT DO YOU DO FOR FUN?

I'm not into flying airplanes or sailing on tall ships anymore —let's be honest; my stomach never was into those things. Now, I garden, and ferry boys and hockey bags where they need to go. I write, and when the words don't flow, I draw or paint. You can check out what I'm working on at www.shellycampbellauthorandart.com.

DRAGONS OR ROBOTS?

Dragons. No contest there. Hang on. I could possibly be swayed by robotic dragons, jet-powered ones.

YOU MIGHT ALSO ENJOY...

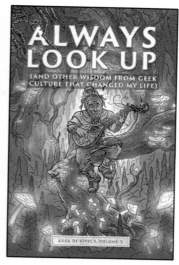

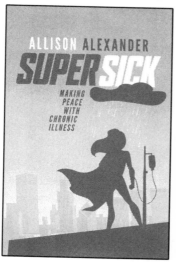

JOIN A
SCI-FI AND FANTASY
COMMUNITY

DISCOVER

new and upcoming books to read.

MEET

other readers, writers, and bloggers.

DISCUSS

worldbuilding and writing.

LEARN

from editors and authors.

JOIN OUR DISCORD SERVER!

 MYTHOS & INK

www.mythosink.com/community

Made in the USA
Middletown, DE
24 August 2021